AMAZING THINGS

Anthony Harwood

Published by Anthony Harwood

ISBN: 978-0-9567479-1-4

For Steve.

Sometimes it is hard to find the right direction. You not only knew the way but drove me there too.

PROLOGUE

The music was Electric Heaven. Dune, the band, derived from Dune, the movie.

Eyes of cold blue, flashing and flaring over and over as they, alone, moved, surveying the city beneath him. His icy skin, pale against the night sky, virtually glowing in the reflection of his own hair and goatee, both seeming to be made of pure electricity, as if every hair was complete, yet made of a strand of that same powerful blue energy than of proteins and fibres dead or otherwise. His clothes, black leather trench coat, snug against his shoulders but playing with the breeze as it fluttered behind him. His tight cotton-lycra suit hugging closely to his skin providing warmth and ease of movement. Its high gloss, however, imparted the notion that it too could conduct the very electricity he grew from his head. His stance was low, crouched, yet ever ready to spring or pounce, whichever the case may be. His sharp features, highlighted by his electric blue eyebrows, were almost elven in appearance, but the lowness and evenness of his brow gave him a sinister look that one could confuse with crazed but silent anger. He was attractive, there was no doubting that, but he was also one not to be messed with by all appearances.

How many other people would be this high in the city and still be outdoors?

He was awe-inspiring. The aura he gave off of complete calm and yet such a sense of absolute power. In a sudden flash of movement, as if his sharp eye had managed to sense another's presence, the Stranger's head flicked around, his steel blue eyes glaring straight at them, barely even looking at them, but registering their presence.

Without a word, or even a sound, he leapt up off his perch and; with a jet of electric embers in his wake, took off. His movement was almost imperceptible. But in a moment, the Stranger stopped again. This time the Stranger stood atop a building adjacent the one he'd previously been sitting on, on the opposite side of the street. His coat, more like a cape, blew against him now; brushing by his leg as it billowed out against the wind. It was an eerie effect, especially with the expression on his face. Even from a distance the sharpness of his jaw, the angle of his eyebrows and the strength of the bones in his cheeks were evident. The only light supplied other than the residual glow of the city below, was from his own making.

His eyes, now partially covered in shadow from his brow were regarding the newcomer with a look that could have been contempt or questioning bravado.

Then the Stranger's thin lips parted into a smile, his pearly white teeth glistening with that same electricity that seemed to reside in his very saliva.

"Welcome," What was it with English heroes? It seemed this Australian city was inundated with them. However, there was the feeling of regality and refinement in this man's voice; one would be unwise to dispute anything about him.

"You're trespassing."

The newcomer obviously didn't know to the full extent with whom he was dealing.

"People own these rooftops?"

Scaling the walls, almost as a squirrel would climb a tree, the newcomer reached the roof of the building he was attached to and stood, revealing himself in full moonlight to the stranger.

He too did not look to be one to mess with either.

"What are you doing here?" His expression was one of pseudo disinterest. His stance, however, was anything but apathetic. His own dark clothing seemed to swallow the light from the sky, having the opposite effect to the stranger's. His frame, being much larger, was also a lot broader. This man had muscles on muscles, perhaps explaining his ability to climb so adeptly and easily.

"I guess you could call it sight seeing. And you?"

"I guess you could call it merely a suggestion that you leave this area."

"Ever the gracious one."

The bigger man smiled, was there humour in it? "I'm giving you a way out. I suggest you take it, or you might find yourself in trouble."

The stranger smiled back and shook his head, "Not tonight, thanks all the same."

And in a flash of blue, he was gone.

CHAPTER ONE

THEN

Edit in the hazy bordering, the surreal and slightly choral music. Dim the lights. Background noise of dripping water. A child crying. Lights up on a room.

Circular, walled with red brick, rotten and mouldy from decades of trickling water. On the north side, a semi-circular entrance to a tunnel. Large, dark, disappearing, almost endless.

Set at even intervals around this large room, eleven all told, large wooden doors, studded and crossed with large metal beams for support. In each a window, a foot squared, barred vertically and set against even more darkness from within.

The main room, large, domed. The centre of the ceiling, the apex of the dome, a simple hole, the only source of light. Whether it is natural or artificial is unknown. Glaring down, it encapsulates a central two tiered dais, also red brick and circular. A slight step up from the damp floor, then a second step, larger than the first to the central platform. One and a half metres in diameter on which an obelisk stood, tapering upward to a point. A reddish brown stone, seemingly carved, but, again, possibly naturally occurring. It stands two metres tall, overseeing the room and those entrapped beyond.

The crying comes from one cell. A child.

Deep down the only entrance, a light flared to life, then another on the opposing side of the tunnel. Shadows began to play on walls that seemed a lifetime away.

And the crying stopped.

Two small hands took hold of the bars. The bars opposite the tunnel, the only thing, other than the door, standing between those bars and whatever it was that was approaching was that one pinnacle of stone. Hardly enough protection from the fear that began to well inside the child.

Then came the footsteps; out of time from the water dripping and getting louder with each beat. Ducking back from the bars and into the shadows of his cell, the child huddled into a foetal position, hoping to enshroud himself in his own darkness, making him invisible.

He knew it wouldn't work.

The footsteps had reached the main room. Through the bars, the child could see shapes dancing across the curved ceiling, vanishing from sight before making claim for its surface once more.

There was a rustling of cloth followed by the jangling of keys. They slid effortlessly into a lock, not his. But he knew who...

A woman whispered her pleas of mercy; begging the unseen for benevolence.

7

The child could tell by the whimpering and the odd high-pitched gasp as the woman was taken away, she was not being heard.

OWEN

Cut to a sunny day. Sky a crisp blue with clouds spotted here and there. A day when children would play and argue about what shapes they could see in said clouds. The city was quiet. A Sunday morning. Trade only in the afternoon.

He stepped off the train and onto the platform. No one followed him so he paused, savouring the moment whilst surveying the sight before him.

It was still a thing of relief. Even after all of these years. To be able to step so freely out of the confines of a cage, such as one could see a train carriage as being. He took a deep breath and moved toward the main entrance of the station.

He reached the street, the cross-walk lights still red as the cars flashed by.

Shortly, the stoplights turned from green, to amber and through to red. An awkward tune played as the green man came to life, giving permission to walk.

Stepping casually onto the street, he crossed to the other side.

He preferred the city in the morning. So peaceful. Hardly a soul around. To think there was such a huge vista of buildings and walkways and, at this moment, most of them were empty; as if he was the only one alive. The only survivor of a long forgotten holocaust. Almost.

He made his way through the newly renamed Forest Arcade, what used to be known as Forest Chase; a large, open aired lot, paved for pedestrian usage and oft times a location where young dance companies would showcase their talent, or lack of, in public displays. Now, it had been lined by a range of shops including places for tattoos, body piercing, and clothes boutiques. A good range, but variable as the general populous that traversed its length was more of the conservative, white-collar variety. Definitely, some would indulge their 'wilder' side by purchasing an ear stud, or perhaps even a nipple ring, but the windows of these shops were more likely to exhibit signs declaring 'under new management' than sport a new product display.

He had to admit, he'd bought a nipple ring and an earring on his upper ear, but that was as far as he would go. No eyebrow ring, no genital piercing or nose studs. Well not yet.

He brushed at the sleeve of his grey suit as he walked, trying to clean it up somewhat. He had to look his best. The employees at the Federal Records Branch would be more likely to cooperate with a well presented youth than a scruffy, unkempt individual. His hair, fortunately, was easy to manage. All he need do with his short cropped bleach-blonde locks was run his hands and some gel through it, allowing it to stand slightly on end, giving him a strange combination of manic, yet neat styling. His small goatee and moustache were also closely cropped and managed; though the darker tinge clashed somewhat with the peroxide effect of his head of hair.

The suit was second hand. Hardly worn by its previous owner, whoever that was. But he had discovered it in an op shop, along with most of his wardrobe. This suit had a strikingly seventies look, minus the flares. But with the maroon turtle neck skivvy underneath, it looked suave and he thought it made him look sophisticated.

Regardless, they would still treat him with more respect than if he wore jeans and a t-shirt.

The Records building, where housing, family and legal documents were housed, was located down the eastern end of the new city. The old city, where much of Perth's life had been located only years before hand, had become a mixture of derelict buildings and slums. People preferred the newer, more innovative designs that had sprung up over the years and insisted on moving there along with their businesses, all to the West. There was talk of demolishing the older end and replacing it with spruced up buildings. That was a long way off, however.

It would take him about twenty five minutes to walk the distance. He was lucky. His natural speed was generally faster than everyone else's. Tending to force anyone he was walking with to put on a small jogging spurt to catch up every once in a while. His fitness was also unique in so far as he could maintain that heavy pace with the greatest of ease. He never bragged about it, but he was proud of that fact.

He turned left from the arcade, heading up the Murray Street Mall, a bricked in roadway now utilised completely by pedestrians. At this hour, it was still pretty deserted, but that added to its charm. The store-fronts were locked; heavy plexi-glass roller shutters in place, allowing partial viewing of what stock lay inside. Even Greyson's, one of the biggest department stores in Australia only had a simple roller door in place. No heavy barring. No 24-hour security guards. Then again, you could be sure of security cameras galore in a place like that, not to mention a fast response police alarm system.

Letting his eyes wander, he perused the various displays including shoes, clothes, sporting goods, health products, vacated jewellery windows where stock had been stored somewhere deeper and safer inside for the night and plastic representations of Japanese dishes to help potential customers decide what looked yummier.

Just as he reached the first intersection, where Murray Street's pedestrian Mall reverted to a proper street, he felt a slight vibration in the ground beneath his feet. A loud rumbling sound followed, tempting him to look around.

Behind him, a fair distance down the street, beyond where the other end of the Mall finished and also resumed its rightful duties as a roadway, a thick plume of smoke was rising from a reddish aura of light, which could only have been fire.

He stopped, thinking about the possibilities.

A demolition crew? In the new end? Not likely. Another explosion? There had been one only a couple of days before hand. A car park. Fortunately no one had been hurt; though rumours were abound about some one who had been thrown clear of the explosion, sent hurtling across the street, landing in a building directly opposite. And survived.

Not likely. Probably the work of the tabloids.

The fire crew would be on site shortly, not to mention the police.

He turned back toward the other end of Murray Street and kept walking.

Again waiting for the man to turn green, he waited at the intersection, though only a few cars actually went by. He wasn't in that much of a hurry. Checking his watch, he still had about fifteen minutes before the Branch opened. It was a government establishment, meaning it didn't comply with the retail laws, enforcing Sunday traders to open at twelve midday. These offices opened nine sharp every day of the week, excepting this Wednesday, which was a public holiday.

If they opened at six o'clock, rather than nine, He would have been there directly on six, if not a few minutes earlier.

They had information he needed and he wasn't going to wait any longer.

THEN

Jump cut back to the circular room. The child, now silent, listening to the soft sobs of the woman nearby.

He forced himself to get up, to move back to the window.

She was being pulled by her hair, her long brown hair, the gentle curls pulled taught by the black gloved hand of the man assaulting her. Even with what little light there was, he could not discern who that man was. But he could see the woman.

Her eyes, full of pain and fear, were wide, searching for anything that could help her, anyone. And when they fell on his, she stopped struggling. All the terror left the depths of her icy blue eyes as she looked deeply into his and was replaced by a sadness. She ceased her sobbing, trying to be strong for him even during her pathetic and painful conveyance toward that ever-dark tunnel. She mouthed to him three words. He wanted to hear her say it, wanted to know that she meant it.

"*I love you.*"

He believed in her, even prayed for her, though he wasn't sure of God. She had tried to explain it to him once. But he never got it.

He felt the tears well in his own eyes. He hated seeing her in pain. He wanted to help her, any way he could. But what could a six year old do to a man like that.

He mouthed back one word. A word he hoped told her everything he wanted to say.

"*Mum.*"

And the tears came, both in his eyes and hers. They cleaned away some of the soot that had covered her face. And she smiled. For the first time in ages, she smiled at him.

And it was the last thing he saw her do.

To happier times. Only months before. On a farm. It sounds like a cliché, but they were a happy family, working hard together, helping each other. Every day was a struggle, but they made the most of it. Him and her and Ryan and his father. All four doing their best to make ends meet.

And they were happy.

Until They came.

He remembered that day. Had seen it in his dreams ever since it happened. It lingered in the back of his mind.

He was in the kitchen with his mother. She was cleaning up after lunch. Ryan and his father had gone back to work outside. He stood in the kitchen doorway laughing at one of his mother's jokes. It was like a dream, even when it happened. She stood, laughing, in front of the sink, in front of the kitchen window, tea towel and dish in hand as she dried.

He liked seeing her laugh. It was her that made it all work, made it all worth while. His father, worn and weary by day's end, always managed a smile when she greeted him at the door. It was her dream that kept them all working. In its own way it was sadistic of her, but she meant the best.

And she made it all worth while.

She had told the joke about the frog. He barely recalled it now. He wished so hard that he could, that he could still hold onto that one sliver of her, the thing that made her who she was. Her good humour. Her good nature. Everything about her was good.

She wore a floral summer dress. Light weight, brightly coloured. Her skin glowed in the sunlight, in her own natural glow.

He had lost himself in the punch line, laughing almost uncontrollably until it hurt. His stomach so tight that he could barely laugh any more, only wheeze in his mirth.

Looking up, expecting to see his mother also caught in the throes of laughter, he saw cause enough to regain control of himself.

She wasn't laughing. She wasn't even looking at him.

Instead she was staring out the window, the expression on her face, not one of humour, but something else. Something he couldn't explain or understand. Something that sent a chill down his spine as he realised this was no laughing matter.

CHAPTER TWO

OWEN

A van charged past. Too fast. Something was off.

But it wasn't the only car going too fast.

He turned to see a small hatchback go roaring by, unable to make out the driver, but positive something was afoot.

A Barina went by shortly after that, its speed was slow, even for the speed limit. But that was unimportant.

Picking up his pace, he hurried after the other cars. He wasn't going to catch up to them, he knew that, but he might be able to see what was going on.

There was a loud screech of brakes a couple of seconds later, followed by a series of metallic clashes as one of the vehicles lost control. It had to be up toward the cathedral. The end of Murray Street, where the road deviated to the right at ninety degree angles.

Breaking into a run, he found himself passing the Records building and continuing onward to whatever it was that was happening.

A second, smaller explosion rang out from the cathedral as he drew closer.

This was looking serious. By the time he made it to the scene, things were getting a little out of hand.

Keeping out of sight, he clung to a wall, watching what was occurring. What he saw was unique to say the least.

At the end of Murray Street there was a cathedral. Tall and gothic, its spires and architecture like something out of the middle ages. All around it, a wrought iron fence, broken intermittently by stone posts reaching about seven to eight feet high. The street curved around to the right, circling the cathedral on one side. On the other, Royal Perth Hospital. People had already exited the emergency entrance to see what was happening. Some were now cowering from the brute force that was being thrown around by the people in front of the church.

Four men. Two against two. One was absolutely huge, the size of a pick-up truck at least. His companion was shorter and a lot slimmer, but was spitting forth handfuls of green bolts. His hands would literally glow green before he released it like a bullet at his target, which happened to be a boy who looked no older than eighteen.

His companion was older, only by several years and was throwing around fireballs of his own.

These were no ordinary people, obviously. From all appearances the larger and smaller man had come from the van, which now lay on its side, severely damaged against one of the cathedral's stone posts.

The hatchback in which he guessed the other two had arrived was parked on the side of the road.

Behind that, a chunk of wall had been torn away, showering the road and the cars on it with white powder. That must have been the second explosion.

He watched in awe as the largest man lifted both his hands high into the air and brought them crashing down onto the grass on which he stood.

The very ground began to shake as a result, but instead of dissipating, the vibrations continued, increasing in intensity until it became difficult to keep ones footing.

It wasn't hard to gauge from the demeanour, clothing and actions of the men who were the good guys and who were the bad.

The younger one, who also had a reasonably largish nose, was far too anxious about the whole situation to be meaning to do any harm. His companion, though wielding forces with potential far beyond the levels he was using them at, was too controlled to be set on destruction.

The other two seemed to disregard the whole idea of human life. An example of this was evident now. The vibrations were reaching unstable proportions. Actual chunks of brick were breaking free from the buildings around them, those from the hospital threatening to crush innocent bystanders.

Something had to be done.

He ducked away, finding a small nook to hide in for a moment.

This was all so superman-ish, but he liked his privacy; though it didn't matter much. He felt a tingle run through his body, like a surge of static electricity. He was sure if his hair hadn't been gelled it would have stood on end. It only took an instant before there was a gentle flash of blue and he considered how odd it was, even after so many times, that he could manifest a costume at the same time as his powers.

It ran in the tradition of the old Wonder Woman television series, which had worked itself back onto commercial television of late, where she only seemed to use her powers in costume; even if it was the most trivial thing. In one such episode she was viewing the making of a movie. Diana, her human alter ego, spots some scaffolding that is about to collapse. In seconds she has done her little spin and become the mystical and mighty Wonder Woman so she could lift up the scaffolding, fix its damaged leg only to return to the guise of Diana before anyone has noticed.

Pointless? But did the costume give her the power? Or just the bracelets?

He knew in his own case, he was the one with the power. It was only through experimentation that he realised he could somehow alter his clothing in transformation.

It had been a case that he had actually tried on a costume idea, the one he now wore, whilst manifesting his abilities. When he changed back, so did his clothing as if they had been sent off to another dimensional

13

locker. He of course didn't mind. It saved the effort of getting changed every time.

Now he was dressed in the familiar black unitard. His trench coat, which he had also found at an op-shop, still flapped in a resulting wind from his transformation. The boots he wore, running up his calves and shins almost like soccer shin pads, had three buckles behind the calves to hold them in place. He had purchased these from a small Gothic store in the city. Probably the most expensive item of clothing at two hundred and thirty dollars. But they were too good a boot to pass on. The unitard itself he had made. It wasn't hard. After all the alterations and repairs he'd done on his second hand clothes, it was just a case of getting the measurements, making a design and sewing it together. Over the lower half he wore reasonably tight black trousers that tucked into his boots that gave a slight Jodhpur effect.

Though he didn't have the biggest of builds, he had sufficient muscle mass to give him a decent shape. And what he did lack in bulk, the trench coat covered nicely.

He rubbed at his chin. It always felt slightly odd when his hair was replaced. But the sensation of rubbing at his goatee was not unlike the complete cycle of rubbing his hand vigorously on carpet before touching a metallic doorframe.

A third, seemingly more powerful explosion knocked him back further into his hiding alcove. Of course it wouldn't be as powerful as the first had looked from a distance, but from this proximity, he had felt the power behind this last one.

Following the initial burst of sound, he heard loud crashes and clattering as the effects of the explosion encapsulated the environment around it.

Glass shattered and more bricks tumbled in the smoke. He could barely see through the massive black cloud that was rolling down the street toward him.

It was time to make his move.

In a blur of blue, leaving a trail of the same shimmering colour in his wake, he vanished into the smoke.

It wasn't that he actually became electricity, but it sure felt like he was on fire. It wasn't painful, but the energy coursing through his body was so intense, it was almost, to use a ridiculous though accurate description, titillating.

Every sense of what was around him was heightened a thousand fold. His vision became so crisp, so detailed that even moving at such a high speed, he assumed it to be at least three hundred kilometres an hour, he could make out every detail in the bark of a tree he was passing. His aural capabilities were almost sonar-like. Everything that moved, every little sound from the scratching of an ant to a leaf falling from that same tree, he could hear with such clarity. Oddly, it was only when he was in one of these spurts of speed. And these only lasted a couple of seconds at a time. He had tried to sustain the speed, but his own body suffered drastically when he pushed himself. It seemed everybody had their limits.

Even in the smoke, he could hear the movements of the fighters. The larger of them all had stopped doing anything, shocked by the blast and unsure of what to do without being able to see his opponent. The flame wielder was in a similar predicament. Though he seemed more determined to put some distance between himself and the brute.

As for the youngster and the smaller man, they were out of sight, but he could hear them both.

One was by the van, which by all evidence was now little more than smouldering scrap metal. The other was on the other side, between the burning van and the church. He wasn't sure which was which however.

"Stace-" a voice called out of the smoke. The youth. But it was cut short by a bolt of green that flared in the darkness, sending an ethereal glow and a most likely painful weapon through the ashen cloud.

It was time for him to act.

The youth had taken the blow hard, having been knocked onto the floor. It wasn't long before he started choking on the smoke, trying to regain his breath.

In the smoke, the shorter man's hand began to glow that familiar green as he moved in finish the job.

Not if he could help it.

Using one more spurt of speed, he lifted himself into the air. It wasn't like flying, but he was able to propel his body in any direction, sort of like travelling a thin conductive wire. He landed by the boy's head. From this distance, even through the smoke, he could tell he was no boy. He had to be about twenty or so. Only a couple of years younger than himself.

The smaller man had made himself a target by initiating his powers so early before an attack. Maybe he was hoping to see a little better.

All the same, he was a sitting duck.

With a mere thought, he felt his eyes surge with a brief power, sending an arc of electricity at the cold blooded little man. He heard him cry out in pain as his own weapon struck home, sending the man flying backward, writhing in agony.

He wasn't sure just how powerful his electric attacks were, but if it was anything like being properly electrocuted, it had to have hurt.

All the same, he was out for the count.

With one final burst of speed, he headed back toward Murray Street and the same alcove he had first transformed in to reverse that action. He didn't want to get too involved. As it was, he had possibly done too much already, but he had most probably saved a life.

In another flash of blue, he was back in the same grey suit. Once more rubbing at his goatee, he was pleased to find it back to normal. He liked the goatee. He thought it gave him a suave look. It also served as a reminder. He still had unfinished work.

Leaving the four men to finish their fight, he turned back toward the Records building and headed inside.

Like most government buildings, this one had undergone a recent refurbishment. New furniture, new tiles, new paint. And it reeked of that new house smell. It was almost nauseous, or perhaps, noxious.

The lady in reception looked as bored as any government official, though she brightened somewhat when someone approached. It was hard to tell whether it was an act or whether she was genuinely happy to see a fresh face.

"Can I help you, sir?"

He smiled, hoping to come across as charming, knowing his slight accent would help with that a little. It wasn't that he was actually English, but elocution classes had somewhat instilled it in him.

"I made an appointment yesterday."

"And your name, sir?" she had already bent her head to her book as if pre-empting his name.

"Owen Bowman."

THEN

"Owen!"

His mother turned from the window, the horrified look in her face sending a jarring sensation through his body.

He immediately wanted to know what she had seen through the window that had scared her so badly.

"Run!"

The kitchen window exploded inward, his mother, still holding the dish in her hand, leapt for cover. Owen himself ducked into the doorway, covering his head from thousands of minuscule shards that sprayed through the room. The wall opposite erupted in a ball of flame, also exploding into the kitchen, sending plaster and wood over the recently cleaned tabletop and linoleum.

Something swept by the window; it made the sound of a vacuum cleaner, as if it were a motor muffled somehow though working under high pressure.

He turned to see his mum already back on her feet, keeping low as she ran for him. Sweeping him up in her arms, she hoisted him over her shoulder in a fireman's lift. He had never known her to be so strong. She had only recently started joking with him about how big he was, always pretending to crumple under his 'growing weight'. But she lifted him now as if he was a rag doll.

He screamed in terror as a second explosion all but destroyed the kitchen table. The wall where the first impact had hit had already caught fire.

16

Outside the roar of Dad's tractor was drawing closer. It could never move fast, but it sounded like it was making good time now.

Then it stopped, its homely chugging replaced by a staccato beat of gunfire on its hard hull.

Owen was carried down the hallway toward the basement stairs.

"What's happening?" He cried out over the racket from outside.

"Hush, honey. Everything will be okay," She said it so calmly, he almost believed her. Almost.

She had only made the first step down when the front door was blown from its hinges, narrowly missing her as she shut the door behind her. The basement stairwell was located beneath the stairs up to the first floor, which were located in the main entrance.

She slammed the bolt closed on the door and continued to run down the stairs. Owen was slightly winded as he bounced on her hard shoulder. He knew she didn't mean to hurt him, but he cried out anyway. He was too scared to do anything else.

Above them, someone was trying the door. The handle rattled a couple of times before the whole frame was jarred as someone outside tried to break in.

His mum reached the bottom of the basement stairs just as the upper door was also knocked from its hinges. Wood splinters shot down at them like daggers, some cutting into her skin.

She didn't make a sound as she charged into the cellar, spinning as she did so to lock the bottom door.

This one would hopefully hold better.

She lifted Owen down, taking hold of his hand as she backed away from the door, eyeing it for any movement. She jumped slightly when the first impact came. Owen felt it in her hands. He also felt her pulse racing. She was scared, almost more than he was.

She squat down to face him, turning him so he could look into her eyes. His own wandered to the door. She shook him slightly to regain his attention.

"Owen. Whatever happens here. Remember we love you. Your dad and I. And if you get away, we need you to get to Aunty Helen. Will you do that?"

He nodded, obediently. He knew where Aunty Helen was. She wasn't really an Aunt. More of a family friend. Even Owen knew she wasn't really related, but she and Mum had always acted like sisters.

His mother smiled, brushing one of his locks of hair that had fallen loose out of his face, just as a second crash came from the door.

"Now, I want you to find somewhere to hide. Anywhere you can."

"But-"

She shook her head and he didn't argue, "No buts. Go."

17

The basement had to be the largest room in the building. He had played hide and seek down here with Ryan. There were a lot of old tool chests, machinery parts and cupboards to vanish inside or behind.

Without looking back he disappeared into the shadows. He didn't look back again, even when he heard the door give way under the attacks from the other side. Nor when his mother cursed those people on the other side.

He ducked behind a large tool chest and tried to squeeze himself into the tightest ball he could. And he listened.

CHAPTER THREE

OWEN

He was led through the building by a Margaret Henders. She had been summoned by the receptionist and promptly arrived. Her role was dual in so far as she aided in maintaining records as well as maintaining the security around them. There were tight regulations pertaining to some of the more 'unknown' and 'mysterious' records.

Owen knew what he was looking for wasn't the most common of items. By all accounts it shouldn't even exist. He still wasn't sure if it did, but he had to find out. He had been given a name and a date. Hopefully putting the two together would bring up something.

After going up several floors in the elevator in complete silence, Miss Henders, she wasn't wearing a wedding band, indicated for him to step off on the fifth floor.

He found himself in a second reception area. Smaller than the first and a lot darker. In one corner, a fluorescent light was starting to give up as it flickered in and out of existence. The hard wood walls, covered in a thin layer of dust, reminded Owen of one of those gritty lawyer shows on television. The only thing not wooden in the room, besides the lights and a slowly turning fan in the centre of the room, was a small metallic swipe box beside the only door out. Henders removed a card from around her neck and ran it through the slot.

A green light checked on before the door, rather than simply unlocking, actually slid out of sight. A bit more high tech than it all appeared. Owen began to wonder about any other hidden gizmos. He assumed there would be cameras hidden here and there. Probably trip lasers as well.

There were a lot of documents in this building and some of them were highly classified. That was probably why the building they were housed in was pretty nondescript externally as well as internally.

The room he entered next was like a massive library. Aisles and aisles of boxes. What one would expect in an evidence storage room at a police station. In front of the door there were eight work-stations closely grouped together, divided by high wooden panels for privacy. At each was a computer terminal, a pad and pen. Simple and probably deceptive. The information stored on that terminal would most likely be extensive and possibly destructive if the wrong stuff got out. Owen was sure there would be monitoring programs in place to make sure he looked only at what was relevant to his request. Similar to that used on the Internet to prevent people going to specific and undesirable sites.

"Most information has been stored on our database. Copies of relevant papers have been made. If it is missing something, you will find it in one of the boxes. References will be given on the database. You will only check what was requested on your application. You will be monitored."

He nodded, moving toward one of the stations. Before he sat, he looked up; "Can I get copies?"

"There are print options on your terminal. There is a printer over there," She indicated a smaller work station, one he had failed to notice on entry, mainly because it sat in the front corner, out of the way, "Some items are restricted and can not be printed. If you require anything else, there is a button located on the keyboard marked RA. Just hit that and someone will be with you."

Her formal manner somewhat clashed with that of the receptionist. It also explained why the other lady was happy to see a fresh face. If everyone in the building was like this Miss Henders, you'd be happy to meet a cockroach.

She left quickly and quietly.

Owen took his seat and let his eyes wander around the room, taking in every nook and cranny, spotting every camera, hidden or otherwise and running over the dozens of aisles of information. He couldn't even begin contemplating what was in here. And this was only level five. There were at least another seven floors of information besides this one.

As the silence set in, he began to feel slightly uncomfortable, so he hit the space bar on the keyboard and watched as the screen came to life. As he had guessed, it was only in stand-by mode.

The program that was on screen was simple. A search engine, much like one found on the Internet. It had specific requests such as Name, Address and Date. Beside date was a pull down menu with options such as Sold, Purchased, Birth and Death. He only had two pieces of information and he wasn't even sure what the date stood for.

Entering in the Name window 'Ethelbridge Holdings Estate', he tabbed down to the date and selected the Sold option before typing '19th August 1988'.

Clicking on search, a second window appeared instructing him to wait, as if he had anything else to do.

He could hear the terminal clicking over, scanning all of its files for related information then scanning the main server.

Surprisingly it didn't take long for the overlaid window to disappear and be replaced by another declaring several items had been found. He selected the first on the list by double clicking on it.

The source was a science magazine that had gone out of print several years ago.

'Ethelbridge Holdings Estate – The agreement to unite between Landsdown and Lester Farms and Minister of Agriculture Karl Horrigan saw the dawn of a new era in pharmaceutical and naturopathic science. Minister Horrigan, also the Chairman to recently established Ethelbridge Holdings Estate, has revealed plans for a newer and better equipped set of laboratories to be established on Landsdown's farm land as the two companies finalised their merger.

"'The acreage shall provide adequate space for the development of the plants found to be rich in medicinal properties as well as room enough for our new base of operations," Minister Horrigan told the guests at a gala opening for Horrigan's newest branch of Ethelbridge Holdings – Jackson's Veterinary School of Science.'

The article continued on about Horrigan's other investments. Obviously this was before a bill had been passed making it illegal for any parliamentary member to have substantial shareholding.

The article was relatively short and low on details. It did, however give other avenues for searching. Owen knew he had limitations on his perusal of stored files, it had been explained to him in detail over the phone. But part of his leeway was the fact he was able to follow a limited number of attached leads, such as Minister Karl Horrigan. This gave way to the idea of freedom of information. They, by law, didn't have the right to totally restrict all available information, but they did their best. What they didn't consider too closely was that by allowing attached links to be followed is that each link leads onto another and, hence, on again. If one had the time, one could look through the entire database because it is all linked so neatly together. Much like the Internet, without the porn attachments, however. Though it had also been made clear he was only allowed a handful of link searches.

Returning to the search screen, he erased Ethelbridge and replaced it with the minister's name.

Again, the wait window came up. And it took longer for it to vanish. Obviously it had to do a bit more digging for this particular name.

When, eventually, it did disappear, the computer informed Owen it had found over one thousand six hundred and eighty two related articles.

"Woah. Who's been a busy boy then?"

This would take some time to get through, unless he could narrow the search.

Clicking on the pull-down menus, he scanned the list of options. It didn't take long to find the appropriate one.

A third window appeared with the heading of 'Refined Search'.

'Include-' and again it had a pull down menu giving options such as Keywords, Topics, and Links.

Selecting Keywords, the window expanded, giving him room to add at most eight words or sentences to add to the search.

The only thing he could think of adding was 'Ethelbridge'.

He did so. And the computer began to click over again.

To be honest, Owen had never heard of either Horrigan or Ethelbridge. Maybe he had been too young at the time. But surely, if Horrigan had been such a humanitarian, he would be well remembered. As for Ethelbridge, it had only happened by chance that he discovered them. That and a little coaxing out of his Aunt had brought him to the Records Agency.

She didn't want him to come. Practically begged him not to, but his mind was firmly set. He had to find out for himself.

This was the only way he had left to find out what was actually going on back then. For Ethelbridge Holdings Estate was somehow responsible for what occurred sixteen years ago. Responsible for what had happened to him and his family. Responsible for all those nights locked in that cell and for that one night he watched as his mother was taken from him for the last time.

THEN

That was the last time he cried. Watching as she was dragged by her hair, swallowed by the darkness beyond the monolith. Not once did she scream after that, nor even whimper. She was strong. She had always been strong. The anchor of the family.

And now she was gone. They were all gone. He hadn't seen his father or Ryan since the afternoon of the attack. It was possible they were in one of the other cells, having watched his mother being taken away and not being able to do anything about it.

That was the worst part. Wanting to reach out, to at least hold onto her, hold her back. Anything to stop the darkness taking her. But he couldn't.

He stared out into the circular room for minutes, maybe hours. Hoping she would come back. Hoping they would return her to her cell.

But she never came.

The light in the next room began to dim, that central pillar being consumed by the invisible night above as the sun set, leaving the only light source without power.

Now the shadows were everywhere.

He moved away from the cold bars. More afraid now of what was beyond them than what was in his cell. But he didn't cower anymore. He moved back to what had passed for a bed for so many nights now he had lost count. And sat, watching the still outlines of the bars, wondering if they would come for him next.

He prayed that they did. He prayed that he would soon die. Even that would be better than this. The impotence of his situation, the futility of it all.

Daring not to close his eyes, he sat the whole evening on that bed, watching for the sunlight to appear once more and bring with it the same messenger of death that had taken his mother.

OWEN

Two hundred and thirty six. Two hundred and thirty six items linking Horrigan and Ethelbridge Holdings Estate. That too, would take some time, but it was better than thousands. He shifted slightly in his seat and called up the menu, listing all relevant articles.

Listed alphabetically, Owen scanned over it first. And he stopped about half way down.

'Landsdown and Lester Farms Amalgamation turns Hostile.'

Double clicking with the mouse, the item was retrieved.

Another article from the same magazine dated only eleven days later.

According to what was written, the deal between Ethelbridge and Landsdown encountered some 'differences of opinion'. Following a heated argument between Horrigan and Landsdown's CEO, Lorraine Parks. Parks decided to null the merger of the two companies. In retaliation, Horrigan initiated a hostile take over by instigating a massive shopping spree on Landsdown shares.

Ethelbridge swallowed Landsdown in a matter of days, continuing on with its original plan to develop the site.

Horrigan didn't appear to be the perfect angel after all.

At the end of the article were several links. One included the proposed designs on the site.

Once again using the pull down menu, Owen crossed to that site and set the machine to print, even before the page had finished loading.

He had a hunch and he was going to follow it.

As the machine in the corner began to spew forth paper, Owen let his eyes play over the pixilated images on screen. They were fairly extensive. Six buildings, several floors in each, then there was the land planning, such as the layout of the plantations, the location of the research compound, as each building would be linked to the others via an integrated walkway system, effectively making it a veritable spider's web design.

Whilst the printer reproduced the screen, Owen returned to the previous page. Another article had caught his eye.

"Minister Dies in Landsdown Explosion"

Following that link, the screen reset itself and revealed, line by line, the same title set underneath the front page heading of the State Newspaper. This had been a huge news item at the time, obviously.

Owen let his eyes dance over the small print as beside it, a picture of the minister himself was unravelling.

From all accounts, there had been an explosion at the Ethelbridge Holdings Estate on the twenty-second of June sixteen years before hand. The minister, who had been attending a shareholder's meeting on the premises, had been killed in the blast, along with the eighty or so other stockholders. The explosion was attributed to a disgruntled employee of the old company having been laid off after the take over. He too died in the blast, supposedly.

"Convenient," Owen whispered aloud.

He scanned through a few more articles before finding one that was dated only three months ago. Opening the link, he found 'Ethelbridge bid for Power'.

The article spoke of Ethelbridge's financial revival. A new, unnamed benefactor was encouraging the company to diversify into power supply. They had placed a tender bid with the state government to provide a newer, cheaper power for the people of Perth. As for what the actual source of this power was, it wasn't made clear.

Something chimed and Owen looked up from the screen. It sounded as though it came from the door.

Leaning back slightly on his chair to get a peek of who was coming; all he could make out was the edge of the door disappearing into the wall.

He'd need to stand up to get a better look.

The door was sliding closed as he got to his feet. And when he looked around, no one was there.

"Hello?"

He wasn't imagining things. The door had opened. And closed again.

Maybe they had changed their mind, didn't want to come in after all.

He shrugged to himself and moved toward the printer. There were at least seventeen pages out already. By all accounts there would be the same left to print. They were detailed schematics. Air conditioning ducts, gas lines, all sorts of electrical circuitry. All included.

He sifted through the pages he already had. There were several write-ups throughout on the architects as well as the proposed purposes of some of the facilities. This was obviously what was given to the planning commission. Each paragraph was a butter wouldn't melt description of, to Owen, what sounded like vivisection. Animals would be housed in some of these buildings, experimented on to test the developing pharmaceuticals. If the public today got word of this, they would be up in arms. But according to the article, they were given the green light in 1988.

One of the terminals, he figured his own, clicked over noisily, probably reverting to standby mode.

"You really shouldn't be sticking your nose where it doesn't belong."

Owen pirouetted around to see who spoke. In the low light, he couldn't see anyone. There was no one by any of the terminals, nor the door.

"You could find it being…broken."

Someone in the aisles. He wasn't close. Perhaps on the opposite side of the room.

Slowly, Owen retrieved the next few pages that had printed out, stuffing the bundle in the back of his trousers, under his jacket.

"Or burnt."

The speaker was moving. Along one of the aisles.

In the gloom, however, Owen spotted a little flash of light behind one pile of files. He was right. Whoever it was was across the room from him.

24

He could make the door. But he would lose the rest of the pages, not to mention be giving up a chance to do further research. There were hundreds of files still to go through.

The light fizzled out and he lost sight of whomever it was that was speaking.

"Some people aren't pleased with you."

There should only be another five pages or so to go, Owen thought to himself. Hopefully he wouldn't need to move until he had them all.

"You're very quiet."

What was this man trying to prove? Was it some sort of psychological game he was playing? Trying to psyche him out? It wouldn't work. Besides his lines had been rather corny so far.

"We know who you are."

'And where I live, no doubt.' He thought to himself. A load of lies.

"You disappoint me."

The printer stopped, reset itself and fell silent.

Owen grabbed at the remaining sheets and slid them alongside the others.

"I expected something out of you. A little bite. Too bad."

And one of the shelves erupted in flames as a stream of fire arced from behind it straight toward the printer.

Owen jumped out of the way, not quite surprised, but amazed at the golden tint to the flames. Fire, normally yellow, was also normally hot. But this was something more. The golden hues were sparkling, giving off a great deal more light and a hell of a lot more heat. He had to shy away from the searing air that enveloped the printer and its cubicle.

When the arc vanished, the shelves around the printer, now a curdling mass of plastic and metal, continued to burn at a surprising rate.

Then Owen staggered backward as that same golden fire flared behind the shelves where the man stood. Not just what had been lit earlier, but the whole stack ignited by something behind it. Something that was also consumed by flames.

That was when Owen caught the first glimpse of his antagonist; having to do so through shielded eyes.

The man stepped from out of the aisle he had been hiding in; his body completely on fire, though the flames themselves did nothing to scar him.

Chillingly, Owen could still make out his face, his smile among the dancing embers that made up his body. It was as if this man was a living towering inferno. The fact he was a good foot taller than Owen added to this notion.

Not good. Every step this man took left a small patch of smouldering carpet that slowly began to spread. The initial flames were also beginning to take hold of the wood panelling of the walls and shelves. The papers nearby, dry with age, were like matches, igniting at the slightest inkling of hot air and setting off a chain reaction as it passed the fire along to its neighbour.

Not good at all.

So, this man had powers. Wanted to use them. Fine, two could play at that game.

Owen flung his arm out, feeling the electricity course through his veins and out through his fingertips. He didn't always transform when he used his abilities. It was more a choice than a definite necessity.

Streaming through the already warm air, his aggressor dodged to the side, easing Owen's fears that his own powers may very well be useless against this fiery monster. The problem, however, was as the Fireman brushed against the wall, it too caught without hassle. Almost as a joke, Owen thought about the nights Aunt Helen had tried lighting a wood fire, only to have it fizzle out. They really could have used this man back then.

"Good. Good. You do have some guts. I was hopi-"

There was a slight crackling sound and the air was suddenly filled with water.

The sprinkler systems kicked into over drive as it tried to counter assault the Fireman and his literal trail of flame. Steam mixed with smoke as the fire started to succumb to the water.

The man roared as he threw his hands pointlessly over his head.

Obviously not the brightest of people, Owen thought, but now he was on Owen's turf. Water was a great companion.

It didn't take long for the carpet to soak through, even in that time, Owen had transformed, The papers, along with his suit, out of harm's way, where ever it was that it went.

Fireman looked up, his own flames starting to dwindle, as Owen's own powers flared, signifying the arrival of his 'battle garb'.

The antagonist had no choice. Power down or be forced to do so by the sprinklers.

It was intriguing to watch as the flames were sucked back inside his body; which reverted to dark burning embers which seemed to show he was cooling and then, in an instant, reverting back to the trousered and jacketed form of this roughly dressed man. His eyes, however, continued to burn that same golden colour. Whether that was a permanent indication of his power, or, like Owen's costume, simply a manifestation when it was in use, Owen didn't know.

Owen could already feel his energy splaying out around him. The currents that coursed through his body in this form were wild and ready to let loose. Around his feet and darting out to the thin streams of water falling from above, small sparks of electricity danced, flashing in and out of existence.

It was time to act.

The man began to charge, his eyes burning bright with rage and power, hoping to take Owen out. Stupid move.

Owen simply smiled, pointed down to the carpet where water had begun to pool and sent forth a small bolt of electricity. He watched with complete and utter calm as it played out of his finger and, once it struck the carpet, trip and dance along the water currents until it snapped at Fireman's leg.

He could only imagine what it felt like. But he watched as the knee Fireman was supporting himself on mid stride buckled and sent him falling face first onto the carpet. Water sprayed up from underneath him as he slid painfully toward Owen, who, now taking direct aim, stunned the 'poor fellow' with one more bolt before hurrying toward the exit.

He could hear people on the other side, fumbling and swearing, probably trying to open the door and failing miserably in their panic.

Before the door started to budge, Owen had transformed back and now waited anxiously for them to get it open.

THEN

The door was blown across the room, once more spraying wooden splinters at his mother. The door itself crashed hard against the wall beside her, but she didn't flinch. Instead, she opened her mouth and screamed.

It was the loudest noise Owen had ever heard. Even behind all the cabinets and storage units, he could feel the effects of her shrill and powerful voice rattling his bones. He had heard her yell before, but this was different. Never before had anyone yelled so loud. And now the other people were yelling, too. Not as loud as his mother and out of pain more than anything else.

Then Owen heard a loud cracking sound and his mother fell silent.

The only noise now was coming from the other people in the room. Swear words, declarations of 'ow' and 'God damn'. And the footsteps. They scuffled around on the bare concrete floor, sifting and stirring through dust. But it wasn't until Owen heard the heavy pounding of feet on the stairs that he truly felt fear.

It was only one set of shoes. He could tell because he had heard his Dad come down like that when Ryan and he had been in trouble for playing Hide and Seek when they had chores to do. He used to come down in that same heavy manner.

But this wasn't Dad. And Owen feared this person a lot more. When they stopped on the concrete below, so did the scuffling about. The room was completely still. Completely silent.

"Take her upstairs."

More movement as, Owen guessed, his mother was lifted and carried out of the basement. The man who had given the order took a few more

27

steps into the basement. Perhaps to clear the way for his Mum and her carriers.

"Find the boy."

That was when the real noise started.

Outside, it was like a demon. A loud roar that couldn't have been human. Something akin to a dragon bellowed as men and women screamed in response. Those men and women had to be the same ones who had attacked the farm in the first place.

So where did the Dragon come from?

Inside the basement, however, furniture began to clutter as it was thrown about, shoved aside and searched.

He pushed himself even harder against the cases and the ground, urging with his mind for it to open and swallow him.

It didn't.

Outside, there were gunshots. More roars of anger and, if Owen was right, pain. They were hurting the dragon. And then there was Ryan.

He was screaming something. And Owen wanted to answer. He wanted to find his brother so they could both escape. So they could both run away and disappear.

"Sir. Over here!"

The man was standing behind him. He had been too busy listening to what was happening outside; he hadn't heard the man coming.

A hand grabbed his shoulder, but Owen shook himself free, flipping onto his back and glaring up at this evil man. He was dressed in army greens, like what he had seen on television. His face was covered by large goggles and a helmet of sorts.

This man had grabbed at him. This man had hurt his Mum. This man would try and hurt him too.

This man would feel pain.

Without even knowing how, or why, Owen struck out with his hand and took hold of the man's leg, feeling his own veins burn with an inner fury. He didn't know what it was until thin streams of blue light shot out of his grip and up the man's thigh.

The man writhed in pain, his body beginning to shake violently under Owen's touch, trying to scream, but his tongue flapped uselessly in his mouth. His saliva flashed that same blue colour, the same blue colour as the eyes that were now glaring at him with such hatred.

Then something hard hit the back of the boy's head and the world finally went dark.

His last thought was that the earth had finally swallowed him, that perhaps now he would be safe.

OWEN

When the door had finally managed to slide open, Owen ran through into the adjoining room, feigning fear. There were already six security guards, two equipped with hydrants, Miss Henders and several other employees looking frantic and eager to get inside.

They obviously took their jobs very seriously. One of the security guards grabbed hold of Owen as he broke through, but he was able to shake him off. Only to move to the centre of the room and double over, hopefully in a convincing display of breathlessness. The fire had pretty much been extinguished by then. A mixture of the hydrants and the installed systems were very efficient.

The guard walked easily up to him, obviously assessing he wasn't a risk, nor that he would run.

"You alright, mate?"

Owen held up his hand as if to wave him away, "Yeah. Fine. Now. Thanks. Yeah."

The guard nodded, keeping his distance, unsure what to do. At least until Margaret Henders stepped out of the records room. She was ablaze herself. Her eyes burning with anger. She stormed over to the mock victim and he fully expected her to assault him.

"What the hell happened in there?"

Owen pushed himself up to look directly at her.

"A… A man. Inside. He was threatening to burn everything down. Then he attacked me. Lit up some of the records. Fire everywhere, I wasn't sure I'd get out."

Henders looked at the guard, "Is this true?"

The guard shrugged, "The smoke blocked out the cameras. Once the fires started, there was no telling what was going on."

Thank god, Owen thought to himself. He'd be dead for sure if they had seen everything that had happened.

That was when two more guards staggered through the door with the unconscious assailant from within. Owen took the time to try and identify him. But he'd never seen him before.

He was a red head, curly. Pale skin, covered with freckles. Not very attractive, but as he'd noted before, the man was huge. Well, in Owen's terms. He was only about five foot eight. This guy was at least six five.

CHAPTER FOUR

KIRRILY

The phone flew through the air before being snapped back and shoved against a blood-flushed ear.

Kirrily had mastered the technique, not that she had practiced. But all she had to do was knock the end of the receiver, sending it cart wheeling through the air before catching it and putting it into position, all the while dialling with her free hand.

Her eyes never strayed from the screen in front of her. If one didn't know otherwise, and if one was allowed inside her tiny office, one would have thought she was about to have a seizure of some sort. She didn't blink, didn't flinch, and beside the interesting dial-up action, didn't move. She just watched the flashing red light in the centre of her screen with two words remaining constantly black.

"Security Breach"

The phone rang once… Twice… Three times before there was that familiar rattle of the receiver being deftly or daftly fumbled with on the other end.

"'Lo."

"Sorry, sir, did I wake you?"

"Hmm?" There was a pause, a further rattling over the line followed by the voice, much clearer this time, "No. Of course not. What is it?"

"Kirrily Briton, Security – Networking division. We seem to have a breach in progress."

"Have you shut them out?"

"Apparently, sir, there was no need. They were cut off at their own terminal."

The voice grunted, "Then there isn't a problem?"

"Just keeping you informed, sir."

"Write out a report, instigate nominal security procedures to procure a tight ship and forget about it," He sounded as if he were reading it from a manual memorised in his own brain. Excepting his voice began to slur once more toward the end.

The line was then cut followed by the ominous tones of an engaged signal.

She hung up just as skilfully as she had dialled.

Some people had commented she enjoyed her job too much. The way she had made everything a test, from following regulations to the letter, to picking up the phone, to writing a report. The voice knew he could expect at least a five-page document on his desk when he came in.

What people didn't know was that she actually despised this job and actually did all those things to spite the people who forced her to do it.

Rather than tests, they were games. What other job would you be required to phone your employer at all hours of the day or night?

Still, it had its interesting moments. Such as this one. And the pay was brilliant.

Entering several commands, she was able to pull up a window on screen detailing all information retrieved by the intruder.

What she found was both fascinating and uninteresting.

News reports, mainly. And some schematics on some compound.

Apparently the breach originated at the Federal Records building. They too were reputed to run a tight ship. Any unauthorised accessing of information would be cut short immediately. But according to the information on her screen, it wasn't the security systems that had disconnected the caller.

Curiouser and curiouser.

So it was an internal alarm. In other words, the files were deemed classified by the company, but those in the Federal Records Database had somehow been overlooked. The company alarm was flashing but Records were none the wiser.

As to why they were classified was another story. According to politics, anyone could rightfully request the base schematics for a corporate building within justifiable reasoning. Their information would be taken into police records, in case any act of sabotage is recorded at a latter date and they would be questioned intensively.

However, who ever it was that had accessed these details had managed to bypass that political system and head straight for the payload without any such divulgence of personal details.

This wasn't making sense. Surely the company wouldn't have overlooked that possibility, whatever it actually was. The CEO was a stickler for running, as everyone now referred to it as, a "tight ship".

But the newspaper articles. According once more to the system, they too were granted a level four classification, which meant that, although they weren't deemed detrimental to the company, they had a high enough classification to warrant an access alert. Then again, there were so many different rules and regulations, not to mention classifications and division in Ethelbridge Holdings Estate's security; one could get dizzy reading the manual, which Kirrily did now and then for a good laugh.

The system wouldn't let Kirrily view the articles. It simply told her the nature of them, such as schematics, newspaper archives and the like, the date of filing and the title. From all accounts someone was researching the old Base of Operations of Ethelbridge before they relocated to the inner city. No harm in that, Kirrily figured, but for some reason, the system didn't like it. Odd. What exactly were they trying to find, or more accurately, what was Ethelbridge trying to hide?

Kirrily knew it was probably nothing, but hey, anything to make the day pass faster.

THEN

The sun did come again. But it brought no warmth to the little hellhole. There was noise. People shuffling in the other cells, trying to breathe in the light. He looked at his hands. They were so pale. Almost incandescent in the darkness. He imagined the glow in the dark stars he had on his bedroom ceiling. He could be one of those now. If only he could sit in the sunlight long enough to soak it in. Then it would be dark again and he would shine like a torch, leading the way for everyone.

He wanted to laugh at that. But his throat was too tight from all the crying he'd done.

No one had said anything. Not when she had been taken. Not afterward. There were others here, but they hadn't said a word.

Maybe they had been crying too.

That made him feel a little better. He wasn't alone. He wasn't the weakest.

He didn't want to be weak. He was small for his age, and the kids had laughed at him for it. So had his brother. But he didn't care. He wanted to be strong. To take it in his stride.

Now he could no longer do that.

He couldn't even pretend to be strong. He wiped his oily hair from his face. It had stuck to it as he cried, attaching to his tears and never letting go.

He felt so useless. So weak. And that made him angry. But what was the use? It wouldn't get him anywhere.

Maybe if he started to yell, they would come for him, if only to shut him up. Or maybe they'd let him holler until he could not.

There was only one way to find out.

He stood up from his bed and moved to the door.

The sun was up, light spilling gently into the cold round room.

He let his eyes survey the other cell doors and could just make out another glow in the dark. A face at one of the other windows. It withdrew quickly, as if it were afraid not only of the Darkman, but of everyone else.

There was nothing else to do.

So he looked back to the long tunnel opening, opened his mouth and screamed. He felt it welling inside of him. A tremendous surge of energy from deep down in his gut that tore through him like a knife.

His skin prickled and he felt a tingling sensation as what hair on his body that was still dry seemed to lift up into the air on its own accord and the sound came out.

Something in the ceiling of his cell began to crackle, spark. He didn't pay any attention. He wanted to let the sound out. But it seemed like an eternity before it reached his lips.

When it finally came forth, his ceiling exploded in a shower of spark as his voice rocketed from his throat and out into the sunlight and even beyond, back into the darkness, daring to go where he would never dream of.

There was a second flash of light, but he felt this one and his cell lit up like a candle, as if his ponderings of before had come true. He had become that beacon of light, lighting the way out of this dreadful prison.

Noise arose from the other cells.

Questions that became mutterings of awe. Mutterings that may have been questions, but could not be discerned from animal growls. Voices. Movement.

That same pale face appeared at the window once more. No longer afraid, but amazed.

OWEN

Helen was waiting. She was standing on the front porch, tea towel in hand, her eyes darting up and down the street.

She was looking tired, worn. Owen put it down to her having another 'episode'. He'd ask her about it later. He knew she would want to hear all about what he'd learnt.

He turned off the pavement and onto the walkway that led to the front door.

It was a quaint little house. Built around the nineteen fifties and with so many coats of paint, Owen believed that there was nothing else there but the paint, the wood underneath having rotted away.

The flooring was wooden on the inside; rugs covered most of that up, though Helen opted for linoleum in the kitchen. The foundations, however, were stone. The columns holding up the porch and bracketing the stairs leading into the house, not to mention the lower half of the entire external wall was stone. On top of this, wood, painted a smooth apricot cream only eight months before by Owen. It had been Helen's birthday present. He would have done it for her even if it wasn't.

The garden was Helen's doing. She loved her flowers and her hedges. They were always neat and seemingly always in bloom, even in winter. Owen had joked several times that she had cheated by planting those fake plastic flowers. Hedge work lined the small path he now walked along, beyond that was grass on either side. In the middle, ringed neatly by a border of broken tiles, a rose garden. Lining the property fencing were more flower gardens of so many different flowers. But to look one way or the other, it looked symmetrical. In fact, the whole house looked symmetrical, apart from the lovers' nook on the front porch. It consisted of a chain swing that dangled from the ceiling. The wall around it was only slightly higher for privacy, but one could still survey the gardens. Owen and Helen, though not lovers, had spent many summer nights there, talking, dreaming, and comforting each other when Helen had an 'episode' or Owen a recurring nightmare. But the nook made it all seem that much further away. Whatever dangers were out there, they weren't really there, just like Owen's dreams. They were just figments of their imagination.

But like Owen's dreams, they weren't. They were based somewhere in reality. His was in the past. Their fears and Helen's episodes were housed firmly in the future and the present.

It was only a matter of time.

"How did it go?"

"I don't know. I got some information," he produced the scrunched up pages, some of which had been soaked from the sprinklers, "but I was interrupted before I could get much else."

"Interrupted?"

He could see the concern on her face. Finally reaching her, he gave her a hug before letting her know what happened. She held him tightly for a moment, as if she were making sure he was real. Her turns could be bad, he knew that. This one had been only mild, it seemed.

Pulling her over to the nook, they sat down before he continued.

"I don't know who it was, a man. He has some sort of power to transform his entire body into some kind of super heated fire."

Her eyes widened in concern and fear, "Are you-"

He nodded, "Fine. He was clumsy. But he prevented me from getting any more information. The funny thing was he said he knew me."

"Probably a scare tactic."

"No. I think he meant it. I wasn't sure if he was part of the Remnants."

She shook her head, "The Remnants hardly ever leave their home."

"One came out last night. I think it was Luka. He doesn't seem to be as sympathetic to their cause as the others."

Helen smiled, her eyes growing distant as if she were looking into a different time, a happier one.

"Luka. No. He was always a bit of a clown. Never too serious. Despite his build, well you thought he'd squash you as soon as look at you, he was always the perfect gentleman. Like a giant teddy-bear," another thought broke her out of her reverie, "What were you doing there last night?"

He shrugged, "I couldn't sleep. I had to do something, so I went visiting."

She said nothing. He was too old for her to reprimand, too old to give a curfew, too old to put on a leash and stop him living his life. Finally she spoke:

"Just be careful."

"I will. I am. Now, tell me, what happened with you?"

She tried to wave him away, but he wasn't having any of that, "No. Tell me."

She sighed, as if the very recollection was painful.

"I saw things," she let out a small laugh, lacking humour in its tones, "I always see things, what am I saying? Just shadows mainly. Whether it was the past or future, I can't tell. Just a room. One big room. But beside it, as if separated, but still part of… A smaller room. Similar, but more like a hospital. Clean, though earthen," She waved him away again. He let her be this time.

It bought back memories of his own. That single room he'd known. He could see it as clearly now as he could back then. It was amazing. Sometimes he could recall nothing. Other times, clear as day. Vivid. And not only the images. He could feel it all over again. It sent a shiver down his spine.

"Are you cold?"

He smiled, pulling her close, trying to comfort her; she was the one that needed it most, "No. Just someone walking over my grave."

She looked at him quickly, concerned, but he smiled, letting her know he was just joking.

Hopefully she didn't know he was lying.

THEN

His life erupted in a ball of blue light. He wasn't even sure where it came from.

One moment his door blocked his exit. The next, it was no more than a shower of splinters dancing through the large central room.

There were screams. Whether of terror or applause, he couldn't tell.

More faces appeared at the windows as he finally took that step, what felt like a giant leap, out of his dank hole. Not all were human. At least they didn't look to be. He let his eyes and mind examine them all. Some had begun shaking the bars on the doors with their hands, pleading for release. He knew what they wanted and how much they wanted it.

But he wasn't sure he could do it.

He tried anyway.

First the meek little face he had seen earlier. He went over to the door and focussed as hard as he could.

The steel bars on the doors began to shimmy; blue lances of electricity prancing back and forth across its surface, and no doubt within its very core. The hinges on which the door rested began to melt, super heated by a blinding flash of blue.

And the door slipped to the floor before falling flat, cushioned somewhat by the thick air beneath it.

The face within had a body. Scrawny, almost skeletal. Its clothes hung loose over its shoulders, hiding what little else there was to see. Sunken eyes peered out of the holes, skull-like. Horrifying.

Owen turned to the other doors, started working on them.

But there were footsteps. People coming. Were they coming back for him? Were they aware what was going on? They were distant yet. Time enough to free the others.

He only had three other doors open before the footsteps were too close to ignore.

He glanced at the tunnel. Still no sign of them, but the constant trudging of boots was easily discernible in the darkness.

The door he was working on finally gave way. Inside, empty. And he recalled. He had forgotten in the moment. It was his mother's cell. She was gone. Not brought back, not replaced. But there was no trace of her.

His anger flared anew. But this time he wasn't alone.

Three others joined him now. The meek little man; bald and pale, though now, his eyes glowed roaring amber. They had come to life the moment he stepped from his cell.

The other two were eagerly at work on the other doors. One somehow managing to pry holes in the doors without actually touching them. The wood seemingly shying away from his touch.

But there wouldn't be enough time to free them all.

"Cease and desist. Or you will not live to see a new day."

The meek little man spoke, "You call this living?"

"It's what you deserve, animal!"

The voice still came from the shadows. The footsteps stopped. Now only the breathing of the prisoners and the invisible people could be heard.

"We've done nothing. Nothing to deserve this."

The darkness erupted with scarlet beams. They shot forth with only a faint hissing sound as accompaniment. One of the others, the man who made holes, was struck by one and collapsed in a heap. The wall beside the other man sizzled as one bolt struck, barely missing the back of his head.

That man turned and gaped in shock at the darkness.

Owen was having none of this. He hadn't made it out of his cell only to be put back in, nothing gained.

It was time to retaliate. Let these men have some of their own medicine.

He couldn't see anything in the tunnel. The invisible ones were careful to remain so. But that didn't mean they were invulnerable. Otherwise, why would they hide?

It was once more time to act. And they would be sorry.

CHAPTER FIVE

KIRRILY

Kirrily hung up the phone once more. In front of her, written in her tiny handwriting on a small pad was a name and address.

O. Bowman. Unit 5 176 West End Terrace, Kelmscott.

The woman at the Records building was very helpful. Unfortunately the address was not. Being an ex-Armadale girl, a neighbouring suburb, Kirrily was well aware no streets, let alone terraces had house numbers going up that far. There were plenty of small streets around. She recalled actually running over a cat down one of said streets in Kelmscott just after she had gotten her licence.

Stupid thing had run right out in front of the car and she honestly wasn't going that fast. All she thought about afterward was the fact the car had seemed to bounce over it at least eight times, as if traversing hard terrain. Very odd for a house cat to have that effect on a car, though she recalled being told that night by a friend that tabbies were known for their hard skeletons.

She wasn't so upset by the cat being dead. But she just couldn't stop thinking about the possibility of some small kid sitting up one morning in bed only to be greeted by its parents with an ever so sad look on their face. And then their hard task of telling the kid the cat was dead and never coming back.

Then there was the whole mourning period as the kid gets used to the idea, possibly blaming its parents, even though they had nothing to do with it. And who would find it, clean it up, and bury it? Dad? Mum? It was a grotesque thought and it recurred through Kirrily's mind for days afterward.

She did stop the car after it happened. Wanted to tell the owners. But who owned it? There were houses all along the street. Was it a stray? Had it wandered over from another road? Why hadn't it been locked inside for the evening?

She thought about it a lot. At least for a day or two.

But no, there were no houses up to 176 in Kelmscott, other than perhaps Railway Road.

So there was the name. Real? Maybe. But why would it be? Fake the address, you'd get found out later using the name. Unless...

She opened up a phone book on the Internet. It took only seconds to load up. Entering his name, she waited.

Sure enough, there were four Bowman, O. s. Two were married. One to a K and the other to a P. The remaining two were single.

Scribbling down both of these address and the phone numbers onto the same pad, she picked up the phone once more. There was nothing else to do, at least until the next hacker tried to break in, but that happened once in a blue moon. And that moon had already come and gone.

Dialling the first number, it rang twice.

"Good afternoon, Bowman Bridal Boutique. Evelyn speaking. How may I help you?"

"Hello, is Mister Bowman there please?"

There was a pause followed by what sounded like a gargle.

"Hello?"

The voice came strained, "Mister Bowman passed away last April. Can I help you at all?"

The receiver was down in less than a second.

Nope, wrong number.

The next number rang seven times.

"Hello?"

A woman. No details given in the greeting.

"Hi, I was wondering, is Mister Bowman there please?"

Another pause and Kirrily found herself thinking, 'Oh, god, not again.'

"Who is this?"

"Ah," Quick, think of something, "My name is Pheobe Cates. I'm doing market research. I'm looking to talk to Mister Bowman-"

"Not interested."

And the phone hung up as quickly as Kirrily would have done. She listened briefly to the engaged signal before hanging up.

Pheobe Cates? An actress of the eighties. How pathetic a cover was that? She almost slapped her forehead for being so stupid.

At least it was a possibility. Of course, there was nothing saying it wasn't one of the married O. Bowmans, nor that it was a fake name. But this was a possibility.

What better way to cover your tracks than to leave a false address, thus people checking the name would assume it too was fake. She had a whole day to test the possibilities. And she would be paid for it too.

"We have a location. We have the designs. What we don't have is any substantial evidence that anything went on down there."

Owen shook his head, "You still want to approach this legally?"

"Not legally, no. But if it comes down to us and them and the authorities, we're going to need something to back us up."

"Isn't the whole idea of vivisection supposed to be against the law these days?"

"But we need the proof."

"And how are we supposed to get that if we don't at least go inside to get it."

Helen sighed and resumed washing up the lunch dishes. Owen had been drying and putting them away as they talked.

"That's why I was hoping you would find something at the Records Agency."

"I did. That someone is onto us, or at least suspicious of us. Our problem is if they actually decide to make the first move."

"We're more than prepared for that."

"But don't you think this could all get out of hand? I mean, just last week, that explosion at a car park. No one's really sure who to attribute that to."

"There was another one this morning."

He nodded, "I know, I saw the smoke. And these aren't everyday human beings involved either, believe me."

"And neither are we. We can't keep skulking in the shadows, Owen. I can't do that for the rest of my life."

He knew what she meant. Being ashamed of being alive. Things were getting out of hand, especially with the recent spate of events. No one was sure who was doing what or who was on which side. It had become not unlike a war. The preliminary stages at least. First starts the subterfuge, then the paranoia, then full blown conflicts. He'd seen evidence of that this morning at the Cathedral. Then at the Records building.

There had already been news reports, government speeches and Vox Pops of everyday people on the street giving their opinions all over the television. Something needed to be done to calm the situation, but all everybody seemed to want to do was heighten the already mounting tension between the factions.

The general public seems somewhat unperturbed by the events, unless of course they were directly involved. But gauging their reactions from what is being shown on the television, Owen knew that if these antagonists kept pushing, it wouldn't be long before everyone has chosen one side or another and the real blatant prosecution begins.

"All I'm saying Owen, is that no matter what is happening today, we can't stop thinking of what happened in the past, nor what will happen in the future."

Again, he knew that. He was one person who didn't need reminding about the past. It clung to his mind like glue. As for the future, he'd learnt to take responsibility for that through Helen and her own unique abilities.

"But what can we do, really?"

"Anything is better than sitting here doing nothing. We can't do that, not when we know what happened may still be happening and will most likely recur once more."

Nodding, he silently agreed. But two of them against this whole movement. It seemed an impossible task. And he knew even Helen's involvement would have to be limited. Her abilities were too unpredictable and debilitating. So it was on his shoulders to get to the bottom of this.

So he'd already checked the Records building. The net came up blank. The only other options were to go straight for the archives of Ethelbridge Holdings themselves. The hard copies. Or to make the move against the compound itself.

They had already hung the pages he had acquired that morning onto the wall in the study. Being basic print-outs, they lacked the full ease of decryption as most blue prints would have. Black lines ran into more black lines and it was hard to tell what was corridor, what was air vent and what was something entirely different. Then there were those that had been damaged by the water. Some portions of the building were unclear.

They had at least found several entrance points, which had allowed them possible methods of gaining entry.

"What choices do we have," he asked after a moment's pause.

She shrugged, weary of the conversation.

"There's enough information here to get me inside. My memory can do the rest."

"But you alone isn't going to be enough."

"The remnants, then? Ask them for help?"

She looked into his eyes. He could see her uncertainty, "Perhaps," and again, quietly, "Perhaps."

THEN

He felt the tingling in his fingers. Like they were itching to explode. Funny, he thought, it was how he felt in his heart. It was beating so hard.

The meek little man's skin erupted. What was once smooth white flesh seemed infected by some horrible disease as large round welts the size of his fist appeared and burst. Long thin spikes, like those on a porcupine, emerged from within. The pain he must have been going through was evident, but he made no sound, the colour in his eyes flaring in intensity even more. Even on his face, small spikes had made their way through, giving him an almost demonic appearance, if not for his small stature.

One of the other occupants had managed to crawl out through the hole made in their door by the downed man. A woman, huge, muscly. She crawled awkwardly out of the hole and regarded the tunnel with eyes full of loathing.

When she opened her mouth, Owen cringed as a roar so loud, so ferocious forced its way out of her throat. It was then that she too began to change. It happened so quickly, her skin sprouting a thick black layer of fur, her muscles melting and reforming, her facial features seeming to flow from her hard, stern features into the angular and regal features of a wild cat. In an instant, her bulky form was transformed into a graceful, lithe, black panther, every bit as big as the woman that had once been there.

The red beams came once more jarring the prisoners to their senses. Rock exploded around them as the shots missed their targets and smashed into the stone walls.

Owen retaliated by releasing the energy within him. Blue electrical currents burst from his fingertips, arcing their way across the circular room and into the tunnel.

Within, he could see shadows cast against the walls as his own weapons lashed out at anyone and anything he could reach.

The panther leapt into the darkness, her dark coat making her as invisible as their opponents.

And the meek little man, now a visage of thorns and spikes launched himself forward also.

Powering down, Owen didn't want to risk hurting his newfound allies. He needed to get closer, get a better shot.

Screams ripped through the tunnel. Who they belonged to, Owen didn't know. He rushed forward, dodging the flashes of red weapons fire, willing his eyes to adjust to the dark. It didn't take too long after being trapped for so long in his cell.

Although he couldn't make out anything distinct, the shapes were there. The savage panther on its rear legs, clawing at the cowering form of the enemy. Other shapes had formed a huddle to one side. A scream was coming from within.

Owen took quick aim and fired.

Blue streaks lashed like intangible whips at the group. Metal buckles and weaponry shone a bright white against the darkness, revealing more of the tunnels occupants. There were scores of them.

A number had already collapsed on the wet earth, gored and slashed by the Panther. Others scrambled for their weapons, hoping to get a shot off.

Owen pushed his power further. And the screams from before were accompanied by several more as the dark troopers succumbed to the electrical fury.

Red beams flashed by him and Owen dove for cover, cutting his attack short.

Pushing himself into the curved side of the tunnel he tried to see what was going on. Some of the troopers had peeled away from the group, overcome by Owen's powers, leaving whoever was below some room to move.

Another round of yelling rose as the group was launched backward from within. The meek little man, his skin seemingly glowing in the darkness, his eyes blazing swung his arms wildly as he emerged, catching several of troopers with his spikes.

The other occupants still locked in their cells were yelling, rattling the doors holding them in. The noise was terrible. Owen wanted to crawl away, cover his ears, even sing a little song to himself.

But he couldn't. These people needed help. There were more shadows coming at them from deeper down the tunnel. How many were there altogether, he couldn't tell.

He needed to get on the other side, so he wouldn't hit anyone he didn't want to.

He pushed himself onto his hands and knees and crawled along the tunnel wall. He could feel the sodden earth below his fingers. Some areas were hard, but made slippery by something too sticky to be water. Something fell against him, hard and heavy, but he managed to push whatever it was off and keep going.

He could hear the panther nearby, sometimes letting off another ferocious roar, other times whimpering in pain as one of the troopers scored a lucky hit. The meek man was still glowing in the darkness, but his skin was streaked with blood. His or the troopers, Owen wasn't sure, but both were fighting on.

Making it past the two other prisoners, Owen managed to ground himself and take aim at the wall of shadows pushing, stumbling over fallen comrades to get into the action.

He felt the energy bubbling within him. A mixture of fear and anger all over again, somehow speeding up every molecule in his body until he was ready to scream himself. In a second flash of white, his body was consumed by his power. His clothes searing and sparkling as his flesh began to glow, his hair burning a shocking blue.

And it kept going. The beating in his chest seemed to multiply a thousand fold as he glared at the army of troopers all clad in black, all frozen in fear of this ball of light that was Owen.

One man moved to raise his weapon, but not in time.

Like opening a floodgate of troubles, Owen let go. Simply let go of all self-control he had and flinched as a blazing wall of white pulsed out of his body at the troopers.

It happened so quickly, he nearly didn't open his eyes in time to see what had happened. A fresh chorus of pained cries rung out as row after row of these shadowed figures were swept off their feet and sent flying backward, convulsing in agony as his onslaught struck.

Behind him, doors exploded from within or from stray weapons fire. It was time for the others to join the fray.

But it was too much for Owen. The light began to fade in his skin, his body reverting to normal and his mind weary from the exertion. A dull throbbing ache ran the length of his body and he was unable to move. No longer could he see the shadow troops as the real darkness consumed him.

CHAPTER SIX

KIRRILY

It was a reasonably pretty house. Set back from the road, unassuming and only slightly distinguished in design. Kirrily pulled up on the other side of the road, removing a street directory from the glove compartment and opening it on her lap.

Winding down the window slightly, she made herself comfortable and let her eyes scan the neighbourhood.

It was all very much like this house. Nothing special, though somewhat noticeable. The streets were spotless, the gardens immaculate and the houses seemed to have recently received a fresh coat of paint. It looked to be something out of some seventies television show, such as the Brady Bunch. Underneath the street sign, a second notice was posted declaring this particular street the winner of the Perth Beautification Award - Best Street 2001, 2002, 2007, 2009.

After making sure no one else was around, she settled herself against the driver's side door and watched the one house she was particularly interested in.

Though it was getting dark, it was still easy to make out the little love nook to one side of the porch. The gardens around it, like the others on this street, were well kept.

Okay, so surveillance wasn't part of her job description, and this wasn't entirely within her occupational hours. But after this morning's little incident and a little research of her own, she had to admit, She was intrigued.

It seemed that although the old Base of Operations of Ethelbridge Holdings Estate was now deemed off limits and derelict, money was still being diverted from the annual budget to a small division of Ethelbridge entitled "Landsdown Acres", a name given to the block of land on which the BO was built. After finding this, Kirrily had dug even further, into some of the older annual budgets, finding the same 'donations' hovering around the seven-figure mark for the past five years.

Something was obviously not right.

Then, having tried the phone numbers again, she had found the married Bowmans to be female, recently deceased, though not that recently, or on the couch watching a replay of the football from the night before, most likely with a pot belly and stubby shorts who were all too happy to recount the game. Which meant she had to resort to the single Bowmans once more. Of course there was no guarantee this would even be the real name of the offender. It was most likely a pseudonym made up like the address had been, but Kirrily had done some study on profiling and figured her guess to be the most likely.

She tried this address, getting the same woman as she had earlier. Using the same cover, though she knew it was ridiculous, she proceeded to call several times adamant she needed to speak to Mr Bowman for market research purposes.

This was hardly an odd occurrence as market researchers could be quite persistent. The woman grew more anxious per call, which was understandable. But more fearful than angry. The majority of people would have slammed the telephone down or insulted the repeat caller; this woman seemed to find it hard to replace the handset on the receiver properly. After the fourth call, Kirrily stopped. Other than the fact she was bordering on harassment, the woman's reaction indicated this was the best lead she had.

So here she was. Carrying out surveillance, the sun going down, and the pathetic array of Sunday night television programs starting their runs.

After the first half-hour, she checked her watch. Six forty-three. The sun was below the horizon already and the deep purple of the night was reaching far across the Eastern sky. Leaning across to a black duffle bag on the passenger seat, she scrounged around for her glasses.

Pulling her hand out, she toyed with a pair of thin-wired frames with dark lenses. Her own design, prescription and all.

Putting them on, she tapped a small almost invisible button beside the screw on the left arm. The lenses flashed to life.

From face on, they looked like ordinary sunglasses. Odd for this time of day, but looking through the wearer's eyes, the night sky was lit up like day, excepting the fact it was overlaid with a heavy green tinge.

Taking into account the top range of the night vision goggles on the market, black or otherwise, Kirrily had spent a few hours developing her own system and micro-sizing it to fit snugly into these tiny frames.

That's what she did in her spare time. Build things. It was a hobby. On lonely nights and quiet days, she found herself researching current technology on the market and taking it that extra step further. It was only a matter of logic, wasn't it? One plus one made two. So it shouldn't be too hard to make night vision goggles, ambient light, microchip technology and optical fibres equal these little glasses. It wasn't exactly one simple sum. She had had to work out several intense equations every step of the way before reaching the final product. She had developed an earlier version that had been somewhat chunky, resembling the disco glasses in retro movies. It had taken a little extra time to work out the problems and put it all together in a more compact and stylised unit.

She was surprised the people developing this stuff hadn't come up with the same ideas.

Of course, she had seen a version of these glasses in the movies, but technical advisers always stated they were currently impossible to make to those specifications and have them working correctly.

Kirrily felt like writing in and showing them how wrong they were, but hey, why bother? She enjoyed using them herself. If no one else had cottoned on, that was their problem.

She was almost blinded when the porch light snapped on. Mewling in pain, she snatched the glasses from her face. That was another glitch she would have to work out. A faster intensity focus or diaptor as it was known. Regardless, someone was opening the front door. Male. Young, well, about her own age. And he was wearing a bright pink suit and sunglasses.

Odd fellow.

"Owen!"

The man stopped, turning back into the house, "Yeah?"

She couldn't hear what the response was, but she got the idea when he said, "Don't worry. I will. It'll be fine."

Shutting the door, he locked it in several places and shut a fly wire swing door behind him.

Adjusting his glasses, he took the steps of the porch two at a time with a jazzy spring in his step. Kirrily wasn't quite sure what to make of him. Blonde, somewhat attractive in a youthful brutish kind of way, but a little out of the loop. Not that she could really talk.

"My god," she whispered as she leant across the passenger seat to get a better look. He looked downright ridiculous, in an endearing sort of way. It took guts to go out in a get up like that. In some suburbs of Perth he would have been beaten up for sure.

The easiest conclusion she came to was he was probably gay. A pink suit for one, the way he walked for another. Hands in pockets, slightly hunched over, defensive, but with that spritely bounce in his stride.

And his boots were immaculate. High shine black army issue. Stunning, even from this distance.

He disappeared around the side of the house, by a driveway that consisted of two gravel strips.

Doing up her own seat belt, she was ready to start the car when she needed to. She half expected him to reappear atop a penny-farthing or a brightly coloured mountain bike of sorts, but the slam of a car door reassured her there was some sense of normality in the man. It was shortly followed by an engine starting and two glaring beams of light spitting out into the street.

The vehicle pulled out from beside the house and up to the road, pausing as the driver checked for oncoming cars.

It was a beautiful vehicle. Oddly enough, or not, it was a Plymouth Hearse; like his boots, highly polished and gleaming in the moonlight and the ambient light from the street lamps hidden behind tall growth further down the street.

With a slight over revving of the engine, the Hearse pulled onto the street heading the same way, fortunately, Kirrily was already facing.

She watched as he idly drove past, unaware she was even there. While he drove, she could see he sat bolt upright, perhaps so he could see over the tall dashboard. He looked somewhat regal in such a magnificent car. It was massive compared to him. There was no coffin in the back, though she had half expected there to be. It seemed completely empty.

Waiting a few moments, she started her own engine and pulled into the street, turning her headlights on as she went. In the distance, she could see the twin red brake lights flash briefly as the Hearse turned right, out of the street.

Keeping a fair length between her own Lantra and the Hearse, she continued to follow him as he headed south toward the inner city. Of course tailing someone isn't the easiest thing to do, especially if they tend to change lanes a fair bit. Then there was the judging of stop signs and light controlled intersections. There were moments she feared she would lose him, but managed to run an amber light or two. Other times she had to pull up behind or even beside him, trying not to peak into his car, looking obvious. At one time she had grabbed a brush out of her bag and started fixing her hair in the mirror, just so it looked like she was going into the city for a good night out.

She wasn't even sure he was looking, but it was worth the effort.

Finally, they entered the inner city limits. Traffic had thinned out a fair bit as most people opted to stay home on Sunday night. But she had to be careful still as she navigated the smaller streets behind him. It was here that it would be more obvious she was tailing him. She was very conscious of this fact as she turned into King Street, a one way street rarely used by cars as it was a restaurant and clothing strip - a pedestrian thoroughfare.

When he reached the first intersection of King Street and Hay, he pulled up at a stop sign. Kirrily slowed, hoping he would pull away before she reached him.

No such luck. Pulling in behind him, she waited for the cars to pass, allowing Mister Owen Bowman to continue onward.

No cars came.

Something was wrong.

The driver's side door then opened on the Hearse and one black booted, pink sheathed leg stepped out, followed by a blonde head, still wearing the dark glasses and the rest of the pink suited body.

Even behind the glasses, she thought she could see a flare of light. It was probably her imagination, but his whole manner seemed aggressive.

Trying not to seem too obvious, she pulled on the hand brake and slid her hand behind her back, as if to idly scratch, but taking hold of one of her many security measures.

Mister Bowman stepped up to her window. It was still partially down. She turned to regard him casually, she hoped, but he didn't move for a few seconds. Finally, he leaned onto the car with his right arm across the top of the window and his head in line with hers.

"Yes officer?" She tried a little joke, though humour wasn't her style. It came out more like a stony sarcastic spit.

"Do you have a problem?"

She smiled, She liked her smile. Her mother always said it was her best quality. Hopefully it would help a little now. She didn't exactly want to get into a confrontation with this fellow, but she did want to find out what he was up to. And starting out with a fight or verbal argument wouldn't help much.

"I don't think so, Officer. Did I do something wrong?"

"I'm not a-"

She opened the door on him, forcing him to step back a bit, "Because I'd hate to think I ran a red light or something. I could have run someone over. That would have been awful," She started getting out of the car. Trying to sound a little frantic.

"No, you misunderstood me, ma'am, I... Look, I'm sorry; I just thought you were following me."

Ah, good, a way out, she thought to herself. Reaching into her trouser pocket, she snapped out a small ID wallet, "Good, because I was." She said, resuming her neutral tones as she flashed her security badge at him.

She found that although it wasn't exactly a police badge, most people tended to think it was either a division of the police, or perhaps the Federal Police and the others never really knew what level of power security guards had.

Even with the dark glasses, she could read him like a book. He was none too plussed with the situation right now.

He actually adopted a semi-fighting stance. Arms at waist height ready to block if necessary; legs spread slightly for better balance. He had obviously taken some form of self-defence classes.

"But I'm not here to hurt you, attack you, or anything else like that. I just want to ask you a few questions."

"That's not a police badge."

"Very observant," She had already deposited the wallet back in her pocket, "No. It's not."

"Then who are you?"

"My name is Kirrily Briton. I'm a security officer from Ethelbridge Holdings Estate's security; Networking Division."

At the mention of her employer's name he stepped back and she could have sworn his eyes flashed a deep blue behind the sunglasses. Shrugging it off, she continued.

"As I said, I just want to ask you a few questions regarding your research this morning."

He looked up and down the street, edging back toward his car, probably checking to see if she was alone.

"I am alone, Mister Bowman. As I said, I'm not here to harm you in any way," Though you seem ready to jump out of your skin, she added mentally. Something was really bothering him.

Granted, she had been following him, not exactly normal procedures. Or legal. But his reaction had not been to her position but the declaration of her employer's name.

Something was a little out of kilter here.

"What do you want?"

"You were doing some research into the company this morning."

"So? I had authorisation," He paused a moment then cocked his head accusingly, "Who sent you?"

Honesty was always the best way, she thought, though so far it wasn't doing so well, "No one. I came on my own accord. Actually that's why I want to talk to you."

He wasn't actually believing her. But he wasn't exactly disbelieving her either. She hoped she seemed honest enough, "I did some follow ups on your research. Found a few inconsistencies myself."

He stopped moving toward his car. Confused, "I beg your pardon?"

"Just as I said. From all accounts you were doing research into the background of Ethelbridge and Landsdown, correct?"

"Uh...Yeah."

"Well, I did some research myself. Landsdown, as you probably know, doesn't actually exist any more. Yet, Ethelbridge is still paying a large sum into their account each year."

"And you're telling me this why?"

"Well, you obviously know something dirty is going down. I think you're right. And I got bored and decided to do something about it."

"But they're your employers."

"True, but they're just employers. The medical benefits are terrible, the pays even worse and, besides, I don't actually need the job. It's more of a hobby. What they seem to be doing could be wrong, even illegal. I guess I got my dad's ethics when I say I can't stand the idea for working for a corrupt system."

"Who did he work for?"

"He was a policeman. By the way, I love the suit."

She wasn't sure if she had won him over or not. He had stopped retreating, which was a good sign. But once more she could see his point. Why dob in your boss? But as she had told him, she didn't need the job. She made most of her money out of selling some of her designs. Mostly harmless little things for toy companies or large electrical appliance manufacturers, but enough to leave her a well developed nest egg, not to mention enough to continue her own private research for years to come.

The Hearse's engine seemed to idle for a moment before humming back to life as they stood in silence for a couple of seconds.

"Well, can we talk?"

The humming was intensifying.

"I guess so."

It was actually getting quite loud, "Good," She started to raise her voice, "I could do with a cup of-"

She didn't get to finish her sentence. Or more appropriately, couldn't. Not that there was any point. He couldn't have heard her anyway.

Two massive arms had grabbed her hard around her chest, under her armpits, squeezing all the air out of her lungs as she was jerked into the air. But she didn't stop rising. Whoever it was that had a hold on her was lifting her higher and higher.

"No! Wait!" Bowman yelled from below, but she couldn't hear him for the second she got her breath back, she started screaming.

OWEN

One moment she was standing there, a very attractive young lady, though somewhat strange, the next, she was being hoisted into the air by Reebo, one of the Remnants.

Owen should have known from the humming. But it had happened so quickly.

It was Reebo's wings that had caused the hum. They were insect like, beating at what seemed to be a million flaps a second. And, like a bee, he buzzed when he flew.

The scary thing was Reebo also had a temper like a bee. Aggressive and territorial. Protective of the hive, which was located only a couple of blocks away. Owen wasn't sure, however, if Reebo was protecting the hive or if he was looking out for Owen. Sure, the Remnants had never been good friends. Most of them were wary of Owen, but they knew he was generally a good guy, or so he hoped.

He had tried calling out to the winged ambusher, but the girl had started screaming.

Of course, one could hardly blame her. Being yanked off your feet by some one and lifted high into the air can be very disconcerting. As far as Owen could tell, Reebo wasn't going to stop his ascent.

There was only one thing for it.

His suit vanished in a shock of blue light, replaced by his costume. His skin became somewhat translucent in the dark, but his eyesight increased dramatically. He had no problem seeing Reebo in the night sky, nor the flailing body of the security woman.

Owen pushed hard off the pavement with his toes, launching himself into the air.

He couldn't fly, especially not like Reebo, but he could certainly travel a fair distance in a short time.

The world around him blurred, his objective the only thing staying clear in his sight.

Hopefully Reebo would keep hold of the girl, not let her go.

Feeling himself slowing, Owen took hold of a small window ledge on the building beside him. He had cleared half the height he needed to, but Reebo was still going.

"Reebo! Bring her back! She's harmless!"

It was worth a shot.

But the insect-like man was having none of that.

At least she had stopped screaming so much, having redirected her energies to breaking free of her captor's grip. Probably not a good thing being over sixty feet above the ground.

He tried another burst, shooting himself higher; over the roof of the building he had landed on, keeping in mind he would need to find a second place to perch in a matter of seconds.

But something was happening over head.

The woman had pulled something from inside her jacket. A gun of some sort. But she wasn't aiming it at Reebo. Of course that would have been suicide. Instead she targeted a nearby wall above her and fired. There was a muffled "pfft" sound as something shot out of the weapon, burying itself deep in the concrete.

With his sharper vision, Owen could see a thin wire attached. With another flick of a switch on the weapon, it began reeling in, jarring Reebo's ascension to a halt as he sped past the point where her anchor made contact with the wall.

She was resourceful, he'd give her that.

It would certainly make it easier for Owen to catch them.

Landing once more on a narrow ledge, part of the design of the building, Owen halted his own ascension. Maybe she'd be fine without him. But would Reebo?

The pulley system she had in her grappling gun was working hard against Reebo's powerful wings, but it was making progress, pulling her down and toward the safety of the wall.

It was only a matter of seconds before Reebo, frustrated with being pulled backward, let her go. She screamed once more as she dropped several metres, never letting go of her pistol. Swinging down, she was heading straight for a glass window, of which she was bound to smash straight through.

Owen had no choice but to launch himself up once more, hoping to judge the whole manoeuvre correctly.

As she swung toward the window, Owen aimed for the closing distance between them. It wasn't a difficult task, but he didn't want to injure her on impact.

It was funny how he perceived things differently in this state. Although he was moving at god knew what speed, he still perceived it as if he were simply running. Through air, admittedly, but running all the same.

Carefully, he reached out for her as he came into range, and wrapped his arms around her. She was still screaming and it seemed to raise an octave or two as he took hold of her. He knew it wasn't from pain. He had learnt to control the effects of his transformed state. It was more for show than anything else, though he had to admit it must have been pretty frightening.

"I've got you, he whispered," and she seemed to quieten down a bit. Maybe it was the tone of his voice, hoping it was reassuring and not threatening.

Changing his own direction, he grabbed for her anchor rope and took hold, stopping this latest spurt. Reaching his feet out, he made contact with the wall and eased himself and his passenger back against the wall.

The humming had dissipated for a short time, but was steadily growing louder once more. Reebo was coming back for seconds.

"Reebo! Wait! It's me!"

The insect man zoomed in from the night sky and hovered a couple of feet away from where Owen was perched. The girl was shaking, but it was hard to tell whether it was fear or anger. She didn't exactly come across as someone too easy to scare. Sure she had done some screaming earlier, but who wouldn't have?

"We were just talking."

"Why's she here?" Reebo wasn't the most eloquent of people. In fact, Owen wasn't entirely sure he had received any formal education at all. Nor had many of the remnants, "Why's you here?"

"I'm here to see you. All of you. As for her, I'm not too sure-"

"I can speak for myself, thank you," She brushed her hair from her eyes with her left hand, refusing to let go her right's vice like grip on Owen. He could tell now, she was definitely angry.

"What the hell were you playing at," She demanded of Reebo, "You could have killed me if I didn't kill you first! You're lucky to be alive, thanks to your friend here."

He poked a finger at her, as if testing her substantiality, "Why's you here?"

"I'm here to find out what the hell is going on around here! No! Actually, as far as I am concerned, it's none of your damn business!"

"Look," Owen tried; the remnants were not known either for their social graces, "I'm sure he meant no real harm."

She looked at him incredulously, "He was trying to kill me! You think that implies he's a pacifist?"

"And you were following me! You had no right to be here in the first place!"

"If you want to argue about this, then screw you! I simply wanted to find out what was going on behind Ethelbridge's closed doors. Obviously you're not going to be any help, so if you'll kindly take me down and I'll leave you alone."

"Ethelbridge?" Reebo buzzed. His vocal chords had somehow been affected by his own abilities for he had a tendency to hum at the back of his throat, not to mention linger on his "s's".

"That's right, Ethelbridge. But if you want to play like children, that's your choice," She turned back to Owen, "Now. Take me down or am I going to have to find my own way?"

Shrugging, Owen did as she asked.

Letting go of the chord, he let himself and the girl fall. It was at least a seven story drop, air rushing past them at a tremendous speed, even Owen could feel his stomach lurch slightly, but she never made a sound.

For the last couple of metres, Owen triggered his powers once more, using the wall beside him, he boosted himself upward slightly, acting as a reverse thruster of sorts to their descent and they landed comfortably back on the pavement, almost exactly where they had left off.

As he landed, Reebo's wings folded behind him, vanishing below his clothing, or seemingly becoming a part of it. It wasn't easy to tell.

The girl, Kirrily if Owen remembered correctly, gave both men a rather scathing look before heading back to her car. Her eyes, even without the mystical flare Owen's own eyes had, burned into him as if she shot lasers out of her very pupils. He felt himself instinctively lean away from her, in case she could, in fact, do that.

"Kirrily, wait," He was saying that word a lot lately.

"What the hell for? So I can be air lifted up another thousand feet and left on top of some building or possibly dropped instead? How do I know I can even trust you?"

That was going beyond the limit. Trust?

"Where on Earth do you get off talking about trust? You who's been tailing me for the last half-hour or so. Then you proceeded to lie to me, playing some stupid little game, of which, by the way, I could see right through-"

I wasn't the one who was breaking into classified files now was I?"

"They weren't classified as far as I knew!"

She stopped and turned on him. This woman had spirit, He'd give her that, "Why the bloody hell should I care? I was just doing my job!"

CHAPTER SEVEN

KIRRILY

Okay, that was a lie. But what could she say? She'd behaved very stupidly ever since she started making the phone calls. Which she didn't even have to make. All she had to do was write the blasted report, have it on her CO's desk and forget all about it. But no, she had to do what he had said, play stupid little games.

"Boy what a fool I was!"

"I beg your pardon?" He asked, a little confused by her change of tack.

"I guess I was bored, I don't know. After finding out about the fire at the records building, the fact you'd been followed inside by one of Ethelbridge's security details, I had to find out what was going on."

"He was from your company?"

She was surprised he hadn't known this. Well, she hadn't either without looking into it a bit further. Mind you, his details were incomplete. As for his arrest that morning, Ethelbridge only had to pull a few strings to get him off. That's exactly why her father got out of the force. Corruption. Someone had to have been bribed or something.

That was also a reason she had followed up on this. If there was corruption involved on both sides, the Police and her employers, she was going to get to the bottom of it.

"Of course he was. What did you think? He was a tourist with a penchant for pyrotechnics?"

"So you know of his abilities as well?"

This stumped her, what was he talking about?

"I beg your pardon?"

"Whoever he was, he burst into flames right in front of me."

She cocked an eyebrow. Was he serious?

"Like Spontaneous Combustion?"

He shook his head, "Like I'm doing right now. Physically manifesting an elemental force."

To be honest, she hadn't even realised. Now that he'd mentioned it, she had to think how blind she was. There he was, all aglow and mysterious in the night; his fabulous pink suit vanished from sight.

"Hmm," was all she managed.

"So you didn't know?"

"No," She wasn't sure exactly what he was asking in regards to, his own abilities or the guy Ethelbridge sent. Either way, she answered correctly.

"Then what's going on?"

"I was hoping you could tell me."

The guy with the wings was getting impatient. They had started to flutter once more, an unconscious sign of agitation.

53

"We best get out of sight," He buzzed.

Mr Bowman nodded, thoughtfully, "Agreed," Then he looked straight at her. His eyes still the sharpest blue she'd ever seen, drilling into her like needles or scalpels dissecting her thoughts, "Your place or mine?"

"I think we best return to mine," The insect man said, "You know where it is."

He launched himself into the air, disappearing into the night. Kirrily watched him go, trying to see how to follow him, but when she gave up and looked back at Owen, he was wearing that old pink suit again.

"Neat trick. You'll have to teach it to me one day."

He smiled, "You got some neat tricks of your own."

"You like?"

His nod was only slight, part amusement, part respect. She could tell. Though the sunglasses were back on, his smile read like volumes.

"So, which way, Mister Bowman?"

"Owen. Call me Owen. And you can follow me."

"That's what I've been doing all along."

THEN

The lights were buzzing, flickering as one would imagine in a horror film. Hard neon tubes hung from an unseeable ceiling above a cold hard table on which Owen was strapped. He couldn't even feel the edges, though his tiny hands kept searching, hoping to find something to hold onto. But there was nothing, other than the tight straps restraining him.

Water dripped in the distance, pinging in a pool of water, yet echoing as if it were in a bucket. He could barely open his eyes. He was weary and sore. Every muscle was aching, and his head throbbed like the drum of some cannibalistic tribe during a jungle ritual.

He wanted to cry, hoping it would take the pain away, wipe clear the nightmare he was in. For that's what it felt like. As if running away, but you weren't getting anywhere, the monsters coming for you steadily gaining. And you scream, but nothing comes out. Then, suddenly falling, the ground giving way beneath your feet and you fall and fall, no end in sight as you keep trying to scream.

And yet he was stuck to the table, unable to move, too tired to even try to scream.

And there was another sound.

Crying.

Someone was crying and it wasn't him. Letting his head fall sideways, he blinked a couple of times, hoping to be able to see.

But there was nothing there, no one.

A breeze ran through the room. Only slight, as if some one opened a door. He could feel the hairs on his skin stand on end, goose bumps prickling in reaction to the chill.

Somewhere, an explosion. Someone screamed. Then silence. No more light, other than the tubes above him, which he strained not to look at.

"Hush little baby, don't say a word..."

A second explosion, closer.

"Mamma's gonna buy you a mocking bird."

He wasn't sure if he was singing or someone else. It was a hollow voice all the same. Lacking in variations in tone and feeling. As if remembering a time when all was bright, but now, all gone.

Someone yelled incoherently nearby, only to be cut short in a loud gurgling choke.

"If that mocking bird don't sing..."

It wasn't him. Someone else was singing. And he knew the voice.

"Mamma's gonna buy you a diamond ring."

Something growled in a room adjacent. Perhaps that black panther. Perhaps another nightmare being spawned. All the while, the singing voice coming closer. It was within the room. And he could hear movement, scratching, like a cat at a door, trying to get out.

"If that diamond ring turns to brass."

"Mum?"

"'s Gonna buy you a looking glass."

He strained, trying to see her. She was in here. It was her. Wasn't it? Or was it a trick? Was this all just another nightmare?

"Mummy."

"If that looking glass gets broke..."

He felt a cool hand take his. Gasping in fright, he turned his head to see the palest of skin reaching from the gloom. But he couldn't see her clearly. And once more he felt a tear. He wanted to see her again. Her happy smile, her bright eyes. He wanted everything to be back the way it was.

He tried to speak, but it caught in his throat, coming out as a strangled sob.

The voice changed, lilting slightly, more soothing as it began the song again.

"Hush little baby don't say a word..."

Another hand appeared and undid the strap around his waist, which also restrained his forehands.

And he snatched at her wrists, wanting to hold onto her and never let go.

"Shh. You have to go."

Her free hand undid the rest of the straps, not once did she enter the light.

"You're coming too!"

She lifted him off the table and onto his feet in front of her, but still he could not see her. She kept him in the light, making it hard for him to refocus.

"They'll be coming for you soon. You need to run."

"I don't know where to go."

A door opened to the room. A dull light shone in from a weak globe hanging from a cord in the hall beyond. His mother shied away from the light. The hand in Owen's felt odd now. Slightly larger, hairier.

"Go. Now."

The voice had changed timber. It was deeper. It wasn't his mother. But it was still familiar. He knew it just as well.

"Owen. You have to go," With the extra light, he could see now, it was his father. Sweat covered his skin. But there were aspects to his face that were his mothers. But they were disappearing, as if he was changing from one form into another, his own form. He was tired, haggard and worn. But Owen could see the same love in his eyes as he had in his mothers, and that was no copy, "Go."

Weakly, his dad turned him toward the door and gave him a gentle push. He wanted to stop, to fight. Argue with his father to come with him. But he could tell he wouldn't get anywhere. His father had always been like that. Once he made up his mind, don't argue.

But this was different. This wasn't a case of go to your room or you'll get a spanking. This was the choice of staying by him, or possibly never seeing him again. Owen knew that. He had learnt a lot within the time he had been kept here. But he had also learnt that no matter what happened he had to keep going. To fight. A figure, a silhouette stepped into the doorway, but Owen knew who it was.

The little pale man. He wasn't glowing any more. He simply extended his hand to Owen and the boy had no choice but to take it.

"Get him out of here," His father pleaded and the little man nodded.

KIRRILY

They parked on the street. Kirrily pulled her own vehicle in behind Owen's Hearse. She'd have to ask him about that. Not many people drove Hearses. She wasn't even aware they were for sale except to funeral parlours. But it was a beautifully kept vehicle. The finish reflected every particle of light off it so cleanly, if it were in the middle of a discotheque or nightclub, it would act like a mirror ball. After she had gotten out of her car, she activated her security system, another one of her own developments.

The building they had parked in front of was old. Well, not old as in centuries, but in terms of decades. The design would have been fifties although it did stand fifteen or so stories high. It hadn't been well maintained as the paintwork had started peeling, rust had taken hold around the window frames and door not to mention the concrete having been water affected and pock marked. All the windows were dark, either painted or boarded closed from within. It was actually quite odd for a building looking like this to be left untouched by restoration or the heritage society of Western Australia. Sure, if it had been located on the Eastern side of the city, it would have fit in perfectly. That was referred to as the Old City. But over this side, it was the glitzy steel and glass towers or refurbished building fronts that had dazzling buildings built behind them, claiming to have kept the historic aspect of the building, when in fact using the facade as that exactly, by concealing the modern steel and glass that lay within.

But this, this was truly amazing. She was surprised she hadn't seen it before. Or that there wasn't an uproar about it from the public. Unless it belonged to someone. But even then, the public would make their feelings known.

It really did stick out like a sore thumb now that she thought about it. In fact, she found herself staring at it for a good while, trying to let the whole thing sink in.

Where on earth had this building been all these years?

"Kirrily?"

"Mm?"

"Coming?"

"Mm."

She felt a hand take her by the elbow and pull her along. She nearly tripped over her own feet as she moved; trying to keep an eye on the structure, as if it would pounce any second and she wanted to be ready for it.

He led her to the front door. And she was finding she was having trouble concentrating on anything but the building or his pink suit. Both were inappropriate really, and both were surprising.

"Your suit…"

He was nudging the door with his elbow whilst toying with the lock, "You like it?" He didn't wait for a response, "Spray paint. It used to be khaki, like a safari suit. I didn't like the colour so I spray painted it."

"Pink?"

"It looks better than Khaki."

"Doesn't it go all hard from the paint?"

"A little and starts to fade a bit but it loosens up a bit after a while."

The door snapped open and Owen nearly tumbled inside, "Have you tried dying it?"

He collected himself and indicated that she should enter, "I was going to, but haven't got around to it yet."

Reaching around in the dark, he flicked a switch and the light snapped on. Several floodlights on the ceiling lashed out revealing a massive lobby. It looked more to be a replica of a New York subway station with the dowdy tiles and columns. Off to the right was a small security station. It had to be an old apartment building. That was where the doorman sat, making sure no undesirables got in without permission. It was empty and dust covered now. In fact, the whole room was covered in a thick layer of dust. There were, however, several sets of footprints down the centre of the room, leading from the elevator and stairs to the front door.

"What, no welcoming committee?"

Owen looked at her and smiled, "They'll be waiting for us upstairs."

He started to lead her toward the elevator, before turning sharply and heading toward the stairs. Kirrily managed to suppress a groan. She hated stairs. It wasn't that she was unfit, just the opposite. She kept to a strict work out regime that kept her in top form. But stairs - there was just something about the whole climbing thing that annoyed her; for one thing, her mother had always told her that too many step walks can cause a big buttocks. Not that she was fussed about her appearance, well, not that fussed.

Besides, if there was a lift, why not use it?

"How far do we have to go?"

Without looking back as he started up the first two steps, Owen replied, "Top floor. Only seventeen flights."

She felt her jaw clench involuntarily, jutting forward, perhaps like an angry ape threatening what Kirrily saw to be an invisible predator. But of course, no one would listen to her complaining, so she set herself for the long climb.

The stairs wound round, half the stairs between floors going one way, onto a landing and then the rest of then reversing back on the others up to the next floor.

The stairwell itself was grotty. The corners were infested by spider webs, dirt and rubbish that had been either left by vagrants or simply kicked out of the way. The dust layer seemed thicker here, though the evidence of previous occupants on these stairs was more than evident. And the railings, she flinched every time her mind slipped and she took hold of them to help her up the next flight of stairs. She practically had to pry her fingers off the sticky bars, dragging dark brown residue along with her. She was going to need a shower after this. The lights still worked, but only just, flickering in and out of power in their little wall mounts. The globes were hidden by the mounting's shells, whether they too were encrusted with dirt or whether it was part of their design, she couldn't tell.

"So," Kirrily almost jumped when Owen opened his mouth for the first time on the fifth floor. So she reached round to her back and took hold of her weapon, just in case, "Why on earth would you risk your job for this? Ethelbridge are ruthless. Who knows how far they'll go to protect themselves."

"No one is beyond the law, Owen, no matter what they think," She answered matter of factly, "I don't hold with corruption. And I abhor being a part of it."

"You're from security, right? That'd hardly make you a part of-"

"Letting them get away with it is just as bad. It's almost akin to standing by and watching a sexual attack take place."

She couldn't see his face, but he was obviously taken aback by her opinion.

Shortly, he spoke again, quieter this time, "Do you even know what this is about?"

By the way he had asked she knew it was personal to him. But the truth was she had absolutely no idea. She figured they had run some sort of scam, like a money making deal and run off with all the investor's money. That had happened several times in the past and been reported widely. Most offenders had gotten away with it by running off to another country and feigning illness to protect themselves from deportation back to Australia. Others claimed memory lapses as well as the bad health in court, thus delaying the trial, giving them time to stash the money in foreign accounts or in their ex-wives' bank vaults.

"I thought I did, but now… I'm not so sure."

"I didn't think so."

"That's not to say I don't care."

He shook his head, "How can you really care if you don't have any idea."

"How can I have any idea unless you tell me? I thought that was the whole point of this exercise, regardless of what they did, was to let people know. If they've done something wrong, people should be told. They should be held accountable."

He stopped a few steps above her, several short of the next floor, he wasn't exactly angry, more trapped, "But what if people don't care? That's what we're facing. That something did happen, something horrible, and yet people aren't going to want to listen. Apathy is worse than sitting by and letting it happen. But we're risking that, because we've got no other choice. We're tired of sitting on our backsides and dwelling on it. It's time to do something."

Owen was right. If what he was saying was true and they work hard to reveal whatever it was that had gotten them on this crusade and no one listens, well that would be a lot worse than having put no effort into it at all. Then again

"At least you would have tried."

That hadn't sounded as good as she thought it would have. She could tell that in his face he didn't exactly believe it either.

"Thanks," was all he said before turning back toward the ascent.

"What I meant was-"

"I know what you meant. And you're right. But we aren't going to lose faith now just because we aren't sure if anyone will actually care or not."

She let silence fall between them again. She wasn't going to push him. She was already pretty much an unwelcome visitor. She didn't want to be dropped from mid air at a thousand feet by some guy with wings.

The funny thing was the insect man and Owen hadn't exactly been best of friends themselves. They obviously knew each other, respected each other. But there didn't seem to be any love lost between them.

She listened to the sound of their footsteps echoing through the well. It was a hollow sound, hers seemingly louder than his. He was taking particular care to soften his footfalls. She wasn't sure if this was a natural instinct or what. She could already feel her own legs tiring. Eight floors and, by looking up between the stairs, she estimated another eight or so to go. He had said seventeen, but already it seemed to be more than two dozen.

"So what is going on with Ethelbridge? And does it have something to do with Landsdown?"

"Sort of. Ethelbridge swallowed Landsdown over fifteen years ago in a hostile take over. Keeping Landsdown's name and property, Ethelbridge developed a research facility, claiming it to still be run by Landsdown as a fall back for their own protection."

"Why-?"

"Why would they need protection?"

"Exactly?"

"Because, although they claimed to be doing pharmaceutical research on plants and lab animals, much of their work consisted of vivisection and other horrible experiments."

She could tell by his tone of voice that this was something more than animal rights, "Not just on the lab animals?"

"Right. Around that time, there had been an anomaly showing up in society. People exhibiting, let's just call them 'talents'."

She was getting the picture now, "You're telling me-"

He cut her off again. They were on a similar wavelength, finally, "Yes."

She wasn't sure how to phrase her next question without sounding like some kind of lecherous journalist, "And you were a part of that?"

He paused a moment in his climb, resuming his step shortly after, "Not entirely. I was going to be. But my parents. Others in there, they got me out. And not just me. Enough of us got out to scare Ethelbridge into supposedly closing down the facility, fearing we would open our mouths," He sounded ashamed when he continued, "None of us did, though. We were too scared. We had all seen what happened inside. We didn't want it to happen again. And if we drew attention to ourselves, well, I knew I was afraid they would come and find me again."

"So you kept quiet?"

"But I have reason to believe they're starting again."

"Isn't there an easier way to go about revealing this than snooping around, drawing more attention to yourself as you go?"

"We need evidence. We can hardly burst into some police station or offices of some politician and declare our intentions without any substantiality to our claims. For one, we'd be a laughing stock, for a second, we'd blow our cover completely and for a third, we'd face legal action ourselves for defamation or slander. We can't afford that in any regard."

"Lawyers?"

"Too risky. And I doubt too many would be interested in our skeleton case."

"So why are we here?"

"These people are what's left of the break out."

"Why are they hiding here though?"

"After everything that happened, everything we were told, I really don't blame them. It was all part of the conditioning. They taught us to fear them, to be afraid of people. It's not so much the fear, but trust. After all that was done to them, to us, how can we really be expected to trust normal people anymore? Few of us managed to get past most of that. Others found it too hard, so they came here."

Which Kirrily still found odd. Hiding in a derelict building in the better part of the city, "In plain sight?"

Owen seemed to chuckle, "Hardly plain sight. Have you ever noticed this place before?"

Kirrily answered honestly, "No."

"Exactly. These people have talents. Some of them are powerful, others, not so. But they all do their best to stay invisible. No one knows they are here and that's the way they like it."

The walls were getting darker. More lights seemed to be completely out of commission as they got higher. Less flickering and more gloom. She was hardly one to be scared of the dark, but it was more than the dark she was worried about.

Her grip on her pistol, still holstered under her jacket, had grown firmer and warmer. She could feel the sweat in her palms, but refused to let go to wipe it off. They weren't going to catch her unawares this time, even if they were good guys.

"Is it really necessary to have the mood lighting?"

She could still see Owen in front of her, but he was becoming more of a shadow than a person, "If you'd been there, you would understand. Not everyone is ready for the light."

Finally they stopped. Or at least Owen did. She bumped into him as she continued, unable to hear his almost silent footsteps cease.

Mumbling her apologies, she could hear his sharp breath as he chuckled at her.

He was whispering now, "Try to stay quiet, let me do the talking. Try to stay by me."

She nodded; a useless gesture in this light.

A door handle creaked as it turned, followed by a sharp click as the latch slipped out of its nook and the door inched its way open.

There was slightly more light inside, flickering as those in the stair well had. Kirrily guessed it to be candlelight.

She wasn't far off.

Inside, there were hurricane lamps hanging from the ceiling and small glass encased tea-candles burning on various levels throughout the open space that was the seventeenth floor. It appeared that the majority of walls had been removed, or at least had passages knocked into them. There were only several separate rooms within the main floor. It was like walking into an archaic church, if somewhat industrial looking.

Directly opposite the door to the stairs was what looked to be a shrine of sorts. Broken furniture had been rebuilt and moulded into a raised platform around the sides of which were small carvings. At this distance, Kirrily could only just make out a faint pattern in the light. On top of the platform was a chair. Or more accurately, a throne. Black in colour, it looked most uncomfortable. There were pillars set evenly around the area, also painted black. It seemed to be the preferred colour.

But apart from the insect man who stood beside the throne and a cowled figure who occupied it, there was no one else in sight.

Owen walked calmly, with even steps, almost as if he had measured each one earlier, practicing a ritual and now, actually partaking in it.

Kirrily tried to mimic him. Step calmly, showing no fear on her face, yet hanging slightly behind his right shoulder.

They both stopped when they were about a metre from the platform.

She could make out the carvings now. She had half-expected psychotic designs and squiggles or depictions of human beings writhing in agony. What she hadn't expected was a series of childlike images of smiling faces, people playing, being happy. In a depressive place like this, it was hard to believe anything happy could survive.

"You will be hard pressed to find evil here, Miss Briton."

The voice echoed throughout the room, but no more so than in her own head.

"I'm sorry, I was just," She faltered. She hadn't said anything. Her name, anything. But strangely, it felt right that this man had known it. A familiarity that washed over her as if they were friends from long ago and she had shared her most intimate secrets. But that clashed with her natural feelings. She didn't know this man, as far as she could tell. She had never told anyone her most intimate secrets, having never really had anyone to tell nor would she ever allow herself to be so familiar with someone. It was some kind of trick.

"No trick."

Owen was looking at her. She could imagine the expression on her face. If it was anything like what she was feeling. Awe, amazement, horror, even violated. The only thing she could think of doing was projecting her thoughts out at him, '*Get the hell out of my head!*'

But the voice had gone. So had the strange sensation of knowing it, like she would a friend. It had obviously listened to her.

"Kirrily?" Owen was whispering to her, concerned, "Are you okay?"

Had he heard the voice? The way he was looking at her, it was like he had no idea what had happened.

"She's fine," it was a woman's voice this time, "We've just been conversing."

He looked back toward the cowled figure. If his voice was any indication, he wasn't impressed, "She's not like us. She's not ready for that yet."

A short sarcastic laugh leapt from beneath the dark hood, "She's more like us than she lets on, Owen."

The hood turned to regard her, she still couldn't see who was beneath it, not that that mattered. But whoever it was spoke with a female voice, yet spoke to her mind as a male.

"Or than she even knows herself, it seems."

Owen looked back over his shoulder, very quickly before looking back, "Regardless, that is not what we're here for."

"I know what you're here for."

"Great, then this shouldn't take too long."

"You can't have them."

Owen stepped forward, determined, "You didn't even ask."

A thin pale hand moved from beneath the robe and pulled back the hood. Kirrily imagined it happening in slow motion, but that could have been this person playing with her mind again.

"I don't need to ask," The hood slid back easily, revealing a small round face, pale, probably due to lack of light, but freckled. Her hair wasn't exactly short, but stood wildly on end, each inch a different shade of red, similar to a flame building from the roots up. Her eyes were small and widely spaced and her mouth, like her eyes in size, was hard, pursed.

Kirrily could imagine this woman, barely so, as some sort of freaky night clubber, jiving away, her laugh, thickly draped in the Australian ocker tones, ringing out in a staccato of life, having fun.

But here she was, barely past a third of a century old, and sitting in the dark, the world on her shoulders.

Then again, looks can be deceiving.

"I can tell as plainly as I can tell how desperate you are getting."

"But, it-"

"May be happening again. I know. But these people don't want to live that again. They've been through enough."

"And now more are going through it. And they're going to sit back and idly let it happen?"

"They had no one there to help them."

"What are you saying? That only those strong enough to survive in there, deserve to survive out here?"

"No. Simply that those that have survived what happened in there, wish to continue surviving out here."

"You call this surviving?" Kirrily was surprised to find it was her speaking.

The other three pairs of eyes fell on Kirrily as she stepped out from behind Owen. She looked at their reactions. They were lightly shocked, caught unawares by her vocalisation.

But she'd started and there was no point holding back now.

"I don't know what your deal is, what exactly happened where ever, but I do know this is not a way to live. This is what pigs do. This is what homeless people without a choice do, not that I'm saying they are completely without a choice. But basically, slumming like this, it's for bums who won't take responsibility for their lives."

The woman stood, her hair seeming to ignite in its depicted element, "You're damn right you don't know what's going on here! How dare you be so arrogant to waltz in here without a clue and cast accusations of irresponsibility and idleness. If you knew what these people had endured."

Owen stood forth this time, "I DO know what these people endured. I was there, remember. But look at me. I didn't run away into a hole and cower. Kirrily is right. It's not survival here. It's wasting away, simply biding your time until you die. And then what?"

"We will not be getting involved. And that is final."

"Um, Miss," Kirrily's head spun to regard a new speaker. He was actually surrounded by other people, still hiding behind the columns and few remaining walls, trying to get a look at what was going on, but remain as invisible as possible. Looking around, Kirrily found they had been surrounded. But this fellow, the speaker, was big. Muscles abound and yet he seemed like a giant cuddly teddy bear. His eyes were soft and sparkling, as one would expect on a small happy puppy, "Some of us don't agree."

The flame-haired woman's attitude changed, her hard manner drifting away to one of compassion, warmth, not unlike a mother talking to her children. But Kirrily had always hated the way they patronised her when she was a child. She felt her own teeth gritting as this woman spoke.

"Luka, you don't understand. They want you to go back in there. Risk going through everything all over again."

The big man shook his head, "No. They want us to help. Not just these others in trouble, but ourselves," He stepped further into the room, indicating Kirrily and Owen with one hand whilst turning back to those others around him, "They're right. This isn't life, skulking away up here. What we need is some sunshine, some excitement," He paused dramatically before speaking again, "Some life," and his eyes settled on Kirrily's knowingly. She could picture him giving her an exaggerated wink as if to say, 'That'll get 'em'.

CHAPTER EIGHT

THEN

There were more noises coming from all around them as they ran. Owen struggled to keep up with the man, his little legs racing as fast as they could. But he was already weary from his energy burst. He needed time to build his strength. He let his tired mind wander to thoughts of sleep back in his bed at home, the large snoopy doll beside him. He had received that for his first birthday and it had stood a few more inches taller than him. It was the closest thing to love at first sight a child could ever get. As he grew older, he had grown even more attached to the white furred friend to the point they rarely went anywhere without him. When he hit five, however, he knew it was time to start moving on. Find real friends to play with.

But what he wouldn't do to have snoopy here now, just to squeeze tight and reassure himself everything will be all right. Even if Snoopy couldn't say it, Owen could always tell when he was around, that everything would be fine.

Looking up at the pale skinned man who had a firm grasp on his wrist, trying to drag him as gently as he could through the maze of corridors, he could almost imagine him as a giant version of Snoopy. Minus the fur of course.

This let a little giggle through, lifting his spirits and pushing him onward.

There was a loud bang around the corridor behind them and Owen stumbled again as the floor beneath his feet seemed to rattle and shake. A cloud of dust caught up to them and he started coughing on the brown grit.

"Keep moving."

"I'm trying," he replied, forcing himself to stop choking.

"Freeze!"

Someone was behind them. The meek man turned his head to look over his shoulder, not slowing up at all.

There was a loud zap and the dim corridor lit up like a red neon tube. Meek man pushed off the wall beside him, catching hold of Owen and rolled with him down an adjoining corridor that had luckily been there.

As the man pulled Owen to his feet, he realised it wasn't a corridor, but a massive hole that had been blown in the wall. The fighting had already spread this far.

Another wall ruptured in the old corridor where the gunfire hit.

"Come on!"

Without a word, Owen followed the man deeper into this new room.

It was dark in here, like most of the compound, but he could see long strips of metal reflecting what little light was around. It looked to be shelving in a storage room of sorts. Feeling his way ahead of him with one hand as the meek man pulled on the other, he let his fingers run over cardboard boxes and papers that were stacked on the lower shelves.

It all seemed to be organised in rows that ran parallel to the corridor they had just come from.

He couldn't even begin guessing how high the shelves ran, but they were definitely long. When they finally reached the end of the first row, Owen found a small table in his way and carefully followed meek man around it. It seemed this man could actually see more clearly in the dark than Owen could. It must have had something to do with his strange eyes.

They passed a couple more rows before ducking into another corridor of shelves.

Meek man managed to locate a small space on one of the lower shelves and ushered Owen to crawl inside, all the while making almost inaudible "shushing noises". When he was sure Owen was safe, Owen watched his pale white legs vanish from view.

There was a crunch of concrete on concrete as a heavy boot stepped on some of the remaining rubble by the opening to the room. The guy with the gun was coming.

Somewhere above him, amongst the shelves, there was a slight rustling of paper. Poking his head out of his hiding hole, he craned his neck to see what was going on. In this light, he couldn't tell a thing, except a white shadow was crawling along the sides of the shelves. He obviously didn't weigh much as the shelving units themselves weren't even swaying.

Down one end of the rows, he heard boot-steps and quickly pulled his head back inside.

They were coming toward him, down the corridor. He couldn't tell if he'd been seen or not, but he did his best to squeeze himself further into the hidey-hole. His heart began to beat louder and faster. Blood rushing through his body as he felt himself start to panic. It wouldn't be long before the boots were next to him. Their hollow step was already half way there.

Holding his breath, he wished he could become invisible. But that wasn't to be.

A heel clacked next to his head and a foot came to rest. Its partner stepped in beside it.

Turning ever so slowly, Owen tried to see how close he was, or whether he was facing the shelves or not. What he hoped was that he wouldn't turn and see the man squatting in front of him, gun pointed directly between his eyes.

Resisting the temptation to squeeze his eyes shut, Owen found his eyes had adjusted somewhat and was able to make out the boots, still facing down the isle, but standing still while he imagined the owner surveyed the situation.

What he didn't expect was a loud tearing sound, followed by a watery squelch. The boots flexed, their toes lifting off the floor as if someone had loaded his heels with more weights as one would a seesaw. The body attached crumpled to the floor and Owen looked away as he realised the head hadn't come with it.

A couple of silent moments later, a hand appeared in the darkness, "Come boy. Let's get out of here."

OWEN

Owen had expected at least some support from the remnants. But when Myrl, the elected leader of the group, gave her initial answer, he was sure that would be the end of it. Then Kirrily opened her mouth. Perhaps it was because she was an outsider, or more likely because she hit a few sore points, they started putting their hands up left right and centre.

Of course, Owen would not expect them all to follow through. Especially the older and the weaker individuals. Not everyone was battle hardened, nor ready to strike up a fight. But their moral support would mean just as much.

There were children hidden among the remnants, newborns and toddlers alike. They had never known the prosecution and hostility their parents had faced in the compound. Owen didn't ever want them knowing. That's why he understood Myrl's stance. It was her responsibility to watch over them. But it should also have been her responsibility to ask them how they felt. Sure, she was a telepath, but even she was surprised by both Kirrily's reaction and then that of Luka which set forth a cascade effect around the whole colony.

Having given in to the over ruling opinion of her people, Myrl had nominated only a handful of men and women to join in the rescue attempt. They still needed the security here, to keep those that had already escaped safe. Of course, they would probably be safer in plain view, living normal happy lives. But Owen knew they had to take it all one step at a time.

The group had taken recess in one of the small rooms that was still intact. Lit by a single table lamp and several small candles, Myrl, Owen, Kirrily, Luka, two other men and two women knelt around an ovuloid table. Lengths of the legs had been cut off to adjust the height. It seemed the whole culture around here had taken on a primitive feel, but Owen knew this wasn't entirely so. There were sixteen other floors to this building. Hidden on each were personal quarters, recreation rooms and numerous other facilities.

This was where Myrl received guests. It was more for show than anything else. But it was effective.

What amazed Owen the most about the situation was Kirrily.

Only a while ago, she had been following him on his way to this very meeting. All along he had thought her a hostile, even after their initial confrontation. But she had done more for his cause then he had. She was totally amazing, and quite attractive to boot.

He hoped Myrl hadn't caught the end of that thought.

But Kirrily was really getting into it. Even sitting opposite him, beside Luka, who looked like a reject from the world wrestling federation because he was too big and a woman who had a slightly green tinge to her skin, not to mention rather large hooked claws in place of her nails. But she was getting along well with both of them, as if none of that mattered. She was currently recoiling in laughter from Luka after one of his little jokes and her head turned, her eyes landing on Owen.

He held her gaze for a moment, unsure of the effect, before looking back to Myrl.

He could feel her eyes on him, unsure whether to look back. What did it mean?

Games of the mind and heart, he told himself. He wasn't even sure if it was wise to get involved, even if she was interested. Who knew what was going to happen?

"That's life, Owen. You should know that by now. You really should practice what you preach," Myrl was speaking in his mind. He knew that for she had not moved her lips except into a curt little smile.

When they did open, it was on another topic, "We are waiting for one more. And I believe he is here."

Everyone turned to regard the small opening, unsure of who to expect. When the frail little hand appeared, taking hold of the frame of the door, Owen jumped to his feet. It had to be…

The meek little man stepped into the room, looking as small and thin as ever. But his red eyes glowed with a vivacity that made sure everyone knew he wasn't as weak as he appeared.

"Alexander!"

Owen scrambled past the others in the room to greet the fellow.

The pale man smiled warmly in response, remembering perhaps Owen as he used to be, comparing that to who he had become.

"You do me proud, boy. You've become the man your parents would be proud of."

Owen simply nodded, embracing the man, though gently, as if to avoid breaking him.

No matter what he had seen, Alexander still seemed as brittle as a twig and Owen couldn't help but treat him so.

Perhaps it was the respect he felt for him. Regardless, Owen was overjoyed to see the man who had saved his life.

"It's good to see you again. It's been too long."

"You never call," the man joked.

"When you get telephones or telepathy, I'll call."

They both laughed, but it was cut short by Myrl clearing her throat.

The men assumed their seating places, allowing her to continue.

"You know why you're here. You know what Owen is asking of you, and yet, you are all still willing to go along with his plan."

There was a murmur of agreement through the gathering. Myrl looked each one over individually, probably probing gently, trying to see whether or not they were being honest. If they hadn't been, she would have singled them out and ejected them from the meeting. Owen knew that. And he would hope so. He didn't want anyone going along who wasn't up for the challenge. His only problem was the actual plan hadn't been formulated as such.

"The problem we have, however, is Owen doesn't have a complete and accurate floor plan of the compound. There are no traces of the underground cells we were kept in. There are no indications what adjustments, either by mechanical or natural means have occurred within the structure, nor where the most likely or logical place of entrance would be."

He had to answer those accusations. They were accurate to the very letter, but they were counting on him to lead them, or guide them toward whatever was coming. He couldn't expect them to go in blindly. He would not risk their lives like that. So his only choice was to be as honest as Myrl had been.

All eyes were on him, even Kirrily's, though her expression was one of encouragement more than expectation.

"No. But this is something we can work out. We don't have to go rushing in straight away. We need to plan. Research. There was no point me assuming I had you on my side and designing a completely inappropriate course of action. Without you on my side, there would have been no point. But that is why I am here. That is why I do need you. I've already talked the options through with Helen, of whom most of you remember. The two of us on our own were stumped. There was nothing we could do. But all of us," he indicated the gathered; "We stand a chance of doing what's right. Of helping others like us, in the same position we were in all those years ago. We can't let them suffer. And I won't let them suffer."

It had become somewhat like a patriotic dedication to the country speech. He had imagined a flag unfurling behind him, the national anthem blaring out around him, and fought the urge to raise his fist to his heart. Something akin to Tim Brook-Taylor's over dramatised monologues from the old television series "The Goodies". But he had meant every word. If he hadn't he would have been ashamed of himself. This was a serious situation.

Helen had been having precognitive visions of what was going on inside the "compound". Some of what she saw and described, Owen knew were more like memories of what had already happened. But She was describing new things. There were aspects to her visions that only she could read and she was certain something was going on again.

He was about to continue, "So-" when the screaming began.

Glass was shattering outside as the inhabitants of the meeting rooms scrambled out the small exit.

A mixture of bullets, fire and other energy beams were streaming into the Top floor of the building. The throne was one of the first things to vanish in a blaze of super heated fire. And Owen knew immediately who it was.

How did they find them? With all the psychic screens and the electro-magnetic shielding provided by Elisha, there shouldn't have been any way of discovering this place. Unless…

He tried to find Kirrily but she had vanished among the panicking inhabitants.

Did she have something to do with this?

Some of the Remnants had started returning fire, whilst others were ushering the weaker and younger of the group down the stair well.

Kirrily had said this guy was from Ethelbridge. Did she somehow lead them here?

One of the support columns nearby shattered under the power of one of the flaring energy beams that lanced into the building. Whether it was from an energy weapon or not, Owen couldn't tell. But he wasn't going to stand by and let anyone get hurt.

In a moment, his suit had vanished for the second time this evening. His black costume in its place, he was ready for action. Every fibre in his body was tingling from the transformation and he was charged for a fight.

The attack was coming from two locations. Both outside, one on either side of the building. The amount of wind that had suddenly picked up, Owen could only assume a pair of helicopters had come to play.

He had already noted which side the "Fireman" was on. He took aim in the general direction of the first helicopter and fired.

Electricity arced out across the floor space, it's blue light adding to the myriad of colours being fired in from outside. It pulsed from his fingers and he could practically feel it as it searched the air for its target. Flaying wildly at the end, he adjusted his aim until he struck gold.

The night sky outside was lit up by the rupturing of electronics on board the helicopter. Obviously Fireman hadn't informed them of his capabilities.

The attack from that side ceased abruptly as the copter swung away from the building. One down, one to go.

He turned away and started to make his way across the floor to the other side. People were still rushing by but the majority had already made it to the internal stair well. They were safer in there than anywhere else. But they would have escape plans of their own. He was about to fry the second helicopter when the floor behind him erupted in a ball of fire.

Diving for cover, he rolled across the concrete flooring and jumped to his feet. Obviously the Fireman wasn't out of commission.

Focussing, he could still see the first helicopter swinging wildly outside. It was like a sick bird trying to keep itself aloft and doing a bad job of it.

It rotated one way, then the other. As it began to swing back once more, the Pilot over compensated, lifting the copter higher and around over the building. From above, there was a loud scraping noise as the undercarriage intersected with either the roof of the building or one of the many communications towers left over from when it was in use.

The floor beneath Owen's feet shook as the pilot lost his struggle above. The copter came crashing down, hard, smashing through the ceiling. Sparks flew as metal clashed with metal and several stray bullets flashed by when panicked fingers closed on their weapons. The circular chassis of the copter plummeted through the hole like an egg being laid and almost continued its journey through to the next floor, but, instead, caught on some of the support beams in the ceiling and jarred to a halt.

Fire from the floor and from the electrical flames that had ignited on the helicopter was starting to spread and the smoke along with it. It was making it harder to see if anyone else was left.

The gunshots continued to volley in from the remaining helicopter, but some of the Remnants were already dealing with that. He could see several of the more aggressive individuals taking aim with their own powers, unleashing them as best they could on their attackers.

The fires from the downed copter were growing in intensity. They were a lot hotter than they should be and Owen knew why. He wasn't sure how many people survived the crash, but if Fireman was doing what Owen thought he was, he was pretty sure not many would survive the aftermath.

Sure enough, the metal of the chassis turned a dull shade of red, the paint bubbling and frying off the surface. There was an acrid odour of burning plastic, wood and hair.

The remaining walls on this floor were all just about wiped out. Most were cindered remains, some were bullet riddled and looked more like colanders than anything else.

There was little cover for anyone.

Smoke was billowing from the ever growing fires, but the rotor blades from the remaining helicopter was causing sufficient wind flow to send it swirling everywhere. At times, Owen was standing in a bubble of clean air, but seconds later was squinting his eyes to prevent them from burning or stinging from the smoke.

The metal of the Chassis had started to melt from Fireman's attempt to escape.

Owen had to get moving.

71

He turned and hurried back toward where the last of the Remnants were dealing with the helicopter.

"How's it going?"

"They're hurting as far as we can tell," one young woman replied.

"But they aren't giving up."

Owen could see the helicopter wasn't fairing well.

But he could also see that the targets of this attack were unscathed.

As far as Owen could tell no one had actually been hurt in the assault. Bullets, fire, all manner of weapons had been used, but it was the building itself that had born the brunt of the attack. Even now, bullets were flying by, but missing the columns behind which the Remnants were hiding.

Something was going on.

"Owen?"

It was Kirrily. He couldn't see her through the smoke, but she was close by. Not seeing her, however, made it harder for him. He wasn't so sure if he could trust her. Had she brought them here? Somehow guided them to this building?

"We have to get out of here," She coughed a couple of times from the smoke.

He reached out for her, "Something's not right," he found her elbow and pulled her closer. He could just make her out, "What's going on, Kirrily?"

She was squinting back at him, "What do you mean?"

"How did they know we were here?"

She shook her head, "I don't know. But we can't stay here. This whole floor is becoming unstable. The fire is eating away at it."

She was right. The building was creaking under the strain. There was a definite orange tinge to the air as the fire had spread out of control.

"How did they find us?"

She was pulling her arm away from him, but he tightened his grip, "I don't know. We can find out later-"

There was a loud pop of air and flash of orange-white light as the Fireman escaped the metal cell of the downed helicopter.

Even through the smoke, Owen could see his body blazing brightly. He was pulling himself free of the chassis.

Kirrily was right. They didn't have time to work this all out.

"You lot, get out of here!"

The Remnants grunted their affirmative before their shadows vanished into the smoke.

Kirrily pulled her arm away, "You're hurting me!"

"You stay where I can see you."

Her arm disappeared behind her back and Owen was ready to defend himself. She whipped out a mean looking pistol and pointed it in the direction of the Fireman.

72

"One thing you're going to learn, buddy, is no one tells me what to do."

She let loose a round of what looked like a puce laser beam, but the recoil on the weapon itself flung her arms back against her body. She staggered back slightly as the beam was launched toward the helicopter that had crashed. As it went, it seemed to enlarge, like what you saw on cartoons, the sonic screams coming out in waves, starting small near the mouth and becoming massive circles of black lines by the time it strikes its target. Instead this was a puce circle and by the time it struck the helicopter, it just about filled the floor from ground to ceiling.

The helicopter burst into flames on impact, crumpling backward like a cardboard box that had been kicked in. Someone screamed from within. It had to be only one person.

Owen couldn't help thinking to himself that perhaps he had her all wrong. Maybe it was a fluke they found this place. But there was still something nagging at the back of his mind.

She turned to him and began to speak, "Let's get out-"

A bolt of green energy knocked into her from behind, sending her sprawling along the floor. The back of her jacket, though intact was smouldering slightly.

First hit on the good team. But it was one of the bad guy's own, possibly. Had they recognised her, deemed her a traitor? He didn't know.

It didn't matter. The second helicopter was still attacking.

Owen launched himself from behind the column he was standing and let loose a wide spread of electrical attacks as he ran to cover Kirrily who was starting to attempt getting to her feet.

Once more, Owen's attack hit home, sending the helicopter wild. The pilot on board this vessel, however, wasn't as lucky as the last, if you can call him lucky at all.

The rear of the copter lifted high and flew straight toward the side of the building.

Metal and concrete collided for the second time. This time, however, was a lot less subtle. Having gained momentum on its approach, the copter's impact crumpled the side of the building. In a mass of twisted metal and clouds of smoke and dust, the fuel tank exploded.

Owen dove over Kirrily's body, knocking her back to the floor as the initial shock wave washed through the air.

The air around them sizzled and burned as a wall of flame rolled after it. Unfortunately what wasn't burning already ignited under the searing heat. The smoke was getting to be almost unbearable.

Something hard nudged Owen's gut. Kirrily was squirming beneath him.

"Get off me!" She was not happy. Whether it was his accusations or the hit she took, he wasn't sure.

He was starting to get up when she managed to flip him up and over onto his side. She was quite strong. It was only a matter of seconds before she was on her feet again, gun in hand.

She was about to offer her hand to Owen, when they both heard the creaking from behind.

They both turned to see what remained of the second helicopter inch its way out of the little nook it had created for itself in the side of the building and slide out to open air.

"It's going to fall!"

Owen launched himself forward, using his burst of electrical speed, but felt something pull back on his shoulder.

His legs slid out from underneath him as he was jerked backward and he felt the floor beneath him come flying at him.

He landed with a thud on his backside, Kirrily still holding onto him.

"What are you going to do? Go with it?"

He was amazed. No one had ever caught him mid burst.

She juggled her weapon in her hand with amazing speed and drew out the same grappling gun she had used earlier.

Taking quick aim, it fired, launching an almost invisible length of cord at the copter, which was gaining speed, as it moved.

Owen was about to protest, telling her that she would go with it herself, when she aimed the other end of the gun toward the central elevator shaft and pressed a second button. Another grappling hook and cord shot out from the handle, striking home at both ends. The cord pulled taught, but it was a lost battle.

The helicopter had slowed its movement, but only slightly.

Owen launched himself to his feet again, "It's not-"

The first helicopter erupted, much like the second one had, in a ball of fire. But there was a second explosion as its own fuel tank caught fire.

Both people jumped for cover as two more waves of fire swept toward them. The first was hotter than the second. Hotter than normal flame should be, well, than Owen thought it should be after experiencing the initial explosion.

There was a loud twang as the cord gave way under the heat and Kirrily yelled out her annoyance.

The second helicopter lost its grip on the building, with a little extra push from the second explosion and slipped almost silently out into the night.

When the fire had cleared somewhat, Owen looked up once more and saw the Fireman standing, free of any clutter or cages. This was not good.

And it was about to get a lot worse.

The fire had weakened the floor and the buffeting it received from the explosions hadn't helped it any.

It had already started to creak under the strain and Owen could tell it was becoming a hazard to walk over.

But the Fireman did so. He moved slowly, but deliberately toward them. Which was quite odd considering his powers all seemed to be range based. Perhaps he wanted a better shot. In the smoke, however, Owen's own glow was making him an easy target, so he powered down.

"What did you do that for?" Kirrily whispered beside him.

He put his hand against her back and started directing her around and away from Fireman and toward the centre stair well. They both stepped carefully over smouldering flooring and watched for weakened points in the ground.

"He could see me. I think we'd have a better chance in the smoke without me shining like a Christmas tree."

But as they moved, keeping an eye on their opponent, Owen could see he was still following them. He could still see them through all the smoke.

Perhaps he had some sort of Infrared sight allowing him to see their body heat. And then it made sense. He would also be seeing the warmth in the air, the flames making it hard to make them out properly. That was probably why he was moving so slow, trying to get a proper baring.

"Slow down," he told Kirrily, "He might not be able to see us."

"He's following us," Owen hoped they couldn't be heard over the crackling of the fire and the moaning of the building.

"Just do it."

Without another word, they slowed their pace considerably. Inching over the short distance that remained ever so carefully and comically as if in a slow motion video.

A stream of fire shot past them, missing them by a couple of metres. It was working. But if Fireman got angry enough, he could probably lay down a stream of fire to wipe them out.

But even then, Owen wasn't so sure. No one had been hurt. Even Kirrily's wound was superficial. If they had been serious about the whole thing, there probably would be dead bodies strewn all over the joint.

A second jet of flames roared past, closer this time. The heat was intense. Any closer and they'd feel the effects for sure.

Something cracked in the floor around them. They both stopped, anticipating the worst. There had been a noticeable lurch underfoot and the world seemed to grow an inch or two around them.

A third spread of fire was coming at them, but wasn't fast enough.

The ground gave way beneath their feet and Owen found himself grasping at air. Fortunately this air was fresh. The heat of the smoke kept it from being sucked down to the next floor.

He felt his feet make contact first, but they soon disappeared from beneath him and he went sprawling across the debris strewn tiles of a sixteenth floor bathroom.

Coughing from the dust as much as the smoke, he looked around. It was dark, but the flames from above were sufficient to give suitable illumination on the subject.

Kirrily wasn't there.

It wasn't until he looked back up to the whole he saw her legs dangling in the air.

She had managed to grab hold of the side of the hole. Lucky, but unlucky.

Jumping to his feet for the umpteenth time in the last couple of minutes, Owen reached his hands up and grabbed her calf. She squealed slightly.

"Drop. I've got you."

He had expected some hesitation from her, but when she did exactly as he told her, he nearly lost his balance again. Managing to keep his footing, he caught her before she hit the ground.

She smiled at him before pushing him away, "Thanks. Now, let's get the hell out of here."

CHAPTER NINE

THEN

It seemed like an up hill climb. The floor had begun to slope awkwardly and Owen's legs were already tired. But there was no point complaining. Alexander, as he had finally introduced himself to the boy, was determined to get out of here and wasn't going to allow anything to stop him.

Owen accepted that somewhere deep inside, but his legs still ached for him to cry out in frustration. Like a baby.

But he wouldn't. What would his parents think of him then? A wimp. He had to be strong now. Had to get out of here as his father had said. Thinking about his father brought back the illusion of his mother in the same room. Had he been dreaming? Was his mother actually there or was it just his father. He couldn't remember. Everything was happening too fast and he was scared. His heart was still thumping in his chest and he feared every corner they approached, worried something would jump out at them. He was no longer afraid of the weird looking monsters in nightmares. They had helped him escape, like the panther lady and Alexander. He now considered them friends. It was the men in the black suits that he was afraid of.

Strange, he thought. All his young life he thought he could trust people and now he was running away from them.

It couldn't be far now, could it?

A little sob of pain escaped his lips and he wanted to hit himself. He felt ashamed that he would show weakness now.

"Come on, little buddy," Alexander's thin arms wrapped around his body and hoisted him up. Owen wrapped his arms around his neck thankfully but didn't make another sound. He was glad Alexander wasn't angry at him for being weak.

Alexander picked up pace, not having to hang back for the young boy's slower speed, and Owen felt himself getting bounced around, but he could endure that. He had to. He felt safer in this man's arms. He knew he would be protected no matter what. This man had promised his father.

It wasn't until Alexander stopped abruptly that he got worried. Wriggling around in his perch, he tried to see what was there. He half expected row after row of men in black jumpsuits to be standing there, guns in hand, ready to wipe them out.

But all there was was a large steel set of double doors. They looked huge and strong. Large diagonal beams of metal were bolted on for support, creating a massive V formation. The actual seam was virtually invisible. They looked impregnable.

But Alexander only hesitated for a moment. Outwardly calm, though Owen could feel his heart beat against his own chest, the pale man walked upright and strong toward the doors. Owen himself was willing them to open, to let them out. He hoped that beyond those doors were sunshine filled meadows, like at his home, where he could run forever, arms outstretched like a plane soaring on the wind. He even thought he could smell the fresh scent of the brilliant green grass and the flowers that spotted the carpet-like spread. The soft ebb of a scent from one of his mother's rose bushes. Something, anything his mind could remember.

It seemed so long ago. The kitchen. His mother wiping and washing up as they joked. His father and brother-

Ryan.

Where was he? He was only a couple of years older than Owen. Was he also here in the compound? Had he escaped? His father had to have looked after him. He would never let anything happen.

But it did happen. Those men had broken into their house. Hurt his mother. Broken up his family.

Something had happened and now Owen's family was no longer together. He didn't know when they would see each other again, and deep in his stomach, he could feel the butterflies flying around like Kamikaze pilots. Would they ever see each other again?

There was a loud clicking sound followed distinctly by three more, like giant locks being turned. A distant rumble as machinery turned over and the faintest of hums as the massive doors began to slide open.

A miracle perhaps?

Owen held his breath, only wanting to breathe in again when he could smell the flowers.

He could see the deep green meadow form within the ever grown gap in the doors. Almost picture it there.

Spots of white, like stars lit up the field beyond, blinking on and off. And Owen was set to burst out in laughter.

It caught in his throat. What felt like a massive brick dropped in his stomach.

There was no meadow.

As the doors opened wide enough to see in, Owen saw no trees, no grass, no flowers.

There was plenty of green, and those white lights flashing on and off. But what he saw was a huge open hall. Just in front of the doors, a long railing ran a perpendicular course to the hall they were in.

Alexander hesitated once more.

But he had no choice. They had to go on.

He stepped through the door and the sound of his footsteps became metallic, hollow. They echoed around the chamber he had just stepped into.

Alexander lifted Owen away from his body and set him down again.

They both looked over the railing at what was there.

The room was at least three stories high. A wider walkway with intersections running from either end forming a giant cross was above them. The walkway on which they stood ran the length of the walls and was considerably thinner than that above them. There were two sets of stairs on this end leading down to the ground floor and an identical pair on the other end.

As far as Owen could tell, the green light was coming from a multitude of tubes that ran in lines from the floor below up to the ceiling. There were eighteen on each level, nine on either side of a main path. There were more on the levels above; facing the walkways that ran parallel to the one Owen was on. The glow from the tubes was brilliantly reflected off the silver walls.

These tubes were about two metres tall and metre in circumference, filled with a green translucent goo which was giving off the eerie glow. And in every tube, as far as Owen could see, were people.

It was like something out of a cartoon. A mad scientist's lab. But instead of rats and mazes, there were human beings.

Owen's mouth dropped open. He was speechless. Not that he wanted to say anything, but there was an urge to do something, even to run. Alexander took hold of his hand, squeezing it gently to reassure him. Of what, Owen didn't know. That everything would be alright?

He only had to look at these people to know that wasn't true.

But Alexander was there. And Owen settled with that. He wasn't alone any more, stuck in a cold dark cell. He had someone here to protect him. Even if he was a stranger of sorts, it was better than being alone.

"We have to go down. It's the only way I can see."

Alexander was right. There wasn't another exit on this level, and Owen couldn't see a way up to the third floor. This looked to be more of a service ramp for the tubes on this floor.

Alexander led the boy toward the metal stairs and down them. They tried their hardest to make the least amount of noise. Like a game, Owen thought, but it wasn't fun.

The stairs twisted around tightly, like a tube of its own. That thought sent shivers up Owen's spine. He didn't like the idea of being stuck in one of those. And as they started to walk past them, still creeping along, Owen had to wonder whether the people inside even knew where they were.

He felt them leering at him and tried not to look. But it was as if they were staring at him, yelling at him angrily with silent voices. A nightmare he was living.

But this was all a nightmare. One horror after another.

They were about half way down the corridor between the green cells when the urge to look became too great.

Owen turned his head slowly, leading with his eyes, trying to catch a quick peek.

The first thing he noticed of the first man he saw was his eyes were closed. He must have been asleep or perhaps dead. But his hair was drifting aimlessly through the goop in which he was suspended, sort of like Luke Skywalker in Empire Strikes Back. But there were no cords or tubes. This man simply hung there unconscious. He, along with the woman to his right and the other man to his left, was wrapped in a dark body suit of some sort and Owen could see his muscles rippling underneath as if fighting an unseen foe. One moment his arm would tense up, and then relax as his leg would take up the strain.

Did they know?

Owen looked up at Alexander, who was also looking at those contained within.

"Can we help them?"

Alexander didn't look at the boy, "I don't know how."

"Can't we turn off the machines?"

He still wouldn't look at him, "I don't know how."

"We could break the glass!" Owen was becoming more insistent. He didn't like seeing the people this way. It was wrong. Worse than he had experienced.

"It might hurt them. Possibly even kill them."

"We can't leave them here."

The man finally looked down at the boy. There was something in his amber eyes. It was hard to tell, but it looked like tears, "We can't help them, Owen. We don't know how. If we tried, we could do more harm than good."

He broke free of the man's hand and ran up to one of the tubes, trying to find a button to press. There's always a button to shut it off, "This isn't good," and to emphasise the point when he couldn't find a button, he turned back to Alexander and repeated louder, "This is not good!"

Alexander reached for his hand once more, "I'm sorry, Owen. There's nothing we-"

Owen pulled away, "No!"

He was going to refuse to leave until they had gotten these people out.

KIRRILY

Kirrily pulled open the first door of the bathroom. It led into a smaller antechamber of sorts. More of a privacy screen so passers by don't get an unwanted glimpse of what was going on inside. Owen followed closely behind.

He would have preferred leading, but Kirrily wasn't up for that idea. She had her pistol in hand and at the ready. She was also trained in security measures to some degree. It was all part of the course. At least they were both ready to defend themselves no matter which direction the attack came from.

Carefully inching open the second door that led out to some abandoned offices, She made sure the coast was clear. Not a sound or a movement.

Ushering Owen through after her, she checked both in front and behind. That guy upstairs was far from contained and although Owen claimed he couldn't see them, she was sure it wouldn't take long for him to work out where they had gone.

What did grate on her was the fact the ceiling above them, the floor through which they had just fallen, was unstable. She could see cracks in the plaster above using the sunglasses she had pulled out of her pocket. They were slightly cracked after landing on them earlier, but they were still working.

The area in which they now found themselves was large and well kept for an abandoned building. Old pieces of furniture still stood here and there, such as desks and filing cabinets. Obviously not wanted by the firm that had moved out last. The walls were of thin wooden panelling, above which, about a foot and a half of glass. It looked cheap and tacky, but it meant she could get her bearings from the scorched hull of the first helicopter. She could see it only a short distance away, a bulb of metal sticking through the ceiling.

The floor was littered with cracked plaster, some of which had been scorched underneath. The fire was certainly having a good time up there.

Their best bet was to find the stairwell and get out of there. Hopefully the others had found a way out, or already had escape options. But Kirrily was left wondering the same thing Owen obviously was. In fact, she knew what he thought of the matter and she was only slightly offended. Of course, she could see his reasoning for suspecting her, but she had nothing to do with leading them here. Unless they had bugged her car, but she would have been alerted to that. She had enough security on that vehicle to have been placed in the front lines in World War two. A simple tracing device would have set off a surface alarm, or at least a frequency scan would have revealed the minute signal it would be giving off. There was no way.

Right now, however, it didn't really matter. They had to get out of here before the ceiling caved in and before that psycho upstairs came after them.

Roughly estimating the central stair well in relation to the helicopter debris, she started off down a maze of corridors. Thankfully for the glass over head, she could keep a general idea of where she was going. But it was a literal twist and turn of small rooms and long corridors. Every couple of metres was either a door or an off shooting corridor that looked identical to the one they had just left. She would have hated been caught in here without any way of marking where they had been or where they were going.

Increasing their speed, she hurried down one hallway after another, sometimes scraping her arm against the corners of the wood panels, not actually wounding herself, but it was damn annoying. She wasn't a fan of tight spaces and mazes had never been her thing as a kid.

The other option was to take aim and fire a direct path through all the panels to the stairs. That was the good thing about her hobbies. Made some things a whole lot easier. The pulse-pistol in her hand was one of her favourites. People used to say even the idea of a pulse rifle was impossible, but it was pure logic, when you thought about it. One scientific equation after another. And it all came to her in flashes of inspiration. Once she'd set her mind to it, there was no stopping her. Of course, she would find herself having to clock in at work and sitting around there running more equations and theories through her head, but once she got home again, away she went. This little beauty had taken a whole week to finish. One of the longest periods she has spent on developing something. Of course, it had to be done by hand which made the procedure a lot more difficult, but with most of her other inventions she had other equipment of her own design or from the market to help her. Such as Wolftan III, but that was another story.

Although the pistol was no where near as powerful as a rifle would be, it was a lot more convenient to carry around. And she fashioned it with material mixtures of plastic and metallic alloys that made it undetectable by metal detectors and security screens whilst maintaining its durability and efficiency.

Still, using the weapon would prove a bad idea. For one, it would pinpoint their location, two, it would allow the flaming guy to realise they had actually fallen down to the next level and three, could possibly prove fateful to the building's structural integrity.

Besides, this was peoples' homes she was thinking about. Who was to say one of these Remnants or whatever hadn't set up home in one of the small offices around here? She could end up destroying everything they hold dear.

So the maze it was. From Owen's half giggles behind her, she had a feeling he was enjoying himself.

Rounding another bend, she finally found a glass door in her way. The backward writing on it in black sticker letters had used to say WHETHERBY, ELLIOT & NEST. LAWYERS AND SOLICITORS. LIMITED. Most of the letters had been scratched out to reveal a new message - HERE LIES YER DOOM. Of course it looked a bit awkward and took a while to work out, but Kirrily figured it had to be a child's handiwork. The maze here had probably been a playground of sorts. She remembered stories from kids at school about a maze in one of the theme parks in Perth where you could get lost really easily. She always knew, however, that the best way to get out of a maze was to stick to either your right or left and just keep doing so. You would eventually find your way out.

But if you were in a maze as big as several city blocks, you may end up dying of thirst or starvation first, having to go down every corridor until you find the way out. That was the price you paid for being so easily amused.

Still, she smiled a little before opening the door. It led out to small t-junction that was attached to a further, larger corridor on either side of which was an elevator shaft. Beside one of these, was a stair well. Their exit.

She was a little unnerved at how quiet it had been. There hadn't been any more explosions from above, nor any trace of the flaming guy.

She decided to voice her concerns before they entered the stairwell.

"Something's not right," she hoped it wasn't an omen for anything to come and felt obliged to knock on the wooden panel that framed the door to the stairs.

Owen nodded, his eyes darting this way and that. He had removed his sunglasses, obviously as they didn't have the same effect as her own.

She couldn't help noticing he had cute eyes. Even when they were glowing she thought so, but even now, there was just a look to them, almost maniacal, but gentle at the same time. This man had seen a lot in his life, and had done his best to keep seeing the good side to it all.

She hoped he wasn't gay and had a feeling he wasn't from the way he had looked at her upstairs in the meeting. She had kind of liked it, in fact.

"We don't have much choice, though, do we?" He asked.

"I guess not."

She touched the back of her palm to the door. Checking to see if the flames had reached the stairs yet, or whether that flaming guy was lurking beyond. It was still cool. Obviously the fire proofing was still suitable.

Slowly, she opened the door inward, surveying the stairs.

Looking up, she could see haze from the smoke. The walls were losing their battle to keep the fire out, but for now, it would suffice. They only had to get down these flights of stairs and to the bottom floor to get out and the stairs should last long enough for that.

She almost groaned at the idea of having to walk down all those stairs again. She would prefer dropping if it weren't that the fall would kill her.

Owen carefully shut the door behind them, hoping to keep the noise down.

Kirrily had already started down the stairs.

Other than their own footsteps, however, everything was silent. The others had obviously escaped.

After the first couple of flights, both Kirrily and Owen began taking the stairs two at a time. It was a lot more awkward, but seemed to be getting them there faster.

It wasn't until they reached the twelfth floor that they heard noise from above them. Stopping for only a moment, Kirrily leaned slightly over the railing, into the gap that ran down the centre of the stairwell and looked up. With her glasses, she could see several shapes and shadows moving down after them. They were going to have to hurry. She was about to start moving again when she decided to look down as well. Same thing. There were several people coming the other way.

"Owen!" She hissed. He stopped, looking back at her.

"What?"

"We're trapped. They're coming from both sides."

He took a quick peep over the edge. She wasn't sure if he'd see anything, but now that they had stopped moving, the faint rattle of feet could be heard. They were doing their best to keep quiet, but not good enough.

"Come on," He said, moving down to the eleventh floor and pulling open the door leading out. This was getting ridiculous, she thought to herself. They could end up stair jumping and bullet dodging all night. There were plenty of places to hide, but there was only so long they could do so.

Besides, how had they tracked them down before? Is it possible they could track them again now?

Was one of them wearing a homing beacon of some sort?

She followed him into the green darkness of an unlit floor. His hand fell on her shoulder.

"You're going to have to lead me. I can't see a thing."

There wasn't much to see. The floor was not unlike the top floor. Virtually devoid of walls. There were several partitions making up a number of large rooms that could have been boardrooms of some sort. The floors were dirty, but swept aside by footprints. There was little or no furniture around. Only broken remnants of chairs.

Putting one hand on his and keeping her pistol in the other, She led him into the gloom.

"Where are we going?"

"We need to find a window."

"What for?"

"We don't have much choice."

She looked back at him. But his face was the blank expression of a blind man in a new location. It looked expectant, but totally void of any knowledge of what exactly to expect. She would have chuckled if the mood had been right.

It didn't answer her question though. A window for what? Sure, if she had her grappling gun still, they would have been able to use it as a flying fox from this building to a neighbour. The only other thing that came to mind was to fly.

She looked back at him again.

84

That was it. He was going to try and carry them both out.

Well he'd done it before, only earlier this evening. It had been a weird experience, but it was doable. She didn't have any qualms about it. But was he up for it. They were eleven stories high. He'd already had a bit of a fly with her, not to mention everything that had happened upstairs. He didn't exactly seem worn out.

Everything would be fine.

They found a window. Well, a wall full of windows. It looked out onto the street below. Owen could see now, and they both went to get a close look of what was happening outside. Everyone looked like ants, but with a slight adjustment to the glasses, the magnification increased by four. It was only limited, especially with all the other capabilities included. She'd need full size binoculars to put it all together effectively.

There were several black vehicles below, including the Hearse. People were moving backward and forward, some dressed in black army fatigues, others she recognised as members of the remnants. Most of the latter looked to be being led by the prior for support. They seemed to be doped up or something.

Not good.

"They have the others. Possibly gas or some other knock out agent."

Owen only looked down briefly. He was more interested in the buildings around them.

The view was nice. Some buildings still had their lights on, left for the weekend or the cleaners. Cars were driving by on distant roads, some slowed down on the road they over looked to see what was going on before quickly picking up speed and zooming off.

Perth was a beautiful city in its own way. Bright lights, busy streets. But nothing you couldn't see in any other city, such as New York. Except here in Perth, there was no Statue of Liberty. In fact there were very few landmarks or monuments of note. That had been Australia's fault. No original ideas, no great heroes to signify or honour. They used to have a statue of an aboriginal leader who had been killed by having his head chopped off. The statue suffered the same fate. And every time it was replaced, it was only a matter of days before it happened again.

The latest monument was a bell tower of glass, surrounded by two bronze coloured sails. It was erected more out of beautification purposes, but everyone knew it was more for the glorification of the state premier.

Perth, no, Australia, didn't really have an identity. It may have housed the largest city in the world, although it was not the capital of the country and was practically forgotten by the rest of Australia, it even had several more impressive monuments in Sydney and Melbourne. But there was absolutely no unity of spirit or objectives in the Australian people. No ideals of the Three musketeers running through the veins. It was more the cry of - "Every man for himself!"

And that was how it was. Australia, every man's land, according to every man.

"There's another helicopter. They dropped the people up top."

"Wonder how they got through the fire."

"Does it matter? Our only chance is to get out of here, somewhere safe."

This stumped her.

"What about the people down there. Aren't we going to help them?"

He shook his head, seemingly ignoring what was happening below.

"There's nothing we can do."

What? She asked herself. The man who wants to stand up and fight the monstrosity of Ethelbridge is backing down.

He finally looked at her, noting her expression, "They could be hurt, even killed if we try."

"And if we don't, what then?"

"They'll be taken away."

"To Landsdown's Compound, right?"

He shook his head, not to disagree, but as a sign of resignation, "We can't just rush into this."

She was disgusted with his attitude. She thought he was more of a man than this. Not in a gender specific way either. The guy was losing his nerve, it seemed. She knew it wasn't so. He was just being logical. But he wasn't thinking about the whole picture. Then again, she thought to herself, he didn't know the whole picture.

She had another plan forming in her head. She pulled the sleeve on her left arm back to reveal a small electronic keypad and started typing. A small colour display lit up as she worked, sending commands through her own personally rigged network.

"Fine. You get us out of here and down to street level, let me do the rest."

"We can't go after them-"

"Not like this we can't, but don't worry, I've got back up."

CHAPTER TEN

THEN

There was no fighting Alexander's strength. Owen was amazed how strong he was compared to how thin his physique. He had wrestled Ryan who was proportionately better built than this man and won. But there was no arguing with the spindly but powerful arms that scooped Owen up and hoisted him into a fireman's lift.

"We don't have time to argue, boy. We have to go. I'll come back for them later."

Owen struggled against the man until his arms grew tired, which wasn't long after all his earlier exertion.

All he kept thinking was "It isn't fair. It isn't fair."

As Alexander began to move, Owen could only see the white tiled floor racing below him. Before they stepped through the next door and out of the chamber, Owen found the strength to look up and back at the rows of glowing tubes, each one a prison he had thankfully escaped, but many others hadn't. He wanted to scream, to fight back. But it was useless. Alexander was muttering calming words of nothing, trying to get the boy to settle down. He was awkward at it, not quite as soothing as a father may have been, but it was having the desired effect. Owen fell back into Alexander's arms and ceased his struggling. There was no point arguing anymore.

He let his eyes close only for a moment.

When he opened them again, he was some where totally different. He must have fallen asleep, though he had dreamt of nothing.

Alexander had slowed down, either out of his own tiredness, or out of caution.

It was darker here. Light fixtures were dim, the walls were a shade of grey that bordered on black and along either side were long thin rails. The floor underneath Alexander's feet was metallic, grating which made each step ring through the immediate area like an owl's call on a quiet night.

Noticing his charge was awake, he slowed down to lift the boy onto the ground.

"Are you okay to walk for a bit?"

Owen nodded, still a bit groggy from the past few hours.

It had seemed like an eternity that they had wandered these corridors. It was quiet now, no traces of fighting or gunshots. How many others had made it this far, he wasn't sure. And how far had they actually come?

He was starting to lose confidence in the hope of finding a way out. It seemed behind every door there was a slim possibility of an exit, but it always ended up being another corridor or room.

There was a sharp smell in the air, and as they continued onward, it began gnawing at Owen's nostrils. He tried to smell it more, sort of like an addict craving another hit. It stung a little. Like smoke, but more acrid.

They came to a junction. Four paths converging on the one point, in the centre of which was a stair well made of the same grating as was underfoot. It ran up and down, though Owen didn't want to imagine what was below. He automatically headed up and was happy when Alexander followed him.

Although he knew it was the obvious choice, at least he was able to make one.

It wasn't until they were halfway up that Owen looked up to see what was ahead. The smell was a lot stronger now and he could even see little wisps of smoke hanging almost stagnant in the air above, clinging to the metal grating like fog to water.

Every time he let out a breathe, the smoke would curl away gently before seemingly freezing in place. It was funny. He'd never seen smoke behave like that before. It was as if it was smoke, yet it grew hard like jelly if you let it settle.

He was about to step onto the next floor when there was a low grumbling sound from somewhere nearby. It reverberated off the metal and down the corridors, making it hard to pinpoint.

Alexander wrapped one arm over Owen's shoulder, pulling him back to him.

His eyes darted back and forth searching for whatever made the sound.

Owen figured it to be some old machinery hidden away somewhere, but a little part of his mind knew that was only wishful thinking. That started a whole new train of thought. After everything he had seen so far mixed with the imagination of a young boy lost in the dark, and you got a crazy mixture of possibilities. He saw giant monsters the size of buildings striding like Sumo wrestlers toward them. Or billions on billions of little rats with their skin ripped off and bone showing through as they moved as a collective down the corridors toward them, scuttling over one another fighting for the first bite on his pale skin.

It was warmer here, too. Sweat had broken out on his forehead and he could feel Alexander's clammy arm against his cheek.

"What is it?"

"Hush," was Alexander's only response. It wasn't hard, just plain and simple. Owen understood.

With the smoke lingering around, the already low light was diminished even more.

There was a low, sharp grunt, perhaps a snore. And Alexander moved himself around to be in front of the boy. Holding him closely behind with one hand, he began to move again. Owen tried to peer around

Alexander's waist to see what was going on, not that there was much to see.

Something moved off to the left, in front of one of the new sets of corridors. Hopefully not the one that led out. There were still more stairs to climb, Owen noted and that seemed to be the way Alexander was leading him. They crab walked until Owen could feel the first step leading up behind his calves.

"Go. Slowly."

Whatever it was sniffed at the air. As well as the smoke, it must have caught a whiff of something else, because it grunted again. A huge black mass began to unwind itself as Owen took that first step and then the second. Alexander stepped up also.

There was a flash of white accompanied by a loud hiss as lips curled back from what looked to be a ferocious set of fangs.

Whatever this thing was, it wasn't human.

Owen took the next few steps even faster, turning around to make the job easier. As he reached the half way point, he turned back to see Alexander still moving slowly.

A metallic tick clacked through the corridors several times and Owen imagined razor like claws tapping away like his father's fingers on the tabletop when he was waiting, or angry.

Owen remembered in movies, how there was always something to give away someone's location. Every time they were sneaking by a sleeping monster or a murderous person, they would always kick a can or knock something over. It was horror film etiquette, though he never knew what that word really meant. His mum and dad had been discussing it while they watched a video they had gotten out with Jamie Lee Curtis in it. Owen hadn't been allowed to watch it, but he had refused to go to bed. He sat drawing instead in the kitchen, listening to them talk.

But the conversation sprung to mind now. Walking by a sleeping monster, if it was sleeping at all. He made extra special care not to make any noise. Alexander was doing the same.

As it turned out, it didn't make any difference.

As Alexander made it to the mid-landing of the stairs, the shape had finished uncoiling. But it didn't stop there. The white fangs were bared again as the creature let out a strangled growl from the back of its throat. It knew they were there and was looking straight at them.

"Go! Run!"

Owen bolted up the stairs almost exactly as Alexander yelled the order. The creature sprang forward. There was a loud clanging sound as it must have made contact with the stairs and Alexander grunted. Owen spun around to see his friend lying sprawled on his back across the landing. He couldn't quite make out the shape of whatever it was that had attacked, but he could see it was somehow wedged between the railings.

It groaned, perhaps in pain, a couple of times before lashing out. A thick paw, that may as well have been a small tree trunk struck out at Alexander, shiny black claws flashed briefly as it arced upward and swung down.

But the meek little man was ready. Several thin spikes appeared out of the side of his leg and he rolled onto the opposite side, hoping to avoid any contact at all.

The paw came down on mostly metal, but one of Alexander's own quills had been caught. The creature yelped loudly, lifting its front leg up once more, perhaps to attack again. But Alexander wouldn't allow that. Continuing his roll, he pushed himself up onto his feet and ran up the rest of the stairs, grabbing Owen along the way and planting him safely on the next level.

Owen had a feeling there was still a long way to go.

KIRRILY

Not eight blocks away below the city streets, several halogen lamps snapped to life along with several items of machinery.

The room was massive. About the size of a small air-hanger.

Cabinets lined the walls, some labelled with part numbers, and others remained blank and locked. At one end of the hanger was a large workshop. Several benches of microscopic and electronic gadgetry was sitting idle; behind that, a heavy duty mechanical operation had been abandoned mid procedure. A vehicle that resembled a giant rodent of sorts, hung limply on the vehicle hoist. Tools were splayed over another row of benches that had been covered with grease and engine parts.

There were several small doorways along the walls of the hanger, all of which glistened with clinical cleanliness like the hard metallic walls that supported them. Several small vehicles hidden in plain sight under large drop clothes took up much of the remaining space, while a massive custom designed sixteen wheeler sat facing a large roller door. The vehicle was majority dark blue; the trailer a shade even more so. The cab glistened with polish adding to its already sleek spaceship appearance. Silver streaks swirled down the side of the cab and along the trailer. A small concertina connection between the rear of the cab and the trailer gave easy access from one to the other.

A single computer work station that looked like some multi levelled pianist's set up crossed with the helm control on the USS Voyager in the Star Trek Series of the same name, began processing data as it received it directly from a tiny wrist component elsewhere in the city. Simultaneously it pinpointed the wearer's location, body temperature, heart rate and all other vital signs. Only meters away, the truck's engine turned over. The rear doors of the trailer opened under mechanical guidance and a sensor scan swept the storage hold. Once completed, the massive roller door in front of the vehicle began its journey upward, rattling slightly as it went. Headlights flashed on and the gear changed. In a matter of seconds, it was on its way up a little known access ramp. At the end of which, a second roller door was lifting out of the way, allowing access to Milligan Street, only minutes from Kirrily's current location – considering her only way out of the building.

It was simple enough to blow the window out. Either one kick, one shot or one zap could have done it. But they weren't going to draw attention to themselves until they were ready to move.

Owen had already suggested a plan of attack. Heading straight across to the building opposite. Sure they'd stand out like a Christmas tree against the backdrop of the night sky, if anyone was looking, but they would be free of this building. Hopefully there wouldn't be many more attackers to quickly come after them next door. The other option was to take them straight down to ground level. This meant confrontation which, at this current point of time, was not a wise idea.

Checking her wrist display, she received an ETA from her truck. She didn't have to worry so much about it finding its way. Nor having an accident. It had an automated computer guidance system on board utilising satellites already in position over head. There were also numerous sensors on board checking proximity of objects, walls, vehicles and people five times every second. If there was any indication of collision, the CGS would compensate in plenty of time. As for red lights, most were run, which wasn't a worry at this time of night on a Sunday, the only concern being for police patrol vehicles catching sight. But even that could be used to their advantage. How would the bastards below react to an approaching siren?

There wasn't time to worry just now. They had about twenty seconds before the truck arrived. They had probably less before all the doors were closed on the vehicles below and perhaps a fair bit more before their current location was discovered by the others in the building.

"We need to move. Help will be here in a bit, but we need to get down there."

He nodded, stepped away from the glass and gave her one quick look, "We're going down, in a round about sort of way."

It was his call. She'd be ready for it.

She checked her weapon. There were only eleven shells left. That should suffice with the modifications she had made on the pulse-pistols firing mechanism. As well as the shell, it released the distinctive pulse wave when the trigger was pulled. She claimed it as her trademark, but it was only present on this miniature version. The rifles were standard issue. Automatic, standard pulse shells, bigger magazines, more impressive impact from the directed pulse reflex. It was less noticeable, being more concentrated, seemingly only a rippling effect in the air, but no less effective.

Owen's transformation was swift. She felt a now familiar tingle as he latched his arm around her waist. It was like a gentle surge of static electricity. Odd as she normally associated a static charge as being sharp and sometimes minutely painful.

She recalled people telling her it doesn't hurt. But in her own experience, she had felt a number of zaps that bordered on a sting. But this was almost a tickle around her mid drift. Lifting her arm around his neck, she braced herself for the jaunt.

He simply pointed his finger at the window frame and let lose a spray of electric current. In seconds the glass cracked as the frame distorted. Then shattered, exploding out over the street, hopefully tearing the bad guys to bits below, but Kirrily knew that to be wishful thinking.

Her stomach lurched as Owen pushed off the floor, launching them out into the night.

He was going slower than she had seen him move before, probably for her benefit. She wasn't even sure if she could survive his normal speed.

But she could feel the effects of this one. She tightened her grip on both the weapon and his neck, still being careful not to choke the trigger or his air passage.

Everything was a blur. Even though, outside, there wasn't much to see, the distant lights of the street and other buildings became a kaleidoscope of colour as they travelled tens of metres in seconds. The already gusty wind was like a thick wall of snow they were charging through, nearly choking her, but rather than worrying, she was exhilarated. Flight without wings or a jetpack. To be able to leap from building to building. What a power to have. She was in awe of this man's abilities. He was like Superman in his own way.

She felt their course take a minor change as Owen compensated slightly for the wind and their intended destination. The glass wall of the intermediate building was fast approaching and Kirrily prepared herself for a jarring change of direction. But it didn't come.

Making only the briefest of contacts with the metal frame on the other building, Owen stopped only momentarily before taking off once more. They had dropped a number of floors already. But this transition was almost imperceptible. She had expected the gut wrenching and nauseating effect one would receive from spinning around on the spot and suddenly stopping. But there was nothing, just a cool change of wind direction.

One more smooth change like that and the next stop would be on the ground.

But of course, they could never be that lucky.

Added to the already speeding lights came flashes of red. But instead of zooming by on the horizontal plain, these were shooting past them vertically. They were being shot at from below. Obviously the shattering glass had caught someone's attention or someone had radioed down to the other bad guys in the street that they had made their escape.

It would make the journey down just that bit more jarring. She could already feel Owen tense under her arms as he dodged any oncoming assaults he could see. It wasn't until some smart bugger from below had a good idea that Kirrily got really worried.

The glass pane Owen had been aiming for exploded as it was struck by one of the red beams.

This time Kirrily did feel the jolt in her system as Owen's journey stopped mid flight.

It was near enough to suicide.

They fell short of the glass and the wall by several metres, not to mention the ground by several stories.

Like a cartoon they lingered in mid air for the slightest of seconds that seemed like an eternity as everything began to register at sonic speed in both their minds. In that time, Owen looked at her, wide-eyed. He had nothing to push off from, she knew that. She was pretty sure from the look in his eyes he couldn't jump-start himself without some sort of boost.

The drop was a lot less comfortable than the electrical jaunts Owen had taken her on. For one, the wind was racing at them straight up their nostrils, making it hard to breathe let alone scream.

But she wasn't in the mood for screaming anymore. One bout of humiliation for the night was enough.

Instead, she tried to look below, keeping one arm firmly around Owen. The street was directly below clear of vehicles and people. So Kirrily did the only thing she could think of.

With her right arm around Owen's neck and his left around her, she aimed her own left hand at the pavement.

It was coming at them possibly even faster than the wall had been just seconds ago.

She pulled the trigger.

The recoil jarred up her arm. Even the suppressants she had installed in the weapon did little to prevent her shoulder aching in response.

The shot bolted out of the weapon, drilling a hole through the grey bitumen the size of a baseball. Along with it raced the same circle of puce light that had erupted from the weapon before. Her trademark.

When it struck the bitumen below, it sent a small shockwave of warm air back up at them, giving them a small boost from below. For a moment the ground beneath them hesitated before starting its climb again. The bitumen looked a lot worse for wear. The radius of the pulse burst had cracked and charred. Several more shots like that and they'd be lucky if there was any ground left to land on.

The vans nearby were just about full size. She had to time this next burst just right.

Firing once more, she was slightly more prepared for the recoil, but pain lingered in her shoulder joint and probably would do, if they

93

survived this, for a long while. A second baseball sized hole was punched into the bitumen as the weapon unleashed its third volley for the evening. The pulse wave was more concentrated this time, the distance between the weapon and the ground being so short, the bitumen erupted in a cloud of dust, some of which was swept upward in the resulting heat wave.

It was a damn fine weapon and powerful to boot. Kirrily was proud of it.

Their feet touched terra firma just as they began to fall once more. They were able to compensate by bending their knees on impact. At least they were grounded. Problem was, when they looked up, there were at least twelve weapons trained on them. Looking across at the still glowing Owen, She could see little red dots dancing around his black costume.

She hadn't paid much attention to it before, but he did look good in the lycra suit. He wasn't overly big in the muscle department, but he filled the suit well enough. She was almost embarrassed, but now wasn't the time.

Just down the road at the first intersection, a pair of headlights turned into the street.

"Right on time."

The people bearing guns, both men and women, looked at each other, unsure of what to do.

"Pull out."

Someone hidden behind the vehicles called out.

There was no argument from the soldiers. They vanished into the vans before Kirrily could even think about their options.

Owen, who still had a hold on Kirrily went for another burst of speed as one of the black vehicles came tearing toward them in their haste to get away, and probably in an attempt to run them down.

Kirrily found herself standing on the other side of the road, the headlights of the newly arrived vehicle heading straight toward them.

"Who are they?" Owen asked.

She beamed. Easy mistake, "That's my truck," she boasted, almost like a child. She was proud of all her inventions, but this was the epitome of her hard work. She couldn't wait to show him around.

He'd be the first person living to see inside what she had been working on for months.

The vans were disappearing quickly.

The truck, as Owen could now make out, slowed to a stop several feet away and Kirrily pulled on his arm, leading him toward it.

"Hurry up. We're going to have to follow them."

He cocked an eyebrow as he moved, "What, no tracking device?"

She smiled, "Yeah, but only a limited range."

She opened the driver's side door, ignoring the fold out rungs that appeared from within the panelling that would make her entrance easier.

She didn't have time. Using her right arm, she hoisted herself into the big rig and flicked a number of switches to turn off the CGS.

Owen had powered down by the time his backside hit the leather upholstery. She threw the vehicle in gear and it sailed smoothly after the little red tail lights that were disappearing down the street.

OWEN

The cab was cushy. Instead of being unlit or having the small light sitting in the centre of the roof glaring, there was a gentle and somewhat eerie glow coming from several points. Around the door edging, above the windscreen, a blue-white light glimmered from what looked to be ordinary metal.

He couldn't stop himself looking around. This was like no other truck he'd seen before.

The dashboard was massive. There were several sets of buttons, some labelled with small writing, others with numbers. LCD displays gave readings on the engine temperature, Revs per minute, speed to the third decimal point and other readings he didn't know anything about. There was a monitor display sitting on a support arm facing the driver. He could only just make out a map revealing their current location and perhaps that of her tracking device.

The seats were overly comfortable. He could imagine sitting in the one spot for days on end and still not wanting to move.

There was a space between the driver and the passenger allowing for some movement between the front of the cab and the small sleep out in the rear.

Leaning around, he peered into the dark little nook and was surprised to see a heavily sealed door at the back.

"Where does that go?"

"Hmm? Oh, back to the trailer."

He was impressed, "It's connected? That's pretty cool. Saves having to hop in and out all the time."

"Tell me about it," As far as Owen could tell she hadn't changed the gears yet.

"Is this an automatic?"

She didn't take her eyes of the road, though he had a feeling with all the gadgetry, it wouldn't have been a problem if she had taken her hands off the wheel. It had driven itself all the way to meet them without her, why couldn't it keep doing so.

"It can be."

He nodded and looked back out the windscreen, "This must have set you back quite a bit. I wasn't even aware they had these on the market."

He could see her smile and blush a little through the corner of his eye, "It isn't. Not yet anyway. I designed it myself, had the parts made especially and put it together."

95

"Like a giant jigsaw."

"Exactly," he looked at her again, a little shocked. He had been joking. She was serious and very proudly so.

"You're telling me you built this thing from the ground up, by yourself?"

"Well, I had a bit of assistance from some of my earlier inventions."

"Robots?"

She laughed, "No. Just several devices that helped with the precision work and of course the manual labour. I may be strong, but I'm not that strong."

She was right there. She was strong. She'd taken a fair beating already and had barely broken a sweat and Owen suspected that was only because of the heat from all the fire.

"So this is like a hobby or what you really do for a living?"

"Both. I work as a security guard, generally on the killer shifts nobody wants. Such as this morning when you broke into the records-"

"I didn't break into anything. I received permission-"

She smiled again. It was a nice smile. Even, like the rest of her face. He'd almost say flawless. Well, probably would. If he was asked, of course. But no one had, so he would just think it.

"It doesn't matter. I don't work there anymore after tonight. Either by choice or because someone here recognised me, I won't be going back. But that doesn't bother me."

She rounded a corner with such ease. Owen nearly laughed at the comical look of this woman easily turning the massive steering wheel of this massive hulk when greater men had wrestled a similar machine as if they were fighting a bull with their bare hands to do exactly the same thing.

"I have my hobby to back me up. I make things. I even sell some of them. I've managed to accumulate a fair amount of savings from it all."

"What, to the military?"

"No!" She looked at him sharply, "I don't support any of that. Sure I make weapons, but they're for my own usage. Not that I've ever really needed to use them before. But just in case. Like in the case of a war. I want to be ready. But not just weapons. I've helped design several pieces of medical equipment developing from the MRI's and other scanning machines. They're on the market, but they fetch too rich a price to be in most hospitals yet. That wasn't my idea unfortunately. The buyer of the design set the price and is refusing to lower it."

He was amazed. This woman was unique. She was obviously very talented, very intelligent.

"How did you get started?"

"I already had a small workshop set up, but it was no where near enough. Then out of the blue, I received a phone call. Some guy wanted to sponsor my projects. He said he'd get me set up. Then it'd just be a case of me paying back the money borrowed and then a small percentage of my profit. I thought, 'fine'. He hasn't hassled me since. He does check up on me at times to see if I need any assistance or the like, but I'm okay."

Strange wasn't the word for all of this. He'd known strange. And unique, as he'd used earlier in his thoughts, was a far cry from what it really was. But he couldn't put his finger on it.

Then he remembered what Myrl had said earlier. Something about her being like them after all.

He kept looking at her for a moment, without saying a word. Not meaning to stare, but just looking. Maybe she was like them. That could be where all this sprung from. Maybe.

"Now, a question for you," she said.

"Shoot," He was more than happy to answer anything she asked. Within reason of course.

"The music. What is it and where does it come from?"

"I beg your pardon?"

She looked at him again, "Whenever you do whatever it is you do, there's this music. It's only really faint, but it is there. At first I thought it was a radio somewhere, but it's not."

He almost blushed. Owen knew about the music. He thought it was only in his mind, sort of like a dream. A glorified dream, as kids run around playing superheroes singing their themes such as "Spiderman, Spiderman, does whatever a spider can…" and so on.

"I honestly don't know," he explained his own theory on it possibly being radio frequencies he was picking up.

She was intrigued, "So you're not carrying some sort of mp3 player?"

"Uh-uh. Not on me."

"Okay. It's pretty neat anyway."

He looked at her, stunned, "Neat?"

"What?"

She wasn't aware of what she said, or was she?

"You said neat. My god, I haven't heard that in years. Neat, Mintox, Buntox. All words from Primary School."

"Oh," He had hurt her feelings.

"No. It's great. I love it when people do that, just out of the blue, something different."

She simply smiled and continued to concentrate on the road.

There was silence for a while. Owen found himself wishing he knew what button to press to turn the radio on, if what he thought was a radio was in fact that and not some other device. After catching only a glimpse of her ordnance, he wouldn't have been surprised if she had a number of rocket launchers concealed somewhere on the truck. It certainly made him feel safer being in her company.

It amazed him she seemed to have the ideals of a pacifist if she was willing to withhold all the weaponry she had developed from the military and yet was actually in the market of building the things. Even so, she was digging herself in deep with the company if she decided to continue along with him. Why should she help anyway, it wasn't any of her concern. Sure, she had moral and ethical standards of which her employers seemed to have broken through, but that was no reason to join in waging a war against them. What really did she have to gain? If she was doing it for him or for anyone else, she was practically committing suicide for them. And that wasn't right.

He had started to say so when she decided it was time to speak as well. It was a comical and awkward moment followed by a few seconds silence before they both asked the other to speak. Just like in a Hollywood movie.

"You go," He enforced.

"How did they get you? When you were younger, I mean? How did they find you?"

It wasn't what he had been expecting. It was a little too deep and personal. He tried to answer a couple of times, his mouth moving but words refused to come out.

"I'm sorry if I'm prying. Don't worry about it."

The words finally came, "No. It's okay. It's just... Hard. To remember."

"You've repressed the memories?"

He laughed, but there was little humour in it, "I've tried to do that. It's not easy to do. Your mind keeps wandering back to it, reinforcing the events in your mind. It just hurts. In a way."

"I'm sorry," She apologised again.

"No. It's fine, really. I was five, nearly six. My parents owned a small farm in the country, past Meekatharra. My older brother, Ryan, he was helping Dad with the machinery. I was in the Kitchen with my mum."

"Did they know you were different?"

He didn't mind her interrupting. It helped put a little distance between himself and the flow of events.

"They were too. I don't know about Ryan. But Mum did things with her mind. Telepathy, Telekinesis. Dad, I found out later, was a shape shifter. He was able to take on practically any form. My Aunt tells me he used to turn into a bright golden dragon for my mother. He was restricted in size as far as she knew. Couldn't really break the twelve-foot mark in height or length. I never saw any of that. But there was one time when I was escaping. I thought it was my Mum. Then my eyes started playing tricks one me. And then it was both Mum and Dad at once. I didn't know what to think. My Aunt says it was probably my Dad trying to calm me with a soothing environment. I'd always been closer to Mum and he knew it. So he was trying to reassure me."

He stopped for a moment. He had never been sure. But when Helen had told him that, he didn't care which one it was, he loved them both and missed them equally as much.

She paused a moment, giving him time, perhaps testing the waters before going any further, "What about your brother?"

"We couldn't find him. Alexander helped me get out. But once I was out, he went back in with a few others to try and help the others. There was no sign of Ryan."

"I'm sorry to hear that."

Owen nodded. He had nothing to say about the matter that hadn't been said. He missed his brother as well. Wished there was something he could have done, even if only to find out hat had happened to him. But there was nothing and that made it even worse. Was he alive somewhere? Perhaps in those tubes, unknowingly kept prisoner whilst unconscious and devoid of knowledge of what was going on around him.

It was his turn to ask the questions.

"Why are you helping us?"

Her brow furrowed for a moment. He wasn't sure if she was considering the question or if she was offended by it.

"Why shouldn't I?"

He opted for the latter.

"I mean, aren't you risking a lot to help people you hardly know."

"That's what I thought we were just doing. Getting to know each other."

"You know what I mean."

"And you have no idea what I'm about, do you? I'm not doing this just for you. I'm doing this because of me, my father. A whole range of reasons. It's my choice. I'm not being forced to help you so don't question it and don't look a gift horse in the mouth."

She had gotten a little riled in that little speech and there was another awkward silence. This was happening a fair bit. Tension was mounting and he wasn't even sure why.

Finally it was up to him to break the quiet, "What does that mean, anyhow?"

"What?"

"That gift horse line? I know I've never received a horse from anyone."

She giggled. He liked that about her. She had a tendency to giggle like a little girl at the dumbest of things. He didn't think that detracted from her in any way. It wasn't a flaw. It was a unique ability to find humour in some things other people are just too stupid or serious to realise. Owen couldn't help himself; he let out a little chuckle of his own which set her off into a proper laugh.

Things were going to be okay.

CHAPTER ELEVEN

THEN

They had opted to take the corridor directly in front of the stairwell leading down. It seemed as good a choice as any. And Alexander hadn't disapproved. What they found, however, was a twisting corridor with dozens of doors lining the walls. It was hard to tell if any one of these could lead to a way out. It was also hard to tell if the corridor they walked down would take them back where they began or not. The number of times it rounded a corner to the right was frightening to Owen. What if it did just that, take them back to the stairs. Would that mean every corridor would do the same thing? Then they'd have to check every door along the way to make sure they weren't hidden doors to the outside.

It was getting pointless. There were any number of options to take. Keep on going, go back and check the doors. After a number of minutes walking, Owen couldn't help himself. He stopped in front of one door and Alexander kept going. He knew it was stupid to get lost so if the man kept going, Owen would call out to him to stop.

He reached for the handle and turned. It clicked loudly down the corridor, getting Alexander's attention. The man stopped and looked back at him.

"What are you doing?"

Owen looked at him and said simply what was on his mind, "It might be a way out."

The man came back as Owen pushed the door open.

Inside was dark. Alexander's long arm reached into the room and felt around for a light switch. When it flickered on, the boy could see he had made the wrong choice.

This wasn't the way out. This wasn't the way anywhere.

It was a small room. A simple double bunk sat in one corner, the sheets pulled taught. A small table sat in the middle of the room. Two chairs on either side. Two stand up lockers and foot trunks lined one wall but there was little else in the way of decoration. There was, however, a smell. Perhaps an aftershave that made the room smell lived in.

"Barracks," Alexander noted, "Those people sleep here."

"Does that mean we're close?"

Alexander smiled reassuringly, "Could be."

Owen ran out of the room with the man hot on his heels. He had a burst of hope and energy.

His enthusiasm was cut short when he rounded the next corner and slammed into something big and hard. The force behind his impact worked in reverse and Owen was sent flying backward on his bottom, stopping only when his back made contact with a wall. Pain had jarred up his spine as he fell, but it made him more angry than sad.

He looked up to see what had gotten in his way and nearly choked on a scream.

He had heard stories about Death. A skeleton in a big black hooded cloak. All Owen could see now was the cloak. Beneath the cowl was shadow. His mind worked at a thousand miles and hour as images of what may lie beneath took hold of his imagination. Bugs crawling through the empty eye sockets, maggots dripping from rotted flesh still clinging to the base of the skull.

Then the arm moved. It reached out for him, a hand gloved in black lunged at him. Or seemed to. Everything around him was a blur as he pushed himself up and away from this horrible creature.

We were so close, was the thought racing through the mind. He knew he didn't know that for sure, but he wished it so hard.

"Alexander!" He screamed as he bolted toward his friend.

The man caught him and held him to his side, trying to calm him with one arm as he craned his neck to see what was there.

Owen peeped through half shut eyes as the Grim Reaper stepped around the corner.

"Neil?"

"Sorry to have startled the boy, but we must hurry."

Owen looked up at his friend. Neil? Who was Neil? They seemed to know each other.

"Agreed," Alexander said simply. He bent down and took the boy's shoulders in hand and looked into his face. Owen couldn't help staring at the cloaked figure that had stopped coming toward them, but still seemed to be staring at them through the shadows of the cowl.

"Owen. Owen, look at me," reluctantly, he did so, "Owen. This man can show you the way out. Follow him."

"But what about you?"

Alexander shook his head, "You were right, we can't just leave them. I'm going back down."

The Grim Reaper named Neil spoke, "Is that wise?"

Alexander stood up once more, "As I said, we can't just leave them. Take the boy. Get him to safety."

The hood nodded and the arm extended out once more.

"Take his hand. He will show you the way out."

Owen timidly took the hand. It was cold, but more so from the material than from what lay underneath it. He could imagine those same bugs crawling around over the bones, as if the man was actually made up of a gigantic colony of wasps and bees and ants and worms. But he wouldn't let go of Alexander either.

The meek little man had to pry himself free before heading back down the corridor, "We will see each other again, Owen. I promise you."

"No! No!" It was useless. Neil was too strong for him as he fought to go after his friend. Alexander disappeared around one corner and Owen had a sick feeling in his stomach that he may never see the man again.

Neil half pulled, half carried Owen along the rest of the corridor until he came to a lift. It was recognisably so by the button that sat on one side of the sliding double doors.

Neil pressed it, keeping a firm grip on Owen's arm with his other hand.

"Please, boy, it'll be easier if you stop fighting me. I'll have you out of here shortly," The voice didn't match the look. He sounded kind enough. But was it a ploy of Death's.

"I don't want to die!" Owen wailed.

"If you keep yelling like that, you're bound to find someone else who disagrees with your opinion."

The Grim Reaper's free hand lifted to its head and brushed the hood back. Owen flinched away, afraid of what would be underneath. Those same bugs crawling through hollow eye sockets, razor sharp teeth smiling a horrid grin of evil.

The doors opened with a small chime.

"Owen. Owen!"

The boy forced himself to be strong, to look. Alexander had trusted this man. He had to believe it was the right choice.

When he looked, There was no skull. No bugs, bees, wasps. Just a normal man. Blonde, oldish. A couple of wrinkles, but not enough to make him ancient in the eyes of a child. He wasn't angry, he wasn't smiling. But he was concerned. Owen could see it in his eyes.

This wasn't Death. This was another human being. Probably one to be trusted.

He ceased his struggling, of which Neil was grateful. He led the boy into the lift and pressed the button marked G.

Looking at the other options, Owen could see that the lift went all the way down to B6. Above the doors, which had shut, was a series of lights covered with the same alphanumerical numbers as the buttons. Currently, B2 was lit.

Neil pushed Owen behind his cloak, out of sight for when the doors opened.

The boy cowered there, holding tight to the material, not daring to look around any more. He just wanted to get out of here. He'd had enough.

The doors chimed once more as the indicator hit 'G'.

KIRRILY

"What I'm still wondering is how they found the others."

102

Owen regarded her. She meant it. She had no idea. If his theory about this Myrl woman using her abilities to shield the building from everyone's presence was true, how did they find them?

"I'm not sure," He sounded as if he wanted to keep speaking. She left him to continue at his own pace, "Look. About earlier. My accusing you. I'm sorry. It's just-"

"No. Hey. No, you were right to think like that. I guess that's how they survived so long, being somewhat paranoid and protective. But I didn't do it. I promise you. But I am intrigued. How did they find you when you were younger? They have to have some way to know how to tell between... Well, normal and not normal."

She turned a corner that led onto one of the freeways. This one led to an extended underground tunnel to bypass the main city road network. A much faster way out of the city.

"I don't know that either. I don't think we ever found that out. Maybe they have some sort of scanning device. Or perhaps my parents had records. People knew about them. Some of the remnants were friends of the family, though they don't like talking to me any more. Maybe there's a mole. Someone feeding them information."

"Is that likely? Betraying your own kind?"

He cocked an eyebrow, "What are you doing now?"

She shook her head, speeding up slightly as the cars ahead of them began to gain some extra distance along the freeway, "That's different. A job is not like a family. Sure, it can be sometimes, but when you live with someone, or are friends with them, it just doesn't sound right. For one thing, you risk a larger backlash in your life."

"Unless there's some sort of benefit for doing so. A bribe, a job promotion."

"True. But would it really be worth it?"

They were coming up on the tunnel, the vans having disappeared inside.

"You saw what they were living in. Not everyone's made for that. I know I wouldn't be."

"Hmm," was all she could say. She found it hard to believe someone could do that to friends, especially those that could be so much like family. Sure, she had had a close relationship with her own parents, but surely there were limits to what you could do against them, even in the worst of households.

"So you really make all this stuff yourself?"

"You don't believe me?"

He hastened to assure her he did. And it was true or he was a very good liar.

"I'm just surprised you could think all of this stuff up. I mean, it isn't stuff you see every day. Pulse guns, I think you called it, your grappling gun, this truck. Everything. It all seems way too science fiction."

"That's the way of the future, don't you think?"

He nodded. She wasn't sure if he liked that prospect. A mechanised reality. Many people dream of it. Such as Star Trek. Everything automated and done by a friendly sounding computer. Others seemed uncomfortable for the whole '2001' reason. Machine destroys man. That could only happen if man became too lax in their designs. Kirrily had built way too many fail-safes into her systems, not that she had fully delved into artificial intelligence. Of course, she had dabbled.

That whole Terminator Judgement Day hogwash was a possibility but an unlikelihood all the same.

The other concern was getting too dependent on machines. She agreed with this. But again, only within a person's own judgement of their own abilities. If people let themselves get lazy, that was their responsibility and their own fault. Not her's, not the machine's and not the designer's. It was easy to blame everything else for human failure and that was one of the real bad notions arising from a mechanised future. Too many ways of getting into and out of trouble due to human failure. Not mechanical, but human.

She realised that he was looking at her intently as if listening and her attention drifted to find she had been talking this whole time; her own arguments had been spewing forth unconsciously. She didn't mind because it was how she felt. He seemed intrigued by it all as well, so no problem there.

Kirrily looked out the windscreen again and started slightly. The cars had pulled further away. Most of them had vanished around one of several bends in the tunnel. At least she could keep following the last couple. The lighting in the tunnel was supposedly "adjusting" It started on entry with two bright lengths of lamps illuminating the road. As it continued onward, one strip of lamps dulled to yellow before complete disappearing. The second then started to dull also.

Kirrily figured the purpose of this was to adjust your eyes when heading back into the darkness. But during the day, it was a real pain in the cornea. Your eyes did adjust to a lesser amount of light and then - BANG - your eyes are hit by a wave of bright sunlight on re-entry from the tunnel.

Following the curve around, she could see that several of the vans had actually made a get away. There were only three vehicles left in front of her now as far as she could see. One was a van probably carrying some of the Remnants. The other two were black sedans.

There were several other cars of other colours, but these were simply your casual driver. It was rare seeing so many black cars, so this lot stood out like a blister on your heel.

"Something's up," she could feel it in her gut. She had seen a couple of sedans at the building, but they had been further up in the convoy. Somewhere along the tunnel, they'd done a bit of car swapping.

They were nearing the final bend in the tunnel before it ran straight for a short length and entered the open air.

Indicating to change lanes, Kirrily sped up, overtaking a car that had pulled in front of her earlier.

It was a dual lane system with a third emergency stopping lane running the whole left hand side of the tunnel. It was also a dual tunnel system. There were in fact two separate tunnels running beside each other heading in either direction, thus they couldn't see any cars coming in the other direction.

Feeling a little uneasy, Kirrily kept applying a bit more pressure to the accelerator. The faster they were out of the tunnel the better. There wasn't much manoeuvring space in here, especially for a full sized sixteen-wheeler truck.

At the mouth of the tunnel, it began another curve that ran around to the left slightly and up an incline so as to rise for the approach of a bridge that crossed the Swan River. It basically meant all Kirrily could see was the road curving out of sight and a little of the concrete barricade erected for reducing noise pollution and supporting an off ramp that lead from the other direction up onto a semi direct route into the inner city.

The air in the truck cabin had grown quiet and almost tangible.

They were catching up to the convoy once more, but only the same three cars she had seen earlier. The other must have made an early escape by speeding up behind one of the tunnel's bends.

That was one of the reasons she was not happy. Why leave these three behind? They must have had intercoms or two ways in their cars or more likely mobile phones. They had to be up to something.

Instigating the main CGS system, she flicked several other switches.

The dashboard's light changed to a deep red, the subsequent glow seemed to cover the two occupants in blood. Over the muffled sound of the engine, a new buzz rang out.

She had designed contingencies for any occasion. Or at least she hoped she had.

They were seconds from exiting now, but they could already see what was outside. As the final van disappeared out of sight, the two sedans managed a hand brake turn that sent them skidding onward and turning around in an almost synchronised movement, effectively cutting off both lanes.

That wouldn't have been a problem for the truck if there weren't five more parked along the road just behind them.

Ramming through all that could send the truck on a crash course, possibly into a roll.

"What do you say?"

He looked at her, his eyebrow cocked as if asking the question she had just answered in her own mind.

"Probably not."

"Is it worth a try?"

"Anything's worth trying once, don't you think?"

He smiled and braced himself against his seat for impact.

She did the same as she all but slammed her foot on the accelerator.

Rather than the slow choking crawl of a truck, Kirrily's custom made vehicle kicked to life. The speedometer raced upward as the vehicle sped forward.

People had already stepped out of the cars, their weapons trained at the windscreen.

Kirrily kept sitting upright. She was safe in the cab. Bullets would do little now. Owen gave her a quick look, as if trying to take cue from her, but remained upright also.

She wouldn't have blamed him for ducking. He wasn't knowledgeable on what this girl could do.

She flashed on the high beams, illuminating the black squad ahead of them, forcing the people around them to flinch away.

If they weren't careful they'd miss their opportunity to jump.

Kirrily counted the metres down and silently prayed everything would work out right.

With just less than a metre to go, the CGS kicked in. The truck jolted sharply as the automated system argued with the manual controls Kirrily was feeding it. But her foot and the pedal pressed hard below it won over.

The cars at the receiving end, however, weren't so lucky.

There was a flash of blue-white light as the CGS field snapped out a large discharge of energy, lifting the front of both of the first vehicles up off the ground and backward under the impact of the truck itself.

As metal clashed with metal, the chassis of the two black sedans gave way, crumpling the engine cavities in on themselves as the rubber on the tyres remaining on the bitumen fought to resist movement. Tyres burst left right and centre as they gave way under the pressure of both car and truck. And sparks flared out when the side CGS fields kicked in, dragging the two vehicles behind it before giving them a sharp boost of electrical current, shoving them away. The car on the right managing to tip over and roll onto its roof.

Then the shooting began.

The men and women from the other cars reacted professionally. Their weapons flashed brightly as they ejected a mixture of bullets and the same red energy beams Kirrily had seen earlier.

Behind them they could hear civilian cars screeching to a halt as they encountered the first two cars and possibly reacted to the bullets that were now ricocheting off the minor shielding that encased the truck. A semi-force field Kirrily had developed several months ago.

It wouldn't last long. It was a massive drainer on the batteries she had installed in addition to the Truck's own power systems. And under the pressure of attack, it would drain even faster. It wouldn't be long before they started breaking through.

As the massive truck drew closer to the remaining cars, a few chinks appeared in the windscreen. Obviously it was breaking down faster than she had expected.

But that didn't matter. They were already starting to dive for cover.

The next impact wasn't as friendly on the truck as the previous one.

The cab lurched as the boot of one of the cars crumpled beneath its attack, jacking the front right hand side of the truck up. Kirrily could feel herself floating for an instant before the car beneath her crumpled back onto the road, scraping metal against the pavement as the truck struggled to move onward.

But it was already slowing down as shrapnel locked the front wheels in place and the car that had become more of a door stop continued to give way under the weight of the truck and yet caught along the road, creating too much friction for the already battered truck.

Bullets continued to ring out against the side of the cab as they travelled past the old occupants of the cars. One managed to break through the shield, shattering the window just beside Owen. He quickly shielded himself against the spray of small glass fragments that covered his pink suit.

Things were getting worse.

The remains of the first car still wedged under the cab collided with a second car whilst the other side of the cab connected with a third.

Kirrily found herself wishing she had designed a monster truck instead of this one. There wouldn't have been a problem if she could have crawled straight over them.

One of the remaining cars barked to life, the driver having remained inside. Kirrily willed her own vehicle onward, but didn't like the chances.

If they were to falter here, they would be at the mercy of the gunfire.

She had back up plans of course, but they were all in the back of the truck.

"Get in the back. Find something to hold onto, strap in whatever."

Owen gave her an odd look, which she couldn't quite discern as she wrestled with the steering wheel.

"Just do it."

Without waiting to be asked a third time, he undid his seat belt and awkwardly hopped into the rear of the cab, the sleep out. From there he disappeared into the accordion like pathway between and into the trailer.

What was left of the car wedged beneath them broke free, most of it spraying out onto the road beside them, some of the remains slipped underneath several of the sixteen wheels, knocking the truck about, sending it into an awkward swerve that Kirrily battled to control. The wheel under her hands was covered with sweat as she struggled to compensate, turning it this way and that, trying to straighten out their path.

Bullets still rattled against the truck, most of them breaking through the shielding now, but finding a hard task of cracking the thick metal hide of the vehicle.

The truck swung out and clipped the rear of the fourth car that had parked along the road, even under the slight impact it spun awkward out and back, slamming hard against the trailer. Kirrily hoped the weight in the back would stabilise it and not send it into a roll.

She could hear the bullets echoing from the trailer now; they had left the shooters behind.

But there was still the fifth car.

Kirrily floored the accelerator pedal once more as she continued to fight the steering wheel in her hands.

It was sliding awkwardly under her sweaty fingers, but she was starting to regain control, she hoped.

That was until that fifth car slammed on its brakes and the driver jumped out of the driver's side door, rolling away toward the concrete barrier dividing the two sides of the freeway from each other.

She didn't have enough time to react.

Once more the truck clipped against the vehicle, but it was the truck that gave way this time. The combination of the shrapnel caught in the front tyres and the rubber that had burnt off it as Kirrily pushed onward had worn the tyre thin. As it knocked against the final car in the blockade, metal was torn asunder from the rear of the car and the under carriage of the truck, piercing what was left of the tyre.

It burst under the pressure, rocking the cab upward like a wave before it dropped heavily against the bitumen. Sparks flared once more as the undercarriage continued to grind against the road's surface and the hub of the wheel fought for purchase before the suspension corrected itself. The cab continued to bob up and down, but that was the least of Kirrily's worries.

The car lurched forward and into a spin right in front of the truck. In seconds the two collided, the latter launching itself awkwardly into the air as the smaller vehicle was belted into a roll like a golf ball hit by a club. It flipped several times, clanging against the road and lifting up into the air, bouncing down and streaming forward on its shredded roof along the road.

The truck lost its balance finally as it's driver lost her grip on the wheel.

The steering column cracked loudly as something gave way underneath. The cab was the first to go, lifting high into the air despite its weight and spinning off to the side. The whole truck lurched to the left, heading toward the outside edge of the Freeway.

108

The drag of the cab pulled the rest of the truck with it. Accordion passage twisted, almost yanking free from both sides, but managing to hold in several points before the trailer lifted off its right tyres and onto its left side. The weight from its cargo gave the added momentum to keep it moving.

The weight of the trailer then took over as it continued the roll and the cab was pulled after it.

The steel girders that lined the external lane of the freeway collapsed, slowing the roll slightly but not enough to stop it.

Kirrily let go of the useless steering wheel and wrapped her arms across herself as if to reinforce the seat belt that already held her in place. Scrunching her eyes closed, she tried to pretend this was all a wicked dream. No such luck she found as the ceiling of the cab was belted against the hard terrain, jarring its supports and shattering the windscreen and the remaining driver's side window. She felt glass cut at her arms and face as her stomach lurched once more when the cab was snapped over onto its disintegrating undercarriage and lifted once more into the air to begin another cycle.

OWEN

Lights had flickered on as soon as Owen entered the trailer. Fully automated. Pretty decent.

What he found wasn't what he had expected, though he was hardly surprised.

The first half of the trailer had been made into a camper option. A small kitchenette with dining area. Beyond that was what a bathroom cubicle and a bedroom. A door separated the first half from the second, so he didn't quite know what was beyond, but he had a feeling he would find out if they got through this.

The dining table had been folded away into the wall of the trailer and he noticed the two bench seats had seat belts installed. A little odd, he thought, but no more so than the desk set up just behind the kitchen counter. It was locked into place against the wall; most of its implements were stuck down or packed away in the drawers. There was actually little lying around that could come loose if driving. There were several pieces of note paper on the floor.

In front of the desk was what looked to be an orthopaedic chair, but it too had a seat belt. The base of the chair was bolted into the floor. It looked to be the safest option around.

Struggling against the movement of the vehicle, Owen slid this way and that as he made his way over.

There was a rattle of weaponry against the outside of the trailer, causing a natural instinct to take over. He ducked slightly, but the walls were holding.

He managed to lay a hand on the chair and haul himself into it. Once in, it was an easy job to cross the belts over and join them together in a small catch that sat just below his chest, not unlike an air force pilot's safety harness.

This woman was amazing. She had everything. Or at least she did before he came into her life. If anything went wrong now, it would be his fault. She had no reason to be here, let alone to help him.

But she had chosen to.

He hoped they made it out alive. There was a lot more he'd like to learn about Kirrily. Get to know her better, maybe.

There was a loud clanging from in front and the trailer lurched slightly as the cab dragged it down. Something popped and the truck swung wildly once more.

For an instant, Owen could swear they were airborne and he pictured in his head an angel coming to take him up to heaven. That they were already dead, but the truck was actually going with them. And there she was, the angel, standing before him.

And it looked just like his mother.

CHAPTER TWELVE

KIRRILY

The truck continued its awkward movement, tyres flying into the air and around to buckle beneath the weight of the vehicle as it briefly righted itself. Most had already blown out, the remainders spun wildly as Kirrily's foot jammed against the pedals, scraping at the air to drive them forward but, finding nothing there, they rotated hopelessly, pathetically in an attempt to escape the flailing vehicle.

Breaking away from the freeway, it continued its roll, now reaching a downward slope that gave them even more momentum. The incline was quick to grow steep and the truck was lucky to stay in one piece as it bounded down it, at times bolting into the air like a spritely lamb before the hard reality came crashing down and both bodies inside were knocked wildly around in their seats.

It wasn't long before the grass they were rolling on became a hard white concrete, stained with age and cracking under the weather. Massive chunks joined the cacophony that was the truck before it finally slowed its turn. The cab managed to twist itself upright.

Like a struggling whale the trailer tried to roll over once more and right itself, but giving up and rocking back down to earth on its side.

There was only the gentle swaying of torn metal dangling by threads and the twinkle of glass as it settle within and outside the cabin.

White dust, almost phosphorescent in the night lifted into clouds around the now blackened truck before settling down around it to a stillness and silence one could easily associate with a tomb.

OWEN

The darkness split in half, right down the centre and withdrew, as a lift was known to do. Stark white walls, ceiling and floor greeted him now.

Someone was silhouetted against bright lights of the same colour a score of metres down this corridor. A woman.

"Kirrily?"

Was this the experience of death? Going toward the light? It was too much of a cliché for Owen to believe. Besides, he didn't feel dead.

In fact, something felt decidedly off. As if a switch was flicking on and off in the murky clouds that currently passed for his brain.

Kirrily?

His thought found voice, even without moving his mouth. Echoing hollowly down the corridor.

She hadn't responded. Simply hovered in mid air, her form, now clearer, surrounded by a billowing dress, semi transparent against the backing light.

It wasn't Kirrily. He could tell now, but whoever it was was familiar.

Owen?

The word echoed, it's pitch changing even as it was spoken as if someone were speaking for the first time, having found a voice after a long silence.

It too was familiar.

Mum?

And in a flash, she was there. One second a number of metres away, the next, he could feel that same dress as it brushed against him in the non-existent wind.

And then her hand against his cheek. It was if he was a child again, her smiling down on him. Not patronising, but loving. He felt it even more so now, as if every fibre in his body was sucking the emotion out of her.

His mind was overwhelmed. Her beautiful face, radiant in this dream or whatever it was.

Not dead but standing, or floating rather, right in front of him.

He took hold of her hand as it moved down to his chin. She felt so real, warm... alive.

His vision blurred as memories flooded back of their times in the kitchen, of family holidays, Christmas and birthdays. Happier times. His throat caught as he tried to speak, knowing he didn't have to, but wanting to all the same. A tear broke free from the water rim underneath his eye and met her fingers as they finally drifted from his skin.

"Not alive, Owen. But I'm here."

In voice and mind, he couldn't find words, only emotions and her smile broadened. She read him like a book. She always had. They understood each other. He knew that.

"I never left you. I never will. We're waiting for you. But not for now."

How?

"You never really die, Owen. You move on, you become a part of everything around you. A telepath like I am, I found ways to navigate, to find you."

Why?

The simplest of questions but not what he wanted to ask. Wanted to say.

"To take you back, to reassure you. You've a long way to go. And I'll be with you every step of the way. I must go. Someone is waiting for your help."

'Not yet,' he wanted to cry out. He had so much to say.

But she smiled as she started to move away again. And before the doors of darkness closed once more, he heard her speak once more.

"I know."

And then he opened his eyes.

The world was on a ninety-degree angle. His head lolled uncomfortably toward one wall, the straps of the chair dug into his skin.

Wiggling his fingers to see if anything was broken, he made contact with the wall of the trailer.

He felt okay. A number of bruises, probably some cuts and a lot of body ache but nothing serious.

The engine had stopped. Either that or the cabin had been separated from the trailer. It was hard to know which. As well as hard to know how long he'd been out for.

The dream - no - vision sat square in his mind. But so did the urgency of the situation.

He fought against the muscle tightness in his arms and reached for the release catch for the harness.

With a click that seemed much too loud, he found the wall of the trailer fly at him faster than he thought even he could travel.

Fortunately for Kirrily's cleanliness there wasn't too much debris. The surface beneath him was, however pockmarked and even torn in a number of places. The truck itself had not fared well at all.

Kirrily?

Struggling to stand, he found it awkward to keep balance; the dull ringing in his ears throwing his senses off slightly.

A door had closed over the entrance into the cabin and it took a little effort to lift. But when he looked inside, all he could see was the black ribbing of the accordion passage. There were several holes where the strain had been too much, but the rest had corkscrewed around relatively unscathed.

From the direction of the rotation, it seemed the cabin had somehow righted itself, possibly snapping the undercarriage that held the trailer in place.

He had to crawl through. It was going to be a tight squeeze, but he'd make it.

He felt the black tubes scraping against his back as he wiggled through. It wasn't long before he could push his upper body through to the other side, getting a clear view of the cabin.

Or what was left of it.

The windscreen had blown out as the supports for the ceiling collapsed under pressure.

The entire roof of the back sleep out of the cab was crushed down, making it impossible to even get close to a stand. If he had remained in the passenger seat, he would have been located somewhere outside of the vehicle now as the plot where the seat had been lay vacant, bar some snapped struts, rails and other shredded metallic protrusions. The cabin floor was littered with glass from the windows and the displays on the dashboard. Fire still smouldered in the electrical circuits now bare to the world in front of the driver's seat, supplying the only light in the cab, casting eerily moving shadows across the cramped quarters.

And most importantly, in the driver's seat, slightly illuminated by the flames, Kirrily's shoulder was visible.

Owen's heart pumped as the worst came to mind and he struggled to pry himself from the black cage that gripped at his body.

When he made it all the way through, he used the dashboard for support and turned to face her.

Blood trickled from somewhere in her hair line and several small cuts covered her right cheek, probably from her own window blowing out.

She looked okay. As if she slept, though her arms were hugged around her, protecting herself, her hands tightly gripped to her own straps. Her knuckles were white with tension and she smelled of a mixture of aromatic perfumes, sweat and dust. He figured the last to be from outside.

There was a rumble in the near distance. He wasn't sure what, but he figured they hadn't finished with them yet.

As he looked back at Kirrily, he saw her eyes snap open and felt a sharp pain along his cheek and jaw as her left hand connected with his face.

"Oh man, I'm sorry."

"'S'okay," he shook his head, "You okay to move?"

She took a moment to think, probably testing herself out, "I think so."

"Good, we have to get out of here."

The driver's side door still faced the highway. The best way out would be the passenger side. Using the steering wheel, which was relatively unscathed, he kicked at the already dented door. It only took two solid connections to send it flying off its hinges and onto the grass below.

Kirrily undid her belt as Owen jumped out.

When he turned to see if she needed any help, he saw only her back as she reached into the sleep out.

"What are you doing?"

What she pulled out was not what he had expected. But then again, he should have expected that by now. She was far from ordinary.

The rifle was more than just a simple pellet shooter.

It looked heavier than the truck itself, though she hoisted it into her arms with such ease and care, you would have thought it to be a baby.

There were three separate nozzles at the end. One large enough to stand out as a grenade launcher of some sort. The other two, he hoped no one would ever need to find out.

It was one high-tech, multi panelled and evil looking contraption. He was just happy to have her on his side.

"I thought we might need this."

There was a shower of sparks on the opposite side of the truck as a bullet ricocheted off the cab.

He took her elbow and pulled.

"Move!"

THEN

The lift doors opened. Gone were the dark and dank corridors from before, replaced by sterile white linoleum and tiles. Owen couldn't help but think he'd gone through a magical teleportation device. It looked like he was in a hospital of some sort.

Stepping out of the lift into a small foyer, he saw there were three other elevators around. There was also a modicum of decorative plants, several small landscape paintings and photographs that looked as though they most likely came with the frames.

Neil moved slowly around, checking the available exits cautiously. Owen clung to one corner of his robes.

The hallway moved off in two directions, with a third minor corridor just beside one of the elevators. Doors with numbers and plaques stuck to them lined the hall to the left. To the right, it curved around and out of sight, the floor turning into a thick blue carpet. It looked far less clinical than the foyer in which they stood, and a lot more inviting.

Owen, taking advantage of the fact he had a firm grip on Neil's robes, tugged in the direction he wanted. He wanted the soft carpet, the friendly faces, and the way out.

Neil either interpreted the tugs in the wrong way or simply had a different idea. He took hold of Owen's hand and led him in the other direction.

"What about that way?"

Neil hushed the boy, "It's not the way we have to go."

"Then where are we going? I want to go home!"

"I know. But you're going to have to be patient, and very quiet. We still have a long way to go."

All but hugging the walls, the man dragged the mutely grumbling boy behind him.

His legs were sore, his head ached more than he had ever remembered it doing so and he missed his parents. There was only so long a kid could stay clammed up, he seemed to reason to himself. But Owen knew this was too serious to be joking about. He had to do as Neil said. Stay quiet. Stay patient. He would look after him, though he'd prefer if Alexander were here instead. He felt like he trusted the pale man more. The idea that a man who dresses up like death was looking after him in a strange hospital of some sort sent tears burning into his eyes, but he refused to let them fall.

He had to be brave. They had to get out of here and the only way to do so was by keeping quiet and doing what he was told.

It was hard. He was lost, no idea where his home was, or his family. He was so close to losing control, but he had to hold on.

It wasn't until Owen heard the metallic shrill of a screwdriver that he really started to panic. Not because he was scared of the tool, but because

Neil began ushering him back the way they had come, hiding the boy behind his cloak.

"You're a fool. You have no chance of getting out of here."

Neil continued to move, carefully, making sure Owen wasn't trying to peer around to get a look, which of course, the boy felt compelled to do.

"We can see you, everywhere you go. You think we're so stupid as to let you all simply walk out of here?"

The man in black didn't say a word, just kept retreating. Owen wanted him to say something. To argue, to respond. His silence was too much like fear, and Neil being scared made Owen even more so.

The boy found himself clutching tighter to the cloak, willing it, if not Neil, to speak.

"The little one. He more so than you, we've kept an eye on."

This other man spoke funny. He said words that reminded Owen of television comedies from England. The toffee nosed men who had lots of money, but without the accent.

The drill whirred some more, louder this time.

"Give him to me. We may come to some arrangement with yourself."

OWEN

The night was dark; barely a star shining in the sky was visible as a cloud bank crept over them; the moon's silver glow was hidden behind the hulking frame of the power station. The truck had come to settle within the boundaries of the disused landmark and there was little else around.

Kirrily had broken free from Owen's grasp and was making her own way along the broken concrete.

Taking only a second to do so, Owen looked up. To their right was a tall tower, a silo, at least seven stories high – some sort of conveyer belt encased by galvanised iron ran from high up on the end the main station building to the upper reaches of this separate silo. Some sort of delivery system for fuel or for refuse, Owen wasn't sure. Above them, a patchwork of rusting beams and sheets of loose metal loomed. It looked to be an old section to the greater building that had fallen away to the weather. It would only give them limited shelter and they would be found too easily if Owen took them that way.

It looked like the only way out of this mess for the time being was into the rickety old station itself. He knew to their right, over a chicken wire fence that encircled the property, was the Swan River. This was the body of water on which the city had been built. Fortunately up this end, it was mainly used for recreational purposes and this late on a Sunday night, it wasn't likely to be populated. The other way was a steep incline that led up to a big, new construction site. They were planning on building even more residential flats around this asbestos infested, run down old heap. Typical government mentality. But it was open ground – no cover. So toward the building they ran. Kirrily had obviously reasoned the same things.

Light flared onto the situation nearly causing Owen to misjudge his footing. Quickly compensating he glanced over his shoulder. Two bright headlights had crested the rise from which the truck had rolled. They weren't going to give up, it seemed.

There were already several people standing by, weapons in hand, their silhouettes looking like foreboding giant toy soldiers with big rifles in hand. It was only a matter of seconds before the beams came flaring at them once more.

Sure enough, the ground beside Owen's foot ruptured under the force of a crimson bolt. Shards of rock and dirt spun free, but Owen managed to keep upright and pushed on. Against the already dark outline of the station, Owen could make out a large chunk of wall that had fallen in. A makeshift entrance if he'd ever seen one, but he was still a number of metres away and with the light on their backs they were sitting ducks. Several more bolts flashed past him, striking the already crooked and cracked ground sending further rubble into the air, one or two narrowly missing himself and Kirrily.

Swinging his arm around, he let out a tongue of lightening from his fist, angling toward the vehicle. In seconds of it making contact, the headlights surged and exploded casting them into darkness once more apart from the odd red beam illuminating the night. They'd be harder to hit now.

Owen was only a number of steps from the building. He had a clear image of it in his mind. It was a number of decades old, well weather beaten and worn from the many years of abandonment. It looked as though many different entrepreneurs had tried to bring it back from the brink as its design was a mixture of styles. Concrete made up the majority of the building, much of it having collapsed or been eaten through by rain and rust. The sturdiest part of the building was red brick that made up a considerable portion of the north side. The rest was a maze and mass of iron and steel sheets that had been bent, broken and torn in many places but still offered suitable shelter. Of course there was plenty of asbestos there too, possibly attributing to its latest closure over twenty years ago. With all the holes and damage to it, the station would have been useless as a hideout during the day, but at night, the shadows could prove impenetrable. The only thing Owen wasn't sure of was the condition of the inside – whether it was multi-levelled or if the inner levels had all collapsed in on themselves. There was nothing he could do about it now, however, and he would be finding out in a matter of seconds.

He watched as Kirrily swung her arm out and grabbed hold of the broken wall, allowing it to act as a grounding as she swung herself around behind it as cover. She was amazing.

Owen felt the shot before he even saw or heard it. The bolt tore at his upper right arm, shredding and singeing the pink sleeve and digging into his flesh. All sensations fell on him at once, the pain flared through his arm as he watched the bolt flash past. He heard it finally as if as an after thought, a metallic zing through the air followed by a crisp odour of ozone, scorched wool and seared flesh and hair. It reeked, but it hurt even more.

No time to worry about it now. He dove for cover into the darkness of the building and for an instant listened as the shots surged and then stopped altogether. They could tell the two of them were inside. He only hoped they didn't have any huge artillery to blow the place up.

"Over here."

Kirrily had moved into the darkness, not stopping for cover behind the wall. Owen had a vague notion where she was and pushed himself to his feet.

From what he could tell, the insides were worse off than the outside. He stepped carefully over broken beams and rubble where the upper levels had given way but it was anybody's guess as to how to get outside again.

He felt an arm touch him on his shoulder, "Here."

"We have to keep moving."

"Duh. Keep quiet, hold onto me and do exactly what I tell you."

No argument from me, he thought to himself. He went to grab her with his right arm, but hissed in pain as fabric scraped wound. He opted for his other hand instead.

The people outside hadn't given up yet. He could hear their footsteps, crunching through the concrete. The problem was, although Kirrily was barely making a noise as she moved, he sounded like an elephant stumbling through thick shrubbery. Broken bits of wood and metal grinded under foot as he did his best to tip-toe through the wreckage.

CHAPTER THIRTEEN

KIRRILY

Her glasses were helping somewhat. Every so often they would fritz out and Kirrily was just as blind in the dark as Owen was. They had been damaged in the earlier skirmish; the subsequent crash hadn't been any more merciful. She pushed past a hanging beam, somehow connected to the level above by rope or cabling of some kind. Holding it back, she led Owen past.

He was hurt. She could see him well enough to know he was favouring his arm, and even in the stench of mould and rust, she could smell the sickening smell of scorched flesh and hair. It was not a nice combination.

The problem they had now were the torches. If they didn't get further into the building, they would be sitting ducks. The ceiling where they were was low and there were only a few thin support beams around providing little to no cover. Further inside, she could make out the ruins of what looked to be old and wasted machinery, not to mention several sets of stairs to take them up if needs be.

She took hold of Owen's hand and pulled him faster. It didn't matter that he was making noise at present, once they were behind cover, they would be a lot safer, they may even be able to find a nook to rest in, or another way out.

This was not the way she had expected this to play out. Sunday night, normally she's working on some new device or other. She still had an updated version of her wrist computer to complete. After tonight, she'd have a whole lot more work to do. Repairs on the truck for one. She was quite pissed off about that. Sure, it would be fixable, but it wouldn't be the same. Not original.

Then again, she'd be able to make some adjustments, fix up a few of the systems, and perhaps add a few more defensive articles, though it had done pretty well for its first field test. She had built many things made for assault or defensive purposes, but never fully run tests like these. That was an obvious failing in her work and if nothing else, she knew now that she had to think more practically.

She hefted the rifle in her right arm and pushed onward. It wasn't far now, but then again, neither were the people hunting them. She didn't even know how many there were but that would most likely be answered soon enough.

Light had already started dancing into the darkness, dust particles glittering in the bright white like tiny snowflakes. The additional light helped only slightly with the night vision glasses. From the angle of the beam and it's width, Kirrily could tell they were almost at the entrance.

Supporting him as he moved, she pushed Owen onward, "Go, I'll catch up with you."

"But-"

She knew what he was going to say, but she wouldn't take long. He cut himself off. There was no point arguing, besides, it would give their location away. Stepping uncertainly, he moved on. Kirrily, on the other hand, stopped and turned. Bracing the rifle against her own shoulder, she aimed at the doorway. Gently squeezing the trigger, several automatic rounds launched from the smaller barrel and sprayed the wall and the ground near the makeshift entrance. There was no silencer on the weapon, so its rumble rang through the old building and echoed as if she were standing in the middle of the grand canyon with stereo playback.

The torchlight flashed about for a moment as the owners were startled. That would at least give them second thoughts about entering. Turning back, she took a couple of steps to catch up with Owen.

Then she found out they were willing to play her at her own game.

There was a loud popping sound, as if someone had opened a can of Pringles chips. Looking back, she had no idea what was coming.

There was a dull thud followed closely by a chink of metal on metal before her glasses erupted in a flash of green light.

She couldn't help but yelp in pain as the flare sent her eyesight on a spin before the glasses went completely black. But the space around them was still burning bright. And burning it was.

It was Owen this time that took control. A loud boom erupted as a second flash of light was discharged, this one however, was not simply a harmless ball of light. Flames mushroomed out of the grenade, consuming the old dry wood around it as it swelled upward and out.

Launching his body forward, he dragged Kirrily with him. Once more, she felt herself being pulled to the ground and found him lying on top of her for protection. She had to admit it was very chivalrous, but she could take care of herself. Besides, he knew more of the situation than she did so it would be best it he came out of it relatively alive.

Over the roar of the explosion, she swore she could hear someone screaming. But they weren't inside the building, otherwise it would be echoing like nobodies business.

Perhaps one of the people outside got a taste of their own medicine.

The flames fell short of their location by a few feet, allowing the two to make the most of their cover and the additional illumination. Pushing themselves up, they ran for the machinery.

Behind them, the floor boards of the level above had burst into flames as had several of the surrounding support beams. Not a good thing. This place was already a fire trap, any more explosions like that would either bring the building down or start a blaze that would be difficult to control even with the entire fire service present.

As the echoes of the explosion levelled out, Kirrily heard the scream getting louder, almost like a siren. She would have thought it was quite comical, if it had been a moment she could laugh in. She shrugged it off.

Perhaps it was a siren. Someone would have found the wreckage on the freeway by now.

Regardless of that, they had to find cover and quickly. With the added light of the fire, it would be easy for their hunters to find them in the relative open they were in.

Owen had powered up; his transformation was instantaneous and still surprised her. It also sent a strange tingle through the air that she felt in her teeth, similar to that she experienced when she ran her nails down a black board or scraped at cement flooring.

Facing toward the entrance, she fired further short bursts, preventing their entry for a little while longer. She swivelled the weapon from side to side, allowing a slight spray as she stepped backward and behind a large furnace casing.

Further dust and concrete erupted into the air, adding further cover as it formed a cloud in front of the doorway.

"I can't see anyway out of here."

She hushed him, "You haven't been looking hard enough, obviously."

Easing carefully forward, she peered around the side of the furnace. The entrance was being sprayed with laser bolts. Whoever these guys were, they sure had funding. Not to mention technological know how. She'd been trying for years to come up with a working laser pistol but the closest she came was the equivalent of a four kilogram cigarette lighter. It still needed a lot of work.

The scream ceased for a moment, ending on a sharp "T" sound.

"What is that?"

"I have no idea, but it's getting closer, fast," Owen replied.

No sooner than he finished speaking than they were answered.

Accompanied by an enormous crash, the roof shattered inward on the north side of the building. Moonlight burst through what was now a considerable sized sky-light, not to mention a second more powerful beam of light. A spot-light of some sort that wobbled momentarily before swooping off and away.

"Helicopter."

"Doing what? Bomb?"

Kirrily wasn't sure until she heard the scream again. This time it echoed loudly through the station. In the new light she could see something scrambling though the debris as it fell from the roof, trying to get a hand hold on something to prevent it's fall, legs flailing wildly.

She watched in horror as who-ever it was crashed into the first of several levels of flooring between the ceiling and the concrete ground. The wooden slats erupted with splinters and dust as the person continued to fall, their decent unhindered by the obstructions. One after the other, they sped through the levels before landing, hard, on the concrete. More dust filled the air as fragments of the ceiling and the subsequent damage showered down on the body, now out of sight.

"Oh my god."

Owen had seen it too, having stuck his head around the side of the furnace to see what was going on.

"There is no way anyone could have survived that."

He shook his head, "No one deserves that, whether its them or us."

Sure enough the shooting had stopped as had the grenades as everyone seemed unsure what exactly had happened or how.

Apart from the odd tinkle of broken glass or clunk of settling wood, there was not a sound or movement.

Then somewhere out of the rubble came a voice, "Woah. That was not nice."

A second voice, female responded to the first masculine one, "Got to keep moving."

Somewhere behind the smoke and the fire, Kirrily could see something move. Wood scraped against cement and clattered to the floor as whoever it was tried to stand up.

To Kirrily's amazement whoever it was managed it, heaving the debris off their body. She could see it's skin reflected much of the bright moonlight that streamed down the newly created air shaft from the ceiling, almost as if they were wearing some form of body armour.

It wasn't until the second person got up was she surprised. There had only been one person falling, as far as she could tell. Where did this second individual come from?

Kirrily was about to call out, to see if they were okay, but she was stopped by a white spotlight that ignited through the upper northern windows. She hadn't noticed before, but along the upper levels were a series of square holes, similar to Morse code. Dot - dash - dot all the way around, but the wall to the north had an intricately inartistic design in which windows were spotted all over the place. Granted, some of them may have simply been holes knocked through the cement work, but the rest were definitely windows. On the south wall, however, it was like a church. Three vertical rows of windows peering out into the night sky, through which the separate silo was barely visible through the dust encrusted glass.

The smoke that was quickly filling the upper reaches of the building refracted the glow from the beam.

Outside, although not making any sound, Kirrily could make out the vague outline of a helicopter. She had had enough of those as well, but there was something different about this one. It was nothing like the other two they had come across back at the Remnant's building.

Well, whatever they wanted to throw at her, she had more than enough fire power in her hands to give as good as she gets, not that she was entirely sure she could withstand a missile being launched at her.

"It's back," Owen said.

"Who's that? Who's there?"

The female was asking.

And the laser beams came again.

All hell seemed to break lose at that moment. The light from above completely destroyed any chance of hiding, the beams of red laser continued to slice through support beams and wall as the army outside continued their assault and these two people who had literally fallen from the heavens ducked for whatever cover was available amongst the rubble and the smoke.

Kirrily pulled back behind the furnace, "I don't think these two are with your friends outside."

"I'd have to agree."

She removed her glasses, useless as they were now, and put them in her jacket. Looking back in the direction they were heading.

From the glow Owen was radiating, she could see that old oil pools littered the floor as well as covered various broken lengths of wiring, tubing and plating. There was little chance any of the machinery in here would work without extensive overhauling, but already in her mind, Kirrily could see exactly how to do it. Calculations regarding the schematics and specifications of new and additional parts flooded her mind as she saw the designs literally building themselves in her imagination. She knew they would work, regardless of whether she decided to try it or not. It was how her mind had always worked. Every little invention from the juicer/toaster she had built as a child to the truck had been based on looking at something small and mechanical and letting her mind's eye do the rest. She had an affinity with machines that she couldn't explain. When it came to the electrical aspect, it just seemed to fit right in there along side the rest. From there, all she had to do was surrender her body to her designs and away she'd go. One morning she had found she had developed an entirely new engine for her moped she was driving at sixteen. It had taken her all night and had fallen asleep just after completing it. And all she had planned for that evening was to tweak the original engine slightly.

One thing she was worried about at the moment, however, was whether or not Owen's little sparks would set fire to the oil, though it was old. Then again, with part of the building already on fire, and rapidly spreading, she wouldn't have to worry about that too much. But it also meant the machinery was not the safest place to hide, especially with him glowing like a light bulb.

He pulled her closer to him, pushing the rifle in her hand aside, "You go up. Be careful, it's obviously not too steady. If we split up, we'll have a better chance for the time being."

"But what-"

"I'll check on these two and keep the others distracted," He pointed just past the end of a small access way adjacent to where they were standing. She could just make out a rickety set of iron steps, "Take those. You'll be covered by the wall."

He was right. It was around the corner from the entrance they had used. The building was virtually a giant capital T shape and they had made it around into the long stem, at the end of which stood the mini silo she had seen earlier.

She nodded and moved to the access way. It was a few steps down from the rest of the floor, allowing better access to the base of the old machines. In her mind's eye, she could imagine the ghosts of old workers doing their daily chores, walking with clipboard and spanner in hand making sure the station was in working order. The initial jump down was easy, though she needed to get down low in order to avoid scraping her back against further machinery. Once down she was able to walk normally, her waist now level with Owen's feet.

There was another explosion and she swore she was getting tired of it. There was no creativity in a grenade for one thing. Throw it and it goes boom. No skill. She preferred targeting weapons, things that required a reasonable understanding of how the weapon worked, rather than pull the pin and throw.

Admittedly she had included the launcher on the rifle, but that was only if worse came to worse. For the time being, it was all up to skill.

Her foot kicked against the step at the opposite end. Sliding her arm through a shoulder strap on the weapon, she levered herself up two steps at a time, using her arms as lifts, being careful not to hit her head on the makeshift ceiling of metal. Although she wouldn't be surprised if it crumbled under the slightest contact.

Emerging on the other side, she could see that the fire was now running rampant through the old wood on the north west side of the building. Through the flames and the smoke, she could see and hear the supports cracking and giving way under the heat. And then things managed to get even worse.

On the other side of the access way Owen had been spraying the entrance with electric current, hoping to ward off the attackers from making any fast entries. The helicopter was searching through the factory, hoping to get a lock on it's target. Right now, however, Owen wasn't sure exactly who that would be. It was only a matter of time before they decided to join the fray. It was time to make a move for the two strangers that had most inopportunely landed right in the middle of a miniature war zone. He half expected a bomb to be dropped just as he made a dash for a secondary furnace only a few metres away.

Sure enough, the windows on the north side of the building ruptured, showering the lower levels with glass, wood and cement.

How the hell could anyone tell what they were firing at through the smoke let alone the stagnant remains of the building that was swiftly being destroyed around them?

The people outside opened fire in return, most likely unsure of what they were actually firing at, making for a dangerous crossfire in the middle.

Avoiding a spray of bullets, Owen ducked for cover behind and underneath a stack of piping.

He knew Kirrily was out of sight for now. But these new comers were definitely not out of trouble, yet. Then again, they had just survived a fall of at least fifty metres. They deserved some credit.

The glass on the opposite end of the building shattered as the spray went wild. Ricochets danced of machinery nearby, making the obligatory "Piaoooow" noise, encouraging Owen to duck down even further.

CHAPTER FOURTEEN

THEN

Hiding behind Neil's robes, Owen managed to catch a glimpse at what was coming at them. It wasn't human. Well at least, not all of it.

It moved on legs, metal legs that had pumps all along them like a bicycle pump. They were long and thin and made slight whirring noises when they moved. The boy recalled his father talking about hydraulics on the farm and knew that this was like no farm machine he'd ever seen. A man seemed to be sitting in the body of what looked to be a spider. His legs disappeared into a ball of shiny metal. It almost looked like a mirror, but it was steaming as it moved, frosting up with wisps of heated air.

The drill he had heard was on the end of the man's left hand.

No. The man didn't have a hand. The drill was there instead, large menacing and pointy. It spun faster and faster as he angled it toward Neil, driving him further away. It was a cone like weapon that spun on the end of a ball that would have been a fist. The other hand was there, but it carried a weapon bigger than any Owen had ever seen on television, besides on tanks. It had eight different barrels at once and the trigger was a button pressed by the thumb, which was hovering closely above it.

What was even grosser was the man's face and body. Although much of the man's chest and arms were covered in dark clothing, Owen could imagine what it looked like. The face was half skin, half metal mask. But it sat so close to his face that it looked like it was actually part of it. His left eye was completely hidden by a large round tube that shone a deep blue. And although he couldn't see his eye behind it, Owen had the awkward feeling it could see him, even as he hid behind Neil's cloak.

He was thankful when the man that looked like Death pushed him back and behind his cloak again. He didn't like the look of this man. Neil kept moving backward. They would soon find themselves back in the elevator lobby, which was not a comforting thought. Where would they go then? Back down to the basement? Back down the other way, and what was hiding there to get them?

"You will be free to leave. Simply step away from the boy."

Through the dark fabric of Neil's sleeve, Owen saw a faint light. It was a pale green in colour, muffled by the thick material. If his hand had been in sight, Owen was sure that it would be burning like a fire.

Before the metal man could speak again, Neil's hand shot upward, pointing in front of him. The light grew, spreading through the air like oil through water forming a sizzling green wall across the hallway.

"Interesting," the voice sounded impressed, "But ultimately pointless."

Neil finally spoke, "You talk to much."

Peering underneath Neil's arm, Owen watched as the green wall began to move once more. It was still joined to Neil's arm via a thick green beam, but it began to waver before it snapped itself into a ball, encircling the man-robot.

"Move," Neil hissed at Owen, pushing him back the way they came, "I'll follow."

Owen began to do so, edging backward, but much like in the cartoons, this evil robot began to laugh. A deep throaty laugh that echoed down the hall. It sent a shiver down the boy's neck and he almost stumbled over his shoes.

The gun spun to life. The barrels vibrated and rotated around one another as the trigger was pressed. It howled out the bullets, tearing into the shield, sending sparks sprouting from it as they made contact. Owen wasn't sure if Neil could feel the bullets, but the man shook with every burst, as if struggling to maintain control. He took a step back, toward the boy.

"Keep moving, Owen."

Owen took a couple more steps backward watching as the bad man continued to laugh and fire at the same time. On the ground, the casings and the dented bullets were piling up, but the attack didn't seem to be drawing to a close.

The shield began to waver as the drill came into play. Ramming it into the green enclosure, robot-man fought to free himself.

Holes seemed to be appearing around the shield, flashing in an out of existence as Neil strained to maintain the prison. But the attack from within was too brutal. Neil looked back over his shoulder. He was looking a little sick, sweat covered his face, and his pale skin flushed red.

"Go!"

Owen backed into something and yelped in fear. It was bad enough in that dungeon, but up here, in a clean hospital where it should have been safe, where he was possibly so close to getting out, he wanted to scream again.

His body tingled with energy and he spun on his toes, sending a small charge out to his attacker. A small portion of the wall erupted in a cloud of dust, but Owen didn't care. He turned away from Neil and the scary robot-man and ran back down toward the foyer.

Instead of choosing the other way or heading back down the lifts, he opted for the smaller corridor.

Behind him he heard a pop of air, like a balloon, and the bullets continued for a couple more seconds before both their rattle and the man's laugh ceased altogether.

Neil was gone. He had to be. Owen was alone again and he was determined he was going to find his way out.

The corridor was thin, enough for one adult to walk comfortably down, more than enough for a child to sprint down. It reached another t-junction that split to the right or left.

Left was the way Neil said was out. Left it was. His shoes skidded slightly over the linoleum as he changed direction. Behind him, he could hear the ticking of the man's spider legs. He wasn't far behind.

The lights dimmed slightly as an alarm began to sound. It was an alternating ring of a bell, two different tones almost like a police siren.

Owen's sneakers were squeaking across the floor, his breath was rattling through the air as his chest felt like his heart was going to break through. There were very few options in the way of directions down this corridor. It seemed to be a service way of sorts, for here and there were thin black tyre marks from trolleys. The few doors that did line the walls were all marked storage of one sort or another. This was like a secret tunnel the public didn't know about. Off limits. Authorised personnel only as Owen recalled signs reading. His friends wouldn't believe where he was, nor what was going on.

The corridor cut around to the right and Owen had no choice but to follow it.

As he rounded it, the wall beside him snapped concrete and paint at him as bullets rattled along it, taking a part of the corner with it. The man was too close behind.

He had to get out of this tunnel, give him the slip.

Yanking on a door handle, he pushed it open and continued to run down to the next door. Once more he pushed the door open, but this time ran after it, hauling his small frame around its edge and gently eased it back to its closed position, making as little noise as he could.

Seconds later, the hall outside boomed with gunfire. Owen knew the man was close. But he was trapped in this room.

It was dark in here, but the light seeped under the doorway, giving a little visibility.

It was a cupboard, about two metres square. Shelves lined the walls, but there was a small standing room, where Owen was now.

But what caught Owen's eye was a small grating underneath the bottom shelf in the back corner of the cupboard. It was very small, but he might just be able to fit.

Outside in the hall, there was a second burst of fire resulting in a loud cracking and banging. Perhaps he had blown up the first cupboard, which didn't give Owen much time.

He pulled on the grate, expecting some resistance, only to find it swung upward with ease, revealing a more than adequate mode of escape.

Something scraped along the floor just outside the cupboard as he dove head first into the thin metal tunnel. Even for him it was a tight fit, but the smooth surface and his clothing working with his momentum and pushed him a few feet into the ventilation shaft. As the grate slammed shut behind him, he heard the door rupture under the assault of bullets, the grating fortunately preventing shrapnel from finding him.

Wriggling his body onward, he felt the metal crease and crinkle underneath him, but the din of the gunfire covered the sound of it more than adequately. He only stopped moving when the robot-man stopped firing. He had to stay awfully quiet, hope that he moved on.

There was movement in the cupboard. Wood scraping on lino. The man was searching for him.

He had no choice but to keep moving. Looking up ahead was a cross-junction. He could see it went straight ahead or to the left or right. It wasn't far. All he needed was a little boost and he'd be there.

Something bumped the grating behind him.

If he opened it, Owen would be seen for sure. Be shot. Or worse, recaptured. He wanted all of this to be over, to be safe at home. He was tired, worn out and trapped. And he was going to die.

Owen felt his body jolt to life, like it had down in his cell; the metal around him sizzled with energy as his skin turned a strangely translucent shade of white.

It was time to move.

He launched himself forward and his feet and hands didn't have to do anything. It was as if the energy that surrounded him acted like billions of tiny fingers, hauling him along the metal at such a rate, he would make the cross-junction, no worries.

Then he heard the gunfire once more and the grate behind him vanished in a cloud of cement and metallic shards. The vent behind him rattled with more bullets as the man aimed his weapon at the boy's feet.

But in moments they were gone as he managed to manoeuvre his small body around the corner to the left and hopefully to a way out.

Back in the cupboard, the man stopped firing and withdrew his arm from the ventilation shaft. He had to have hit him.

His legs arched outward as the spider body lowered itself, allowing him a better chance to see down the rabbit's hole.

As the smoke cleared, all he could see were the pockmarks in the metal sheeting from his last spray of bullets.

No blood, no body. Nothing.

The hydraulics whined as he righted himself, holding back a howl in his throat. He had to find the boy. He was essential. And now he was missing.

OWEN

The two newcomers were huddled by a support beam that had started to smoulder. Flames were spreading quickly upward and starting to envelope more of the wooden levels above. She, who seemed to be covered in some sort of metallic armour, shielded the man from any bullets that may come their way. They were talking to one another over the noise, Owen could make out nothing.

He tried to get their attention by peering carefully out of his hiding hole but they didn't notice him. It was time to try something a bit more noticeable. Reaching out his hand, he let lose an arc of electricity toward the entrance, just a short one, hopefully enough to grab their attention.

It worked. She was eyeing him wide-eyed and warily but something in Owen's mind told him she would not be hostile toward him.

He indicated for them to make a move toward him, take cover with him. As he did so, the pipes he was behind erupted with ricocheting bullets. The woman had not been the only one to spot him. The helicopter's light vanished from view as it moved upward and over the hole in the ceiling. It was now or never.

"Now!" he shouted and through the smoke, he wasn't sure how but the girl vanished from sight.

Owen paused for a moment. If she could do that, why hadn't she done so before?

The man made a move. He moved toward Owen's hiding place, careful to avoid any stray laser beams, favouring his right leg somewhat, probably an injury from the fall. His armour slowed him down a little and when he made it to Owen he kept his distance as he slid in beside him.

It wasn't until he had stopped moving that Owen noticed it wasn't body armour at all. The man's skin was made of some sort of organic metal fibre. Impressive defensive mechanism. But also susceptible to Owen's own powers. He decided to turn his down for the time being, get some information.

"Welcome to Hell. I'll be your guide for this evening," He quipped. The man smiled at him.

"Thanks. I don't know who you are, but we could use a little assist right now," It was the woman again. The guy's skin seemed to shimmer slightly before it began to flow from his body. It rolled to the floor before reshaping into something resembling a person. In a matter of seconds the woman had appeared once more, looking as normal as any person would regardless of having formed herself out of ooze. "Okay. That must come in handy with this crowd chasing you."

"They're not all ours. Who are the guys with the laser pistols?"

"No friends of mine, but I take responsibility all the same."

"We better keep moving," The man spoke briefly and quickly. Almost shyly. Ironic for such a bulky man. Actually, now he was closer, Owen could see he wasn't exactly what he had appeared to be. Much like the woman. He had lost a considerable amount of weight since she had decided to detach. The armour was obviously her, but she must have to maintain a specific body mass. Now, although he had a considerable muscle tone, he was a lot smaller than he had originally looked.

130

"He's right. We need to get out of here. It's only a matter of time before this place burns down, and us with it."

The Helicopter had taken position over head and had started shooting more of the ceiling down.

Owen pointed toward where he and Kirrily had been hiding previously.

"Over there. There's an access way that'll take you to some stairs. If you can get up to the upper levels, you may be able to find my friend. Either way, head to the end of the building. Try your luck in the silo. I'll keep them busy down here."

She nodded, "Thanks," before vanishing once more. The man, once again covered in metal, pushed off from the concrete and half ran, half limped toward where Owen had pointed.

Now he had to think of how he was going to do what he had just proposed. Distract a horde of laser toting bad guys and a helicopter. He just hoped Kirrily was all right.

KIRRILY

The stairs were in a terrible condition. The railing on one side, although connected further up, had broken away from the stairs. Rust had also made its presence known on every step, making the safety of the journey upward questionable. Then again, the helicopter had joined the battle with its machine gun and staying put would be suicide.

How did she get involved in all of this? If only she hadn't been so inquisitive. She'd never curse her father or the gift she inherited from him, but she was very close to it.

It was a Sunday for goodness sake! People were meant to be relaxing in front of the television, not running for their lives. She tested the lower step with her foot. It creaked a little and seemed to move slightly but it was capable of holding her.

Taking hold of the rail that was still attached, she began her careful, but pacey climb up the rickety stairs.

Like a fire escape, the steps folded back on each other as they reach the next level, it wasn't long before she had made it to the first step on the second floor.

It seemed water had made itself known here, having reacted with the oxygen and the metal steps. Rust completely coated the next flight.

"Things don't get any easier, do they?"

It was at that moment, through the din of machinegun fire and falling debris, she heard someone below her. Owen? She couldn't tell. Trying to get a glimpse of whoever it was over the side of the steps was pointless, but whoever it was moved slowly and deliberately.

"Damn it," she whispered to herself as she set herself to keep climbing.

The first three steps held her, although somewhat precariously. When she put her foot down on the fourth step, it held tight. It wasn't until she pushed off for the next step that the rusty joints gave way and the ground vanished from beneath her.

Her hands slipped and slid over the railings and felt the metal scratch at her hands as she scrambled for a hand hold. It wasn't until her backside was almost sitting on the Fifth step which groaned threatening under her wait that her left leg managed to floor itself there and halt her fall.

The remains of what was the fourth step clanged loudly on the floor below, prompting the light from the helicopter to flash in her direction.

"Damn it!" She hissed at her clumsiness. Whoever was below her stopped momentarily. She didn't have time for that herself.

Hauling herself up with a combination of pulling with her arms and pushing with her left leg, she managed to get back upright. Her right leg had been scratched as she fell, but not badly enough to warrant her favouring it. A Tetanus booster would definitely be necessary.

She pushed onward, using the railing as much for carrying her weight as she did the steps, hoping to even out the load. Not that there was much of a load to worry about, she thought to herself.

The fire was getting a firm hold on the wooden floorboards on the upper levels, she noticed. There was nowhere to hide for the glow was too bright.

Making it to the third floor, Kirrily found there were rooms, perhaps offices and locker rooms located here and there on the upper levels. Good hiding spots, but death traps when the fire got closer. The only option was to keep climbing. Looking toward the long end of the building, she could see down to where she had come from.

The machinery from the old station seemed to glow like a rainbow. Each and every piece of equipment was spewing forth designs at her, ways to be fixed, to be manipulated to be more effective, even to be altered to become something much different than was originally intended. Even from this distance, she could make out details and blue prints, that was until she saw Owen's signature glow racing between the machinery.

Approaching, but not daring to lean on the railing, she could see more than hear the laser shots as they flashed from one end of the building to the other. Their pursuers had made it into the building, the helicopter, whoever or whatever its purpose was, continued to send volleys and bursts of bullets into the building, striking nothing in particular, but surely making Owen's progress a lot more difficult.

OWEN

The roof was collapsing. Owen wasn't quite sure how much longer before the building followed suit. Much of the lower level was consumed by fire, making the upper levels less stable, having no lower support. The upper levels were already shot to buggery as far as Owen could tell and everything was either exploding, groaning or creaking.

He was beginning to question the intelligence of sending them upstairs.

At least his glow would more than distract the attackers. That was the main idea. The problem being Owen had been unable to cover the entrance for long with the helicopter shooting down huge chunks of ceiling over him. The men on foot had scrambled through the hole in the wall and taken various positions in front of the fire. That made it harder for them to hide, but with the onslaught from their laser pistols, that made little difference to Owen. He had lost ground to these guys.

Now he was hidden behind what seemed to be a conveyer belt of some kind, he had powered down, hoping he could hide a little better, get some rest. His arm still stung from the earlier hit, the smell almost unbearable, especially knowing it was his own flesh that was burning.

A laser beam cut closely by his head and he ducked down further. He couldn't tell where Kirrily or the other two had gotten to, but he hoped they would find a way out soon. There was no telling how much longer he could hold these guys.

His estimation was cut even further when he heard the sound of glass shattering from the opposite side of the building. Footsteps soon followed as people charged the building from that side. It wouldn't be long before he was surrounded.

A burst of machine gun fire cracked the floor a few metres away from him, he dove to one side to avoid several ricochets off both concrete and metal. This was becoming a death-trap, reminiscent of one he had been in before.

Pushing up onto his feet, he kept low and moved further down the length of the T. Hopefully there wouldn't be any surprises waiting for him there. He found, not for the first time this evening, that he wished he'd worn something a little more practical and a lot less garish. Sure, he hadn't expected World War 3 to land on his doorstep, but a Pink suit stands out at the best of times.

To his left, Owen heard a metallic clunk. Without even looking, he launched himself forward as the air behind him sizzled under the impact of a laser beam. He pushed headlong into a tangle of old wires and insulated cables, connecting with the back of a cupboard of some sort.

"Perfect, a dead end," he thought to himself. He wasn't going to be able to stay here long and he knew he had to make it out of the building ASAP.

People called out, obviously alerting each other to his presence.

He wouldn't have much time before they had him completely surrounded.

Turning awkwardly around amidst the tangled cables, he searched for a means of escape. The cupboard was barely a metre deep and most of that was taken up by the rubber-coated twists of old metal. Much of that rubber had rotted or wasted away. There were no exits, bar the one he had come through. He was well and truly trapped.

THEN

Owen found the burst of energy ebbed away. He was too exhausted to keep going much further. His legs ached from all the running and walking he had already done and every other muscled seemed so worn and tired. It would have been nice if he could just curl up in this vent and sleep. But with the robot-man out there, he couldn't do that. He had to find a way out.

The notion of "left" was imprinted on his brain. It was the way Neil had gone and it was the way he had to go to get out of here. But he was a lot further from the exit now than he wanted to be. He knew that from the way he had come. Heading into the vent had taken him in the opposite direction from where he should be heading, but the turn to the left might lead him all the way back again.

There was a cool breeze blowing up from behind him, whistling slightly as it forced its way past him.

Maybe he was heading in the right way then. It would be easier going with the wind than against it, he thought. Like when he used to run on the farm. Sometimes it blew so hard he couldn't breath as he ran into it. But when he was pushed along by it, he moved faster and easily along the paddocks.

So with it he went.

Straining against the pain in his arms and legs, he wiggled onward into the darkness. With the loss of his energy, he had lost all light as well. Before hand, the vent had given off a faint glow. Now it was pitch black. That would have scared him earlier, but now he knew there was a way out there somewhere and when he saw the light, that would be it.

The vent creaked slightly with every move, but he wiggled forward. He made it a few more metres before he felt he had come to another junction. Heading left would take him back to that hallway, he knew that. Back to the robot man. The right would take him further from where he had to go, so he kept moving.

Minutes passed as he struggled onward. Hand over hand, he clutched at smooth metal, pushing with his feet, barely able to bend his legs enough to give him a real push. Then, unexpectedly, his next grasp for metal met with thin air. The ventilation shaft disappeared.

Another junction? The end of the road? Maybe even the way out.

He stopped momentarily thinking about what to do. Keep moving onward, go back? That was all he could really do.

Edging his body carefully forward, Owen tried to keep his weight back on his lower body as he groped for whatever was in front of him. Most of his upper body was over the hole by the time he discovered he was still inside the vent and just in another junction, this one had a vertical connection running both up and down.

His hands grabbed onto the metal corner on the other side. Without the ability to really push off with his legs, he knew he would have a hard time pulling himself over the gap, especially the way his arms were crying out for rest. He felt tears come again as the thought of further physical exertion came to bear on him. He had always hated doing the hard chores on the farm and he hated this even more. Tears had helped him when he was younger, his Dad giving into his wishes to run off and play. There was no one here now to feel sorry for him and tell him he didn't have to do it.

He bit his lip and readied himself for the effort.

It was hard to get a proper grip on the sheer surface, but he tried digging his nails in all the same. He pulled and pushed simultaneously, hoping the sheer effort would launch him across.

No such luck.

Keeping his weight on his legs and arms as his body crossed the gap, he managed to lower himself on the other side, the cool metal almost refreshing after the strain.

But when he pushed off with his toes from the other side, his hands slipped on the metal and his muscles gave way. Both legs crashed down into the hole, kicking the vertical ventilation shaft and jolting his body backward.

With what little energy reserves he had left, he clawed at the metal to find a hand hold, to no avail.

The rest of his body slipped down over the side and he narrowly avoided jarring his chin on the edge.

He wanted to scream for help, but all that escaped was a yelp of pain before his fingers snagged the sharp edge once more and brought his descent to a halt.

Tears threatened to come now. He bit his lip even harder, desperate not to give in to either the fear or the pain. His knuckles turned white as his thumbs slipped, leaving him dangling by his eight digits.

One by one they lost grip and he cried out in petition as his body began to fall once more down the vent, back down toward the hole he had woken up in that morning. It seemed like days ago.

CHAPTER FIFTEEN

OWEN

Owen was blown back against the cables and the back of the cupboard as the machinery opposite him exploded in a ball of fire. The explosion looked a lot like Kirrily's earlier blasts at the door. She was obviously still looking out for him.

He smiled in gratitude, even though he knew she couldn't see him. His smile was repaid by a second blast. This one was different.

The left over oil in some of the machinery must have reacted to the flames. Owen couldn't tell where the second explosion was, whether it was a chain reaction from Kirrily's assist or from the fire that was encroaching on the rest of the building. Perhaps the Helicopter had more fire power than they had anticipated.

Men screamed and yelled from around the building as chunks of brick and plaster collapsed from above, shaken loose by the blasts.

The helicopter ceased fire as Owen poked his head through the cables to see flames consume the entire north side of the building in a mushroom of amber and orange. Perhaps there had been some old flammable liquids down that end that had finally given up the ghost. He couldn't worry about that now, Kirrily had given him a distraction, as had whatever else had gone off and he had to make use of it.

He felt energy course through his body as his pink suit was once more replaced by black coat and trousers. He needed a burst of speed and he used it to launch himself away from the cables and down the opposite direction from whoever had fired at him moments before.

They must have been distracted as there was no follow up fire.

It was time to get out of the building before there was nothing left of it to escape from.

Heading further down the building, he kept an eye out for an exit of some sort. It was only seconds before he spotted a small room toward the end of the building. Before that was a set of stairs that lead up to an exit onto the roof just above that room. That looked to be the safest and quickest way out at the moment. It was just the problem of getting there as it was located on the other side of the building, near where the second assault of laser pistol totting weirdoes had burst in.

It was a chance at least and if he could keep moving, he'd be a hard target.

One thing he had to admit, being on the defensive all the time was becoming a real pain in the arse.

"Legs, don't fail me now," he joked quietly to himself as he launched himself toward the stairs. It took a short while before he was spotted again and the few men who had recovered from the blasts were even able to try and take aim. Beams of red licked at his heels and flashed in front of him as he bolted to the exit.

When his hand closed around the railing of the stairs, he used it as a lever to swing himself around and up. He was going so fast he nearly passed the door, but he managed to grab the handle and turn.

Locked.

"You've gotta be kidding me!" Who would lock the door when you've got so many holes in the building? He asked himself. It didn't matter now. He had to get out before they could take aim once more.

He sent a bolt of electricity through the handle, superheating and melting the lock. He shouldered the door and it gave way under the force of the blow. The hinges broke free of the jam and Owen nearly tripped over the door itself as it travelled with him unexpectedly. Instead, he stepped onto the door and ran up it as it collapsed onto the roof. The platform he had just come from strobed with enemy fire, some managing to shoot through the door and onto the very small balcony on which he now found himself.

The door connected with the balustrade of the balcony and bounced back up before sliding down to the roof. Owen launched into the air before the makeshift platform made its final descent and found himself careening over the side of the building.

"Oh SH...!" He yelled as he fell back toward the gravel beneath him.

On the bright side of things, he was out of the building. He readied himself to roll with the landing which he managed to do so, sending a cloud of brown dust into the air. Tumbling up onto his feet, Owen continued to run away from the building, down a steep grassed embankment toward the foreshore of the river. He could see in the light of the fire that the banks had a number of shrubs and trees which offered a degree of cover. He could only hope they would at least keep following him, forgetting about the other three and that they could make it out safely before the building gave way.

Shouldering her rifle once more she charged up the stairs. If she hung around too long, they'd discover where she was and that would defeat the whole purpose of Owen staying behind. It seemed the Helicopter crew weren't fortunate enough to have either Infra-red or night vision goggles to aid their aim, or perhaps the heat from the fire was distorting their view, but they couldn't located either Owen, the newcomer or herself.

As she stepped onto the next flight, the stairs beneath her shook with the force of a second explosion from god knows where. She collapsed face first onto the metal steps, cracking her cheek against the grated metal. Her head rung with the impact and the world spun momentarily before a wave of heat washed over her.

Regaining her bearings, she saw the floorboards toward the north end of the building of the floor she was on and the one she was heading to were engulfed in flame which was spreading fast.

The railing, which she grabbed onto to try and help her up, had buckled and detached from the stairs, much as the earlier flights had done. Carefully pulling herself up once more, feeling the blood trickling from the cut on her cheek, the world seemed to sway slightly from her dizziness. It wasn't until she looked down for the next step that she realised the whole staircase was moving and not just her sense of balance.

Whoever was coming up after her, whether they were good or bad, had better watch their step or the whole thing would collapse, she thought to herself.

Stepping onto the next floor, or what was left of it as much had been eaten by weathering, rust and now fire, Kirrily noticed there was a small service-way that ran around the walls toward the other end of the building. From what she could tell, it had been used in the past to service the conveyer belt to and from the silo. That implied she would be able to get from here to there along the same belt, as long as it was strong enough to support her.

She had no other options as the fire was spreading quickly and she needed to get out of the condemned building. It had been in no good state before and in the last ten or twenty minutes its degradation had increased exponentially a thousand-fold.

The service-way was made of steel, hopefully making it safer than the rest of the flooring. Her only concern was that she would be completely in the open for about thirty metres or so.

The boards beneath her feet creaked eerily, helping her decide. Forgetting decorum and discretion, she ran straight along the wall, despite the rattle she made she remained unnoticed.

It wasn't until she reached the south wall and headed toward the large cylindrical conveyer dump that she was spotted.

Their attack was futile. Although they had the technology to make laser pistols that packed quite a punch, their range was still limited. Most of the shooters were located toward the other end of the building. Add several floors between them and the beams became little more than flashing lights dispersing into the darkness.

She had already seen ways they could improve the designs to help with that flaw from when she had seen the weapons earlier, but she wasn't about to go spreading trade secrets with the enemy.

The dump itself was as high as the building, sitting dead centre of the south wall and was approximately two metres in diameter. The door to the dump was a square slat of metal latched closed by a small hook and eye mechanism. Primitive to say the least. She unlatched it and pried the door open. Using the shoulder strap, she hung her rifle off her back allowing her to use both hands against the rusted joints.

138

Inside, although dark, she could make out a ladder against the main wall. This lead both further up and right down to the base of the dump, each rung was a half-rectangular bar studded into the brick. It would have been a much safer option than the stairs she had just climbed. At least she would have been unseen.

Putting that thought out of her mind she grabbed onto the nearest rung and stepped onto the ladder. Despite their age, they were firmly secured to the wall.

From here she needed to reach across to the conveyer belt. It was within arms reach and would only require a slight effort to pull her body onto it. The end of the actual belt protruded about half a metre into the dump.

Within seconds she had relocated herself from the ladder onto the belt. It was sturdy under her weight and looked to be in similar condition up the entire length.

On her hands and knees, Kirrily began the crawl up the incline. It wasn't too steep and a set of small rails allowed her easy hand holds and a sense of security as she hurried. She couldn't take too long or they could make their assault from the silo end. It was possible they were already there waiting for her, but she liked the chances they would assume she would climb down the dump, forgetting the conveyer belt was even there as it wasn't even visible from inside the building.

She reached the other end, arriving in another 'room' much like the dump, yet this one had a secondary belt that ran vertically. Along the length of this one were large scoops that were used to lift the coal and dump it onto the belt she had just climbed. From the look of it, this was still in working order. All it would take was a flick of a switch and away it would go. She could tell this simply by looking at it, not that it would come in handy right now, except for alerting these guys to her position.

Instead, she used the scoops as a ladder down. It was a fair climb, but she managed it quickly and as quietly as she could. At the base of the tower, there was no sign of the enemy or no sound of them either.

Of course it was entirely possible they were waiting to ambush her, but she had other plans.

Lifting her arm, she looked at her wrist computer again. With the press of a button, the backlight clicked on, allowing sufficient light for her to see what she was typing. Then it was a case of several simple commands and the display altered, allowing a small but distinct video relay image.

Back at her truck, several tell-tales came to life on the outside of the trailer. Most of these were located on the vehicle's side and thus concealed in the dirt in which it lay.

Then came the hydraulic whine as three mechanical arms, one located at each end of the trailer and one in the centre, extended themselves from the main body, unfolding and elongating, all the while pushing against the earth beneath.

The trailer lurched once as the computer calculated the amount of pressure required to lift the trailer's weight. Compensating sufficiently, the hulking container was pushed up from the dirt and righted to its proper axis.

The minute all its tyres made contact, the suspension thus kicking in as the trailer's weight transferred to its rightful position, more equipment came to life inside.

The driver of the black car and three men left behind as rear guard jolted to attention at the noise. Several other men who had arrived in the back-up vehicles shortly after the crash made their way toward the trailer to investigate.

All they could see was a simple, albeit large trailer gently rocking side to side.

They exchanged curious and cautious looks as they moved in on the vehicle.

Some could swear there was a noise coming from within. One was about to say so when the back doors on the container erupted outward and was followed quickly by a six-wheeled vehicle like none of them had seen before.

Almost like an open-air tank crossed with a quad bike, on its back stood a large triple-barrelled weapon on a thick swivel turret. The contraption landed on the concrete, bouncing several times before grinding to a halt. In shock, the men watched as the turret turned, surveying the area before pointing directly at two of the men standing closely together.

"Move!" The two men leapt for cover as the weapon fired a single shot. A tiny ball of blue light shot out of its upper most barrel. The men narrowly avoided being hit, but the bolt snapped passed them, colliding with the hill behind.

The air reverberated with the impact. A flash of the same blue light, a wash of searing heat and a considerable chunk of earth burst skyward and rock, sand and plant matter was blown scores of metres into the air before gravity managed to grasp them and yank them back earthward. The men were showered with debris as the vehicle began its journey once more.

It seemed to ignore any bumps or cracks in its way as it sped over to the tower in which Kirrily was concealed. The turret continued to survey the area, what it saw instantaneously transmitted to its controller who was currently trying to prise open the door to the silo. This one was lower, against the ground and swung upward like a flap of sheet metal. Although the joints were loose, there had been a considerable build up of dirt on the outside. Once more using her complete body weight, Kirrily forced the door open in time to see her pride and joy round the corner. Wolftan, she had named it. This was, in fact, Wolftan 3 as it was the third design, this one being considerably different from the first two.

Without the slightest hesitation, she leapt onto the vehicle, taking her position in the driver's seat. Snapping her handheld rifle into position by her leg, she took over the manual controls.

Now to find Owen, she thought. He had to be out by now.

She was proven correct when she saw flashes of red and Owen's unmistakable bolts of energy exchanging volleys down toward the river's edge. She couldn't head down there and help him just yet. A small alarm and a flashing light on the dashboard told her she had problems of her own.

OWEN

It hadn't taken them long to find him. He had to admit, not powering down the minute he got outside was a little foolish. Having made it to the foreshore, Owen had positioned himself behind a sand bank and a fair bit of shrubbery, hoping to see whether or not the others had escaped.

What he saw, however, was like watching rats abandon a sinking boat. Men in black clothes, suits or otherwise, seemed to pour out of the makeshift entries and years old holes in the wall, chasing after him. How could so many people work for the wrong side, Owen wondered. The answer was obvious. You just had to look at the weapons they carried. Money. This organisation was well funded, supporting what he had discovered in the records. There was a higher power behind it all. Initially Owen had figured it to be government funded. It wouldn't have surprised him in the slightest. But now, having seen the weapons, he knew otherwise. The government didn't have this sort of technological research capability. Sure they were looking for new ways to blow the possible enemy up, but they were no where near this level. Laser rifles and pistols? They were still considered things of sci-fi novels and films. Then again, a man turning into fire, let alone electricity isn't that normal these days either.

"Fan out, he's out here somewhere." He couldn't see who spoke, but the men followed the order. It was like a sweep. They spread out evenly and moved toward the river, combing the area thoroughly.

It wouldn't be long before they found him and there was still no sign of Kirrily or the other two.

Then he heard the shot from near the silo. Something was going on up there. First there was a bright flash of blue light followed by the sound of gunfire. Shortly after that a tremendous 'bang' echoed through the night. Then on the wind, Owen could hear a vehicle moving around. Kirrily? He couldn't be sure. It didn't matter now, these guys were far to close for his liking.

The problem was he had no where to retreat to. Either way was simply sand and scrub, no real cover and behind him was water, murky and cold.

He shifted his weight slightly and very fortunately because one of the men had spotted him and fired.

The bolt narrowly missed his ear.

It was time to run. There was no other option.

Owen shot back, knocking the man to the ground with an electric charge. It would stun him momentarily and give him a hell of a hangover, but that was about all.

And it was on for young and old. The air came alive with searing light as the virtual army of black-clad men fired at him.

It was a miracle he wasn't hit as he bolted across the sand. The unsteady texture made it hard for him to find footing, let alone run properly but that ironically helped him dodge several close shots.

Firing blindly behind him in retaliation, he sent weak bursts of static charges at his assailants before realising he had only one option. One that he'd never thought to use as it was too much of an uncertainty. The river.

Water was unpredictable with electric current. It conducted it no problems, but what would be the effect of a man effectively made of electricity launching himself into a body of water? Would he be discharged, forced to revert to normal as had happened to the man of fire in the records room. Owen had found that water level sufficient for his own attack, a heavy, but by no means drenching torrent of sprinkler water, but swimming in this form is something he's never tried. Or would he simply super charge the whole river, physically dispersing and ceasing to exist. Then again, his skin still had some tactile essence to it. He couldn't be completely electrical.

A shot passing right in front of his abdomen helped him decide.

Turning toward the river, he used his electric burst to launch himself high into the air to instigate a dive into the deeper waters.

His hands made contact with the chilly river first. The hairs on his forearms sizzled as they followed shortly and then quickly by the rest of his body as it submerged in the dark waters. His head erupted in pain as his facial and cranial hair, now completely electrical, arced out into the depths. But rather than finding the water slowing his progress through the water, the electric current around his body seemed to act in a similar way as to when he had been in the vent many years before. Like thousands of tiny feet, it pushed him through the water. Not quite as fast as a bolt of electricity but at a speed even Olympic champions would be envious of, Owen was launched forward. Consciously making a decision, he directed his body back up toward the surface and toward the opposite side of the river.

He would have been yelping with joy if it didn't hurt so much. He could feel his electrical energy, where ever it manifested itself from, was seeping quickly into the conductive waters. It was draining him fast and he wasn't sure how much further he could go. He was about to convert back to his pink suit when his hands made contact with the sandy bank on the other side of the river.

Hurriedly and painstakingly, Owen hauled himself out of the water and onto the shore. He could see flashes of electric blue coursing over his skin, evaporating the water on his clothes and body, each drop felt like a needle prick, his clothes like a malfunctioning electric blanket, practically burning him.

Unable to take the pain any more, he reverted to the other suit. The transition dried him completely. Miraculous, he wasn't sure, but a relief all the same.

Looking back over the distance, it had taken seconds for him to cross the several hundred metres from one side of the river to the other. But it had certainly taken its toll. His muscles felt lethargic and worn and he had to take several deep breaths before he could move.

On the other bank, the laser fire had ceased, but had resumed back toward the silo. Kirrily was in trouble. He should never have left her.

Owen was about to stand when something hit him from behind. The laser fire, the power station, Kirrily and the world was left behind as he fell into darkness.

CHAPTER SIXTEEN

KIRRILY

Motion sensors, proximity alerts, energy tracers were going berserk on the dashboard. She floored the accelerator in the nick of time, only to feel the warmth of a laser bolt against her back. In the glow from the burning station, she could clearly make out several people approaching, weapons raised. Some had even emerged from the building. It wouldn't be long before she was inundated with unfriendly fire.

Spinning the handles, Wolftan fought to keep all six wheels on the turf. She angled the vehicle back around the tower, placing it between herself and the main building. Windows were exploding both inward and outward as the old frames reacted to the growing heat inside. The roof must have caught as well as the sky was aglow with amber smoke and embers. In the distance, she could already hear the sounds of police and fire engines, probably soon followed by ambulance. She was surprised it had taken so long, especially considering the fact there had been a considerable demolition derby on the freeway already. Then again, people tended to be so self-involved these days, they've probably driven past the destruction agape with amazement and gone home to tell their families rather than the authorities.

Taking her left hand off the controls, she programmed the pulse cannon to fire at random heat signatures of 37 degrees Celsius. The night was chilly making people a slightly better target although the heat from the fire would be more than confusing for the sensors.

The cannon jumped to life, its three barrels alternating shots, allowing for cooling after each one. Explosions rocked the compound as round after round of blasts struck either earth, building - Kirrily tried not to think about whether or not the cannon would actually hit its target.

Odd, she thought. A weapon of war and she hoped it was ineffective. Unfortunately, she knew her handy work and her skill. There was no doubt there would be some casualties, either through blast concussion or collateral damage.

She tried not to think about it.

She heard yells and screams, there was also a whirring in the air as those still standing or those under cover tried to retaliate.

Wolftan didn't offer much protection, being an open-air vehicle. Her legs were protected, folded back and supported inside braces; much like one rides a motorcycle. This allowed her to hunch over the controls, keeping her low and little of her body in line of site. The windshield and much of the vehicle was protected by a similar energy field she had on the truck, although a little more primitive.

With turret extended, the vehicle stood approximately 1.7 metres tall, 1.8 metres long and 1.2 metres wide. The engine, her own design -

actually a combination of three engines she found in abandoned vehicles - was capable of speeds in excess of 235 kilometres an hour on 85 kilometres a litre.

She was proud of this version, mark III, but she already had plans on a fourth. More defensive capabilities for one.

Right now, she had to get away. Running a quick search, she found Owen's unique energy signature had moved from one side of the river to the other. She wasn't sure exactly when he'd made the transition or how, but she had to worry about getting herself out of this mess.

Men from the foreshore were joining the fray around the tower, having lost their initial target and more were coming down the escarpment from which the truck had rolled. That left only the area to the west. From memory it was simply a new development site. The land had been flattened and covered with a fresh layer of sand for foundations, but she couldn't recall if any construction had actually begun there or not. She'd simply have to risk it. Wolftan was practically an all-terrain vehicle; it should be able to deal with a few bumps and scrapes.

Kicking the machine into gear, she let some volleys fly to clear her way. Black figures leapt out of the pulse rounds' way not to mention Wolftan's which she had kicked up to 78kmph. Despite the suspension and tread on the tyres, the result was bone jarring as the ATV bounced its way across the broken concrete and into uneven terrain. Grass flashed red as the attackers followed through.

The building was beginning to cave in on itself, she could hear walls crumbling behind her and more screams as people tried to avoid the falling debris. There may well have been people still inside, but when she heard another explosion from within, machinery and oil tanks finally succumbing to the blaze, she didn't hold much hope for their survival. Had they known about this sort of work when they signed on? They were possibly leaving families behind and yet the others kept coming.

This struck Kirrily as a little odd.

Sure, in movies, the bad guys keep coming whether it was due to revenge or money or just bad writing. All things considered this evening, they had a very good chance of being injured or killed. It was almost mercenary, their behaviour, to the point of psychotic or obsessive. Even those that narrowly escaped being hit by her pulse weapons, they simply got back up and came after her again.

Was money that powerful a motivator? Or was there one hell of an insurance coverage in their job? If so, she was working for the wrong company, not that she'd have anyone to collect if she was one of the unlucky ones.

It just didn't ring true for Kirrily as she heard her own weapon let loose several more rounds only to be echoed by screams of shock or pain. This simply wasn't natural.

As flames billowed out through what used to be the ceiling of the station, Kirrily could make out a slight gully before the ground curved back upward toward the new development. But at the top of the rise, she could just make out a chicken wire fence.

Wolftan could make it through, but she couldn't risk getting jagged, or a wheel blow out as a result and so far, her weapon was doing a damn good job of deterring her assailants.

It wasn't until she surveyed the gully that she saw part way down; a small concrete dividing wall had been set up. It was as old as the main building, and although separate, was obviously part of the flow of things. From this divide, she noticed another conveyor belt, this one was open to the air and angled itself upward to the overhanging metal beams both Owen and she had run under to enter the building before hand. What its purpose was for, she didn't know, but on the opposite side there was a tunnel of some sort. A delivery system by the looks of it.

If she could make it inside that tunnel, she'd have better cover, the ability to defend herself not to mention time to think of a way out of this mess. Who knows, maybe the tunnel was still active and there was a way out.

Turning the handles once more, she aimed for the edge of the gully that would allow her a little lift to clear the wall. Her added weight on the front of the vehicle would help balance it in relation to the turret meaning it wouldn't land head over arse or vice versa.

The earth fell away from below her and she tensed herself, ready for the hard fall.

Tyres squealed as the rear four made contact with remnants of whatever was on the divide. This left the front on a kind of free fall for a few seconds as it tried to find its own landing.

Kirrily's bones rattled as they finally made contact and found purchase on the surface below. Thinking quickly, she slipped her other foot hard onto the brakes as Wolftan, grinding slightly out of control, careened toward a second wall, this one made of brick.

The vehicle screeched to a near stop before she regained her bearings and boosted the ATV into the tunnel. The laser shots had ceased momentarily as she disappeared from their line of sight and once she was inside the pitch black tunnel, they were almost forgotten.

Now that she was no longer an open target, she switched on the four headlights, revealing the tunnels length to be quite considerable. Ten or twenty metres down, however, she could see it had collapsed, most likely from the machinery that had been working above to smooth the earth for construction.

She pulled up as close as she could to the break before stopping completely. Jumping off the vehicle, she found the ceiling was just tall enough to allow her to stand.

Moving quickly, she hopped behind the front of the vehicle and out of sight.

Now it was a case of waiting to see what they would do. If they tried to come in after her, then she'd just have to fight back. If they opted to leave her alone, all the better.

What was about to happen, however, she didn't consider an option and thus didn't entirely expect.

THEN

It wasn't a long drop. Owen could tell. But when his feet finally made contact with the vent below, it was still sufficient for him to cry out as they gave way beneath him. His left ankle roared with pain, which was matched only by his right knee as it connected hard with the metal floor.

He curled himself up into a tight ball, back against the vent wall, his legs up to his chest as much as his injuries would allow. So tempting to fall asleep. It was dark, quiet and they had no way of finding him here. He was safe for now. If only he felt that way.

He had to move.

He shuffled around in order to move forward, the way he had been heading previously before the drop. But his hands met only cold metal.

The vent didn't follow the same direction as the one above.

He pushed at it, to make sure it wasn't a dream or a secret door. All it did was clunk and bend slightly as he did so, not giving into his persistent, if weak attempts.

Giving up, he turned his attention to the other four walls. To his left and right, there was empty space. In front and behind, there was only metal.

Left then, he thought. Back to the hall, but not quite. He was under it now. The man had no way of finding him. Maybe he would find a way out this way.

Carefully, trying to avoid pressure on his ankle or knee, he manoeuvred his body to find the new path and set out once more.

Minutes passed, although they seemed like hours. Making sure each hand fall was on metal and not into another hole, he tried his hardest to see in the darkness, even squinting, hoping it made a difference. No such luck, until, finally, he looked up ahead and saw something. Light. Only faint, but light all the same.

Nearly laughing in relief, he hurried his crawl to near spider-like run. But as he got closer, he realised it wasn't a way out. It was a way down. A mesh plate in the floor, part of the air conditioning system.

But it was light, all the same. Moving closer, he slowed to his normal crawl until he neared the plate.

Peering through it, he could see the room below. Well lit, once again reminding him of a hospital in its clinical appearance. Every so often a reddish hue was cast over the room as a flashing light was going off. Some sort of alarm system.

There were several machines and consoles down there, men in white coats rushing backward and forward amongst them. Other men were piling papers and files into boxes, yelling at one another as they did so. The room, from what Owen could tell, was fairly large, about half the size of his parent's house but just as tall.

A door opened on one side of the room. Owen could only see the bottom of it as it slid into the wall. A woman rushed in with a trolley. The men with the boxes converged on her at once, vying for room to dump their loads before hurrying back to fill up more boxes.

These people were leaving in a hurry. Maybe the fighting from below had gotten up this far and they were evacuating.

The woman looked at her watch before she started yelling at the others in the room, "Fifteen minutes, people. I suggest you move your arses."

Then the door opened again and this time everyone in the room stopped moving and looked at the newcomer. All Owen could see were the tops of their heads, but he could tell these people didn't like what they saw.

And when he heard a familiar hydraulic hiss and whirr, he realised exactly what they were looking at.

A long thin mechanical leg stepped into the room, followed by another and another until all eight legs were inside.

"Don't mind me. I have some work to do. As do you all. I suggest you finish it."

As if their motors were started again, the people in the coats started rushing around again.

The Robot man moved further into the room, looking around.

He was looking for Owen, he just new it. Holding his breath, he shuffled back away from the plate, only enough so he could still see the Roboman with one eye.

The mechanical man froze, his head slightly cocked. And then that horrid blue eye was staring right at him. The Robot Man knew exactly where he was.

Owen yelped and pushed himself away from the grating.

No, he thought to himself. He had to keep moving. He was a sitting duck here.

The air around his body sizzled to life once again, Owen feeling his head swim slightly as it did so. He wasn't going to be able to do this for long, he knew it. He was running on empty of whatever juices kept him charged.

He pushed himself forward, feeling himself shoot over the grate and into the darkness ahead once again. Behind him he heard a loud roar as the Robot man fired at the grating. A rush of hot air came up behind him

148

as he darted forward, the vent vibrating beneath him as a result of the gunfire and his own abilities.

Just under the gunfire, if he had been listening, Owen would have heard the groan of metal as it twisted and buckled. But that didn't matter, he could feel it around him. Something was wrong. The vent wasn't steady anymore.

Just as his power cut out once more, he felt the tube around him lurch awkwardly followed uneasily by his stomach.

Light ripped into the vent as the welded seam just ahead of him tore lose from above, the lower seam screamed as it bent on itself, but maintained its grip.

Once more, Owen found his legs falling. So too was the vent behind him.

Lashing out at the walls around him, Owen extended his arms, lodging himself firmly in place as the vent behind him connected with the floor, creating a very slippery slope, like a slide. His whole body rattled and vibrated along with the tunnel around him.

Looking up, he could see he was only an arm's length from the rest of the vent that disappeared into the wall. Behind him, of course, was the robot man and the floor.

He could already feel his tired arms start to slide.

CHAPTER SEVENTEEN

KIRRILY

There was no gunfire, not that she could tell. But at the end of the tunnel, she could see something moving. It was bright, like flame and it's resulting glow flickered like a candle.

Her glasses would have come in handy right now to see exactly what it was, but Wolftan's own sensors would have to suffice.

Using her wrist computer, she linked into the vehicle's database and ran a scan on whatever it was that was coming down the shaft.

It was human and yet, much like Owen, had a completely different energy signature. Surprisingly very similar to Owen's despite the obvious difference in the basis of their powers. She didn't need Wolftan to tell her that whatever it was was super heated, she could already feel it in the air. The tunnel which was damp and dank for the most part was starting to heat up considerably.

A slight hissing was coming from the intruder's direction; she figured it to be steam as the moisture in the ground reacted with the heat.

"Oh, damn," she whispered.

"Your boyfriend isn't going to help you, lady. He's a bit indisposed at the moment."

She scoffed at his remark. Sexist prick.

"I can look after myself."

"Ooh I'm sure you can," he laughed. The undertones in his voice working their way up her spine.

She hated men like this. The type you could imagine meeting in a biker bar or something. A woman, unless weighing eighty kilograms and wearing leather riding gear with big hair and bad make up, was nothing but a sex object for these pigs.

"Don't believe me? Try this."

With a flick of a couple of buttons, she altered the heat targeting to the 60+ degree mark and in automatic response, the turret swivelled and let loose three rounds simultaneously. Wolftan's brakes had to fight against the recoil, Kirrily found herself being knocked back slightly as the loose ground beneath the tyres gave way under the pressure. The rock around her practically hummed with the pulse rounds; loose stones from above raining down on both woman and vehicle.

Regaining her footing, Kirrily peered over the dashboard at the result of her attack.

Dust and debris mixed with steam, but still she could make out the distinctive glow of whoever it was that was coming after her. She had to admit he had been knocked back by the concussive blasts, but he was still on the approach.

She heard the voice rattle back at her as it laughed, "Nice try."

The man was drawing this out. He'd proven her weapon was ineffective and she already knew she was cornered. If he wanted to, he could probably kill her with a single blast of whatever it was he was made of, if, of course, he had projectile abilities like Owen did. Or he could charge at her and fry her with a single touch. She knew this, and although it scared the hell out of her, she had a feeling this man was either a very sick bastard who liked pulling wings off moths, or he was actually hesitating for one reason or another.

The latter wouldn't have surprised her simply for his sexist attitude. As a female, or in his eyes, a sex object, she wasn't a significant challenge. She was almost demi-human, unlike a male. No risk. In other words, he was possibly a traditionalist who believed women and children first when the chips are down. Women are made merely as entertainment figures and breeding grounds. Not made for war.

Of course, she could be way off the mark. The other guys outside she had already agreed with herself that they had suicidal tendencies or were being paid a fortune. The same was probably true for this guy, if not more so. Psychotic or highly paid.

Not good qualities by themselves or as a combination of the two.

She had to stop him and she knew the equipment on hand wasn't sufficient. Next time, she would design Wolftan with a flame retardant of some sort.

And then she had an idea.

If not water, what else can you use?

Switching off the heat targeting system, she took over the manual controls of the turret. On the wrist computer's display, she magnified the image slightly.

It was definitely a man and he was encased in fire and yet she could still make out his features through the flames.

"Freaky."

A change of co-ordinates and a final hit of the enter key and once again, she found herself on her backside.

The tunnel roared as the pulse rounds launched together at her selected target. It continued to roar as they made contact with the stone above the flame-boy's head.

She heard him scream as the tunnel above him exploded, showering him with rocks, stones, dust and pebbles.

However, he was not the only one to feel the results of the blast. The direct hit on the tunnel was much like the vibration of moving machinery used in construction multiplied several times.

The tremor reverberated back toward Kirrily and Wolftan.

Pebbles were already shaking lose from above, raining down on Kirrily.

Problem being, unlike the last shower which had stopped reasonably quickly, this debris kept falling.

"Damn it again!"

Grasping at the rocks, Kirrily hauled herself back at Wolftan and dove under its chassis.

Being only a small vehicle, it was a fairly tight squeeze, but she managed to drag and squirm her whole body underneath as the slight rain became a torrential downpour of earth.

The tunnel growled, as if in anger and pain, as the ceiling began to collapse in various sections up and down its length.

Above her, she heard as well as felt Wolftan receiving a fair dose of dirt, the suspension rocking the vehicle up and down, scratching at Kirrily's back.

She hadn't even considered this as a consequence. You're an idiot, she thought to herself. A single shot would have done it, but loosing the three barrels combined was too much for the old tunnel.

The fear of the flame-boy was quickly and severely replaced with the fear of being buried alive.

THEN

That same drill sound from earlier echoed up the vent. Looking down past his feet, which were wildly kicking for foot holds and finding nothing but smooth metal, he could see the almost hypnotic glint as the light in the room reflected off the quickly turning drill.

"Give it up, boy. There's no where to go."

His arms held him still, even though he could feel the burning sensation already tearing through his upper arm. His elbows were quivering and his shoulders were threatening to give way.

The walls around him rumbled and the vent lurched suddenly as something connected with the middle of the tube. The already tenuous link it had remaining with the rest of the building creaked and moaned awkwardly as it started to resettle.

Owen's arms gave way momentarily, allowing him to slide a few inches before he pushed out once more, this time, his feet finding a join between plates.

One more hit like that and he was gone.

He half expected a hand to reach down from above, to pull him from danger. He'd seen it happen at the last minute in a number of movies. The hero comes and saves the day.

And then he thought about it for an instant.

On this occasion, Owen was the hero. He was the one who had to vanquish the evil robot man. He was the one with super powers that could destroy the secret lab and save the world. It was up to him.

But the Roboman didn't seem to be aware of that. He battered the vent once more and Owen's strength failed him completely. He groped for anything to stop his fall, feeling the slick metal sliding past, every so often broken by the same joins his feet had caught hold of.

One such join wasn't sealed smoothly and Owen felt a sharp stab of pain as his palm slid over a torn shred of twisted aluminium.

He gasped but did not yell. Owen saw light approaching. Not the bottom of the makeshift slide, but the grating he had peered through before.

A hand hold.

He dragged his fingers along the metal, feeling the ends of them burning slightly as he did so, but soon found the smooth texture replaced by the almost train track sensation of the grate. He pushed his fingers in harder and found purchase, jerking his body once more to a halt.

But even as he grabbed hold, he felt something take hold of his ankle. A hand. It wasn't warm like a normal hand. Instead he could feel a harsh chill through his sock and pant-leg.

"Let go. Don't make this any harder."

"Leave me alone," it was simply a whine. He didn't have the strength for anything more.

The grip on his leg tightened, hurting slightly. It was almost too much to bear. Everything he felt was pain. The pull increased, but he dug his fingers further into the grate.

"Leave me alone!" He kicked at the hand with his other leg but ended up hitting the vent more than anything else.

Obviously unimpressed, the fingers squeezed into his leg, cutting off the blood circulation to his foot and forcing a cry out of the young boy's mouth. The Roboman said nothing, He just squeezed and pulled. Owen was sure the man could break his leg if he really wanted to.

Owen's fingers were no match, the combination of his body weight, the drag and the sweat that now covered his hands, he was losing it.

He slipped, no more fight in him. His body limply sliding down the rest of the vent slide only to be swept back up again as he reached the bottom.

He wanted to scream. He wanted to cry. But all he could do was close his eyes and wish he were in a better place.

Images of his parents, their farm. Anything he could remember. His brother. He hadn't seen his brother since he got here. Was he okay? Did he escape?

No. Don't think of that. Think of the sunshine, the animals on the farm, their dog barking every morning, the whirr and hissing of the Roboman's legs and body as he moved from the room into a darker room.

Owen didn't see where they were going. He didn't care.

Even with the metallic clicking as they moved and the odd clank, Owen found himself drifting off to sleep. It wasn't long before he was complete unaware of what was going on around him.

KIRRILY

A dim green glow from her wrist computer revealed to Kirrily that there were still pockets and small tunnels amongst the rubble. She had no idea if they led anywhere, nor if she had any chance of escape at all. But she was not going to give up that easily. She also noted that Wolftan was giving off a dim eerie white glow. She had no idea where that came from.

She coughed again, the air still heavy with unsettled dust and sand. Rubble was still rolling and trickling around and above her, emphasising the instability of what remained of the old tunnel.

Wolftan's tyres had held up. The probability that they would have burst and the chassis buckled were more against her, but the night had to give her a chance at some stage. She didn't expect any more such freakish favours.

At least a minute had passed already. Perhaps two. Time was losing meaning, but not importance.

There was likely to be limited air in here with a possibility it will be polluted by other gases, whether from a broken fuel line in Wolftan or old works around the tunnel or new pipes for the new development above.

If she could wait till morning, she was sure the owners of the development sight would be rightly cheesed off with the collapse. He'd have a right to sue the surveyors for not seeing the structural weakness or predicting the use of a pulse rifle or two in the vicinity that would cause further damage.

She almost laughed.

There wasn't that much time. She had no idea where Owen was. His energy signal had vanished from her computer sensors.

So had that of her mysterious assailant. Whether he was taken out by the collapse of the tunnel or if he escaped and reverted to a more natural guise, she had no way of finding out.

Typing into her computer, Kirrily tried to raise any sort of response from the vehicle which now acted as her only protection.

There was a whine of servos as they strained to move and respond, but nothing else. The cameras had been destroyed by falling debris. All she could see was static.

"Damn it!" She'd been saying that and thinking it a lot tonight.

It's not every night you have helicopters falling down around your ears. Not to mention men turning into various elements of nature, laser pistols firing and high-speed car chases.

Sirens were audible now, even through the thick rock. She didn't hold much hope of them getting her out.

Time to think!

The easiest way out would be up. There was less earth that way then toward the way she had come. The problem was it was highly likely that she move some of it and there will be tonnes more ready to cave in on her. She could always risk using her pulse rifle. Then again, if she did, she would also risk blowing out her ear drums with the pressure wave.

However, if she could fine tune it a little. Tighten the focal point, effectively creating a mini jack hammer. The problem would actually be getting to the gun. It was on the other side of the vehicle and chances are it was damaged by debris.

Her chances were looking slimmer, but Kirrily was always up for a challenge. This one just seemed to be getting worse and worse. She so wanted to use a tag line from a Bruce Willis movie but it seemed a little out of place. He had just killed a bad guy. Kirrily on the other hand had possibly killed herself. Maybe Disney would be more appropriate.

"Zippedy-doo…"

There was a sound from above. Dirt trickled down the sides of Wolftan.

There were more sounds and each was followed by the fall of more dirt. Were they trying to cave the rest of it in?

Seconds turned to minutes and the sounds got louder and louder.

Finally there was a metallic clunk and Wolftan's chassis vibrated around her.

"Are you alright down in there?"

She didn't recognise the voice. It was female with a slight huskiness which implied either a smoker or a little age. The question was should she answer?

"Miss Briton, you have nothing to fear. We're friends of Owen's."

Kirrily had been independent for too long to trust that line, but she didn't have much of a choice.

"I'm fine. Nothing a little head room wouldn't fix."

"We'll have you out in a jiffy."

Sure enough, her make shift shelter began to rock above her, dust clouded around her forcing her to cough.

"Impressive."

"We can discuss that when she's out."

She knew the other voice. It wasn't hugely familiar, but, then again, she knew the other one as well. She had talked to both only recently.

Wolftan vanished from sight, but Kirrily had to cover her eyes from falling sand and stone. A bright light flashed into the hole in which she now found herself.

"Give her a hand, Luka."

A massive hand grabbed her by the scruff of the neck, catching and pulling some hair forcing her to yelp slightly.

She felt herself lifted and she kicked lightly, trying to find some steady ground. Luka placed her on her feet.

Vanity and the need to regain her sense of independence forced her to quickly brush herself down, get rid of the dirt that had caked her clothes. She'd need a heavy duty washing machine if she survived the evening.

"Ms Briton. I'm Helen Indolini. I believe we spoke on the phone earlier. I apologise for my curtness."

Kirrily took the lady's hand and shook it gently, "Completely understandable. I would have done the same thing."

Helen nodded.

"Good to see you made it out, Luka."

The big man looked almost ashamed.

"Otherwise I'd still be under those rocks. I appreciate the help. Though, I am still wondering how you knew where to find me."

Helen didn't smile. Kirrily wasn't even sure the woman was able to for her face was so creased with worry, "We all have our own talents. Mine is a form of precognition. I just wish I was able to react sooner, but I am afraid my abilities have a side effect."

"Do you know where Owen is?"

There was a hollow silence in the air. Luka scuffed his feet.

"He, along with the rest of the Remnants are being taken to the old site of Ethelbridge."

Not good.

"Then I guess I'll have to meet him there. Excuse me," Kirrily turned and headed back toward her truck.

"Do you know where it is?"

She froze.

"I've uploaded the details to your system."

Kirrily turned to regard the older lady. She could smile, by all appearances.

"Technology isn't only for the youngsters."

"No. No it's not."

Turning back toward her totalled vehicle, Kirrily had only one problem.

How was she going to get there?

Wolftan was gone. She could tell when she was stuck underneath it that it wouldn't run again without extensive repairs and she didn't have time. The truck. That was a foregone conclusion.

The only other option, as far as she could see, had just appeared in sight, lights flashing red and blue just on the rise where Owen and she had taken a dive.

Three Police vehicles had arrived, accompanied by two Fire Engines and a Fire Utilities Vehicle. In the distance, the distinctive ring of an ambulance and several other emergency vehicles were on their way not to mention the less obvious journalists and town officials.

Kirrily would prefer a more inconspicuous means of travel, but the siren may come in handy to achieve high speeds, if she could get away with it without instigating a second chase.

Torches were darting left, right and centre along the banks of the foreshore and around the burning remains of the factory.

156

It had been a beautiful, if not terrifying vision. The sky was lit like day as the fire had reached its climax. Embers of all sizes had flown through the air like glowing fairies. The crackling of both flames and the old timbers as they snapped and caved in rang through the night, now sizzled and snapped, periodically interrupted by the last supports succumbing to the still intense heat.

There was going to be little or nothing to salvage from this mess. All traces of the machinery inside had melted or been completely destroyed. Kirrily couldn't even get a sense of the images she had seen earlier that evening when she had looked at the broken down, dilapidated building and its equipment.

It was a shame, to say the least. The building must have stood for decades only to have been completely destroyed in one night.

Sticking to what cover the sparse shrubbery allowed, Kirrily managed to evade several policemen and women as they searched the grounds.

After tonight she was going to have a hell of a lot of explaining to do to the authorities. Explaining her truck, her weapons inside the truck not to mention the remnants of Wolftan.

Weapons.

She closed her eyes, almost rolling them underneath. She's going to need weapons of some kind if she's going to help the Remnants and Owen. Which meant she was going to have to get to her truck. Already there were plain clothed and uniformed officers trying to get inside. Obviously they had deemed it safe enough to attempt an entry. Of course, they could have easily gained entry to the living compartment through the connection between the cabin and the trailer.

If only she could do the same.

Perhaps another ploy. It was going to be even harder to convince these guys than it had been to fool Owen. And that hadn't even worked.

Then again, another option.

She was still in the ditch that ran the length of the new construction area. She had to make the right decision at the right time.

And she could see her opportunity coming right at her.

A police woman had obviously come to a bright conclusion that one of the only possible places to hide successfully would be the ditch. Women still had the brains in this operation, Kirrily mused to herself, although it was hardly a brain twister to come to that conclusion.

The officer was angled a little to the south of where Kirrily was hiding.

If Kirrily had gone for the Police instead of security, things would have been a lot easier. Now she was going to have to mug a cop and face even more criminal charges.

Oh well. The things we have to do to survive, she thought.

The officer was only a couple of steps away from the edge of the ditch. Pulling her pulse pistol out from its holster under her jacket, Kirrily aimed it directly at the woman.

As she looked over the edge, the officer shone her torch first to the south and then directly at Kirrily who crouched low, hidden from the sight lines of any other officers. The woman was about to yell but Kirrily put the index finger of her free hand to her lips, indicating for the woman to stay silent.

Wisely, she did so. Kirrily motioned for her to approach.

The officer stayed on the ledge, ensuring she was in sight, thinking that would save her. She had no way of knowing Kirrily had no intention of even hurting her.

When she was in earshot, Kirrily whispered to her, "Do as I say and you won't get hurt."

In the glow from the flashlight, Kirrily could see the woman was terrified. She felt absolutely horrified for having to do this but Kirrily had no choice.

"Kill the light and come down into the ditch. Slowly."

The torch light died, Kirrily blinked momentarily to get her eyes adjusted to the light. She heard the gravel give under the officer's shoe as she slid into the hole.

"Turn around and get down."

The officer hesitated.

"Now," Kirrily added harshly. The woman complied.

With her free hand, Kirrily unclipped the holster and removed the gun. The holsters were designed for quick draw, but surely didn't help when you had someone pointing a gun right at you.

She shoved the pistol into her own belt and went back for the handcuffs.

Debating whether or not to go the whole hog, Kirrily flipped the cuffs over in her hand. No. She could do without the uniform.

She placed the cuffs on the officer's wrists, keeping them behind her.

Now what? Stuff a sock in her mouth to keep her quiet? As soon as she was gone, the officer would be screaming blue murder.

"I'm sorry," was all Kirrily could whisper. The woman was about to speak and turn around but Kirrily used the butt of her pulse pistol and clipped her sharply across the back of her head. Not too hard but it seemed sufficient in knocking the woman unconscious. She slumped forward and sideways.

Carefully, Kirrily checked her pulse. She was alive, thankfully. Finding her wallet, Kirrily checked it for police ID, slid it out of its envelope and into her own wallet. It would look more believable if she had her own driver's licence on hand rather than this woman who, on closer inspection, had very little in common in appearance with Kirrily.

Now for the big test of her acting talent. She picked up the torch, re-holstered her pistol and moved the police gun around to the back of her pants.

Flicking the light back on, she stood up and ran the light along the ditch. Satisfied that the search looked genuine, she climbed out of the ditch and made her way toward the people milling around her truck.

THEN

Owen came to on a hospital gurney. All he could see were the bright white lights of a hallway passing over head. He flinched with each one, unable to cover his eyes as they seemed to be strapped down beside him. In fact, he found he couldn't move at all. He wasn't sure if that was because he was so tired; every muscle ached from all the crawling and the transformations. And from the fear. He was so tired and worn out from fear it was as if he had spent all his energy on being afraid..

He didn't know where he was, where he was going or why, but he couldn't feel that almost sickening twist in his stomach, the pain in his heart he had felt so much today. All he felt was the constant throb in his arms and legs, especially his knees and hands. And the sharp stab of light against his eyes. He could have closed them, but then he wouldn't know what was going on.

Lifting it slightly, Owen found his head was still mobile, allowing him to turn it left and right to see who was with him. Someone had to be pushing the cart.

Sure enough, three men in white coats were around him. One on either side and, with a bit more strain, he could see the hands of the third as he pushed the end behind him, steering the Guernsey down the hall.

There was a loud clunk as the bottom of the trolley collided with a door. The men pushed it aside as they too passed through. The lights above and the walls around him disappeared. In its place was a grey concrete ceiling which seemed to be put together with large slabs, the seams clearly visible.

A bright wash of light seemed to be coming from somewhere, and the smell in the air was familiar. It was cool, fresh. It was outside. Not as nice as on the farm with its mix of animal and plant smells, but it sure was nicer than down in the prison.

More banging and the trolley stopped moving. Lifting his head once more, Owen could see the top of two large doors swing apart and reveal the inside of a truck. They were going to put him inside.

No!

He tried to transform again. But he couldn't. He tried to muster up what little strength he had left and turn into the blue light, but nothing happened.

But nothing needed to happen.

There was a yell from above him. The man pushing the trolley disappeared. The one on Owen's right vanished as well. The third man collapsed, falling over Owen's body before sliding off and out of sight. There were footsteps as the other two ran for cover.

159

"Get the boy out of here!"

Someone appeared where the third man had fallen. They reached over and started to loosen the straps holding him down.

Words came, but not to his ears. They seemed to flow straight into his head along with a sensation of a calming presence. Even though he felt no fear, he now felt a lot more relaxed.

"Don't worry, little one. You'll be home soon."

Owen couldn't smile. He already knew that was a lie. He wouldn't be going home. No where would be home now. His Mother and Father were gone. He didn't know where, but that didn't matter. They weren't coming back. He could feel that inside, too. And his brother...

Where was he? Why hadn't he seen him? He wasn't gone. He was somewhere inside this building.

The person, a woman, he could tell now. A woman with red hair. She was not as old as his parents.

She didn't smile either. But once she had him loose, she picked him up and carried him, much like his mother used to with him sitting on her hip, arms around her neck. She smelled sweaty, but that was ok. She was like Alexander. Like Neil. She was here to help.

She ran. Not very fast. She couldn't, not with the extra weight, but she did her best. She ran toward the light. The outside. Sunshine.

The concrete ceiling was left behind them as she ran, Owen watched as it turned into a massive white building.

It stretched on for ages. It had to be almost a kilometre, at least to a child's perspective. Then there was the height. It was about four stories tall at some places. Having lived on a farm, Owen rarely saw this kind of building. It was covered in white walls and silver glass. It was no wonder he couldn't find his way out. It was too big.

The ground began to crunch under the woman's feet, having turned into a loose, grey gravel. There were other people around now. And trucks. Lots of cars and trucks were moving around the building. People in white lab coats, black military style coveralls, a mix of people who clearly weren't a hundred percent human and those that looked like terrified passers-by. Most likely, like Owen, having escaped the prison below the ground.

No matter who it was, everyone was in a panic. There was no more gun fire, no more attacking one another. Just running.

The woman spoke into his head again, "I need you to move on your own? Can you do that?"

Owen nodded into the pit of her neck, not really wanting to let go, but knowing he had to, "Yes."

In one smooth movement, the woman lowered him to the ground. His legs nearly gave way, but she took his hand and that seemed to give him the strength to move.

They were still going slowly, because of his pain and his height, but they were moving faster than they had been.

Owen could see there was a group of people gathered further ahead. One man had turned to watch them, motioning for them to come.

"Hurry!"

Owen wanted to yell at him, tell him they were going as fast as they can, but before he could even open his mouth the world around him exploded in a flash of light.

The ground gave way beneath him and he went sprawling head first into the dirt, grazing his face and already lacerated hands.

A wave of heat rushed over head as he felt the woman jump on him, covering him from the blast.

The building behind them erupted upward and outward in a massive explosion. Glass showered out and over everything for miles. Flames licked out past the gravel, melting what little metal content remained inside it and congealing it into a molten pavement, reaching further onto the field on which Owen was sprawled, charring the earth, dissolving the plant-life, its effects dissipating as it spread out.

Owen's feet felt like they were burning. He hated to think what the woman above him was feeling. She screamed over the din as the explosion roared and echoed over the terrain.

Owen felt his own body wracked with pain, not from any external physical stress but from his own brain. The woman had somehow, most likely unintentionally, transferred part of what she was feeling into his body. He cried out as well but his voice, too, was lost. Bricks, mortar, dirt, metal glass showered down around them, like a vicious and deadly rain. Owen could only imagine the unfortunate people caught in the flames, or under falling debris. Human and unhuman alike were suffering. Those that had suffered already having escaped found only more of the same. Those that had caused pain were getting a taste of their own medicine.

Never before had he had such thoughts of anger, of vindication. He didn't care anymore if he got out alive. He just hoped that robotman and all his people were still inside or nearby, feeling the fire, getting cut to pieces by the shards of building materials. He wanted revenge. He wanted them to pay for what they did to his family and for everyone else that was there.

And he heard a simple word in his head. Like the woman's but not her voice. It was his mothers. She said it. That one simple word. Not angrily, just earnestly, honestly.

"No."

And Owen understood. Even amongst the running, the screaming, the pain. The world around him vanished. There was no more shaking around him as the explosion acted like a seismic charge, shattering and distorting the Earth around it. No heat, no burning. Just that one word and a complete sense of calm.

And then it all came crashing back down. But it no longer had that edge of hatred to it. He just wanted it to be over. And he knew, soon it would be.

"We have to move!"

The woman hauled Owen to his feet by his shirt and he allowed himself a quick glance back to see what was happening.

And he saw why they had to move. The ground around the building was splitting, cracking, falling into a chasm. Pits appeared all around them as the earth exploded upward, spraying them with dirt and smoke. It was a veritable mine field as they launched themselves forward toward the group which had taken cover over a rise.

The air was thick with heat and ash, making it hard to breathe and see, making even the simplest of foot-falls into dangerous leaps of faith whether the ground would give way or would erupt.

CHAPTER EIGHTEEN

Kirrily wanted the Earth to open up and swallow her. It was bad enough that she had to knock the poor policewoman out. The majority of the police were milling around the cab of the truck, trying to see inside.

She pulled her wallet from her pocket and flipped it open at a plain clothed guy who looked like he'd watched too much television. The whole trench-coat and oversized notebook look was almost too comical to be believed. He was more interested in his notebook that he only barely glimpsed up to see her and didn't even bother examining the badge when she showed it. He "harrumphed" and went back to his pad.

She re-pocketed the wallet and quickly punched a control on her wrist. One of the back doors, having closed themselves after Wolftan had made its escape, clicked open. She casually strolled up to it, opened it and jumped inside, miraculously unseen by anyone.

Once inside, she locked the door once more and turned on the light. She was amazed it still worked. But even before it flicked on, she had made her way to a line of weapons lockers on the left hand side. She could see through the wire grating at what she wanted and shook her head to clear her mind of the multiple images of possible upgrades and mental blueprints that raced through it.

Using a small touch pad she typed in a six digit pass code and three thin sets of double grates snapped open.

She whipped off her jacket and pulled out military style webbing, wrapping it around her torso over the shoulder holster that was already there. Deftly, she attached several extra clips for her pistol, an extra holster and pulse pistol, a fully automatic .45 calibre pistol of her own design and a grappling attachment.

Following that, she slipped her right forearm into a metallic gauntlet much like the wrist computer on her left. She pulled her jacket back on over the top. It looked a little deformed; she didn't think the officer outside would notice.

Into one pocket she put an older and bulkier version of her night-vision glasses. Another three small thumb locked grenades and two flash grenades.

She wasn't leaving this truck until she was fully stocked. So she put a miniature pistol – a sonic pistol from which she had derived some of the basics for the similar pulse one – into an ankle holster and picked up a simple double edged knife about seven inches long, handle included.

This was a present from a friend of hers years ago. An awkward present she knew, but it was around the time she was considering Wicca as a possible religious choice. Her friend, a practicing witch at the time, had brought it as a sign of friendship, of hope, too, she figured, that she might join the faith. Religion had never held with her.

She flipped it in her hand, catching the handle and slid it into the other ankle holster. Ready.

Now for the hard parts.

But one could help the other, not to mention aid her getting working transportation.

Once more turning to her wrist computer, she moved through the menus until she found the appropriate one.

A quiet recording of her own voice began to play within the truck. She knew it would also be projecting outside.

"Warning. Self Destruct in 30 seconds. 29…28…"

Time to go.

She jumped out the back of the truck to stunned looks of a number of policemen. It seems uniforms wanted to get a look at the truck as well. Kirrily couldn't help feeling a little pride. But she wasn't sure if they were shocked at seeing her jump out or at the fact that this thing had started a verbal countdown.

That was something from the films; she guessed that thought was running through their heads. This was going to be an exciting night for them all. Especially if they didn't move their butts and get about two hundred metres away.

One, a less shell-shocked Officer, made to grab Kirrily but she easily evaded him through the crowd.

"I'd move your asses, everyone. Twenty seconds."

Hearing her voice amongst them must have got them going because they all went clambering for safety. Some ran toward the ditch. Good, she thought. They would find the woman. Others ran for the smouldering building while others headed for the water of the river, just in case.

Kirrily was alone in attempting to climb the steep incline up to the freeway. It took her nigh on the rest of the twenty seconds to get to the top and the last two to take cover behind one of the closest vehicles.

The sky, for the second time that night, was lit like daylight as the truck went up.

There would be little in the way of debris, most of it was incinerated by the intense heat of the controlled and localised blast. Anyone who hadn't managed to get about a hundred feet away would have suffered second to third degree burns. Those beyond that, a nice crispy sun burn. Kirrily could only hope no one was that unfortunate.

She would be able to find out from the police band.

Once she knew it was safe, she moved out from behind the car.

She was lucky she had moved behind it. The front paint work had blistered and the headlight covers had melted completely. The tyres were pretty useless as well.

The cars were parked three deep. With a quick glance, she could tell the cars she had hit with the truck were still scattered on the freeway.

Spotting a dark green unmarked Commodore toward the back of the mess, Kirrily made her way over to it. Luckily, the door was unlocked. Jumping behind the wheel, she disarmed the immobiliser with a short frequency scan with her computer. Then, reaching under the steering wheel, she managed to hotwire the car.

Things were too easy, she found herself thinking. It was true. Yes, it had come at a cost, but it was still far too easy.

She kicked the car into reverse, spun the tyres before launching backward onto the freeway. Knocking it back into second, she lurched the vehicle forward and raced them through the numbers as she pushed the car up to and beyond 120Kmph.

Discretion wasn't an option. She had to find the signal again before they had the remnants and Owen completely out of range.

She guessed that they would be maintaining a decent speed so as to not attract attention. That meant at her current rate, she should catch up with them in about fifteen minutes, or at least have them on radar in ten. That's if they don't turn off onto the side streets.

In the car, she saw means of escaping being pulled over for speeding. The flashing lights sat on the dashboard flat against the windscreen. The switches for it and the siren were easy to find and she had to suppress her childish urge to let them fly. That would draw unwanted attention and make her far too obvious if she caught up to the ones she was chasing.

Her calculations were slightly off. She heard her wrist computer begin to beep in response to the tracking device in just under 5 minutes. It wasn't until she checked the speedometer to see she was well over 140Kmph.

She hadn't realised she was such a lead foot. But then again, she was anxious to get Owen back. Her brain faltered for a second. Owen.

And the Remnants. She had to get them back too.

"Damn it," she smiled to herself. That wasn't meant to happen.

In the distance she could see the convoy. The vans, the black cars. She slowed down accordingly, maintaining a couple of hundred metres distance between herself and them. There was no way she could manage an assault on the convoy in this vehicle with her small arsenal.

She maintained her distance. It was dark but there were still too many street lamps to even think about being sneaky. She had no idea where they were going but they were already over forty minutes from the city central.

Dropping back slightly, she tried to stay concealed behind the odd car that separated between her stolen vehicle and theirs.

A few minutes passed and she saw the convoy turn right onto a secondary highway, making a move north. This highway, she knew, intersected with a third major road that led to the outskirts of the city or back into the heart of it.

As she rounded the corner after them she remembered something of the files that had been accessed by Owen earlier in the day. He had retrieved designs of one of the company's facilities. She couldn't remember the exact location, but she knew it was located on the outer rim of the city. Could that be where they were heading? If so, what then? A one woman army infiltration would be as effective as throwing rocks at her truck. So would an attack on the convoy in this stolen police car. What she wouldn't give for a couple of vehicle mounted rocket launchers, a remote all terrain vehicle like Wolftan and an extra twenty clones of herself. She, of course, did not support cloning, but right now, she was very nearly considering it as a temporary and viable course of action.

Maintaining her distance, she opted to simply keep following. Who knows, she might get lucky.

THEN

Smoke was still stirring, earth was settling and people were moaning and crying. Some in joy, others in despair and pain. Owen managed to dislodge himself from the arms that were holding him. They grabbed for him but he managed to shake them off and sit up. The woman with red hair was lying next to him on the ground; several people had already started tending to her. She was awake, but barely. Owen moved away; letting the people get to her, help her. He crawled, as he didn't have much strength to do anything else, back toward the thicker area of smoke, up the small ridge so he could see what was left of the building.

The ground was soft, broken. He felt the sand and grass stick between his fingers and come away as he moved on. His eyes were stinging slightly from the fumes but could make out shapes in the gloom. People were spotted to the left and right of him, but in front of him, even though it was almost pitch with ash and soot, he could see the hospital had been replaced by a crater the size of a football field, perhaps even larger. He wouldn't be able to tell until the smoke had cleared.

Spot fires were flashing around the carnage, some beginning to spread on the shrubbery that had managed to stay above ground, others flaring only briefly before ebbing away into darkness. The ground itself, whether it was due to moisture content or some other source, was steaming and smoking. Whoever stepped on there any time soon would probably melt their sneakers. If they weren't wearing any, thought Owen, they would have very badly burnt feet. But...

What happened to Alexander? And Neil? Where was Mum and- Owen couldn't follow the train of thought without more tears welling in his eyes. He realised he was already teary because of the smoke but the lump in his throat had returned with a vengeance making it most difficult to breathe and swallow. Where was everyone that had been held below in the rooms? Did they all get out? How many of them had been trapped underneath the ground?

He almost screamed when a hand touched his shoulder. He hadn't heard her approach but the woman with red hair had crawled up beside him. She didn't say anything. She was simply gazing out over the destruction not looking happy or sad, but it was funny. Owen felt he knew exactly how she was feeling. It washed over him the instant she touched him. A sort of calm relief. As if the world had somehow achieved a balance it was always meant to have. Everything would now be alright.

"Liar!" he could only squeak. Barely audible from his hoarse throat which was getting drier as the smoke rolled by. He pushed off her hand and she looked at him and smiled. Not a malicious smile or evil smile. A smile of understanding, perhaps pity but mainly compassion.

"I'm sorry, Owen. I only meant to help. But you can see through my tricks. No. You will remember this. I wish I could answer your questions. I wish I could tell you what happens now. But I don't know the answers. It is something we will have to discover ourselves."

Again the words came not from her mouth but from inside his own head. She meant each one; there was no lie this time. He could only nod his acknowledgement, his own understanding.

"Come. We will take you somewhere familiar. Somewhere safe, away from this horrible place. There you will have time to sleep, to heal and accept what has happened. You should rest as we travel."

"Where?"

"Think of it as a pleasant surprise, but you can trust me."

And he knew he could. Even now he felt sleep coming. It had pulled so heavily on him for so long but he had had to fight as hard as he could. Now she was giving him permission to give in. He had no fight left. He didn't want to anyway. He would be okay now. She smiled once more as he closed his eyes and, almost instantly, was asleep.

OWEN

The van bounced over several pot holes in the road, the final one lifted Owen's head off the pillow and pulling it down hard. It was sufficient to jar him awake.

His eyes snapped open but everything was dark, blurry. Allowing them to close again he waited several seconds before trying to open them. It was hard work. His eyelids held down by the invisible weights of sedatives.

As he worked his eyes open it became obvious darkness was the most prominent aspect to his surroundings. Every so often a blurry flash of light would light the area around him. Even in those split moments he could tell his eyesight was distorted, affected by the drugs still spinning through his system. He didn't know how long he had been out. He hated that fact. Being unconscious is a scary business. Anything could happen and from the looks of it things had happened he knew he wouldn't like. For one thing he had been strapped down. He felt the restraints against his wrists, ankles and around his waist and neck. There was also something that had been placed around his neck. It was cold, metallic, unwelcome.

For another, he was in a vehicle of some kind.

The base of his skull and the nape of his neck were throbbing. This was a good thing. It gave Owen something to focus on to keep himself awake. The fact he couldn't move meant his body would be more inclined to give in to the drugs again. Mentally, he refused to do that. He had always been a bad one for sleep whether forced or otherwise.

A voice came out of the darkness to his left. One he had heard only that morning in the file room, "Sir, he's awake."

Another voice, unfamiliar, responded over a radio or telephone.

"Fine. Keep an eye on him."

Owen decided against the obligatory struggle against his bindings. He knew it would prove futile. His other option was to power up. Hopefully that would also help rid his system of the sedatives.

Nothing happened.

"How are you feeling?"

"You care?" Owen managed to slur.

The man chuckled, "Of course not. Just formality. I guess you've already discovered there is no point trying to charge up or whatever. The collar on your neck has a similar effect to something you might recall from a number of years ago."

Owen remembered. It was a long time ago, but he remembered clearly. But it hadn't stopped him then. In fact, his powers had been what had destroyed the whole system that prevented his fellow prisoners using their abilities.

"That's enlightening," his control on his mouth was returning.

"I guess they figured we needed you docile for a while. You certainly made a mess of things back at the station. Dead bodies everywhere. Including that girlfriend of yours."

That was not something Owen expected. He hadn't even thought of Kirrily since waking, but he had simply been trying to get his head around where he was and what was happening. She couldn't be dead. Could she? She would have gotten away with all her gadgets.

The idea that she didn't began to sink in. It was possible he was lying but equally as possible he wasn't. It began to form a ball in the pit of his stomach and he felt like he was going to be sick. Owen knew the anger he felt welling inside, but there was something else and he didn't know exactly what it was. He could guess but he didn't want to go there. That wasn't possible, not after everything he had gone through. Much like the fact it was impossible that Kirrily was-

"No girlfriend of mine," he was no actor and he knew he had just admitted his true feelings to this stranger even without having the chance to tell the woman herself.

"Yeah, ok. I'll leave you with that. But doesn't change the fact that right now, you're screwed. We're on our way to somewhere you might remember. Oh it's changed a lot. Been rebuilt for one."

Owen had to focus on the now. Of course he couldn't forget Kirrily but he had to concentrate on the here and now. That way he can find out what actually happened to her.

Well, he was lying on who knows what in a van heading who knows where. He needed some exposition and it sounded like this guy was the one who wanted to talk.

"How would you know?"

Another scoffing sound.

"Obviously," he paused for effect, "I was there."

That wasn't what Owen had expected. He was thinking he'd get some talk about the history of the hospital or the way it had been destroyed in the first place. That all new recruits were given a class in The Evil of Ethelbridge 101.

He couldn't have been there. The guy Owen saw that morning had to be only a couple of years older than he was, if that. And as far as he knew from Myrl, Owen was the only child held at the compound.

"Not from what I remember."

He sounded slightly aggravated by that response, "No. That doesn't surprise me at all."

Ok, that was personal, Owen thought. His eyes were clearing up. He could make out the finer fibres of the lining in the ceiling of the van. Focussing seemed to be having at least one beneficial effect. But seriously, this guy was taking this whole deal very personally. The other benefit of focussing, Owen found, was the fact he could maintain composure in the heat of the situation. Or so he had thought. Owen felt the thought of Kirrily pushing into the foreground of his thoughts but had to keep her out for the time being. That was hard and rather than getting easier, he found himself losing the battle. Even as he tried to speak he felt himself stutter as he tried to keep hold on his vocal cords, not to mention his emotions.

"You've lost me."

"I really couldn't care less. In about three and a half hours you're going to be nothing more than a memory as far as I'm concerned. Time for a bit of pay back I guess."

"So they've rebuilt the place? Who have? What for?"

"Surely you remember what they used it for. Someone had to tell you that sometime over the last decade or so. As for who. I would have thought that'd be obvious. You were doing the work on it this morning, you and your girlfriend. An unhealthy interest you might call it. One that proved fatal for the missus and you won't be too long in joining her. Same stuff different day."

Power. That was what they had been doing all those years ago. Utilising the energies of the Remnants and anyone else who had been unfortunate to be taken captive by Ethelbridge. They were experimenting on ways to harness the energies, even drain them from their very bodies to use as an independent power source. Owen wasn't sure if they had been effective in the original attempt, but now, the way technology had come over the last few years, he knew it was a firm possibility they had found better ways to do the same job. Whether or not they were more or less barbaric, Owen couldn't say until he actually got to see the equipment. Unfortunately it looked like he would soon and be able to experience it first hand.

"What about you? What are you getting out of this?"

"I get to live. Where as your lot forgot about me back then, now it's my turn to forget you."

Emotions were starting to take hold. Not the fear of his situation. That wasn't so worrying. It was the thought of Kirrily, it was his fears for the Remnants. It was the futility he felt.

"What are you talking about," he nearly yelled, "Who are you?"

The Fireman came into Owen's direct vision, looking over him, squaring off. His eyes were icy blue – a contrast to what Owen had expected. He had expected either a deep brown, even the chance of orange or red. Something that matched his powers. But the ice was behind the colour. It had spread across his face like a mask.

When he spoke he had seemingly stolen the focus Owen had until recently possessed. It was a voice of calm malice. Slow, purposeful.

"It isn't going to matter to you soon enough. Nothing is going to matter to you. You don't matter any more."

He had taken hold of Owen's upper arm. He could do nothing to shake the hand off so he didn't bother trying. Instead Owen held the man's gaze. He almost got lost in it. There was something familiar there but he couldn't put his finger on it.

Something stung on his arm for a moment. A needle.

Owen couldn't regain his composure and as the sedative began to wash over him, so too did the suppressed emotions. Before he could give expression to them, however, he felt himself falling into darkness once more.

CHAPTER NINETEEN

KIRRILY

The city had moved, dropping to the horizon. Kirrily looked out her side window and saw the mass of buildings silhouetted by the bright moonlight. She was driving up Welshpool Road East that wound its way up into the hills toward the suburb of Kalamunda. Although Perth had grown as a city, much of that had been vertically. Inner suburban townhouses had been replaced by high-rise apartments. Any urban sprawling had taken place to the north and south. Joondalup, once a small township of its own to the north had been replaced by a smaller version of Perth proper. To the south was Mandurah. Once a popular seaside holiday destination, it had mimicked Joondalup's growth.

Kalamunda, on the other hand, had been recognised through the sixties and seventies as a rural area. Horses, chickens and small market farms mainly. As the eighties hit, Kalamunda and the suburbs around it had seen a boost in population from the rich socialites that wanted to utilise the escarpment of the hills for its views of the city. Now, the once bush covered slope was covered by multi-storeyed monstrosities with decks and stilts. Kalamunda hadn't lost its country feel. It remained one of the few places people could go to the small shopping centre and recognise the people and refer to them by name. A real community – though now it was finally starting to lose that feel as the sprawl made its presence known. The city had to grow and East was the only direction left.

She had kept the convoy in sight for the last hour. As the road reached the top of the hill, it maintained an undulating path into darkness as the street lights thinned to a single light every two hundred metres along the road. Kirrily had to slow down and drop further behind. She was already worried that she was too obvious and had been observed although they hadn't given any sign of that being the case.

She passed a sign that pointed toward the old Perth Observatory which had become a museum in recognition of all the work that had been done in Perth in the seventies and eighties. One of the Astronomers there had plotted the location of every known star in the sky as we knew it and logged them all in a concise folio. His work had been integral in the work of Astronomers for many years, making it a lot easier for them to continue their studies. The Observatory itself had closed down in the late nineties due to the light spillage from the city. It had made it impossible to see the stars clearly in the night sky. The new Perth Observatory was located a further two hours from the city.

It was almost those two hours later that, in the pitch blackness of the gravel roads that wound among the bush land of eastern Perth – Kirrily had turned off her lights and was relying on the bulkier night-vision

171

goggles, the moonlight and the rear lights of the convoy to navigate – that the convoy turned off into a driveway. She could tell it was a driveway because the road was bordered by a high wire fence that vanished to either side and into the surrounding bush land.

She slowed almost to a stop, avoiding using the brakes for the light they would give off, and rolled the car into the shrubbery on the side of the road; far enough that it would be practically invisible to passing motorists.

She turned off the door light and got out of the car. She felt like an idiot with how bulky and awkward she must look, but beside a couple of owls and small bush marsupials and mammals, no one was going to see her.

Tapping a few instructions into her wrist computer, she ran a scan on the surrounding area. Electric currents coursed through the fence. That wouldn't be a problem.

Kirrily could also locate a security grid – difficult but not impossible – and a number of camera points around the perimeter. Harder still. But nothing a little rewiring couldn't handle. Either that or a feedback loop. Redirecting the current in the fence into the security system was one option. Not the one she would take, however. Highly suspicious. All she would need to do is get through the fence and, once inside, find a switch or control box and get to work.

Moving on foot to the drive way she could no longer see any sign of the convoy. They had made their way through heavy bush into the compound. Parrot bush and Hakea plants did their best to protect the bad guys from Kirrily's prying eyes, scratching at her arms and tearing at her legs.

A gate had closed behind the cars and vans and closed the circuit allowing current to flow once more. Thinking about the financing behind Ethelbridge, Kirrily was starting to get suspicious herself. To rely on a simple system such as this was totally uncharacteristic. And for whatever purpose they were using this compound for, obviously illegal for the most part, there was no way they were going to rely on such a flimsy and easily bypassed system. Especially when they have laser weapons.

Something wasn't right. Checking her computer again she ran several scans for variant energy signatures on all frequencies including infra-red, ultra-violet, geographic distortions and microwave.

Jackpot. The electric fence and camera surveillance were real. But that was just the tip of the ice burg. Surrounding the perimeter was an optic fibre with geo-phones stationed at intermittent points so as to make sure it would be difficult to navigate. The fence itself was wired with infra-red, photo-electric and microwave sensors. Getting over the fence rather than through it or under it would certainly be the better option.

The problem there would be the fact she wouldn't be able to simply climb it. It was strain-sensitive and triggered by vibration. The slightest disruption would have klaxons sounding.

So a possible air-lift was one way. In the corners of the property she spotted several air-turbulence detectors. If Kirrily had wished to assault the complex with a helicopter, these would have been most useful, but in a single person infiltration as she was planning, they would be completely useless.

Thankfully the trees provided the perfect bridge over the fence. Rather stupid planning, Kirrily thought. But once over, there were a number of other security measures to by-pass or avoid.

She stayed crouching a number of metres from the fence, contemplating her options. Then something struck her. As she stared, her thoughts were constantly being interrupted by images and thoughts of the goggles she was wearing. Not simply the fact she looked like an idiot, but more to do with how they were made. New designs, old designs variations all ran through her mind like a series of blueprints on a PowerPoint presentation. Perhaps she was looking at these devices in the wrong way.

She turned off the goggles and took them off, blinking a number of times until her eyes had adjusted to the light, or lack of.

When she could determine the different shades of black and grey in the night she turned back toward the fence.

It seemed to shine with its own light. Kirrily couldn't describe it. It wasn't a visible light but some kind of radiance or aura. As had happened with the goggles, blueprints of the multiple devices within the fence and around it ran through her mind's eye. If she opened her mind completely to it, she could see the connections, not simply through the fence, but radiating from within the ground itself.

The video systems, the geo-phones and connected optic fibre cabling. Everything seemed to be disassembled piece by piece, and then reassembled better than before. But it didn't stop there. Over and over, like an ever growing jigsaw, one that was designed to get harder to put together every time but Kirrily had a mental hand book as to how to put all the pieces back together better than before.

This wasn't normal. She knew it. It had always been there at the back of her mind, barely even noticeable. Back at the Power station, she had known how to fix the generators. Even as she worked with her own equipment, she had always seen ways of improving it straight after she had completed it. She had simply assumed it was a natural talent. But what she was seeing now was completely different. Then she remembered the odd light source she had seen emanating off Wolftan. There had been no explanation for it.

What ever it was, right now, it was a godsend.

Within seconds she had made mental maps of the weak points within the microwave and infra-red sensors, navigating paths that would allow her, if taken slowly and keeping a close proximity to the ground, to get deep within the compound.

She didn't need her gadgets to get inside. All she needed was this insane ability. And the trees to get within the grounds in the first place.

Opting to keep the goggles off, Kirrily felt her way toward the fence. Through the radiance of the technology before her, she found she could still make out the shapes of the trees around her. She surveyed them all, trying to find the best entry point.

It was only a few metres down from the main gate that she noticed two trees, one on either side of the fence. Their branches barely touched, but given her weight, it would be more than sufficient to act as a natural bridge over the fence. Before taking the climb, she also made sure that the base of the tree was within one of the handful of safe routes she would need to take to remain undetected.

Reassured by her abilities that her path was clear, she took the first hand and foot grips on the tree and she began to climb. What she wouldn't give for her workshop and a few minutes to whip up any alternative to having to rely on these trees and her own physical stealth to get inside. Kirrily felt very alone. She knew this was the case, but this was different. She had always had technology to help her, but now she felt worse than naked. The only comfort she felt was from the weapons she had strapped to her body which were also radiating a preternatural light.

She found that after a few hand grips and foot holds climbing the tree was hardly a problem. Of course, she would have preferred to have had a set of rappelling gloves of her own design but apart from a few misjudged nooks and crannies and several moments of having to work out which route would be safest and still keep her on track, she managed to reach one of the branches that created a bridge over the fence.

This was the fun part. To try and walk it like a tight rope or to crawl along it. She could barely see the adjoining branch that would take her into the grounds and onto the next tree. It would be a reach but not impossible. Deciding to stick with caution, she held onto the trunk of the tree to steady herself as she straddled the branch. Inch by inch she edged her way along the long piece of wood that would have been only a foot in diameter and thinning out as she moved. Kirrily didn't weigh much, she knew that, but she was not a good judge of trees and how much load they could withstand before giving way. Everything seemed okay for now.

As she approached the fence line, she noticed the branch she had chosen did not allow enough room for her dangling legs. Not a problem. Leaning forward into a more feline position she lifted her feet behind her until they aided in supporting her against the branch. Pushing onward she heard the creak and moan of the wood beneath her.

The tree was already being generous but it seemed it was getting time to leave the party. Just a couple more inches and she knew she'd be within arms reach of the next tree.

Sure enough, reaching out and up, she felt the less than sturdy branch she had been aiming for.

Now for the tough part. There was no way either branch was going to hold her entire weight by itself at this stage. She was going to have to allow each tree to share the responsibility. It was going to be a very uncomfortable job of judging how much weight to allocate to each branch.

She began the process of transferring some weight to the branch with her hands, it being about three inches above her head height. She felt the branch begin to bend a little and she pulled back, replacing some of her weight onto the first one. She used her hands to pull her body along gradually allowing the upper limb more of the load. A few seconds later she was able to swing one leg up and over the new branch and continue the journey toward the trunk of the tree on the other side of the fence. It wasn't as hard going as she had imagined.

She was much happier when her feet were back on solid ground again. The tree itself was providing coverage from one of the video motion sensors that covered the front gate. Because of the other systems she was going to have to tread carefully from here on in, at least for a few metres into the compound. From there it seems they neglected security, believing what they had installed was ample. Kirrily had to admit, it was ample. Or would have been for an ordinary thief.

It was a lot darker now, under the shade of the trees. For the first time since she was a child, she found herself somewhere totally alien. Nature. This late at night, everything was so calm, so soothing. The odd beam of moonlight would shine through the leaves above her. It was so much easier to focus. She had never realised how beautiful it was only a short drive out of the city. People took this sort of thing for granted. It was just a shame that it took an emergency like this for her to discover this other world.

There was work to do. She carefully studied the strange light show that her own eyes were creating for her. It swayed back and forth with the turning of the sensors. At other points it was replaced completely by darkness or the odd beam of light from the moon. It was in these points she knew she had to tread and contort her body so as to avoid detection. Five minutes maximum and she had successfully navigated the security net. From here on in it was knee high shrubbery and some big trees she had to worry about. And beyond that, she had no idea right now.

THEN
Someone had managed to wrangle a vehicle of some sort. The back of the van smelled dirty and smoky. The odours of singed hair and skin

175

wove their acrid way to Owen's nose. He coughed awake as the van rounded a corner. Someone had their arm around him, keeping him safe and warm. There were other bodies around him, some moaning slightly at the jostling. As he gathered his bearings, Owen noticed that the person holding him was the woman that had spoken to him earlier, before he fell asleep. Her red hair brushed his cheek every so often but he didn't bother brushing it away. He didn't want to move. He felt safe for the first time in what seemed like ages.

"Almost there," her voice spoke in his head, answering one of the lingering questions at the back of his mind. She knew he was awake. She also seemed to acknowledge he didn't want to move.

The road beneath the van changed from a smooth surface to what sounded like gravel as it was dug up by the tyres. A few minutes passed and the van rounded a long corner before slowing to a stop.

The back door slid open and bright sunlight burst into the vehicle. More moans from the bodies around them as they reacted to it, still unaccustomed to the invasive natural light.

"Give him to me," a familiar voice. Female. Owen felt himself lifted and passed out of the vehicle into a new set of arms and a fresh, clean smell that reminded him of his mother. Tears welled in his eyes, which he still could not open against the sunlight. But he would not cry.

"I'll take him inside to rest. If any of you need a place to rest, my home is open."

"Thank you, but we had better go," finally the woman spoke in his ears, "The sooner we leave, the less chance they have of finding him and the sooner we can get help for everyone else."

"Good luck. And thank you for bringing him here."

"Take care of him. He's a very special boy."

There was a slight pause before this new woman spoke, "Thank you. I know my sister would have been so grateful for what you've done."

Owen blinked a few times against the light and what had been a shadowy silhouette was quickly becoming a familiar face.

The van door slammed shut, the engine revved and the gravel rattled as the vehicle began to move again.

He felt lips against his forehead, a very tender, loving kiss. The soundtrack at this moment was the dying rumble of the engine and the whistle of a cool breeze drifting across a wide-open space.

"I am so sorry for everything, Owen."

He recognised her now, through all his haziness, he saw her finally. She smiled at him, though her eyes were full of tears. He felt a lot safer in her arms. He kept looking up at her as she carried him inside, through a couple of rooms and finally placing him down on a soft bed. As she was taking off his shoes, he found it hard to fight the pull of sleep. He hadn't been this comfortable in a while.

By the time she had covered him with the quilt, he had left consciousness behind.

When his eyes opened again, he could barely move. His arms were heavy with fatigue.

"Owen?" her voice was a simple whisper. It wasn't this new lady speaking.

"Mum?" his own voice was dry, almost inaudible.

"Shh, Relax, sweetie, don't try to talk. I haven't much time. We are so proud of you, Owen," Owen still couldn't see her. But he could hear her as if she stood right beside him. He managed to wriggle a hand free from the bedcovers and reached out for her.

"We love you, Owen," he could hear that she was crying, her voice was cracking, "We always will."

"Mum!" He called for her, but managed only a throaty croak. She was gone, even though he hadn't even seen her. She had been there; she had been looking down at him. He knew it. But now he felt all alone.

"Owen?" it was his Aunt. He remembered her now. He heard her soft footsteps as she rounded the bed and bent down over him. She could see he was shaken, on the verge of tears. Helping him up, she sat on the side of the bed and wrapped her arms around him, drawing him close to her. But he couldn't bring himself to cry. Instead, he took comfort in the gentle arms of his Aunt.

"You're safe now."

No, he thought. He knew.

"No, what?" She pulled away a little and was regarding him carefully. She was treading so delicately around him.

He shook his head, closing his eyes, letting his head loll forward slightly against her shoulder.

He was tired. Physically and emotionally. He didn't want to move any more. Didn't want to think. Never again. He didn't want to remember.

Finally he looked up and she hadn't moved.

He wanted the bed to swallow him, like a giant monster, like his Dad-

No.

The memories wanted to bite through, wanted to stake a claim in his consciousness, but although he no longer needed to run, to fight, on the inside, he was stuck in an even more horrible battle than he'd ever dreamt of.

All those nightmares he'd had, waking up screaming. Put them all together and that would never come close.

Never would he see them again.

"Owen?"

He shook his head in a form of defiance and in response to the enquiry. It was all he could do.

And resolve gave way. He fell forward against her chest, his arms hanging loosely by his sides, his hands lying palms up on the soft quilt.

And he began to rock. Gently, serenely almost. Back and forth. Over and over again without her help. He wanted to say something but his tongue betrayed him. And he realised he was wrong. He didn't want to say anything. He didn't want to see or hear anything. But most of all, he didn't want to feel anything. But inside him, like a waterfall, it all came flooding in.

She moved. Taking action. She swung a throw rug that had sat at the end of the bed into the air and brought it down around his back, around his shoulders. And she held on tight, rocking with him. Besides that motion, they didn't budge an inch. They remained like that, together, finally, for hours. Helen sobbing gently. Owen, too tired, too weak but too determined not to let anything show.

And they rocked.

CHAPTER TWENTY

OWEN

The cell was a lot different to the one he remembered from his childhood. This was high-tech, state of the art. It was approximately three metres by two metres and only just tall enough for him to stand comfortably. Owen wasn't sure how the others might fare, especially if Luka had been caught.

Metal had replaced the brickwork. Smooth steel walls, a light metal-framed cot to sleep on that had the thinnest of mattresses and little in the way of bed clothes. At least they had provided one. From what he remembered, it wouldn't be long before people were locked into their horrid machines and then their sleeping conditions simply didn't matter.

The door itself was non-existent. There were thin beams of green light that crisscrossed forming a security wall Owen was sure would be lethal on contact. The lack of privacy however made the use of the small toilet and basin at the rear of the cell one of public display, not that anyone would be interested in viewing, and those that could anyway seemed to be in a similar predicament. He could see someone huddled in a cell on the opposite side of the corridor on which his was located.

He stood up from his own bed, his head thumping slightly as an after effect to whatever they had used to sedate him. He was still wearing his pink suit, which he couldn't help smiling at. He must look a right sight locked up in this cage.

Trying to transform was useless. He knew it, but he still had to try. Their dampeners were working. As to how or what actually was creating the field, he wasn't entirely sure. But he was sure that no matter how much he tried, his powers were less than likely to short the system this time. They had had over a decade to fix the problem with their systems and had more than likely come across more powerful people than Owen to test it out.

He stepped a little closer to the green beams, careful to avoid touching them as he could feel the intense heat they seemed to be giving off.

"Hey," he whispered as loudly as he could.

There was no response from the person opposite so he tried again, "Hey!"

Whoever it was turned their head slightly, their eyes peering over their arms as they had sat themselves in a foetal position on their own cot.

"How long have you been here?"

"Too long," a woman. Her voice wasn't familiar and so far he couldn't recognise her from the Remnants, "You're new."

Owen nodded, looking both ways down the cell-lined corridor as best he could to see if there were any guards, "But an old hand at this sort of thing, you might say."

The woman scoffed, burying her face in her arms again.

"Do you know how many they brought in?"

"Leave me alone."

Didn't seem like she was going to be too cooperative. He still had to try, "Well, do you know how many are here?"

"She's not going to be much use."

Another voice, a man this time, came from somewhere above.

Owen hadn't even thought about the possibility that they were stacked one on top of each other as in traditional prison cells. He peered up, noticing the metal walkway that ran around the next level of cells. He had simply assumed it was part of the ceiling for all he had seen.

By craning and bending, he could just make out the new speaker's head. Didn't recognise him either.

"Well, how about you, then? Do you know?"

"Boy, this place is huge. They could have thousands tucked away in here. From what I can tell, from the few times they've taken me out of here, they could have at least fifty of us in this block alone."

Owen knew that couldn't be possible. There weren't that many of their kind in the first place. Even the remnants were of generally small numbers. No more than thirty, really. And they only group together because of what happened years ago. Before that, they may have been aware of each other, but must have been even scarcer.

Perth had a population of over 10 million at any one time. Of those, their kind made up maybe 0.0001%. So approximately one thousand in Owen's reckoning.

Owen hesitated a moment. He hadn't ever considered there could possibly be that many people around with strange abilities. Of course he had only been estimating, but Owen's realisation that there were quite possibly thousands of them here was more than a little frightening.

"How long have you been here?"

"Now, that's the million dollar question. Lights go on, lights go out. Days go by, some long, some short. You never really know. I been here a long time, Boy, and they still keep coming for me and bringing me back again. Some aren't so lucky. They don't come back."

This man was Aboriginal. His accent was reasonably thick.

Owen took a deep breath and let it out as a long sigh. He had an idea why they didn't come back. But what he needed more now was an idea as to how to get out of this mess. He was about to sit back down on the bed when he heard a loud metallic hiss followed by a resounding clunk.

Footsteps shortly followed. Two, maybe three people. Moving back to the security wall, he tried to see the new arrivals. It didn't take long before a man and a woman, both dressed in black uniforms and carrying similar rifles to those carried by the men who had led the assault on the Remnants and the Power Station, walked past. Behind them was a man in a lab coat. In his hand he had a digital palm top computer, casually clicking at it with a small stylus.

Completely ignoring the prisoners, the three people stopped in front of the cell next to the woman who had been less than willing to talk earlier.

"Stand back," the woman spoke, hefting her weapon and aiming it into the cell. Owen couldn't make out anyone due to the angle he had to view. The man leant forward after a moment and tapped at a keypad beside the door before stepping back and aiming his weapon also.

The green mesh of laser light vanished and the man disappeared inside the cell, reappearing shortly after with the prisoner.

Again, this was someone Owen had never seen. A man who looked to be in his late forties. It was hard to tell though as he looked pale, sickly and malnourished. Whether that was a side effect of his abilities or the treatment he received from his captors wasn't clear. His hands were clasped behind his back by solid handcuffs that seemed to weigh him down. Stepping feebly and awkwardly, the man was escorted by the two guards as the lab coat continued working quietly on his PDA.

Owen waited for the sound of the door closing and relocking before he said anything.

It had been like watching a condemned man being led to his death sentence.

"We need to get out of here."

The man he had spoken to earlier chuckled, his voice was echoed by several others from various directions.

"Don't we know it, Boy. What we need is a miracle."

With growing frustration, Owen moved away from the mesh and let his eyes scan his cell. There was little comfort, little detail and no way out. He had been through this before so many years ago. Owen could feel those memories start to creep in. A knot began to form in his stomach as he remembered what had happened back then.

Trying to shake it from his mind, he flung himself onto the cot and thought about the recent past. Keep his mind focussed on something else.

And then Kirrily popped in there. The knot got bigger, tighter. She should never have gotten mixed up in this. Mind you, if Myrl was right about her, that she too had abilities, and the Fireman had told the truth, perhaps she had been given the easiest and most painful way out of the situation.

Owen hated himself for even thinking that. Any of it. He had to believe she was still alive.

Clearing his mind of any thoughts at all, he stared up at the ceiling and at the little halogen lamps that dotted it, washing the room with their bright white light. And as if one of those halogen lamps had switched on above his head, Owen had an idea.

KIRRILY

Kirrily had managed to navigate the shrubbery with only a few minor cuts and abrasions from fallen branches and the parrot bush leaves that seemed to be everywhere, scratching any uncovered surface of skin. She had withdrawn one of her pulse pistols for security's sake, hoping that she wouldn't need it right now. It was useless in a stealth situation.

The effect of the weapon was devastating and the puce light it gave off could be seen for quite a distance in this sort of darkness.

She hung close to the trees, using them as cover as best she could. It wasn't long before she had seen the lights from the compound shining through the foliage. Moving even slower than before, she edged her way closer, noting that her weird sight wasn't showing her any form of security or technology device being present on the exterior of the building. Or buildings.

There were two that she could see. One about three stories high, the other, five. The walls of the smaller were brick with the odd window dotted here or there. It looked more to be some sort of warehouse for industrial purposes. The other was steel and glass. What one would imagine a fairly posh hospital to look like. The main entrance was completely glass with sliding doors and all. In front of it was a drive-through road that looked to be used for dropping off. This steel building was more stylised, like a giant sail, curving from the entrance all the way back to its peak on the opposite side of the building.

Above the entry in bright neon blue lights was a company logo, a diamond with two shaking hands inside and the words Ethelbridge Power Co. underneath.

Now this was a division of the company Kirrily didn't recall. Almost all of the power supply in this state came from one company. Western Power. What's more, this didn't look like any power station she had ever seen. She couldn't even see a transformer station or any means of dispersion.

What she did see were a fair number of guards. They seemed to be dressed in common light blue shirt, dark blue trousers. Hardly expert or combat trained specialists. She was thankful for that. However, if the cars had pulled in here, then the men that had the laser rifles had to be here somewhere too.

That was what she was worried about. That and the fact that she was looking at blatant forms of technology such as the electric sliding doors, the rifles the men and women were carrying, their radios, phones. She wasn't getting anything from them. She was blind to it all. Not even a hint of an upgrade.

Something was playing with her senses, obviously.

Well, she had gotten by without them in the past, it was time to get back to the things she knew best.

From her fairly extensive knowledge of security systems, she assumed that most of the windows had some form of defence. Whether it was proximity alerts, motion sensors, tactile sensors, it didn't matter. The result would be the same, alarms and possible lock downs. What she needed to do was find a different way in. The only one she could vaguely consider, beside strolling through the front door, was to go through the roof.

If one roof, say the warehouse, didn't have an entry, she noted there were several walkways and service ducts joining the two buildings. It would be a simple, cautious stroll from one to the other and then resume the search for a way in. The only problem she would have, beside actually getting onto the roof in the first place, was that the hospital like building had one or two storeys over the other, meaning she could possibly be in plain sight if she weren't careful on the first roof.

Kirrily would have to cross that bridge when she got to it. Checking her armoury and then rechecking her resolve, she made her way back through the trees around the clearing that surrounded the buildings. Admittedly, nature was doing her a huge favour at the moment by providing very apt cover. The lights shone on the trees at some points, but there was too much foliage from the taller wattle and eucalypt trees and several smaller types of plants that deflected most of the light, allowing the shadows to remain mere inches from the edge of the clearing.

The rear of the brick building had several doors. One seemed large enough to fit maybe two semi trailers. The others were man-sized and appeared to be service access. The larger doors would explain why there was a lack of cars outside. Perhaps the convoy had been housed in there.

There were only two guards on this side of the building. A third had been walking the opposite direction around the building as patrol. There were also several flood lights keeping this side well illuminated. Which would mean the best option of accessing the roof would be from the side she had just come around.

Retracing her steps, she noticed the guard she had seen moving the other way was coming back around again. That meant she didn't have much time between patrols.

The second he was out of sight behind the building she would have to make a move.

Biding her time, she prepped the bulkier wrist device she had put on in the truck and watched the man walking almost apathetically back toward the other two guards.

When his back disappeared, Kirrily ran. As she did, she raised her right arm, aimed it at the roof and, using a finger trigger, launched a grappling hook that fired with a minimal amount of sound, whizzing up into the air and catching on the ceiling with a metallic clang.

She winced at the sound but couldn't stop to worry about it. As she reached the wall, with her left hand she initiated the retraction once she was sure the hook had held. She stepped up onto the wall and using the wire to balance herself she began to run up the side of the building as if she were running on a normal piece of horizontal ground.

Underneath her the guard had returned to continue his patrol.

CHAPTER TWENTY ONE

OWEN

Owen had managed to prise one of the halogen lamps and its housing out of its niche in the ceiling using his nails, a spring from the bed and a little ingenuity. What had come with it had been a relatively disheartening small amount of wiring. He hadn't expected metres of it, but enough to be able to work effectively with. What he had he would have had an easier time using tweezers to play with.

Luckily the room was rather short, meaning he hadn't needed to move the furniture around too much and create a commotion. Ironically, that was exactly what he had in mind for the wires.

He quickly detached the light from one of the wires, exposing a tiny amount of copper. Tiny, but sufficient.

Grabbing his mattress, he hoisted one end up, letting the other fall to the floor. This meant there was less weight to carry as he juggled balancing it with one hand and working the wires in the other. Owen made contact with one of the wires with the tip of the mattress material. With his spare hand he manoeuvred the other wire until it almost touched the connector of the halogen lamp.

If there was one thing he knew, it was electricity. He just hoped it would be his friend, powers or not.

Sure enough, as he moved the wire closer he got the result he was looking for. Through the mattress, an arc of electric current zapped between the two exposed wires.

Scorched, but not ignited, the mattress had turned black at the point the arc had connected. Not good enough. He needed something that could possibly react faster. Then he remembered his suit. He wasn't particularly liking the idea of sacrificing it, but the paint would have to add an edge to the flammability of the piece of clothing.

Quickly, he undid the buttons and took it off. Fortunately he was wearing a black t-shirt underneath, albeit a smelly, sweaty one, now.

It took several more attempts with the wires before the paint covered jacket caught and began to smoulder. Willing it to burn with his non-existent powers seemed to help anyway as the paint caught, followed quickly by the material.

Carefully, he dropped the jacket onto the cot itself, it wasn't long before the mattress caught fire and spreading as he had hoped. The mattress was soon fully alight and, as the foam inside began to melt, a foul smelling black smoke was beginning to fill the cell.

With any luck, this would get their attention.

It wasn't long before several inmates started yelling, "Fire!" and variations of.

For the second time that day, Owen heard a cracking sound and the corridor outside was filled with water as a sprinkler system turned on. Fortunately, there wasn't one in the individual cell as it would ruin his plan.

The door clanged open at the other end of the hall as screams began to erupt from around the other cells. Time to assume the position. Owen dropped to the floor, legs toward the grill, as far from the now well burning bed as he could get, and pretended to be unconscious.

Boots hurriedly splashed through the build up of water outside as they made their way to Owen's cell. He could feel the water seeping into his pants as it started to pool on the floor. There was also a faint hissing as some of it was vaporised by the security lasers.

"In here! This one! Looks like he's out of it."

The security grid went down and there was a loud roar as presumably someone attacked the fire with an extinguisher. That was even more handy. First the smoke, then the residue from the fire extinguisher.

The roar stopped and was replaced by the odd cat call from above. Owen felt someone kick his leg, whether by accident or not, he wasn't sure.

A second voice spoke, "Is it alive?"

Charming, Owen thought. Whoever it was would soon find out. He noticed a shadow looming over him and figured it was time to strike.

His eyes snapped open, taking in everything in the tiny cell as quickly as he could.

One guard was leaning down over him, too scared to actually touch him but still having to make sure he wasn't dead. The second guard was standing further back carrying the extinguisher in one hand and was aiming his weapon at Owen.

In one swift move, Owen swung his leg up and around, connecting with the nearest guards knees, knocking his feet from under him. As he fell, Owen continued to swing his legs until they were under him and used them to launch himself up and forward, using the guard, whose body was flailing helplessly for a handhold, as a battering ram against the second guard who was too stunned to fire his weapon.

What Owen hadn't thought about, and seriously regretted, was that he had forgotten the security grid on the other side of the corridor.

As he slid to a stop, the second guard, under the force and weight of the first, staggered backward on the slippery surface and fell into the burning green lattice.

His scream, although it didn't last long, reverberated and echoed throughout the cellblock. The lady, who had been less than interested in talking earlier, began to scream shortly afterward as what little of the man that had actually made it through the grid came splattering to the floor inside her cell.

The first guard, stunned, but not completely out, was straggling for his weapon and sliding foolishly across the slick surface.

Owen lunged for it as well and tried to wrestle it free. Realising that wasn't working, he used his second weapon, his fist and brought it crashing down on the man's face. Pain lanced through Owen's knuckles as he did so, but he knew it would be more painful for the recipient.

Sure enough, he was out like a light.

There were some cheers from the few that had been able to see what had happened, but Owen didn't have time to take the glory. There had to be a way to open the security grid.

He scrambled over to the weapon the first guard had dropped and began looking for an empty cell that still had its grid up. The one directly to his left was just the ticket. He aimed the weapon at the keypad beside the door and fired.

A beam of red energy shot from the barrel and struck the pad. It erupted in a flash of flame before simmering down to a mere smouldering. The grid didn't lower.

"Great. Sorry everyone, I'm going to have to find another way through this security."

He could now see there would be approximately seventy cells in the block, of which only forty or so of them were occupied. Faces were peering out through their green cages; some he did recognise from the Remnants.

Had it been his fault they were here? Had he led them to their hideaway? Or had they somehow managed to by-pass the combined efforts to keep the building cloaked?

It didn't matter.

"I'll be back soon, I swear!" He called as he ran back to the unconscious guard. Checking his pockets, he found a swipe card, a set of car keys, his wallet which simply contained pictures of his family and a few notes and coins. Nothing more of use.

Keeping the card, Owen dragged the man into his own cell and then quickly made his way toward the way out.

It had shut behind the guards, perhaps to keep the water or fire from spreading. There was a port for the card, used much like a chip and pin system for banks, minus the pin, luckily. It took a second for the reader to process the card and Owen was rewarded as the door swung open into the cellblock. Using it as cover, he peered around into the room outside and noticed it was a lot darker than the brightly lit cells. This made it hard for him to see anything.

Taking a deep breath, he readied his weapon and charged through the door and into a control room.

It was semi-circular. The opposite wall to the door was flat with a single door half way along.

Lining the curved side of the room were computer consoles and monitors stationed between the door Owen had just come through and three others like it.

There were four technicians, or lab-coated men and women sitting at the consoles whilst two other guards, including the woman that Owen had seen earlier, had spun around in surprise at their new visitor.

Owen, nerves already on edge, didn't hesitate. He fired, hoping to simply hit the weapons and not having to kill anyone. One shot was true, shattering the weapon held by the female guard. The other shot, not so accurate. The man screamed as his wrist was severed from the rest of his body. The wound itself was cauterised instantly by the heat of the beam. In shock, he fell to the floor cradling his smouldering stump of an arm.

The woman was about to assist him but caught Owen's look. He shook his head and she stepped away.

To the technicians, he said, "If you don't want to end up like him, I suggest you open the cells."

They simply sat there eyeing him in terror.

"Don't make me repeat myself. I'm not the sort of person who likes doing things twice," yet here he was, breaking out of another Ethelbridge prison camp, "Next time it may not be a hand."

One technician turned to his consol and began typing furiously. The large door beside him swung open and he could hear cheers from inside.

"That's one. Three more to go."

The other three got to work. Owen knew it would only be a matter of time before more guards appeared. One of the techies was bound to have set off a silent alarm or a message of some sort to warn of the prison break.

"Now, would anyone here know how to turn off this dampening field you guys have going?"

The response was the same. Blank looks of ignorance. Obviously it had nothing to do with these guys. No matter. They'd make do.

Some of the prisoners had already started making their way into the room. Owen asked the first couple that he recognised to pick up the weapons dropped by the guards. One, Jordan from the Remnants, had the gruesome task of prising the lifeless fingers from the grip of his retrieved gun and leaving the hand on the floor.

"Now, leaving your swipe cards here on the bench, I want you all to move inside this cell block."

The semi-circular room wasn't large enough to fit all the prisoners, but Owen had to get this lot out of the way quickly and safely. He ushered them back into his own cellblock, ensuring they did as they were told, however reluctant they were.

He could see only a handful of prisoners remained and were well on the way out.

"Down the back there. Go on. Once we're out of here, we'll send help."

The six Ethelbridge employees did as they were told as Owen made sure the block emptied. Once he was happy, he pushed his way back into the control room and used one of the swipe cards to shut the door.

It was loud, cramped and hot in the room now as people were still trying to get in from the other blocks.

There was no use trying to yell over the din. They wouldn't have listened anyway. As it was, someone had managed to open the door on the opposite wall and the mass started to pour through into the heart of the facility. Owen couldn't help thinking that these people didn't have a clue what they were getting themselves into. Without their abilities and against armed guards, they didn't stand a chance. There had to be a way to organise them.

He tried pushing his way through, getting jostled and hustled around. It was a pointless exercise, but he had to try. The guards would no doubt be on their way and they were sitting ducks.

It was only a few moments later he began to hear the screams.

"Let me through!"

He was right, they didn't want to listen. He had to get through. People were dying now and he had to stop it.

But the screaming had caught the captive's attention, too. Some had faltered. Others had started pushing back into the room causing an even worse traffic jam.

He tried to find Jordan in the crowd, but it looked as though he had made it out. Hopefully, he would be able to assist those facing the guards. Someone had to. Otherwise it would be a massacre, pure and simple. More death.

Resolving himself, Owen pushed onward, he managed to get to the door. By this stage, the direction of the stampede had changed completely. They were all trying to get back inside the semi-circular room. A few elbows in the gut later and Owen found that everyone had stopped moving. There was no where else for them to go.

At the other end of the kafuffle, Owen could hear more screams, the discharge of weapons and a lot of shouting. He had to get through. He was one of only three with a weapon and had to provide some form of cover.

Time to get aggressive. He started to force his way through, sometimes using the butt of the weapon in his hand to move body parts aside. Injuring them now wasn't a concern he could think about. The minor bruises now would hopefully prevent laser burns and death later on.

People started getting the message, noticing he had a weapon and they started to clear a path. A short while later he found himself at the end of a corridor flanked by Jordan and the other Remnant with the gun, whose name he couldn't remember. They were doing their best in fending off the guards down both directions of the adjoining corridor.

To Owen's horror, he saw that at least a dozen of the captives hadn't survived the first retaliation of the guards. The bodies lined the corridors, some fallen on top of each other, and the smell of burnt flesh was almost overwhelming in the cramped confines of the corridors.

"We have to do something, Owen," the guy whose name he couldn't remember called.

"I know," was all he could say. He didn't have the faintest idea what to do now.

"What?" Jordan asked between shots.

How was he supposed to know? Owen wasn't a leader. He never claimed to be. He preferred working alone at the best of times. His mind was awash with images from his past mixed with what he saw now. The death, the pain. The futility of it all. They had fought all this so long ago and here they were again. Straight back where they started. And what then? If they got out of this, would it start all over again? Who could stop Ethelbridge or whoever it was behind this murder?

The wall beside Jordan exploded under the assault of some unseen guard's weapon.

"Owen?"

His brain refused to focus. Too much had happened today let alone what was happening now. First Kirrily, now these poor people. Some of whom he knew he would recognise. He couldn't look to hard, nor could he take his eyes off the corpses.

"Owen, please!"

"I don't know!" the words roared out of his mouth before he had a chance to stop them. And as they did, everything seemed to freeze. The two men were looking at him, eyes wide. God only knew what they were thinking. And the people cowering behind him, trying to find safety in a dead end. What would happen to them?

The words repeated, a weak whisper now. It was the truth. He'd never felt so helpless. There had to be scores of guards. Miles of tunnels. He'd been through all that before.

"Ah, screw it! Cover me!"

The two men blinked back into life, taking to their corners and firing blindly. Owen squatted down and took a moment before rolling, head under legs, into the junction. As his legs and backside met the opposite wall, he aimed the gun to his right and let loose several shots, taking a quick look the other way as he did so.

The guards on Jordan's side had retreated behind the walls of another room to avoid being hit.

Swinging the gun over his body, Owen looked back down the other way. It was a shorter distance to yet another room. How many people were in which, he couldn't tell. He could see that both directions were strewn with bodies, guards and prisoners alike. That meant that it was going to be a slow trek either way.

Using his feet, he pushed off the wall and rolled back to the safety of the first corridor.

The two men stopped firing.

Owen stood up and turned to the crowd that were all looking at him expectantly. What he had just done was pure show and could quite probably have gotten him killed. What he was about to suggest, he knew was going to get people killed. They had to do something though and his show of bravado would hopefully stir something in these folk.

The onslaught from the guards had resumed, providing audio cover as he told them his plan. What he didn't tell them was it was basically a suicide run. How could he? They all probably knew anyway.

"We run right. All of us. We stay together. Help the weaker along. If you can, grab a weapon and use it. Just keep moving. Once we take the next room, we can decide what to do next," he turned to Jordan, "You give us cover down your side and follow behind us," to the other guy, "You're point. Don't worry, I'll be right with you. Everybody. Watch your feet. It's going to be difficult going."

With that he surveyed the faces of the people he could see. There were mixed emotions. Some completely petrified, others indignantly stupefied at the predicament in which they found themselves. Either way, all of them wanted to get out.

"Right," he turned back to the junction, "Jordan, give us covering fire."

As he did so, Owen began firing his own weapon down the other way, toward the direction they would be making a charge.

"Okay! Let's go!"

Own was the first to leave the corridor in which they were trapped, but, from the primal yelling he could hear behind him as his companions all psyched themselves up for the charge, he knew he was definitely not alone.

KIRRILY

Kirrily hauled herself over the ledge and onto the roof. With the help of the winch, it meant she only needed the smallest amounts of effort to do so. The guard below had disappeared around the front of the building once again, completely unaware of her presence.

As quickly as she could, she unhooked the grapple and reset it back in the launcher. She knew the device so well she barely had to look, instead she surveyed the landscape before her.

There were several air vents and air conditioning ducts. All would provide adequate entry points. Yet there was an even better way. A small hut like structure stood only a couple of metres away. She figured it would be a stairwell down into the building proper, being maintenance access.

Keeping low, to avoid being visible to the ground below, she hurried to the hut, trying to keep it between herself and the hospital building so as to keep herself concealed. When she reached it, she was glad to find her supposition had been accurate. There was a door on the side facing the glass building, which could be a slight problem. The other problem would be the security attached to the door itself.

She crept slowly around the hut and tried to get a look at the door itself, hoping to ascertain what devices might be attached in order to keep her out. There was a small black card swipe block mounted to the side of a big steel door. Easy.

Kirrily lifted her wrist computer and angled it toward the card swipe. She didn't need to get too close, luckily, which meant she could stay hidden against the side of the hut as she worked.

She typed her way through several options before managing to establish an uplink into the security system itself. She wouldn't have tried this with the window mechanisms. She wasn't too up to date with those. Door mechanisms, on the other hand, were child's play, abilities or no. And she had been too far away from the main system to have had any effect on the perimeter systems she had had to climb over.

She followed several links and inputted a command or two before a little red tell-tale on the swipe itself turned green, indicating she had successfully disabled the system. As quickly as she could, she moved around to the door, snapped the handle open and stepped inside, shutting the door as quickly and quietly behind her as possible.

She needed to revert to the night vision goggle again. They were definitely a must for any cat-burglar, she thought.

On switching them on, she could see the steel steps descending to the floor below. The lights seemed to be off down there as well.

As she made the fourth step down, her world was turned bright white. She grunted in annoyance and snapped the goggles off her head. Someone had turned the lights on. No. Someone had turned the lights on and sounded an alarm.

"Great!" Maybe she had missed something. A trip wire, something. She was a sitting duck.

Pulling out her pulse pistol and the small automatic borrowed from the policewoman, Kirrily hurried down the stairs, ever cautious that someone would barge in any second.

When she reached a door at the next level, no one had found her.

Perhaps she'd been lucky. Maybe the system didn't isolate where the break in had occurred.

She tucked the automatic under her arm and reached for the door handle. Opening the door just a smidge, Kirrily peered into the room beyond. It was a shambles.

Some sort of mess hall. Nothing unusual about it. Linoleum floors, several vending machines, a counter and a small selection of hot meals. The people inside it, however, were charging left right and centre. All were dressed in black uniforms and carrying or about to pick up some familiar looking weapons. Kirrily recognised them as the laser rifles the men at the power station had been using. Limited range. Yet, in a building at close quarters, more than enough power to be fatal or crippling at the least.

Obviously something else had tripped the alarm as not one of the people inside were interested in the stairwell. Instead, they were bolting out two large swinging doors.

Maybe it would be better to use the cacophony to her advantage. Dressed in black as she was, who was to know she wasn't part of the crew. Admittedly, her uniform was quite varied, but who was going to question someone running around in the midst of a bunch of heavily armed guards?

Surely no thief in their right mind would be stupid enough to try it. Kirrily smiled at the thought. She was no thief, but she could either do that or wait until everyone but the dinner ladies had left. Problem with that is that she would look far more suspicious stepping out of the stairwell. If she hurried, she wouldn't even be noticed.

Pulling the door open about two feet, she stepped in quickly and fell in behind two guards, one of whom was scoffing down a handful of some pastry or another he had been trying to enjoy. No one had noticed her by the time she followed them into a wide hallway and toward a rough concrete stairwell leading down.

The sound of heavy boots crunching from step to step rang through the building. There had to be hundreds of them, she thought. By the time she reached what would be the ground level, she noticed that they were still heading down.

A little out of breath, not used to the exercise and the reality of her precarious predicament settling into her brain, she continued after them, not daring to turn around for fear of showing her face to the ones still following behind her. Some of them may well have been at the assault of the Remnant's building and could recognise her. She knew none of them got close enough, but if they had found out who she was, it was possible her photo had been handed around. Then again, as far as they were concerned, she was already dead. Buried alive along with that flaming git, hopefully.

Three more flights down and out of the stairwell into what appeared to be a big black hanger. In it were vehicles, including the convoy she had followed, crates of something or other and in the far corner was a large transformer fenced off from the rest of the room for protective reasons. A steep ramp led up to one of the big doors she had seen from outside. On the wall opposite, beside the stairwell she was running from, another roller-shuttered door stood open. This one was about the size you'd expect to find on a double storey two car garage. The stairwell itself was located in the opposite corner to the transformer.

The guards had formed into five different squadrons, the ones in front and behind her hurrying to join them.

Kirrily could see there were men out of uniform patrolling each squadron, which meant she had to get out of sight before she was spotted.

Maintaining her fast pace, she moved toward the convoy vehicles, hoping she didn't look too out of place or suspicious. One of the vans was close by and she fell in behind it.

The heavy footsteps continued for a minute or two more before it seemed all the stragglers had arrived. Once everything had settled there was a series of slow but very heavy steps. As they too stopped, a voice then began to call out. It had to be artificially enhanced as it boomed throughout the room.

"We have a situation. Level two of cellblocks E through H has been compromised. There is a small insurgence. Nothing major. It needs to be dealt with quickly and efficiently. Dead or alive, it doesn't matter. Just stop it. Sections two and three need to secure the other blocks and ensure the generator room is protected at all times. Fall out!"

Instantly the footsteps began once more, hundreds of them all at once resounding and reverberating throughout the room. Using the van as cover, Kirrily tried to count the number of men and women disappearing through the open door. She lost count after thirty-seven as there were simply too many.

As the mass of guards started to trickle off down into the darkness, she waited a few more moments and edged around the van to see if the rest of the hangar was clear. It was. The other men and whoever had done the talking had vacated the hangar via some other means. She hadn't seen them charge into the fray.

Which was good, she thought. Meant she could head after them and hopefully find her way around.

She drew both pistols once again and bolted into the dark opening.

There was another ramp, not so steep, leading down into what looked to be another hanger of sorts. This one, she could see had a walkway around the upper level which also contained some sort of computer work room. It appeared to be empty, which was a relief. There were three doors, approximately the size of a double garage door, leading out of this hangar. There were also two large, industrial looking elevators that looked large enough to fit a small car.

Above the doors, she could see the letters that obviously corresponded with the cellblocks the man had spoken of.

The central door was labelled "E – H". That was where the main fight would be taking place. Did she join it, attacking from behind and most likely get herself killed in the mean time, or did she find another means of righting the wrong?

She scanned the room once again and found exactly what she was looking for. A metal staircase led up to the walkway above. From there she could access the work room. Perhaps the computers in there would have a bit more information for her.

Hurrying, taking the steps two at a time and finding herself rather exhausted by the time she reached the top, she strode quickly toward the workstation. If anyone had been inside, they would have spotted her as the top half of the walls were made of glass, allowing them to oversee what was occurring on the floor below. That would mean they had to keep an eye on incoming prisoners.

She was about to enter the room when she spotted a solitary man standing up, back to her, at the other end of the room. He had to have been working on something or perhaps even been sleeping on the job as she hadn't seen him before.

He was about to turn when she dropped to the floor, back to the door. She had never expected to be in this sort of situation. Shooting people. That wasn't who she was. She made the weapons, yes. But not for her own personal use. Merely for show and something to ease her mind. It was an insane ability she had and she found that when she got bored, her mind would automatically drift to tinkering with various household appliances. So she had decided to focus on something more spectacular. And here one was in her hand. Probably enough firepower in that one small pistol to completely pulverise the man inside.

That was something she couldn't bring herself to do. There was another way to use a pistol and that was what she was going to do.

Standing up again and turning to face the door, the man was standing on the other side of the door, ready to depart. His eyes wide with shock, she smiled at him. Or rather, smiled at the comical situation. He relaxed a little and was about to smile back when she used her booted foot to kick the door inward. It connected with his head and he went flying backward onto a table and crumpled to the floor. He was out cold.

Well, so much for any use of the weapons she had bought at all.

Quickly, she entered the room, closed and locking the door behind her. There were rows of computer terminals. The reason they weren't being manned had to be the fact it was night shift. Granted, that didn't explain the mass of guards on site. Perhaps it was due to the nature of the prisoners they were keeping.

Using her wrist computer once again, she managed to hack into the networked systems.

Running a basic program she had picked up from a friend of hers, she managed to by pass most security protocols. There were five options open to her now.

1. Prisoner Profiles.

2. Procedure & Processing.
3. Out-put & Functional Maintenance.
4. Security.
5. Classified.

The last one was tempting. There were more important things to do though.

She pressed 'one' and her display came alive with self indulgent artistry that most programmers felt obliged to include in their software. As she accessed the information, her own miniature hard disk was saving what was being processed for back up, speeding up the operation time next time it would be accessed. She could also use it at a later stage against Ethelbridge, if she managed to get out, that was.

Scrolling through the names, she located Owen's. Highlighting it and executing the link, she was greeted with a picture of a young boy, no older than six or seven that then flashed into a more recent image of the man she knew. Beside that were his personal details. Name, date of birth, address – or assumed as it was listed as the Kewdale address he had falsely given to the records department – and abilities. It mentioned Electrical discharges, altering physical form and possible dimensional teleportation. That, in itself, was hard to take in. Before today she had never considered any of these sort of abilities as part of her life, of her reality. Again, she had to remind herself there were more important things to do.

Below that was a rather detailed history of the man. Certainly more than she knew of him.

Kirrily was horrified to read of his and his family's capture all those years ago, yet was hardly surprised to find he had been integral to the break out. His Mother and Father had died during or as a result of "procedures". His brother was...

She stopped. It couldn't be true.

There in pixelated text, the words "in the employ of the company".

So he was alive? Working for the company? How could he? His own family were victims of their regime. She wasn't sure how Owen would take the news. She would have to find him first before she could tell him.

At the end of all the information, she found his cell allocation. E 42.

That would put him right at the heart of the breakout below.

A shiver ran down her spine. Was that good news? If he was without his abilities, much as Kirrily found herself to be, he'd be a sitting duck. Yet, someone had been resourceful enough to initiate an escape.

Perhaps the best thing she could do would be trying to find what was causing the suppression of their powers. If it was something to do with the computer program, she should be able to get it off line in a matter of minutes.

Hunting through the other options, she explored option two. It wasn't too much help. It told her of how to "enrol" prisoners and then transport

196

them to their cells. Once there, another list of orders informed Kirrily how they were then moved from cells to "Procedure Rooms". Which sounded rather ominous and far from welcoming.

There were no further details about the procedures themselves. These must have been handled by trained personnel. She wasn't even sure she wanted to know.

It was when she was skimming through option three that she began to get an idea what was actually taking place.

There was some sort of power source below, in a very non-traditional sense. They were skiving power from somewhere and redirecting it outward to the transformer in the large hanger which, in turn, redirected it out to a larger system somewhere else on the property via an underground system of high tension power cables. No wonder she hadn't seen any above ground.

Considering the multi-purpose of the facility, Kirrily could guess where that power was coming from. It was vampiric. Sucking the energies from the captives and somehow manipulating it, conducting and magnifying it to provide electrical currents suitable to power the facility, and from the look of things, the rest of Perth.

She had to do something. Delving into the security protocols, she tried to hotwire the grid to the rest of the other cell blocks. Perhaps if she could release them, the resources Ethelbridge had on hand would be spread thinner, making the escape attempt a little easier.

She was just about to set things into motion when there was a tap on the glass ahead of her. She nearly jumped out of her skin as she looked up. Then she didn't make another move.

Pointed at her were the multiple barrels of a miniature gattling gun that was mounted on the shoulder of a very tall, very calm looking man.

His hair was jet black as were his eyes. His skin the complete opposite, as if he'd never seen the light of day before. There was such coldness about him that Kirrily knew he would have no qualms about shooting her if she moved and a weapon like that would have no problem shattering the control room's plexiglass windows.

Shaking his head, he used the index finger of his left hand to summon her from the room. She hadn't had time to free the other prisoners, but the program was still linked with her wrist computer. It would only be a matter of a few short commands and that would be it. But with the rather formidable weapon trained on her, she didn't like her chances.

Not wanting to die just yet, she slowly set about doing what she was told.

CHAPTER TWENTY TWO

OWEN

The gunfight had been messy. More of the captives joined the corpses that virtually carpeted the corridors. But there were still enough to make quick work of the guards in the next room.

The guy whose name Owen couldn't recall had managed to take out a handful before he had been shot. Someone larger than him had used the fireman's lift to carry him to the relative safety of the newly captured room.

Others had also taken weapons and tried to defend themselves and those around them as best they could. Behind him, Jordan had managed to provide sufficient cover. There had been fewer casualties on that side of things.

As they forced their way through, those with guns tried strafing the remaining guards as the weaponless charged at them maniacally. They had worked themselves up into a frenzy, knowing they were fighting for their lives, some of them not for the first time against the same corporation. The resulting chaos and roar had some of the guards frightened out of their wits and running for their lives.

As the last of the escapees made it into the room, Owen took over from Jordan giving the man some cover as he too bolted through to join them.

They were one step closer. There were quite possibly another one hundred to go, but they would need to take them one at a time and not rush ahead of themselves. Nor could they get too over confident. There was bound to be more resistance than they had faced. By now an alarm would definitely have been set off and reserves would be called up. There must be other measures they had developed in this sort of situation. They must have learnt. Unless they had gotten cocky themselves and thought there would be no way to escape the cells in the first place.

Mind, they were still without the use of their abilities and that made Owen very uncomfortable. They had become a part of his life and not having them felt like someone had blocked his ears or removed his sense of touch. He was sure that his colleagues were feeling the same way.

This space was much larger than the control room they had just moved from. It was rectangular with five doors on each of the longer walls. A herd of hospital trolley beds were gathered around the middle of the room, each looked foreboding with tan leather straps dangling over the sides or lying lazily on the sterile sheets. Obviously these were used to keep the subjects subdued, or at least in place if whatever sedatives they used wore off.

There was something sterile about all of it. The flooring was the same metal plating they had encountered so far. The walls were similarly plated and the doors were like those out of Star Trek – metallic slider doors that appeared to vanish into the walls.

The rest of the room was empty. At the opposite end was a double doorway with frosted windows in their upper halves.

"Keep this door covered, and stay out of the line of fire," Owen ordered Jordan and then pointed at two others, "You and you. Check the side rooms, make sure there's no more of us in there nor any of them ready to try and ambush us."

As they moved to their task, Owen stalked past the gurneys and toward the double doors. Slowing as he got there and moving to the edge of the doorway itself, he tried not to cast a shadow in the glass. Gently, using his spare hand – the other holding the rifle ready – he pulled the closest door open.

Although he couldn't see much, he had an idea what he was looking into. The room was awash in a bright green light. Familiar and far from inviting. The floor was replaced with metallic grated walkways as the room beyond was multi-levelled. In the centre of the room was a large octagonal tower that ran from below the level Owen was standing on and disappeared up and out of sight. Around it, like cocoons, were long curved mounds approximately the size of a tall man. Several were glowing, the source of the green light in the room. Others were dark – unoccupied. There was a fairly loud hum emanating from inside. However, that was quickly replaced by a steady rumble that began to intensify. Footsteps on the walkways. Running. People were coming.

"Damn it," letting the door close, he looked back toward the crowd of people who were staring at him expectantly. The two he had sent to check the side rooms had finished their task. A handful of others had been called over to help a very feeble looking woman who seemed to be heavily sedated.

"Right, anyone with a weapon, we're going to need you. Jordan, keep the other exit covered."

Seven prisoners and the other two both ran up to him. They all looked fairly confident. It wasn't until they were able to hear the pounding of boots on the gangways beyond that their bravado faltered.

"You know how it is, everyone. We need to put up as much of a defence as we can. Use the gurneys to barricade this door and hold until they start making progress."

What he really wanted was to get through the doors into the chamber beyond. That was where he could do the most good. With the imminent onslaught, he just couldn't risk it. Not without his powers. He wondered how many people were already beyond the doors, unconscious and suffering. These monsters where doing whatever it was they had done to the victims of all those years ago, all over again.

Right now, he couldn't think on it. He left the nine to get organised at the door and headed back toward Jordan. He was sweating profusely, every so often firing a shot or two down the corridor in retaliation to the odd shot from the other end. They seemed to have tired or at least were holding back for some reason. Perhaps it was so the new arrivals could finish the job.

Not going to happen.

He clapped Jordan on the back. The man jumped. He was scared. They all were.

"We have a harder task. We need to break back through to the other end."

Jordan let out a choked laugh, "You're kidding, right?"

"I'm afraid not. We have a big problem this way. We might stand a better chance heading back that way. Either way, we need to be able to protect this lot and they might be safer back near the cellblocks. At least there we can make a last stand."

Jordan considered this for a moment then nodded, "Just the two of us then?"

"They're going to need all the firepower they can get down there," he took a deep breath and examined Jordan's face, "Ready?"

The man nodded, also setting himself for the task.

With that, Owen stepped into the mouth of the corridor and began firing. Hurrying forward, he hoped the men at the other end had gotten so complacent with their simple distraction of an odd shot here and there that they wouldn't be ready for an assault.

He sensed Jordan a step or two behind him also firing aimlessly, trying to discourage any return fire.

As they reached the junction they had found themselves at early, Owen ducked to the side and his companion followed closely. The space they had just vacated was filled with a barrage of laser fire. Whether or not they were aware that they were heading toward them, Owen couldn't be sure.

When the firing died off, he loosed another couple of shots down the hall.

It was like a game of tug-o-war. One side pulls, loses power, and relaxes as the other side has a go. As the next round of enemy fire died, Owen indicated to Jordan that it was time for the longer leg of their journey.

Crouching low, He made his third charge into the corridor. They were somewhat ready for it. More shots came his way, but they flashed past him carelessly. The second he saw a hand or body part protrude from behind the cover of the walls, he fired toward it. He simply wasn't a good enough marksman, though it did act as a deterrent.

As the end of the hallway drew close, Owen launched himself forward, twisting his body as he did so. Landing on his back, the metal plating on the ground mixed with the smooth cotton of his t-shirt meant his movement wasn't halted. Instead he continued to slide onward down the hall and into the room. Assessing the situation as quickly as he could, he spotted five guards, male and female.

With the benefit of surprise, he was able to take out two with his laser before the other three were on him.

In one moment their weapons were trained on him. The next, Jordan came charging into the room, surprising them once more. Owen lashed out with his legs, tripping the woman closest to him. She landed hard on her back, smacking her head on the ground. She was out cold. Jordan managed to shoot one of the others as the final guard simply froze as both Owen and Jordan cornered him with their weapons.

"I think you can drop your weapon now."

Jordan had been hit. The clothing on his left shoulder was smoking and the smell was starting to permeate the room. Despite that, he stood strong and waited for the man to lower his gun. Owen grabbed it and kicked all of the others away.

Ushering the man aside, Owen had a quick look around.

This room had much the same sort of equipment as the cellblock control. Just on a much larger scale. A whole wall was covered by what looked to be rows of servers. Beside that was a large metal box with several thick cables running in and out of it and disappearing down two large holes in the wall.

Beyond that, there were simply computer terminals and several chairs. Between two such consoles, a thin metal door, almost like a service door that had been forgotten.

A way out?

From down the corridor, Owen could hear a few screams as the fighting erupted. There wasn't enough time to stuff around. Ensuring Jordan had the guard covered, he hurried to the door and opened it. Behind it wasn't exactly what he had expected. A large storage room that had another door down the other end. Shelves and fridges lined the walls. There was an array of medical supplies, sheeting, cleaning goods, household items such as utensils and toilet paper. Anything necessary to keep the cellblocks, their captives and the staff overseeing them comfortable. Or, at least, alive.

A flick of a handle on one of the fridges revealed small vials of clear liquids marked with tiny labels. Another fridge was filled with pre-packaged food dishes like those you received on an airplane.

There still wasn't time to waste. Darting down to the other end, he was more cautious about opening the door.

A kitchen cum ref room for the staff with two tables and several chairs. There were a couple of air-conditioning controls lined on one wall and a lot of microwaves to process the meals. It was the same stark metallic décor as the rest of the facility. The guards that had been in here had been part of the crew Owen had just taken out.

Beside the microwaves were a couple of ovens, presumably for the guards to use or for particular meals. And where there was an oven, there was a way.

The risk of smoke, especially in such confines as this, would be huge. There would have to be sufficient ventilation in case a meal caught fire or some other catastrophe occurred. Well, thinking of catastrophes, Owen knew what had to be done.

Above the ovens themselves were small fan exhaust systems that would suck up the offending smoke. Beside that, there would also need to be a way to get healthy air down here. And on careful inspection, he spotted a handful of vents tucked away here and there and dotted along the ceiling. As for whether or not they would be able to fit a full grown adult, that was debatable. But it was their only chance as it stood and they didn't have time to stress over the technicalities. It was either a way out or a defendable position.

Charging back down the supply room and to Jordan, he informed the wounded man that he would be back very shortly. Continuing down the corridor he had fought through only moments before, he was glad to see that the men and women at the door were still holding their own against the onslaught from beyond. The doors themselves were still in place, but very much the worse for wear. Holes had appeared, singed and some even burning as their captors tried to take back the room. The glass had melted at points.

The rest of the people were huddled near the entrance to the hall, some crying, others holding them trying to keep them calm. Keeping his voice low, he said to the larger group, "Head back that way. Keep going until you get to the far room. There's another door open, follow it through."

Simple instructions and they didn't hesitate in obeying them. As they moved off, Owen made his way to the gang by the door, holding the gurneys as support against the doors. They stared at him with a mix of resolute determination and escalating fear.

"We may have found a way out," some sighs of relief on their sweat strewn faces, "But, I need you to keep hold here as long as you can. The minute you think you've lost out here, follow us through. I'll come back for you once we've found something."

He waited for their nods of agreement before leaving them, hopefully not for the last time.

The rest of the prisoners were filing through the door as he returned. Jordan had made the guard move his colleagues out of the way and then kept him covered in a corner, keeping the way as clear as possible. The spare guns had been scooped up.

Owen pushed through the crowd. On seeing who it was, they moved aside and aided his passage. Handy, he thought. A change from the first time he had tried getting through them.

The kitchen was half filled as he squeezed through the door.

"Right. We need to get the vent covers off. Someone needs to break through to the exhaust over the oven. We need to find out if the vents can fit any of us through."

They got straight to work. Chairs were hauled over to the higher vents as a rather tall man jumped onto the oven and started knocking the exhaust system aside with one of the microwaves.

From behind the stragglers still heading down the supply room, Owen heard the sound of a rather loud explosion reverberate and echo through the complex. Screams followed and the tide of people surged into the room making it almost impossible to move. Owen jumped onto one of the preparation tables and tried to calm people down. It wasn't doing much good. People simply wanted to get away from the violence.

Concern for the nine left at the door was mounting terribly in his thoughts as Owen started to yell over the cacophony.

"Calm down! Calm down! You'll only hurt yourself or someone else. We need to remain calm."

It was no use. Those that weren't panicking were faced with the limbs of those that were as they lashed out, trying to get further into the room.

There was another loud crash from inside the room and everything went silent.

Owen spun on his heels to see the remains of a microwave and the exhaust system lying shattered on the floor. The man on the oven had done his job.

Unfortunately the hole would have been large enough only for a cat or a small baby to get through. As the rest of the people in the room started to realise this, the panic started to set in again, only to be cut off by someone else calling, "I've got it. Some should be able to make it through!"

All eyes turned to regard the woman who appeared from behind a small freestanding pantry. In her hand was a metal grill, approximately the size of a small television. Blood was dripping across its surface; her finger tips were also bloody, her nails either ripped or broken.

Owen cringed. There had to have been a better way to get it off. Their desperation was become very evident. Owen felt it himself but had done his best to store it away. Perhaps that was what was hindering him. It seemed to help with getting things done. But at what cost, his mind argued. We need to get out safe and sound. Not at the expense of our fingers or any part of us.

"Right. Take it slowly, see if you can fit through. If you can, the first three take a weapon and get moving. Those of you that can't, we need to find another way out."

There was a similar hustle and bustle to get to the ventilation shaft. But the panic had gone, for now. One thing was for sure. Owen wouldn't be going out that way. He'd had enough ventilation shafts to last a lifetime. It would take a hell of a lot to get him back in one.

So he had to find another way out, or at least, find out what the explosion had been all about.

Pushing his way back through to Jordan wasn't as easy. People were too desperate to get out to care who was coming through. He worried that once they were alone in the shaft that they would need to find their own way out. But they had the defences they needed and the numbers. Besides, for now, the majority of the guards would be focussed on gaining control down here again. There should be little resistance above ground.

The point would be ensuring that the guards kept their focus down this side of things.

"Jordan," he called the instant the man was in sight. The flick of his head indicated he had heard. He was now keeping watch on two guards, the woman having managed to wake up, "Can you move those two to the cell block. Lock them up. Then come see me."

The man didn't say a thing, instead indicating with his gun, the guards did as they were told.

Following behind, Owen saw the source of the noise earlier.

Down the corridor, he could see that the two doors the nine had been protecting earlier had vanished. Unfortunately, the explosion had taken a toll on more than the door. Three of the defenders were lying on the floor, motionless. The others had managed to move the twisted bulks of the gurneys back into place. They had provided some protection from the blast, but not enough. There were other wounds sustained. Owen could only mentally commend how brave these people were. They should have left their post by now, but they weren't giving up.

Jordan ushered the guards around the corner to the cell block. Owen was about to run to the remaining six and instruct them to pull back when his vision went white.

A second explosion erupted at the door and the force of it knocked Owen backward off his feet.

Landing hard, his right leg twisted unnaturally beneath him and he cried out in pain. But it lasted for only a split second as his mind quickly jumped to more important matters.

He had to blink several times before he could focus again. When he could, he wished he had kept his eyes closed.

Scorch marks, gore and blood covered the walls and floor of the hall in front of him.

There was nothing left of the defenders.

A knot caught in Owen's throat and he choked in horror. His ears were still ringing as the last of the echoes reverberated around him. Already black-garbed guards were marching toward the flaming doorway.

Scrabbling backwards, almost futilely on the smooth flooring, Owen started calling for Jordan.

He felt hands grab under his armpits and lift. Using his feet to assist him, Owen managed to stand and spin. Jordan was ahead of him, having left the guards back down the cellblock corridor.

They both ran back toward the next room, Owen with severe difficulty due to his leg,

Once inside, Owen was glad to see that everyone had managed to fit into the kitchen.

"Go through. If you can get out, do it."

Jordan was standing, back to the wall on the other side of the doorway they had just run through, "No chance, Owen."

With that, he fired a couple of warning shots down toward their attackers.

He was right. They had no chance. Another grenade or whatever it was they had used at the door would wipe them out in no time.

There was only one way out now, and Owen was going to be fighting all the way.

KIRRILY

Back in the large hanger, Kirrily didn't need her abilities to know that this 'man' wasn't human. No matter what he looked like, he was simply too cold, too technically perfect in his movements, not too mention too strong to be able to carry such a weapon on his shoulder without straining or stooping.

"Breaking and entering is a serious offence, Miss Briton."

That was freaky. Him knowing her name.

"And what do you call torturing and murdering innocent people?"

"The difference is no one cares. No one will find out. Who will you tell? And how will you tell them when you're dead?"

The mind was definitely human. The worst kind. Everything else was a construct. And if Kirrily knew about anything, it was electrical and mechanical devices. Just how that would help her was anybody's guess.

"It's only a matter of time. So many people going missing. Someone is bound to start asking questions," she tried.

"They didn't when we first started over a decade ago. And now, if we can provide an environmentally friendly power source without harming the general population, why would anyone complain? Getting rid of freaks of nature like yourself is doing a service. By using your 'gifts'," he spat the word, "to power the city, we simply kill two birds with one stone."

"The environment? Global warming? That's your defence?" Sadly, it was probably a very good one. With so much media hype about the melting of the polar ice-caps, the lack of rainfall in London, Sydney and numerous other cities around the world, a new eco-friendly power source would be not only accepted but revered. And if a few dregs and freaks in society had to suffer or die for it, why would anyone complain?

His mouth twitched into a mockery of a smile, "We don't need a defence. As I said before, no one is going to find out."

Kirrily heard a loud click and noticed that the shoulder mount had rotated to face her. It was coming. And she had two choices. Stand there and take it, or fight back. She simply needed to avoid his first strike. What was odd, or perhaps a sign of the man thing's arrogance was that he had not removed any of her equipment. She still had a couple of pistols stashed away, not to mention the grenades. With the tech that must have gone into this thing, she was certain he would be completely aware that she was armed. He obviously read the situation and concluded that she wasn't dangerous.

Big mistake.

She pushed her body around with her right leg, allowing her torso to increase the momentum by dipping and swinging her leg backward and up, spinning all the way around until her heel connected with the side of the now roaring gattling gun.

Her timing had been perfect, albeit coincidental. The instant she had swung her body down and around, he had opened fire. Kirrily felt the hot burst of air as the bullets ripped past, narrowly missing her.

Boot crunching against spinning bars of metal and she was sure she had more than likely cracked her heel in the process, she noticed the weapon dislodge from the man's shoulder. It tilted at an awkward angle and the man had to grab at it to steady it, causing him to stop firing in the process.

The hard impact had forced her foot back the way it had come, knocking her off balance. Unable to keep her footing as her leg came down she stumbled to the ground, facing away from her attacker.

Behind her, the man made no sound, She had no idea what he was doing, lunging for her, re-acquiring the target with his weapon. It didn't matter. She had to move.

Pushing off the ground like a runner at the Olympics, Kirrily bolted as fast as she could toward two APC's parked next to each other. She was at least four metres away and didn't like her chances of making it without creating a diversion.

Once up, her left hand groped for one of the thumb locked grenades. She found purchase, initiated its timed countdown and tossed it back the way she had come. The grenade clunked several times on the floor and three seconds later, as she reached the first APC, it exploded.

The noise rang through the hanger, echoing and reverberating for some time after as the force of the explosion ballooned outward, sending with it pieces of shrapnel and bursts of flame. Explosion followed explosion, like a chorus of drums and cymbals in an orchestra of monkeys.

Kirrily launched herself forward, hoping to offer the least amount of body surface to the deadly shrapnel, her target being the under carriage of the APC. Several sharp stinging sensations rained across her back and legs stopping as the hulking vehicle became her makeshift shelter. It wasn't until after she had stopped moving that she noticed that there was more than simply shrapnel from the grenade coming to land on the hanger floor. A car door, scorched and smoking came crashing to the concrete inches from her face, between the vehicle she was under and the one next door. More clatter and rumbling followed as further pieces of machinery and vehicle lost velocity from the blasts and gravity took hold once more.

An acrid smell also began to flow through the air as smoke from the blasts began to circulate due to whatever air-conditioning system they had in place, making visibility a bit hazy, but far from impossible. The main issue was the smoke affecting her eyes. That and the fact she had no idea where the man-thing was.

The second problem was resolved as the chassis above her was rocked by a hail of bullets, presumably from the shoulder mounted weapon. To try and avoid being hit by any lucky shots, Kirrily scrambled forward, away from her attacker and out from underneath the APC. It was withstanding the attack admirably, though she wasn't sure for how much longer, nor how much ammunition the guy had. There was also the fact she had picked up from watching a documentary on weapons created by war. Gattling guns had to cool down after a while, otherwise there was a higher chance of jamming or even misfiring. So he could only maintain the assault for a short amount of time. She hoped.

Withdrawing her pulse pistol from its holster, she stayed low against the vehicle. Kirrily knew she had to move, or else he had her dead to rights. She waited a few moments more and sure enough, her theory was confirmed. The firing stopped. What's more, she could hear the barrels on the gun still spinning, giving her an idea where the guy was.

He had moved, heading toward the rear of the vehicle she was using as a shield. In a few moments he would see her and she'd be a goner.

As quickly and quietly as she could, she began to move toward the front of the APC and turned left, away from where she had been standing earlier and into the maze of vehicles. This should allow her some cover, unless this man thing had some form of thermal imaging, in which case it would be completely pointless action.

Then she had an idea of her own. Her goggles. The older pair. If this man was giving off heat signatures of his own, she could track him. She pulled them from the pocket she had shoved them into earlier and slipped them on as she moved. As the system readjusted to thermal tracking, she could make out outlines of her surroundings. When she took a quick glance back, she spotted multiple heat signatures from the fires, but there didn't appear to be any from the man.

Damn it, she thought. A normal man, she should be able to make out the body shape and the hotter points of the body should be burning red. But this wasn't a normal man. She was looking for the wrong thing. Allowing another quick glance back, she thought she had spotted him. Eleven bright red dots seemed to be floating in the air, moving unlike the small spot fires were around the rest of the hanger. It wasn't much but it was something.

The biggest problem was that he was getting close.

She flipped the goggles up as they were far from conducive to navigating around a cramped and crowded space. She had an idea where he was, that was enough for the time being. Now it was up to her expertise in her weapons to keep her alive.

She made it to one of the convoy vans she had hid behind earlier and stopped for a moment, listening. There was the odd crackle of fire, movement of debris, but no footsteps.

Why couldn't he be like the villains in movies where he needed to give exposition, she found herself thinking, then she could at least pin-point his voice.

She had to do something!

Her mind suddenly switched track. There was at least one thing she could do. Her wrist computer was still on. She could free the other prisoners and create a suitable diversion. The only problem then would be that of stopping whatever it was that was inhibiting their abilities. Something for later. Get them out first.

Her fingers danced across the miniature keyboard as her ears listened for any sound. When it came, she jumped.

"Miss Briton, I suggest you stop whatever it is you are doing."

He was right behind her. Well, behind the van that was behind her.

She entered the last command and turned to face the van. In her mind's eye, she could see the gun aimed directly at her from the other side of the black metal box. The bullets more than capable of penetrating the plating used to black out the windows. That was okay, because so was her pistol.

"Much better. You're co-," she didn't let him finish his sentence. She fired her pistol at the side of the van and squinted as the purple pulse ripped out of the barrel and impacted with the door. With a screeching sound, the door crumpled in on itself where the pulse made contact and the whole van was knocked a metre further away from her, tyres squealing in protest.

Kirrily herself was knocked backward, struggling to maintain a grip on the weapon. Close quarters combat was not what the gun was meant for. The recoil alone was bad enough but the reciprocal force from the initial impact was powerful enough to create the feeling she was being squashed beneath several mattresses.

Blinking a couple of times, Kirrily noted that the door was firmly embedded in the opposite wall of the van, not having made sufficient impact to go through. The fact the van had been pushed away was an interesting outcome. She had predicted the sides to have been ripped apart, leaving a hole where the pulse made impact. Something she would need to experiment with some more, later.

She had to keep moving.

If she could somehow dislodge or even get rid of the shoulder mount, she might have a chance of beating the guy. Or if the people trapped below could make their way out, they might cause enough of a commotion that this guy would lose interest.

An image of what he might end up doing then crossed her mind. It was quite probable he would use the gattling gun against all of the helpless prisoners. Which made it even more vital that she disarm him.

She had the weapons, now it was using them properly. She began to run down the narrow alley between the various convoy cars, back toward the main hangar door that led outside.

Blowing a hole in the door and getting outside might be one of the best things to do, she considered. At least if she could get outside, leave the last two grenades to clear up some mess, she might just help in crippling the establishment.

As she reached the end of the second van she felt something hard connect with her jaw. Her legs continued to run forward, sending her falling hard onto her back, winding her.

The man stepped out from his hiding place, no emotion on his face. He had been fortunate enough to have missed being hit by the pulse pistol. The pistol, her eyes widened with desperation at the thought. She had wasted a few seconds trying to get her breath back and not worrying about protecting herself.

Raising her arm, the man noticed her attempt and stomped down hard on her wrist. Kirrily screamed in agony as she was certain a few of her wrist bones threatened to snap. The computer was destroyed, shards of metal digging into her skin as sparks flew from the crushed circuits and power systems. It had, however, provided a modicum of protection.

"Enjoy pain, do you," he asked, his voice still smooth, cold and modulated.

Only a whimper escaped her lips as she tried to wriggle her hand free. The pistol had fallen from her grasp. In a pointless act, her left arm had swung across to pry the foot from its place. It was immovable.

"You have obviously given up your chance and your right to a swift death. So let us draw this out as long as we can, shall we?"

Her eyes widened in terror. She was stuck. No way out.

The man reached down and grabbed the front of her harness, lifting her up, waiting until the last minute when her broken bones were straining against the underside of his boot before lifting his leg off of her.

In an unemotional act of brutality, he swung her around and slammed her hard into the side of the van, her head colliding hard with the metal.

Struggling to maintain consciousness, she tried to kick at him. Her legs having no effect on him whatsoever. Her left hand was working furiously at his clenched fist. The thick fingers were entwined in the harness and she tried to dig her nails into his skin. No response. With her right arm, she gingerly held onto his arm for support.

"You should have kept your nose out of our business, Miss Britton. Maybe then you'd be tucked up in a cosy bed somewhere, safe and sound."

Through gritted teeth she muttered, "A life like that just isn't for some people."

Kirrily tried to focus on a few things at once. First and foremost was staying conscious, the next was finding a way out of this mess. The third was her left hand. It had changed tactic. Moving from his hand to the buckle of the webbing, she was furious working at it with her fingers, trying to unclasp it. With it pulled so taught from the weight of her body, this was not an easy task.

"Life? You're about to die, Miss Britton."

"To hell with that. And with you!"

Her fingers had worked their magic. The clasp gave way and she found herself slipping to the floor. The holster still caught in his fingers. Although his face didn't register it, he was surprised by her sudden move.

Kirrily, on the other hand, didn't have time to hesitate. She snatched up her pistol as quickly as she could with her bleeding right hand and kicked off for the hanger door once more. Her left hand dug into one of her pockets, searching for one of the grenades.

Behind her, she could hear nothing. There was no indication whether he was running after her or aiming the gun at her. A few metres from the door, she let loose a round directly in front of her. The door screamed in protest against the force of the pulse, a slight tear forming in a circular pattern, but not giving way.

Just as she fired a second pulse, the back of her jacket was grabbed and for the second time, she found her legs moving without her. She had to keep moving. Using the same tactic as before, she tried sliding out of the jacket she was wearing, her left hand releasing one of the thumb lock triggers as she did so.

It wasn't until her arms got caught in the ends of the sleeves that she realised she had acted too hastily. The added bulk of the two wrist computers had made the jacket even tighter around her forearms and, as it doubled back on itself, the material got stuck. Then there would have been the issue of the pistol still in her hand.

"Going somewhere?"

"Somewhere you're not," And she fired a third shot from her pulse pistol trapped in the sleeve.

The pulse erupted, colliding with the man. Kirrily allowed herself to be launched forward as the force ricocheted off the man and back at her. The seams of the sleeves gave way and her legs began to pump once more as they connected with the ground. She only had a second or so to get away before he went sky high.

When she looked back at the door, she saw that there was now a hole approximately seven feet in diameter in the metal. Kirrily launched herself forward as fast as she could go.

As her boot touched the concrete outside, the world behind her erupted in an inferno of heat and flame. The thumb lock grenade she had switched on had gone off. There were also still the last of the thumb locks and the two flash grenades left in her jacket.

When the air around her was consumed in a blinding white light and the roar of three more consecutive explosions Kirrily knew she had to act or she was liable to be fried or turned into a kebab by stray debris. Her eyes already burned from the flash grenades, she squeezed them shut all the same as she leapt to her left side, out of the blast line of the flames spewing from behind the hangar door. The huge door itself bulged and wrinkled under the intense pressure and heat from inside.

Like the earlier grenade, the explosions didn't stop there. The vehicles must also have started to react as at least six more blasts bellowed forth. Each one hitting the door with so much force it began to buckle off its hinges, the flames licking from underneath. At several points, shrapnel impacted with the door creating large dents and in some places even slicing through. One particularly sharp and nasty looking piece bounced on the concrete inches from Kirrily's face and into the darkness beyond.

There was absolutely no way the man could have survived that, Kirrily found herself thinking, or perhaps hoping.

The ground beneath her was shaking furiously. Kirrily rolled over onto her backside and looked up at the roof of the building. With the ambient light from the fire inside, she could see that the brickwork above the door was giving way. A crack had formed in the cement joins and was getting bigger and bigger. It wouldn't be long before the wall and maybe even the ceiling collapsed.

What had she done? She needed to get back inside to try and help the others. If they managed to fight their way through, they would be faced with the fire or worse, a collapsed building blocking their exit.

Unless there was another way down.

There was the other building. Maybe there was an alternate entrance.

Then another notion jumped into the foreground of her mind. There would be more people there too, not to mention guards and they would be coming to find out what had happened. And those that weren't would more than likely be evacuating the other building giving her a little relief from the guards. She had to move.

Scrabbling to her feet, she ran up the driveway and around toward the side of the building from which she had scaled earlier. The orange glow from flames could already be seen in the sky above.

The guards from earlier had gone. Obviously drawn by the alarm. Certainly not all guards would have gone running, however, despite the bells and calls. There would be other security concerns to keep in check whilst whatever was happening below was occurring.

Perimeter guards would be increased. Off duty guards would be called in from home. And with the fire she had started should come the emergency services. Outsiders. Help. Or was that just being hopeful?

She continued to run until she could see the other building.

CHAPTER TWENTY THREE

OWEN

They had to get their backsides into gear. It wouldn't be long before the guards stormed the corridor, perhaps using explosives like they had on the doors. If they did that, there was no way they would survive. But they had to give enough reason for the guards not to go after the other escapees. That meant drawing their fire from the kitchen and holding them at bay for as long as they could.

Owen knew the only way out for himself and Jordan was to climb through the holes in the wall through which the cables ran. There was absolutely no telling where that led to, but it was better than staying here. The problem was making sure they could keep the attackers at bay long enough to give them a good enough head start.

"Keep the corridor covered," he told Jordan. Without a word the man fired round after round down the corridor. The guards retaliated in kind and for every one blast from Jordan, twenty were returned,, destroying what computing equipment was in their path.

Owen moved over to the servers. Beside it, the holes in the wall looked large enough to fit both himself and Jordan one after the other at a squeeze. Mobility would be limited and their going slow. So they definitely needed something to keep attention off them. The best he could think of was a physical barricade.

There wasn't much in the room to use. He hurried to the small door dividing the kitchen from this room. And he remembered.

There was a lot of different chemicals and bits of equipment in here. Two chemicals in particular came to mind. He quickly scanned the contents of the shelves and found several large glass bottles of each.

He started gathering supplies in a sheet to use as a makeshift sling bag. When he had everything he needed, he told the stragglers still in the room to barricade the door as best they could. After he left, he moved back to where Jordan was still holding a meagre defence.

First things first. Hit them where it hurts.

"Don't breath for a bit," he instructed Jordan as he withdrew a large bottle from his collection, the rest he put on the ground. He remembered this stuff from when he was doing science. It used to make the whole class feel ill.

Ironic, he thought, that something so powerful was kept in a glass jar.

With both hands, he took hold of two bottles and threw them down the corridor as far as he could. Fortunately the guards hadn't anticipated the attack and completely missed shooting the jar.

Before they even landed, Owen had retrieved two more bottles. Smaller than the first. He knew what he was about to do could very well kill people. But that was a risk he had to take.

The first bottles shattered as it landed on the hard ground. There were yells of surprise and pain a moment later and the volley of weapons fire stopped.

"Jordan," The man looked over at him, confusion was evident in his eyes, he pointed and called, "Go through one of those holes. Go as fast as you can. And wrap this around your face."

Owen threw him a piece of sheeting he had torn up and quickly wrapped another piece over his own nose and mouth, tying it behind his head.

Jordan stared vaguely at the sheet before Owen yelled, "Now!"

The man moved just as Owen started to hear the cries from the guards. The gas from the liquid ammonia had started to invade their respiratory systems. He was sure some of the men would be vomiting soon.

When he was sure Jordan had a clear enough head start – the man's feet were the only thing sticking out of the hole - Owen launched the second two bottles down the corridor and ducked around the corner. There were three ways this could go, he knew that from chemistry. He had no way of knowing what would happen. If things went completely wrong, he stood a good chance of dying himself.

As the second container connected with the floor, it too shattered, its contents spraying out over the men and the walls around it much like the first liquid. Unlike the first liquid, it didn't simply cover the corridor. This one reacted with the first.

Owen hadn't wanted to stay around as it did so, so he threw two more bottles, one of each chemical, down the corridor and ran. When he got to the hole in the wall, he all but leapt into it and was confronted with a strong blast of cool air.

That was fortunate as behind him he heard yells from the guards down the corridor, many of which fading into coughs and even some heaving. Mixing Ammonia and Bleach could have two different chemical reactions which could very easily result in an explosion. The third was the release of Chlorine Gas which was toxic in large amounts and in prolonged exposure. The short term effects were vomiting, burning lungs and sore eyes and sinuses. Owen didn't want to think of what could happen with the dosage he had provided. Instead he used his elbows and shoulders to wriggle his way into the hole around the cables.

It was quite clear why they needed cool air. The cables, even through the insulation, were running extremely hot. Owen did his best to keep from touching them with his skin. If he had his powers, he could have travelled down the hole in seconds. As it was, it seemed to take forever before he managed to reach the other end of the tight tunnel. It had only been a matter of minutes and a few metres.

Jordan was already out and sweeping the area with his weapon. All Owen could see once he had managed to lever himself out and onto his own two feet again was a largish dark room where the cables united with a tangle of others and disappeared into the ground. The room itself was close to freezing, some form of refrigeration unit cooling the air whilst large fans circulated it and even pumped it down the holes through which the cables travelled.

The only lighting came from faint halogens in the ceiling that cast an eerie white glow over the top half of the room. The light itself dissipating as it fell, leaving everything below the knees covered in darkness. The cables seemed to be steaming as condensation on the rubber was evaporated by the heat. There was also a considerable hum coming from somewhere. Despite this, the two men thought it safer to keep quiet.

Jordan indicated a door that stood inconspicuously on one wall. Owen would have missed it for all the panels that lined the walls, presumably as insulation. Owen nodded and they moved quickly across, avoiding the cables as best they could.

As with a freezer, the handle was one of those large pull latches. Tentatively, Owen touched it to see if it were too cold to touch and then mentally berated himself. What point would there be if the handle would freeze on human contact. It would simply be impractical. As it were, it was covered with a thin film of some sort of plastic material.

He took hold of the handle and gently pulled it open. The door was heavy and it took a bit of effort to move. This was okay as Owen wasn't hoping to burst out of the room and run, he would rather try and sneak out.

Slowly and gently, he pulled the door open. Jordan stood opposite him, aiming the gun toward where the gap would eventually appear.

To assist with the refrigeration, the door was insulated as well and approximately five inches thick which meant peaking through would be a little less sneaky. Owen imagined his fingers and toes were crossed that someone on the other side wasn't aiming a large energy pistol at the gap, ready to blow a hole in both the door and his head.

Edging as quietly as he could toward the gap, he managed to peak out into the next room.

It was the same large room he had seen beyond the now destroyed double doors. Green light spilled into the cooling room and Owen noticed streamers of frosted air curling up and out into the room beyond through the gap in the door. They had to be quick before they were spotted.

As for guards, he could see guards straggling out through those same ruined doors on the right hand side of the room. Some were hunched over coughing violently, others were being carried out by colleagues.

Any guilt Owen felt for causing these guards pain quickly slipped from his mind. These were human beings who had been willing to farm, hurt, maim and even kill other human beings. For what? Money? Because it was their job? Neither excuse was good enough. They could have made moral judgements, quit their jobs, reported it to police. What sort of human beings were these? Bigger monsters than how Owen's friends could ever be perceived as.

But Owen knew he was different. He did still feel remorse for hurting the guards. For killing some. He had hoped he wouldn't have to, but what choice did he have? He'd even had some locked away for their own safety. And he wasn't about to go out there guns blazing and wipe out the sick and injured left overs. That simply wasn't the right thing to do.

So he pushed the door shut for a moment.

Jordan gave him a questioning look.

Shaking his head, Owen said, "We have to wait for a bit. A few guards. They don't know we're here."

"We can't stay here. We'll freeze."

Owen nodded quickly, "I know. But we have to do something about what is through there."

Jordan wasn't clear, "What?"

"They have people in there. Locked up. Somehow attached to this machine. I've seen it before but I didn't know how to save them," he fell silent for a moment as a wave of frustration washed over him, "I wasn't given enough time."

He didn't blame anyone. He didn't really blame himself. He was too young. What could he have done? All that weird technology. Even now he was at a loss. If Kirrily was here, she would know exactly what to do. She knew machines.

If she was still alive.

Yet another casualty in this absurd situation. There was no need for it. People living their own lives away from the normal population. Not hurting anyone. Kirrily was just an innocent bystander who got pulled into it all. And she too had paid the price of someone else's malicious agenda.

So, that was it, Owen told himself, no one else will simply be left behind. These people will be freed. The rest of the people suffering or set to be suffering will be saved. He had failed to do anything as a child, but now he could make up for it.

He went back to the door and had another look through the gap.

From what he could tell, there were a handful of guards standing guard, weapons aimed back into the other room. They wouldn't give up that easily. Once the gas and smoke had cleared, they would be right back inside and ready to wipe out anyone they found.

How to tackle this? If the two of them tried to take on the guards, they were dead. From what Owen could gather, there was no visible way to turn off the tower on this level, so staying here would be pointless. They had to make their way out of here and find somewhere they might actually be able to make a difference.

He was about to close the door again when he heard one of the guard's radios.

"Status report?"

"We've been pushed back from Level 2 Cellblocks E through H."

"Well push back again. You have weapons. They are meat. Pure and simple. Whoever you kill we can replace."

"Yes, sir."

He indicated toward his colleagues and they moved back into the room, leaving the gangway empty as far as Owen could tell. There was too much machinery in the middle of the room for him to be able to scan the whole of the walkway from this vantage point. Besides that, Jordan was right. They would freeze if they didn't get moving.

He looked back at the man who was rubbing his arms and hopping quietly about to keep his blood circulating and nodded. Good to go.

Waiting until Jordan was standing beside him, Owen took a deep breath before swinging the door open and stepping onto the metal gangway. He covered the area he could see with his gun while Jordan stepped through and shut the door. It was clear. There wasn't a sound of footsteps, which was a little unnerving. There was, however the distinct hum from the tower in the middle of the room that could quite easily cover the sound of someone walking. That meant that they were going to have to be as careful as possible.

Well, that was what Owen had thought. When suddenly, like an approaching car, he heard a distant rumble, he knew something was wrong. That sense of foreboding grew when the gangway beneath his feet began to vibrate, and not in a good way.

"We have to hurry," he whispered to Jordan.

As if to emphasise the point, the lights flickered several times. There was a tremendously loud scream of twisting metal, several snaps followed by what sounded like several coins bouncing across a metal surface coming from above and below him.

"Lead the way," Jordan wasn't stupid. That last bout of noise was an omen of worse things to come.

Owen did just that. Heading to his left, he walked away from the scorched doors that led back to the cells. His eyes were busy keeping an eye out for guards and examining the machinery.

They had already passed three occupied pods on this level. It was impossible to see who was inside as the glass was frosted with ice. Along the side of the gangway was a rail that must allow some sort of loading mechanism to access the tower.

What Owen needed was not to physically access the tower, but to somehow access the controls, to turn it off, unplug it or whatever it was that needed to be done without harming the people inside.

Leaning over the side of the railing around the tower, he looked up and down the chamber they were in. He could count another two levels above and three below. But at the very bottom he could see the base of the tower branched out, like roots, out of sight.

"Sir, Levels one and three of cellblocks E through H are secure."

Someone was coming. Owen indicated Jordan back around the tower before realising the voice was coming from directly below them.

"Good work. Split your team. They need help on level two. Send the other half to Cellblocks I through L. We're facing strong resistance there. A through D has been secured already."

"Yes, sir!"

There were eight more cellblocks, however, if they were divided as the ones he had been held in, that meant there were three more towers like this one. There were no other doors to this level that looked to suggest more cellblocks around this tower. And there were three levels worth. He remembered in his own block that his level was double height. That meant two floors per block. The lingering question in his head, though, was how did the others make a break? Good timing? Good luck? Not likely.

Didn't matter right now. What did was that they would very soon be getting some visitors from below.

Owen and Jordan found the entry to the stairwell.

"We're going to have to wait here for a bit," Jordan said.

"We're going to have to do a lot more than that."

Owen's last word was lost to the sound of Jordan's weapon discharging and that of a body falling back down the stairs.

"They're here already."

There was a commotion from below. Obviously the sight of someone falling down dead in front of you in a stairwell was going to raise a little concern.

And then the gunfight began again.

Using the wall to either side of the door as cover, Jordan and Owen made good their defence. But that would only hold until the guards sweeping the cell block opposite realised they had all managed to escape and came back, trapping them between a rock and a hard place.

"What I wouldn't give to have my powers. I'd suck out their blood and feed it back to them," Jordan called over the sound of gunfire. Owen cringed. A little too graphic for his own taste, but he could understand the sentiment.

KIRRILY

The building behind her wasn't going to stay standing very long.

Already massive cracks had formed and continued to creep along the brickwork. If these monsters hadn't condemned the prisoners to death, she quite possibly had done so herself by burying them underneath the rubble.

218

There had to be another way in and out, she told herself and set her mind to finding exactly that.

The front door of the snail-like building was a hive of activity. For a night shift, there were an awful lot of people working. A few dozen men and women were rushing from inside the building. Some to evacuate, others, it seemed, to get a better look at the slowly crumbling but steadily burning building in front of them.

The orange glow from the roof, now aflame, reflected eerily on their faces and the windows of the taller building but only danced several metres into the trees before being consumed by the night.

Kirrily had to make the most of the distraction. She wasn't too dissimilarly dressed to the other guards to attract attention. So she simply jogged toward the building and into the mingling and somewhat confused crowd.

Swallowed by suits and white coats, she pushed her way inside, swiping a security pass badge off two unsuspecting employees as she did so, just to be on the safe side. She was no pick pocket, but their attention was sufficiently elsewhere to make it possible for almost anyone to take their wallet if they so wished.

Double sets of automatic doors stood open, apparently held in position by the fire alarm that she could now hear buzzing from inside. A cool and unemotional male voice instructed all personnel to make their way to the nearest fire exit.

Kirrily decided to ignore the voice and rushed into the lobby.

The room itself was approximately three stories tall, with a second glass wall inside that looked out from the offices and labs into the reception area. Elaborate, yet strangely clinical chandeliers hung four metres from the ceiling, their light useless against flashing orange lights that came from the obscure corners of the room.

The front desk was abandoned, the receptionist's headset sat precariously on the LCD monitor as several stragglers finally made their way out of the building.

Strange, thought Kirrily, there were no guards left inside. Or perhaps they were doing the rounds, checking to make sure all rooms and personnel had evacuated successfully.

She rushed to the receptionist's desk and took control of the computer, keeping low and out of sight of anyone who may decide to peek back inside.

The screen saver took a moment to evaporate, revealing a similar display to the one she had seen in the other building. There were several other options, however, that related more to the building she was in. Personnel locating, Human Resources, Communications (both internal and external). That last one would come in handy. If the Fire Department and Police hadn't been called already by the alarm, one quick call of her own should do the trick. She navigated the menus to achieve an outside line and dialled '000'. An automated recording answered a couple of seconds later. She had managed to put the headset on in that short space of time.

"You have reached emergency services. Please select from the following options. If you require an Ambulance, please press one. If you require the Police, please press two."

Kirrily had worked on the phones long enough to know that these automated messages had become the norm. The fact emergency services had adopted it seemed ironic in this day and age considering the number of jokes relating to this very thing, not to mention the insults and commentary about the lack of service and incompetence of said Departments.

She hit two without any further hesitation.

It rang once before a human voice greeted her, "Please state the nature of the emergency."

"I am at Ethelbridge Power Company, up past Kalamunda. There have been explosions, people injured."

"That's more a Fire Department matter, Miss. Let me transfer…"

There was no way Kirrily was going to stand for that. She needed the Police. They had to be here to protect the survivors down below. If there were any after her stupid trick.

"No! This is also a Police matter. There are people being held hostage inside one of the buildings. I don't know if they are terrorists, but they have guns."

The woman's voice changed noticeably. Whether she heard the desperation in Kirrily's own voice, she wasn't sure, but she started to take the call seriously.

"Ethelbridge Power Co. Terrorists. We'll have Police to you as soon as we can."

The word Terrorist would have rung alarms in whatever systems they had monitoring calls these days. That would go directly to the Federal Police and their response should be swifter than the everyday officers. Or at least Kirrily hoped so.

"Can I have your name, Miss?"

Only one name came to her. One she had recently seen, "Ryan. Cloe Ryan. Could you hurry?"

"Can you stay on the line Miss Ryan?"

No. No she couldn't, "I can't. We're evacuating the rest of the building. I have to go." With that, she pressed the cut off button and returned her attention to the screen. She had been typing as she talked, trying to find any information on the CEO of Ethelbridge Holdings. She already knew his offices weren't in the building.

The thing was, Kirrily had never heard of Ethelbridge entering the Power industry. This was a completely isolated branch of the company despite sharing the same name.

Digging further on the system told her that there were several other divisions of Ethelbridge that flew below the radar, most not even using the name. One example was the Peerson Corporation. It was an ancillary company that fed back into Ethelbridge.

No wonder the company had security tabs on the data Owen had been digging into that morning.

That morning. So much had happened since then.

She shook her head, trying to clear a rush of different thoughts and emotions. There was too much work to do.

The first thing was to try and shut down whatever security systems they had in place. Beyond that, anything she could find to help the people down below and stop the company and get Owen back safely.

As she typed furiously, she noticed that at the periphery of her hearing she could make out a slight rumbling. Moments later it was joined by a vibrating in the floor which grew in intensity. Beside the monitor, a cup of pens began to rattle along with several other items on the desk. Looking up and over the bench that surrounded the reception station, Kirrily could see the security guards trying to herd and contain the personnel away from the opposite building.

Apparently that was where the vibrations were coming from. Where else?

The night sky was awash with the orange glow from tall flames that had all but consumed the building. What brickwork that she could see was starting to crumble and fall apart under the heat of the fire and the strain from the vibrations.

She could hear the panicked calls from people as they started to follow the guard's instructions to move away.

There was a sudden flash of green light that usurped the orange and glared into the main building's lobby like a spotlight, temporarily blinding Kirrily. Instinctively and letting out a short yelp of pain as she did so, she ducked behind the counter. She covered her eyes with her hands, hoping that whatever the light had done hadn't been permanent.

With only her hearing to help her at this time, she quickly picked up that the rumble had ceased and in its place was a squeal just in her range of hearing. This too seemed to be getting stronger and louder. In short time, she moved her hands from her eyes to her ears as the high pitched wail reached a peak.

It was so loud she did not hear the glass façade of the building she was in begin to crack. Nor could she register the wall of force that shortly followed the burst of light from the other building.

What was left of the brick walls was demolished as what could only be perceived as an expanding bubble of dirt and smoke rolled its way outward at an amazing speed. The bricks themselves crumbled under the force. People who had not managed to get far enough away found themselves knocked off there feet screaming until the energy within the blast seared the skin from their bones and turned what was left to dust.

As the shockwave connected with the main building, the squeal was replaced by an all-mighty roar. The glass erupted inward, its shards, bullet-like, pierced walls and furniture alike. What plant life there was in the lobby was consumed by heat along with the upholstery of the chairs and the unprotected carpets.

The chandeliers were knocked from their brackets in the ceiling and catapulted into the upper levels shattering and showering their own glass over the lobby.

Kirrily screamed futilely as she launched herself off the chair and under the desk, smacking her head hard as she did so, unable to see where she was going. Scorched and semi-fluidic glass projectiles punched through the metallic brackets of the counter and into her left arm as it covered her head and her left thigh as she pulled it up into her chest, trying to make herself as small as possible.

The world, a scorching cacophonic mass of twinkling glass, falling fixtures and the roar of the shockwave, shook around her. The air was burning around her and the sweat was evaporating off her skin. She found herself struggling for breathe, but every lungful made her want to gag and vomit. The oxygen itself was being consumed by the heat.

Forcing herself to breathe, she decided to try and hold it for as long as she could, but her lungs couldn't take the combination of gases that she inhaled and she began coughing, bile at first rising in her throat in response to the acrid taste.

She tried to fight the urge to vomit but failed and began to gag on her sputum and the very air she was trying to breathe.

Kirrily felt herself losing her grip on consciousness. She continued to fight as hard as she could, but in the end it was pointless.

CHAPTER TWENTY FOUR

OWEN

The decision to fight was taken from Owen's hands.

The platform beneath his feet began to shake once again, this time more insistent than the last. Along with the motion came the flickering of lights. Even the central column that seemed to be on some sort of gyroscopic correction system had moments of lightlessness.

The guards were already starting to make their way up the stairwell, firing as they moved. Jordan fired back without any regard or particular aim, relying on blind luck. That was all they had helping anyway. It had gotten them this far. Hopefully it would see them making their way out of here as well.

As the shake continued, it actually increased. Owen found his footing slipping several times and could hear the bracketing and supports around the room begin to whine under the strain.

Surely it wasn't an earthquake.

"What are you doing?" Jordan called across the doorway.

Own looked up at his companion, "Something is wrong. It's not stopping."

"More important things right now."

There was a zap in the near distance followed by a short buzzing sound.

A cold shiver ran through Owen's body that didn't seem to go away. Like something in the air had changed. Or maybe something else.

Owen let off a few shots into the stairwell for good measure, not expecting to hit anything. They were going to have to find another way.

The wall beside his right shoulder sizzled and sparked jarring Owen from his thoughts. The other soldiers had found them. They were effectively surrounded.

Jordan was too busy with the people below so Owen took it upon himself to give some cover on their floor, the problem was they were essentially out in the open and stood to be surrounded on three sides if they didn't get moving.

"Jordan! We have to move," But where? Right now the only safe place he could think of that offered any chance of defending themselves or cover was back in the cold room.

Somewhere in the chamber something snapped and twanged loudly. Perhaps a bolt breaking loose and ricocheting. A flash of light from below shortly followed by a loud crack, almost like thunder and another realisation jumped to the foreground of his thoughts even as he let off several shots at the soldiers on the opposite side of the chamber.

This whole place was essentially a power source. Electricity. And Owen knew electricity.

"Jordan. Leave it. Follow me," he could see Jordan hesitate but Owen wouldn't give him that chance, "Move your arse!"

Owen fired wildly in front of himself as he ran back toward the cold room. He could hear Jordan running behind him, still loosing shots in some direction or another.

The soldiers that had been by the blasted door, although greater in number, seemed to be scared of the escapees for they started to retreat back around the platform and out of sight as Owen charged their way.

Why? It didn't matter.

He got to the door they had left minutes before and pulled it open, still firing. He was sure he had hit one or two in his random pot-shots. Jordan bumped into him.

"What…"

"Just get inside and fast."

Having stopped running, he found he was finding it even harder to keep his footing. In his peripheral vision, he could see the metal flooring begin to buckle, its groans adding an eerie chorus to the sound of blaster fire.

As soon as Jordan was inside, he jumped in and pulled the door to.

"What the hell was that?" Jordan's blood was up. His eyes were wide with what almost seemed to be lust or longing.

"We were surrounded, or close enough to it. But we have bigger problems. This room gives us a few moments, at least to think."

As if to either contradict or perhaps highlight this, there was a loud bang on the door. Gunfire? Something else?

"This whole facility is designed as a power station, either to siphon it or to conduct it. Either way, power is usually a form of energy or electricity."

Several other bangs reverberated around the room; the guards must have realised they weren't shooting back. Jordan jumped and, with the unsteady movement of the ground mixed with the ice, nearly fell over. Grabbing onto the wall, he managed to stay standing. Seething, he retorted, "So?"

"Think about it. That whole chamber was made of metal. A conductor. Something goes wrong and we'd be sitting ducks. Not to mention the fact we were outgunned twenty to one."

Jordan's already wide eyes widened even further. He shoved the hand that had been holding him steady into Owen's face, "And what do you call this?"

Looking at the moisture that had melted under the heat of Jordan's body temperature Owen answered, "Water."

"I wasn't the best student but isn't water a conductor too?"

"Yes," Owen started.

"Genius!"

"Did you notice how your hand isn't stuck to the wall?"

Jordan looked at his hand, unsure exactly what he was meant to be seeing, "So?"

"The wall isn't metal. It's a type of plastic. If it was metal, you probably would have lost some skin. We're in a refrigerator of some kind, which should also mean we're insulated from outside."

As if on cue, the whole world seemed to lose stability. Both men's feet flew from underneath them and they landed hard on the ground as there came a tremendous, ear piercing squeal from outside. Even the thick door was having trouble keeping it out.

The pipes and cables in the room squealed under the torture of the shifting walls and several smaller pipes snapped open releasing one gas or another into the air above them. If it was poisonous, they would be in trouble, Owen knew. At least with the hole they had come through earlier, it allowed some ventilation.

Seconds later, the door started groaning on its own as it too started to move on its hinges.

Instead of simply twisting with the wall, it seemed to buckle down on itself as if something hard was hitting it in slow motion from the other side.

Vibrations in the ground were numbing Owen's body as they increased dramatically, he couldn't find purchase with his hands to help him stand, not that that would have gained him anything in the first place.

His hands flew back to his ears when a tremendous roar and explosive crash echoed through the building.

And silence.

The world still shook beneath him, but the noise was gone. Or so he thought. As he lowered his hands from his ears again, he heard a faint whistling. He knew it wasn't the pipes above. It was coming from the hole they had crawled through earlier. And it was getting louder.

Something was coming.

A quick look at Jordan proved he knew it too, his eyes widening with fear with each passing second.

The whistling grew in volume and pitch as whatever it was came closer.

"Down!" was all Owen could think of. It barely came out as a croak as he realised the air was being sucked from the room.

Both men threw themselves onto the floor covering their heads with their arms just as the air above them erupted in a devouring inferno.

It lasted only a split second. Whether it was because the flames had already sucked the air from the room or that the gas above was stifling the flames, perhaps it was Carbon Dioxide, the flames engulfed the upper sections of the room before being swallowed in on itself and vanishing once more down the hole it had come from, taking its piercing whistle along with it.

The room was no longer cold. Ice that had once covered the ceiling had turned to steam and been evaporated. The ambient heat from the flames left the ice around the two men melted and pooling, soaking their clothing. The lights were gone as was every sound, even the gas pipe above had ceased its workings.

But something else was different. He had felt it before, out on the gangway, only now in the peace, in the dark, Owen could feel it even more. Owen could feel it in his blood. He could sense it in his skin.

Slowly, he sat up and tried to find a wall to lean against. He could hear Jordan moving in the dark. Owen lifted his right hand, spreading his fingers and focussed.

It didn't take much. An arc of electricity leapt between his thumb and his index finger and this then continued to his middle finger and all the way from digit to digit to his pinky. The arcs danced along the lengths of his phalanges and he watched with relief.

His powers were back.

In the glow from his hand, he could see Jordan manoeuvring himself to be able to see, quickly followed by the smile of realisation.

"They're back?"

"So it seems."

"Appropriate as it seems the rest of the power in this place has gone out."

"But how?"

Then a terrible thought crossed his mind. The source of the power. Either the link was broken, or the source itself was gone.

Keeping the arcs going, he scrambled to his feet, glad that the air had come back into the room. He was worried they were going to suffocate for a moment, but that worry was overcome by a second horrible thought.

He pushed at the door but it wouldn't budge.

"We have to get out there."

Jordan came to assist, but it made no difference, nor did shooting at it or even using his electric powers. It was jammed shut either through the buckling that had taken place or some other means.

That left the crawl space.

For the second time that night, this time with Owen leading, the men made their way back through toward the cells. As they reached the adjoining room where they had had the little standoff, Owen raised the power flow, allowing more light.

Everything was melted. What wasn't immediately flammable; as those objects had been incinerated; had been twisted and warped under the intense heat of the flames that had engulfed the room. The door to the storage room was a ghastly corkscrewed mass of metal leaving everything inside decimated. The sprinklers for normal fires were inoperable chunks of metal, though Owen guessed the water inside had probably evaporated anyway.

The kitchen door still stood, barely, but it was completely sealed shut by the heat melting both door and frame together.

Heading around to the corridor he had earlier lobbed his chemical bomb down, Owen knew what he saw charred on the ground were the smouldering remains of people.

There wasn't enough left to truly identify them as such, but what else could they have been? Had they been alive before the 'whatever' had taken place or had they been his victims?

He'd never know and he knew that that would haunt him for a long time coming. Even though it wasn't his fault, there had to be some responsibility taken for what happened tonight.

Similar remains were found spotted around the room they had initially barricaded with the hospital beds, where the first casualties had occurred.

Those beds and the doors they had covered were unrecognisable hulks of metal. What had been two or three beds had been turned into one multi bracketed form like a child's climbing frame designed in hell.

Which of the remains belonged to the guards and which were escapees? No telling.

The men kept moving. At least until they got to the hole in the wall that had contained the double doors leading to the main chamber.

There they stopped.

The structure that had occupied the centre of the room, where the people had been encapsulated to draw energy from. Those people that had no chance of escape. It was gone.

It had either been the cause of the devastation, exploding or simply destroyed in the event, but pieces of it had erupted out and infused themselves on the walls of the chamber itself. There were no signs of any remaining life. This escape attempt had been one mass murder instead.

Owen's breath caught in his throat and he couldn't take another. He gasped for air, letting his power fade dropping them in darkness once again as he doubled over, retching.

Jordan simply stood, stunned.

In his mind, Owen kept hearing three words playing over and over. "It's happened again!"

He had failed again. More death, more suffering. He hadn't stopped it. Not the way he was supposed to.

Catching his breath again, he found he was chanting his own word again and again.

"No."

KIRRILY

Kirrily awoke to pain and a foul taste in her mouth.

The glass in her leg had solidified completely but was immovable. If she tried to pull, it only brought more pain. It must have attached itself to

227

her flesh, effectively cauterising the wound, but lodging itself there as well. It hadn't seemed to damage any major veins or arteries, fortunately.

Slowly, she pushed her way out from underneath the counter. She could smell that some of her hair had been singed, but that was almost overwhelmed by the fumes coming from the charred remains of everything else in the room. The seats that had been the waiting area were no longer, nor the odd plant, whether they had been plastic or real, they had been completely vaporised.

Had it been some sort of radioactive explosion, Kirrily wondered. Was she going to die as a result of the fall out? Couldn't think about that now. Had to try and find out what was going on.

But all the equipment was down or destroyed. As was the power. Her wrist computer was no longer working, having been damaged in her scrabble to find shelter it seemed, though there seemed to be some sort of residual glow coming from it. Maybe the screen was still working.

She felt a dull ache throb into her head and she rubbed her forehead.

Where was Owen? Had he survived that blast?

Had anyone?

Slowly limping, trying to ease the pain in her leg, she made her way through the broken glass and burning ornaments until she was standing outside.

The tree line had moved a few metres back, the closer trees having been consumed in fire and reduced to ash. Those that now made the tree line were smouldering.

Where the warehouse building had once stood, there was only rubble.

In the glow of the fires, Kirrily could make out people moving. Some trying to stand up in various places, having either been knocked over or dived for cover. Others were fumbling in various directions amongst the trees. Small crowds of people were gathering here and there, some of these in uniform, but she could also make out people dressed in civilian clothing.

Could they be members of the Remnants? Prisoners who had escaped?

There was a noise from the warehouse, bricks falling onto other bricks. Perhaps they had finally given up on trying to form a wall, Kirrily mused feebly.

She glanced over for a moment before trying to see if there were any other possible groups of Remnants.

What she saw in that moment didn't register to begin with. It appeared to be an undulating mass of bricks initially which, to her current state of mind, didn't seem out of the ordinary.

It wasn't until she started considering that it was more than likely that these civilians were truly escapees that she registered what else she had seen.

Her eyes darted back to where the bricks had been heaving themselves around and confirmed to her own mind that she had seen something else.

A head, metallic and gleaming in the firelight around it. Its eyes appeared human enough from this distance, but this was no human. It was looking straight at her.

By now it had managed to work loose its arms and push itself up.

Something appeared to be wrong with its legs, however.

Quickly, almost without thinking, Kirrily reached for her pulse pistol still in its holster on her webbing. As she pulled it free, the machine had articulated its arm around to point at her. Something unravelled from its outer forearm and let loose a shot.

The impact jarred her wrist and sent the pistol flying from her hand.

It hadn't tried to kill her with the shot, merely disarm her. Even though she couldn't see the eyes clearly, nor would she be able to read their expression even if she could, Kirrily had a feeling it wanted to make her suffer.

She started to back away into the building she had come from.

Something began to sprout from the base of the machine man, where his legs seemed to dangle uselessly. No, not sprout, the legs themselves were changing, folding, separating and mutating.

It took approximately ten seconds for the change to take place. When it was complete, Kirrily saw that instead of the two legs it had had before when she was fighting it, it now had eight long spider-like legs attached to a bulb-like base that his lower body had become.

She hurried her retreat, watching the Machine Man's approach carefully.

Two of the legs didn't seem to work; one on either side; but dragged uselessly on the ground. It took a few steps forward for the Machine Man to discover this as it stumbled over the rubble. It examined its wounds briefly before compensating its walking method and beginning its approach once more.

Kirrily couldn't wait any longer. She had to find protection.

There were audible gasps from the onlookers outside.

She turned, no longer thinking that simply backing away would do the trick. She had to move quickly.

That was a nice idea, she thought, as she winced under the pain scaring her leg.

Half hopping, half running, she made her way back inside, keeping an eye out for any legible signs indicating another exit, or perhaps some stairs. Elevators would be useless now.

The problem was this thing had her locked. It was quite probable it had visual sensors such as infra-red which would allow it to pick up her body signature where ever she went.

She made it to the counter when a small section of it erupted under the impact of another of the Machine Man's blasts.

It was going to toy with her. That shot could easily have killed her.

She turned in the other direction and kept moving.

Past the elevator bank, she saw a larger than normal door that appeared to be a stairwell. She pushed it open with a little effort and found her guess to be true. Wishing she had something to barricade the door for a bit, she pushed it to as fast as she could before painfully making her way up the stairs.

She only had two more weapons that would possibly make a dent on this thing. The .45 pistol she had designed two years earlier and the sonic pistol in her ankle holster. She had to be careful that he didn't try a similar trick of disarming her of those.

If she could get to the first floor balcony before it got to the stairwell, she might be able to get a few shots in.

Knowing that trying to be sneaky would be a waste of time, she let all the pained grunts out as she hauled herself up the stairs using the arm railings and avoiding using her injured leg as much as she could.

When she did reach the first floor, she was glad to see that the damaged legs had actually held the Machine Man up. He had only made it to the waiting area, having come through one of the window spaces instead of the main entrance. It had had to cross the car park and the rubble.

Kirrily stayed low behind the thick concrete wall that acted as banister to the walkway on this level overlooking the lobby. She pulled out the .45 pistol, knowing the sonic pistol was better for close range attacks.

Something clattered below her as the Machine Man moved. Taking a couple of breaths, she used her good leg to lever herself up and fired down at her pursuer.

Being that it was an automatic, she squeezed the trigger for two seconds, five bullets were fired. All but one made contact.

The Machine Man lurched for a second as the majority of the shots impacted his torso. Half ricocheted off, but two penetrated its hard exterior. The expression on its face seemed to register pain.

Then it looked up and saw her.

Strangely, Kirrily had expected some sort of Terminator like skeleton underneath the Machine Man's fake human exterior. But the musculature of both body and face was actually present in metallic or some type of plastic form. It was like looking at a human without its skin, but instead of meat and tissue, there was technology.

Looking at it made her head begin to ache. As she ducked behind the wall again, it smiled at her.

There was a rattle of gunfire and the concrete wall she was using as protection began to crack. He was working at her defences, getting her to move.

The firing stopped. She was about to launch herself up again when he seemed to predict her movement and fired over the top of the wall, forcing her to stay down.

He could see her. In whatever spectrum he was using, he was watching her and predicting her movements.

And she was blind. As it stood, they were at a partial standoff, but she was going to be on the loosing end if she didn't move.

Back to the stairwell, she struggled to crawl. Once behind the fire door, she stood up again and made her way up to level two. By the time she had reached it, she could hear the door from the lobby opening. She had to move faster.

She didn't stop on two, instead continuing up to the third level. From the sounds coming below, he wasn't faring to well on the stairs. That would give her some time to try and find another way down or out. Plus, she remembered something that may help her a little.

The third floor, much like the first, opened onto a similar walkway balcony. In front, to her left, were the elevators, not working of course. To her right the walkway continued before reaching a cross junction. One path led back into the building, but to the left was a bridge that crossed toward what remained of the exterior glass wall and onward to one of the walkways that would normally attach to the other building. This was what she was looking for. She hobbled her way toward the junction.

As she moved, she looked out of the building. The bracketing for all the shattered windows stood fairly firm, a latticework of white now scorched black. Beyond that, she saw the walkway that had led to the other building. The bridge to get across was still intact, thankfully. As for the walkway itself, she couldn't tell. The other end was burning, having once been attached to the now non-existent warehouse. It was bending down in a slight slope, having been dragged down with the collapsing building. This would mean that the structure wouldn't be the strongest, however it was the only way out of the building she knew.

She hurried to the junction and started along the bridge. There would still be plenty of time before the Machine Man made it to the third floor. Or so she thought.

As she reached the halfway point along the bridge, she heard a loud clang behind her.

Something had punctured a hole in the concrete wall and had fallen short of hitting her.

It appeared to be a diamond shaped piece of metal about the size of a fist. At one end, leading through the hole, was a cable.

The diamond unfolded itself into a symmetrical web of claws that, as the cable was retracted, found purchase in the wall.

A grapple of some kind.

Looking over the edge, she saw the Machine Man on the level below. He leapt off the balcony and onto the elevator tower where his six working legs crunched into the surface, keeping him in place.

It was still smiling at her, its expression clearly readable and that made the machine even more terrifying. Kirrily gasped and brought her .45 round to bear. She squeezed the trigger, holding it until the clip was empty. Ten more bullets fired from the custom clip, three went wild as she swung the gun across. The other seven made contact with the mechanism's face. It screamed as one of the eyes was shattered. The cheek below it also collapsed as two bullets made contact there destroying the fake musculature and disconnecting the left hand jaw from its socket. The mouth now hung limply aside, but this did nothing to stop the horrific scream still emanating from where ever its voice came from. The smile was gone now.

The other bullets dented the structure, but made no permanent damage. In its rage, a couple of its legs lost purchase and it began to slip momentarily before it regained its grasp.

Kirrily had to move. The clip was out and she couldn't waste time fumbling for another on her webbing. There were more pulse clips there than .45's and she didn't have time to make a mistake.

She launched herself forward and away from the grapple. The air around her frizzled with pressure as the Machine Man fired off several shots at her. These were actually aimed at her, it seemed. No longer in the mood for toying, it had decided to kill.

As she entered the walkway, she heard a noise from behind. Glancing quickly over her shoulder, she saw it had managed to jump or pull itself onto the bridge and was aiming its arm weapon at her.

Pushing off her good leg, she launched herself forward and twisted her body so she would end up facing the Machine Man, landing on her good thigh and buttocks.

As she landed, she saw him fire. The blasts went over her head as she bent down and retrieved the sonic pistol from her ankle holster.

It recalibrated its targeting as she wrapped her hand around the grip, fingering the trigger.

They both fired in unison.

CHAPTER TWENTY FIVE

OWEN

They weren't out of the woods yet.

Owen felt Jordan's hand on his back. Even in the dark, he had managed to find him.

"We need to move. There's someone here."

Owen stood up, "What? Where?"

"There are a few people; I can sense their blood pumping in the other cells. But there's someone else. He's moving around down there."

Owen ignited his hand again, "Maybe he's a Remnant."

Owen could see the look in Jordan's eye, he was worried about something. He had never understood Jordan's powers fully. He knew that the comment he had made about sucking out the guard's blood was actually possible. He could control blood cells as well as Owen could control electricity.

"It's not a Remnant. I recognise them. It's familiar though."

"Maybe they need help. We need to help everyone else here."

Owen looked out the door again. It was going to be hard going. The gangway that encircled the chamber was badly affected by what had happened. There were grills missing, having been melted through. The support beams were in a terrible shape. They would be lucky if the structure could withstand their weight.

Allowing more light, Owen looked around the rest of the chamber.

The door to the refrigerated room was welded shut from the heat. The concave buckling had occurred from the unsupported centre of the door being blasted inward, melting the metal and pushing it outward.

Parts of the room still glowed red hot.

Now, they could see the stairwell opposite. It was in darkness, but it seemed to be the only way out, for Jordan, at least.

Owen transformed his body, casting obscure shadows around him.

"I'm going to take you across to the stairs. You find a way out. I'll help the others."

"I can't leave you here," Jordan protested.

"We need to find a safe way out. We can't just leave it to blind luck again. You find a way then come back. I will help the survivors. Now grab on."

Jordan did as he was told, his hair standing slightly on end from residual charged energy from Owen's body.

Owen launched himself across the chamber. Not directly, it was too far. He made contact with a wall and pushed off once more as he had done with Kirrily back at the Remnant's home.

Immediately he felt a pang of sorrow for Kirrily, but pushed it straight out of his mind for the moment. Not the time.

As he landed on the doorstep to the stair well someone called from below.

"Owen!"

The voice was instantly recognisable.

"Owen?" Jordan asked, picking up on the worry Owen was feeling.

"Go. Get out of here."

His name echoed up from below again. There was the brute force of anger behind it that hung on the air as it reverberated off the now hollow walls of the chamber.

"Go!" Owen hissed and Jordan did as he was told, starting gingerly up the stairs, ensuring they were safe. Once he was sure, he moved faster, gun ready, despite knowing his powers were back and would most likely offer him more protection.

Owen turned to look down into the chamber.

There was a flash of bright orange before it dulled to an even glow.

It was the Fireman.

"You did this!"

Owen felt like responding with, "No, duh!" but in truth, he hadn't done any of this. He didn't even know what had caused such massive devastation. All he had done was instigate an escape. And they wouldn't have had to do that if this fool hadn't come hunting them down in the first place.

Instead, he stayed silent.

He could help the others escape. Or he could stand here debating semantics. Problem was if he did help the others, it's possible this man would try and kill them all.

The glow began to move, and Owen could see the flames moving between the damaged gangways and the various beams below.

"All of this. This is all your fault," He sounded closer.

Was he reading Owen's mind? He already felt the guilt of these poor people's deaths.

It wasn't until Owen could see the Fireman through the gangway just outside the stairwell that he realised what was happening. The man was flying, or levitating. He must have been using his power to create thermal updrafts or something. Owen was no aeronautics genius, but there had to be some reason. Besides hot air rising, of course.

He was level with Owen, who was still glowing himself, when he said, "It was your fault that they died the first time."

Even through the flames that enveloped the man, Owen could see the anger, hatred and even pain.

"I did nothing. I only tried to save people."

"Did you? You didn't save everybody! You left so many behind. You killed the rest."

"That's not true! I was just a boy!"

What the Fireman said next didn't come out in the same yell he had used up until now. It hissed through his teeth like steam, crackling with tiny embers, "So was I."

The man replaced the volume he had lost with heat. The temperature in the chamber rose several degrees, and even in his electric form, Owen could sense it.

Then the man threw his arm out toward Owen and with it came a blast of fire.

Owen used his speed to haul himself behind the doorframe as the flames connected with the stairs. The heat, hotter than a furnace began to melt the metal framework, a true feat considering the massive blast earlier had failed to do so.

The stream of flames continued for a couple more seconds then ceased, replaced with the wavering lines of heat one normally associated with the desert.

With this man's ability to fly, Owen's choice to go up or down would be redundant. He would simply be followed. There was one other option.

Owen flung himself around the door jam and launched himself forward, firing an arc of electricity at the man as he jetted forward, fists in front of him like a diver who had taken up boxing mid jump. The Fireman writhed in pain but maintained his flames. Owen knew they would most likely burn him so he created a small energy field around him, close to his body, hopefully that would protect him from the heat.

His fists connected with solid matter, despite the man appearing to be made of fire.

The force of the impact sent him backward toward the double doors where the prisoners had died earlier.

The impetus of his leap gone, Owen felt himself begin to fall, but his opponent wasn't having that. He felt a hand close around his wrist and haul him upward until he was hanging like a rag doll in front of the burning face. There was an increase in temperature in the room as the man compensated for the extra weight.

"Nice try. No cigar."

With his other hand, the Fireman punched out at Owen's head, but Owen used his legs to kick off from the man's body. It seemed his energy field was doing its job, something he'd have to remember in future, if there was one.

The force of the kick took him out of the punch's range, but he was still firmly in the man's grip and he could feel it twisting his arm.

Swinging back toward the man, Owen chose another tactic. He grabbed hold of his body, wrapping his free arm around his waist and up over his shoulder like a hug locking his punching arm in position over his own shoulder. He then wrapped his legs around the other man's legs.

It was an odd sensation to be so close to flames and not be burnt. He could see through the flames that writhed against the side of his face he now had pressed against the Fireman's chest. What he could see was a body of burning cinders beneath the flames.

Owen could feel the heat through his field, but it was greatly reduced, thankfully. His leather clothes were steaming slightly.

They were essentially in a deadlock, neither man able to move to attack for fear of giving the other an advantage.

"Let go!" the Fireman bellowed. There was something in his voice, not just anger.

Owen kept holding.

The Fireman tried again, "LET ME GO!"

Fear, but not only fear. Something else. Whatever it was, it stood out more in his tones than the anger. But what was he afraid of?

Owen didn't have time to dwell on the thought as the heat in the room rocketed up, as did the two embracing bodies.

A yelp escaped Owen's lips as he felt himself shoot upwards. The only thing up was a ceiling. What then? Would he stop?

He turned his eyes toward the roof in time to see it peel away in a burning ring like paper after someone has stubbed it with a cigarette.

They weren't going to ram it, but the Fireman was reacting. It didn't seem like he knew how or why, but he was doing something simply because it was the only thing he could do.

Molten earth, metal and concrete dripped past them as they continued up through the floor above and straight out into the night sky where they stopped thirty metres above the ground

Owen could see people gathered around the periphery of what appeared to be some sort of compound. Below him was the rectangular outline of a building that no longer stood, just on the edge of his vision was a second building he couldn't quite see.

The momentary distraction of looking around and being outside was enough for the Fireman to take advantage. He let go of Owens wrist and punched him in the side. Owen's reaction was instinctual.

He let go his arm and fell backward, his legs still locked with the Fireman's for a split second before slipping loose.

What he would give for one of Kirrily's pulse pistols to break the fall.

He couldn't see what he was falling toward, but it could have been a sharp piece of metal, or perhaps back down the hole.

The Fireman wasn't going to give him the chance to contemplate it.

In his eyes, as Owen fell away, he could see flashes of cinders welling. Were they tears?

If they were, they didn't stop him from firing one last blast at him.

Flames engulfed his body in a heat that started to wear his energy field thin. No longer were his clothes simply steaming, they were beginning to char and burn.

If the fall didn't kill him, the flames would.

KIRRILY

Kirrily felt the impact of the Machine Man's weapon on her left shoulder. It spun her sideways and she landed face first against the blackened floor of the walkway.

Like the Pulse pistol, the sonic pistol sent out waves of compressed audio frequencies. In such a state, it must have deflected what should have been a point blank dead-to-rights shot into a wing clipper.

The result of her own shot at the Machine Man, she couldn't know yet with her face in the dirt and more pain erupting from her leg and her shoulder. She moaned as she endeavoured to turn herself over, expecting the Machine Man to be bearing down on her, or at least ready to shoot her.

He wasn't moving. It seemed her own shot had temporarily knocked it out.

Some more time to get away. She forced herself up onto her good leg into a kneeling position and managed to right herself once more into a standing position. As she did so, she saw something bright flash into the sky through one of the window frames ahead.

At first she thought it was a gas pocket blowing or a signal flare.

But when she looked, she could see the distinct form of two people. Someone shouted something and one of the people, glowing blue, began to fall.

Owen. It had to be.

Something whirred behind her. It was beginning to reboot. She had to move.

She hurried forward, feeling the ground beneath her feet wobble, accompanied by the wretched whining of metal straining.

As she advanced along the walkway, she could feel it begin to slant down more and more. Her weight added to the damage the walkway had already sustained was adding strain to an already brittle system of support.

There was a clack from behind and she whirled around in time to see the Machine Man, arm and weapon extended, firing his weapon.

But nothing happened. Either he was out or it was damaged. It cocked its head briefly in a question then bent its six working legs and launched itself forward.

Raising her arms in defence was useless; it only lessoned the blow to her body, perhaps cracking one of her arm bones in the process.

She collapsed under its weight as it came to land, its legs encaging her, on the walkway. The sonic pistol vanished from sight.

There was no quiet whine from the walkway this time. The supporting beams attached to the main building simply snapped and gave way.

The walkway detached from the taller building and began to fall. The side that had just come loose bounced on the lattice framework that made up the shell of the standing building, jarring both occupants, though Kirrily could not move, pinned in place by the pincer-like legs.

The opposite end that had once joined to the warehouse, crashed to the ground first.

Kirrily's jaw jammed closed as her head snapped back against what used to be carpet. The rest of her body slid slightly down toward that end, though found pain shoot through her left shoulder when it struck the front leg of the Machine Man who maintained his position.

The walkway now lay with one end on the ground, the other wedged against the second and third floors of the building, leaving Kirrily lying head first down a steep incline.

She looked up at the Machine Man. He was looking down at her. He didn't need the jaw to be connected to smile. She could see it in his inhuman eyes. And the headache came once more.

The machine man lifted one of its legs, moved it toward the wound in her shoulder and pressed it down firmly into her bleeding flesh.

She screamed in pain, barely realising how similar it sounded to the Machine Man's scream earlier.

From somewhere, it began to chuckle as it withdrew the leg ever so slightly.

It then moved one of its other legs toward the wound in her leg where it proceeded to tap gently, then more forcefully against the glass that was lodged there. She managed to pull it up toward her body and out of its way, feeling the muscle tearing away from the glass inside.

Kirrily gritted her teeth, trying to get her breath to prevent herself from screaming again. She looked up at the Machine Man's ruined face and a lance of pain ran through her head. She squeezed her eyes shut, shivering, but refusing the give in.

And when she opened them again, what she saw amazed her.

The night had begun to glow like a rainbow. Words, numbers and images danced in front of her and all around the Machine Man. It was glowing too, a bright ivory glow that flickered and grew more brilliant at different points around its body.

She was seeing the potential of the technology. How it was made, what it could become.

She could see what each part did, how it fit into the rest of the system.

There was a human brain inside, she could see that now. Her vision showed her how it was being sustained in the skull through electrodes, lubricating conductive gels full of nutrients.

This was her power. It was back. She should have known the second she saw Owen and the burning man. They had powered up, so, of course, had she.

Her gritted teeth turned into a smile and the Machine Man noticed.

It stopped chuckling and cocked its head again as her hand reached down to her ankle where she had one last remaining weapon.

The one weapon she had not designed. The one weapon that did not come with any bells and whistles. The weapon that had been a symbol of a religion that believed in magic. Something Kirrily had grown up thinking was fake.

By the time she had slid the knife out of its sheath in the ankle holster, the Machine Man had started to move.

First it reinserted the front leg into her shoulder, but she continued smiling, refusing to give in. It then started to move away from her, its human brain obviously not sure why she was seemingly happy when faced with death.

But it was too late. Kirrily, with the aid of her 'magical' ability to understand technology, had already seen what she needed to.

The instant her right hand was free of the Machine Man's legs, she swung her arm around and jammed the knife into what would have been the kidneys of a normal human being.

Like a human if struck with a kidney punch, it would be crippled in pain and urinate blood for days. The Machine Man screamed once more, but only briefly as this blow crippled him efficiently and permanently.

The blade sliced between two plates of metal and deep into the inner workings, carving up power couplings, lubricant channels and numerous other items. But the point ended up deep in the centre of a small, highly sophisticated device that was integral to the automation of the Machine Man's limbs, effectively paralysing it.

He simply froze. No big explosion, no twitching. Everything simply stopped moving.

Inside, the brain would still be operating, would continue to do so as long as the power supply and the nutrients were available. But he was trapped in there.

She let go of the knife and let her hand fall back to the floor, breathing heavily as if she had run a marathon. She was still trying to control the pain from her shoulder; the leg still sat inside her.

Slowly and carefully, she grabbed the intruding leg with both arms and pushed it away. It moved with minimal resistance and hung in place where she left it.

Gravity then started to work its own magic as, with nothing to hold her in place, Kirrily began to slide down the walkway.

With the use of her good arm and leg, she managed to manoeuvre herself around so she would land on her good leg and not her head.

There she waited, catching her breath. She was tired, hurting and wanted to go home. But that wasn't what she had come here for.

With a jolt, she remembered what she had seen on the walkway. Owen. Alive!

She pushed off from the floor of the walkway which she had been using for support and climbed over one of the empty window frames to get outside.

239

Looking every which way she could, she wasn't able to see either the burning man or Owen. But she could hear the sirens very close by. Help was here.

OWEN

Owen felt himself getting light headed before he hit the ground. There was no oxygen to breath in his cocoon of flames.

There was nothing he could do. So he relaxed as best he could.

When he finally hit the ground, his body cracked loudly against what rubble there was. Bricks, concrete, dirt. He was fortunate there had been nothing jutting upwards, but he felt a sharp pain in his ribs and his right elbow connected hard with the ground, taking much of the brunt of the fall. His neck cracked awkwardly as he landed also, but managed to prevent his skull making contact with the ground.

He howled in pain and curled into a foetal ball. His power shut off, leaving him back in his normal form. There was too much pain to focus and maintain his alternate form.

Broken arm, broken ribs, he was sure. The fact he could still feel his body was a good sign that he hadn't broken his neck, but it ached with a throbbing sensation that implied he may have scored a degree of whiplash.

The flames had stopped and the Fireman was hovering above him, looking down with those same hateful, haunted eyes. He had lowered himself a score of metres.

"This is all your fault," he said simply, the emotion thick in his voice.

Owen grunted, clearing his throat and fighting through the pain, "How? What did I do?"

"You left me behind."

Owen agonizingly moved his head so he could get a better look at his attacker, "What? I was five. I don't know…"

He realised who he was speaking to.

It wasn't a sudden epiphany; it was a slow dawning realisation. The putting together of the little bits to make the whole.

"You let them kill our parents."

Owen could barely say his next word, "Ryan?"

"If you hadn't started the escape, they would have lived. They told me. Just like they let me live."

"You really believe that?" Owen couldn't believe what was happening now himself. This was his brother. His older brother who had disappeared in the underground chambers all those years ago.

"What else is there? I didn't have anyone else. They looked after him."

Owen used his left arm to help him sit up; wincing against the pain in his ribs, "And look what they do. They kidnap people, put them in cages then suck them dry. These are people you trust? People who really care for you? What happens when they have everyone they need? When you

240

are the last person with powers out there. You really think they'll let you wander free?"

Ryan considered this for a moment.

There was a tremendous noise from somewhere toward the other building, Ryan looked up, distracted. Then he looked back down at Owen, the cinder tears gone from his eyes. He lowered himself to the ground a few metres away from where Owen sat supporting himself.

"I didn't do this for them. I did this for me. I did this for me! To get revenge on you leaving me behind, for killing Mum and Dad."

Owen was in no state to fight. He wasn't sure he would be able to transform even if he needed to. But inside, he felt angry. His own emotions were starting to flare. He had lived with enough guilt over the death of so many people all those years ago. He was going to have to live with the guilt of the lost lives, Remnant or otherwise, tonight. But he was not going to feel guilt for what happened to his parents or to Ryan. That had not been his fault. He had watched his father die through no fault of his own, but through the inhumane actions of these murderous monsters that claimed to be human.

He had been too young to find his brother. He had been herded out of the building by adults, members of the Remnants themselves. But how were they to know where he was.

It had been coincidence, bad luck. Owen had escaped and Ryan had not. How was that Owen's fault? The fault of a five year old?

"Now I get my own back," Ryan extended his arms toward Owen and once more flames licked out from his hands.

Owen's own anger was fuel enough for his transformation. The pain was still present in this form, but so was the energy field. He concentrated hard on a number of things: the field, his form and standing up.

He managed to get to his feet as the temperature around him increased exponentially.

Now he was standing, he turned his attention to his field, extending it out, creating a bubble of air around himself so he could breath. The fire wrapped itself around him.

Owen raised his own hand and fired into the oncoming inferno. The electricity arced out of his spread fingers uniting in a single thick, crackling stream of blue power that cut its way toward his attacker, his brother.

Ryan yelled in surprise, the onslaught faltered and Owen could see his brother writhing in agony. He stayed standing, fighting against the electric charge that ran through him.

Owen moved toward him, one slow step at a time.

When he spoke, he spoke calmly, gently, "It wasn't my fault. How can you possibly blame me for everything that happened? Your people did that. They invaded our home; they took us away from our parents, from each other. There was nothing either of us could have done."

Ryan screamed and Owen knew it wasn't because of the electricity. His assault was crippling but not deadly. He didn't want to kill his brother.

"Can't you see that? All these years, if I had known you had survived, I would have come for you."

With effort, Ryan spoke, "It's too late now."

"No. It's not. You have a family," Owen stopped his attack and his approach. He was now only a couple of steps away, "Please?"

Ryan was bent in an effort to regain himself.

"Owen! No," the voice came from behind him. Owen spun quickly, too quickly for his injuries and he collapsed. It was Kirrily. She stood beside a chunk of wall that had kept him from her sight back at the building, "You can't," She puffed, "It's Ryan. You're brothers."

Owen didn't know what to say anymore. Or feel. Kirrily was alive!

Instead he slowly turned back to his brother and powered down, "I know," he said more to Ryan than anyone else, "We're brothers."

The cinders had returned to Ryan's face. Amongst the flames, Owen could see he was torn.

Things started getting hotter and brighter. Owen raised his arm against the glare that his brother was putting out and felt a hand against his shoulder. It was Kirrily who had managed to squat awkwardly beside him.

"Ryan?"

"No," was all the man said.

Then he was gone.

He launched himself into the air and out across the bush land.

Owen watched him go until he was out of sight.

Kirrily waited a while before she tried to help him up. They didn't say anything but when they stood face to face, each leaning on the other for support, they didn't need to. Instead they embraced each other, carefully so as not to hurt the other, and kissed. It was gentle, but full of enough of the emotion of the night that it didn't need to be any more than what it was.

EPILOGUE

The music was electric. The people were having fun, laughing, drinking, dancing.

Kirrily and Owen arrived at the event arm in arm. Kirrily wearing a small black dress, Owen in black dress pants and a brown shirt. No need for fancy costumes tonight whether they were leather coats or pink suits.

It was Friday, five days after the Ethelbridge incident.

The police, fire department, ambulance and Federal Police had turned up shortly after Ryan left. The appropriate people went with the appropriate department. There were several arrests made. Forty eight people were rescued from the cells below. As well as the rest of the survivors Owen had made crawl out of the kitchenette. There were sixty people that Owen had helped, seventeen of which had not made it out before the blast. The survivors had been taken to hospital.

They only stayed there the next day as they had healers of their own to do the job better.

Strangely, the doctors treating them have no recollection of these patients and the police that went looking for them afterwards always returned to the police station unaware they were meant to be looking for them in the first place.

Myrl was doing her job well, as were the rest of the telepaths that had survived.

Their number was greatly depleted, but the Remnants struggled on. Some of the survivors that had not previously been a part of their society enquired about joining. Myrl informed them that their doors would always be open. As for where, they would have to relocate after the destruction and violation of their old home.

Myrl offered the services of their healers to Kirrily and Owen who graciously accepted.

They had made an awkward escape from the scene in a police car Kirrily hotwired, returning to Aunt Helen's for some much needed care. Helen herself was overwhelmed that they had survived, though Owen left out any mention of Ryan for the time being.

In the days that followed, several board members on Ethelbridge Holdings were taken into custody, though whether they were the truly guilty ones or not, Owen didn't know and vowed to keep an eye out. Several of their smaller off shoot companies also closed, including Peerson Corporation that was being investigated for an incident at the Australia Day celebrations on the following Wednesday.

The site of the whole Sunday night devastation had been closed down and quarantined.

On the Thursday, Owen, Kirrily, Helen and the Remnants held a private memorial service for those that had not survived, both the guards and the prisoners were honoured. In all there were six hundred and forty two casualties that they were able to uncover. Just over one hundred had been guards, the rest a mixture of Remnants or other powered people who had simply been captured. Many of those had been inside the large devices within the chambers that had vaporised.

According to Myrl, the work of Ethelbridge had wiped out almost two thirds of Perth's super-powered population, many of whom weren't even aware they had powers. He didn't ask how she knew.

The service was held at the site of Ethelbridge Power. Owen gave a small speech that was well received by the survivors.

On that day Owen also received a mysterious invitation in the mail inviting both he and Kirrily to a charity event that Friday evening.

Aunt Helen did her research into the benefactor before giving her approval. It was some big money group who were rallying together various members of the public, of whom some were Remnants. Owen had spoken to Myrl about this at the service and she had been more than enthusiastic about their meeting the mysterious group. She said she knew of them, favourably.

They heard nothing from or about Ryan. He had once again vanished from their lives. At least for the time being.

And so it was, the pair who had spent most of the week together, though Kirrily had demanded time to work on some upgrades and new ideas she had been thinking of, walked into a party in the inner city.

They greeted the three Remnants they knew. They sipped champagne that came from the free bar and watched the people around them, both a little wary. There were at least two faces Owen thought familiar but couldn't place where from, but they smiled amicably and he let it pass. They didn't recognise him.

Then Owen built up enough courage to ask Kirrily to dance. She played the "I can't dance card," but Owen insisted and they both cut a mean caper together.

The music was dimmed, but not eliminated as the head of the inviting company was asked to make a speech.

An Alex Lloyd song began and Owen leant over to Kirrily's ear and whispered, "This song."

She smiled, "What about it?"

"Nothing," he said coyly.

She listened for a moment before elbowing him in his now healed ribs, "Shut up and listen to the man talk."

He leant in to kiss her cheek, but she caught him and, this time with the force their first had lacked, but still full of that same passion, they kissed.